PRAISE FOR

TO WOO AND TO WED

"*To Woo and to Wed* is the perfect conclusion to a series I love with all my heart for its deeply swoony romance and fun, supportive friendships that make you wish you were right there in the ballroom with them."

—Sarah Hogle, author of *Just Like Magic*

"With her trademark witty voice and fresh take on the Regency era, with *To Woo and to Wed* Waters once again gives readers a delightful confection of a novel. Martha Waters's books have taken up permanent residence on my keeper shelf."

—Manda Collins, author of
A Lady's Guide to Mischief and Mayhem

"Martha Waters has done it again. *To Woo and to Wed* delights with its clever drollery alongside its sizzling heat."

—India Holton, internationally bestselling author of
The Wisteria Society of Lady Scoundrels

"*To Woo and to Wed* is the perfect conclusion to a perfect series. Martha Waters writes crackling dialogue that's genuinely funny while giving Sophie and West their long-awaited happily ever after. I'm sad this series is over but I can't wait to see what Waters writes next!"

—Kerry Winfrey, author of *Waiting for Tom Hanks*

"Waters concludes her heralded Regency Vows series with the most delightful and emotionally angst-ridden installment yet. Like the couple in Jane Austen's *Persuasion*, the heartbroken bachelor Lord Weston and the widowed Lady Fitzwilliam Bridewell have been separated by circumstance, but not lust, for seven years. Waters's books always give the reader consummate root-worthy characters of whom one can simply not get enough, which makes the appearances here of the beloved couples from the earlier books so satisfying, but Weston and Sophie are the most winning of them all. Equal parts scintillating romance and hilarious comedy, *To Woo and to Wed* is the very mix to win over readers' hearts everywhere."

—Natalie Jenner, internationally bestselling author of
The Jane Austen Society

"Martha Waters remains the queen of the historical rom-com! *To Woo and to Wed* has it all: fake engagement, pining, second chances, pining, wit, charm, heat, and did I mention pining? West and Sophie's story gives this series the perfect happy ending."

—Jen DeLuca, author of the Well Met series

PRAISE FOR MARTHA WATERS'S
REGENCY VOWS SERIES

"Waters has an arch sense of humor and a marvelously witty voice that rivals the best of the Regency authors (see: Julia Quinn, even Austen herself) . . . unabashedly fun and bursting with screwball energy. It's a romp of the highest order, difficult to put down and effervescent with its own abundant charm."

—*Entertainment Weekly*

"I simply could not put [it] down . . . Bridgerton fans will like this one."

—Julia Quinn, author of the Bridgerton series

"Sweet, sexy, and utterly fun. A love story with depth to match its humor, and refreshingly frank communication between its two headstrong leads—I adored it."

—Emily Henry, *New York Times* bestselling author

"Waters's debut Regency rom-com delights with hilarious, high-concept romantic schemes . . . Waters gently lampoons genre tropes without sacrificing genuine feeling. Self-aware and brimming with well-timed epiphanies, this joyful, elegant romp is sure to enchant."

—*Publishers Weekly* (starred review)

"The Regency Vow series evokes a charming Regency-era vibe, complete with colorful outfits and countryside walks sure to delight *Bridgerton* fans."

—*USA Today*

TO WOO
AND
TO WED

A Novel

MARTHA WATERS

ATRIA PAPERBACK
New York   London   Toronto   Sydney   New Delhi

ATRIA
PAPERBACK

An Imprint of Simon & Schuster, LLC
1230 Avenue of the Americas
New York, NY 10020

First Atria Paperback edition February 2024

ATRIA PAPERBACK and colophon are trademarks of Simon & Schuster, LLC

Simon & Schuster: Celebrating 100 Years of Publishing in 2024

For information about special discounts for bulk purchases, please contact Simon & Schuster Special Sales at 1-866-506-1949 or business@simonandschuster.com.

The Simon & Schuster Speakers Bureau can bring authors to your live event. For more information or to book an event, contact the Simon & Schuster Speakers Bureau at 1-866-248-3049 or visit our website at www.simonspeakers.com.

Series design by Kathryn Kenney-Peterson

Manufactured in the United States of America

1   3   5   7   9   10   8   6   4   2

Library of Congress Cataloging-in-Publication Data

Names: Waters, Martha, 1988- author.
Title: To woo and to wed / Martha Waters.
Description: First Atria Paperback edition. | New York : Atria Paperbacks, 2024. | Series: The regency vows
Identifiers: LCCN 2023036828 (print) | LCCN 2023036829 (ebook) | ISBN 9781668007921 (paperback) | ISBN 9781668007938 (ebook)
Subjects: LCGFT: Romance fiction. | Novels.
Classification: LCC PS3623.A8689 T69 2024 (print) | LCC PS3623.A8689 (ebook) | DDC 813/.6—dc23
LC record available at https://lccn.loc.gov/2023036828
LC ebook record available at https://lccn.loc.gov/2023036829

ISBN 978-1-6680-0792-1
ISBN 978-1-6680-0793-8 (ebook)

For Mom, Alice, and every single reader who asked,
"But what about West and Sophie?"

Prologue

Sophie Wexham was quite convinced that a future duke was the worst possible man to fall in love with.

She had no complaints about the gentleman himself: The Marquess of Weston was tall, broad-shouldered, and possessed of dark hair, green eyes, and a stern brow that softened, somehow, whenever he caught her eye. He was polite and interesting, and—astonishingly— seemed just as inclined to listen to *her* speak as he was to offer his own thoughts, a vanishingly rare quality in men of the *ton*. (Or, Sophie suspected, in the male sex more generally.) He was respectful toward her parents and amused by her sisters, and had hinted—multiple times—that he was planning to have a word with her father about a matter of great import soon. Very, very soon.

There was, however, one rather large problem: the Duke of Dovington. The man whose title West would one day inherit. And, unfortunately, a man who Sophie was increasingly convinced did not like her one bit.

"Miss Wexham." Sophie glanced up, startled; she was at the Haverford ball, where supper had just ended, and she was caught in the crowded exodus from the dining room, searching for her younger sister Maria, whom she liked to keep an eye on. The Duke of Dovington stood before her. Dressed in evening attire, he bore a startling resemblance to his sons, though his eyes were an everyday brown, rather than the arresting green that West and his brother had inherited. "I wonder if I might have a word?"

She cast a brief, desperate glance around the room, hoping a savior would materialize, before conceding there was no polite option other than to drop into a curtsey and say, "Of course, Your Grace."

Until now, she'd had no complaints about the evening; the Haverford ball was one of the last grand events of the Season, and she'd arrived swathed in silk and lace, wearing her mother's favorite emerald necklace, loaned specifically for the occasion. She had danced twice with West, and much of the rest of her dance card had been filled by friends of his: his best friend, the Marquess of Willingham, who teased her slyly about West's attentions to her; Willingham's younger brother, Lord Jeremy Overington, who was rakish and flirtatious to the point of it almost—*almost*—being inappropriate; and finally, the supper dance with Lord Fitzwilliam Bridewell, another friend of West's who only had eyes for a dark-haired beauty across the room.

The duke offered his arm and led her from the crowded dining room back to the ballroom, where he began to escort her on a leisurely circuit of the room. "You and my son seem . . . fond of each other."

He seemed to have chosen the word specifically to annoy her, so she merely said, "Rather."

"I understand he has taken it into his head that he might even propose marriage."

"I believe that may be his intent, yes." She and West had been dancing around the subject for weeks; yesterday he'd mentioned his plan to pay a call on her father in the days to come.

There was a long beat of silence as they slowly circled the room, and then the duke said, "He is only four-and-twenty, you know."

Sophie hesitated for a moment; this was not the angle she had been expecting him to take. "I know."

"That is young. Younger than I had expected him to marry. He still has much to learn."

"And I look forward to being at his side along the way," Sophie said. It was odd to hear West discussed in such terms; twenty-four was, yes, younger than men of his station were accustomed to marrying—the general view among polite society was that young men still had too many wild oats to sow at that age, and that it was pointless to expect them to settle down much before thirty—but it was certainly not unheard of. And the burden of his inheritance, of expectation, seemed to weigh more heavily upon him than such things did on other men, making him seem older than he was.

"Mmmm. You have younger sisters, do you not, Miss Wexham?"

Sophie stiffened at this inquiry, but did not allow her steps to falter, nor did she remove her hand from the duke's arm. "I do. Four."

"No doubt you are hoping that they will make successful matches."

"Naturally."

"I understand that your sister—Miss Maria, is it?—has been quite taken with a certain marquess this Season." The duke's tone was idle, but Sophie was not fooled, and she went very still at the sound of her sister's name.

"I fear you must be mistaken, Your Grace." Her voice was cool, but dread began to creep through her.

"I would never argue with a lady, of course," the duke said politely, and Sophie suppressed the strong urge to roll her eyes. "I just know how much you must hope for your sister's happiness, and I should hate for any of these unsavory rumors to get in the way of that—and, naturally, there are your other sisters' prospects to consider as well. I'm told the two youngest in particular are quite . . . spirited."

Now Sophie did stop, turning to face the duke fully; they were slightly obscured behind an enormous potted palm.

"What, precisely, are you implying, Your Grace?" She managed to keep her voice polite, just barely; being the eldest of five sisters, the one who was relied upon to set a good example, had lent her valuable experience in keeping her temper in the face of extreme provocation.

"Nothing at all, Miss Wexham. I merely seek to remind you that actions have consequences. And I wouldn't want you to take any actions without fully considering what those consequences might be."

Before she could respond, he bowed over her hand, offered a curt good evening, then turned and strode away, leaving Sophie batting palm fronds out of her face and with a horrid sinking feeling in her stomach.

"There you are!"

West turned away from David—Willingham (it was still difficult to adjust to his friend's new title, even though it had been a couple of years since he'd inherited)—at the sound of Sophie's voice. She looked beautiful, as always, wearing a gown of light-green silk; her golden hair was dressed simply, with none of the curls that were so in fashion, leaving her lovely face clearly exposed to his hungry gaze.

"Hello." He gave her a small smile, which faded immediately upon catching a proper glimpse of her expression, which was stricken. "What's wrong?"

"I need to speak to you." Her voice was calm, but there was a note of strain that would have been undetectable to someone who didn't know her well.

"Of course." He turned back to David. "If you'll excuse us—"

David nodded equably, his brow wrinkling slightly at whatever he, too, could detect from Sophie's expression. "I'll see you at the boxing match tomorrow?"

"Right, right—" West was distracted; he'd already forgotten that he'd reluctantly promised David he'd accompany him to a boxing match in Kent the following day. He offered his friend a vague wave of farewell, then turned back to Sophie. "Let's find somewhere more quiet where we might speak."

She nodded, and he led her around the edge of the ballroom, out a side door, and into an empty hallway. It wasn't perfect privacy, but it would do in a pinch.

"Your father doesn't want us to marry," she said in a rush, as soon as they came to a halt. He reached out to gently grasp her hands, pulling her so that she was facing him directly.

"Why do you say that?" he asked, a feeling of terrible foreboding building in the pit of his stomach.

"Why?" she repeated, a note of frustration creeping into her voice. "Because he sought me out deliberately to *threaten* me, that's why!" She tugged a hand free from his, pushing a loose tendril of hair behind one ear in an impatient gesture.

West went cold at the words, as slow, creeping anger began to make its presence known. "What do you mean, threaten you?"

"I mean that he asked me to go on a walk about the ballroom and used that time to hint, in oh-so-vague and polite terms, that if I were to marry you, he'd take it out on Maria's matrimonial prospects."

West inhaled slowly; all his life, he'd existed within the carefully drawn parameters that his father expected his heir to occupy, and while he'd occasionally chafed at these restrictions, he'd never found himself feeling truly *angry* about them until now. "I would not allow that to occur."

Her eyes narrowed. "Your father does not strike me as a man who is much concerned by what his son might *allow*."

He could hardly argue with this, but West had spent his entire life playing the dutiful heir, making himself indispensable to the duke. Just this once, he thought, he could push back and emerge victorious.

He had no choice—not when the other option was to lose Sophie.

And he had never wanted anything in his life as badly as he wanted to marry her.

"My father needs to be reminded that I am no longer a boy—that my life is not his to arrange as he sees fit," he said, reaching out to take her hand.

She allowed him to pull her closer, her eyes troubled. "Do you think it will be that simple?"

Truthfully, he did not. But he did not wish to admit any uncertainty to her—could not bear the thought that she would doubt, even for a moment, his ability to give her the future he'd already all but promised her. "I think that my father is a strong-willed man," he said carefully. "But I also think that he has never sought to exert his will over something that mattered as much to me as this does."

Something in her eyes softened at this, though there was still a crease in her brow that he did not like. "You cannot—I know—" she began haltingly, then blew out a frustrated breath, her gaze skittering away from his. "I know that you had mentioned plans to call on my father, but you must know we cannot become betrothed until this is resolved."

His grip tightened on her hand. "Do you not wish to marry me, then?" The words were stiff, his voice quiet.

Her eyes did return to him now. "You know I do," she said softly. "But we cannot risk our marriage ruining Maria's reputation—not when she is still unwed."

"I know," he said, reaching out to touch her cheek. He glanced quickly up and down the hall, saw that they were still alone, and pressed a quick kiss to her forehead. "I would not have anyone in your family suffer because we had the bad luck to fall in love."

The words landed with some weight in the space between them— for all that they had been courting for weeks now, had hinted at a betrothal, neither of them had yet spoken the words to describe precisely what it was that existed between them.

She swallowed. "Was it bad luck, then?"

"No," he said quietly, reaching down to take her other hand, too. He ducked his head so that she could not avoid his gaze. "Meeting you at that musicale is the luckiest thing that has ever happened to me, and I'll be damned if I allow my father to ruin it." He squeezed her hands gently. "I'll speak to him, I promise."

She looked at him for a long moment, then nodded. "All right." They started at the sound of footsteps and laughter drawing nearer, and West dropped her hands, immediately missing their soft warmth.

"I should go find my sister," Sophie said reluctantly, waving away his proffered arm. "It's best if we don't return at the same time, I suppose."

He inclined his head. "Of course," he said, and pressed a kiss to her hand before watching her walk away, the fair skin of her shoulders a tantalizing promise. Her hair gleamed like a coin in the soft candlelight, and he could not tear his eyes from her until she'd rounded a corner and was out of sight.

It was only then, alone with his thoughts, that he allowed himself to lean back against a wall, his head meeting it with a dull *thud*, and mutter, "God damn it."

David found him in the billiards room, where he was not playing but sitting moodily in an armchair, staring into space, a mostly drunk glass of brandy before him.

"Drinking alone?" his friend asked, sinking down into the chair next to him. "Perhaps we'll make a dissolute rake out of you after all." He paused, then added, his tone a bit gentler, "Do you want to talk about it?"

"No." West drained the glass; it was not his first. Nor his second. He'd retreated here after parting from Sophie, his mind occupied by thoughts of how to approach his father—how to make him understand, once and for all, that he was not to interfere. Three glasses of brandy had not yet miraculously provided the answer.

"I thought to take my new curricle to Kent tomorrow," David said, taking a sip from the wineglass in his hand. His golden hair was mussed, and his cravat was askew; West wondered idly whom he'd found to entertain himself with that evening. "It's the fastest one I've ever driven."

"I'd hope so," West said mildly, "if you're hoping to outrun your creditors."

"Ha." David took another sip of wine, staring moodily into the fire. "I could certainly outrun *you*."

West sloshed a bit more brandy into his glass. Held it up, gazing at the amber liquid within the crystal. His head was spinning, and his conversation with Sophie was still echoing in his mind; the looming prospect of a confrontation with his father was like a sudden weight upon his shoulders. He felt frustrated, angry, and—for once—ever so slightly . . . reckless.

He rolled his head against the back of his chair, giving his friend a sideways glance as he took another long sip from his glass.

"Want to bet?"

He did not see Sophie again that evening, instead departing in David's company in a brandy-soaked haze and then awakening the next morning with a splitting headache, in a decidedly ill humor, with a commitment to a poorly considered bet with his friend.

Tomorrow, he thought; he'd go to Kent this afternoon, and then speak to his father and call upon her tomorrow.

But he did not see her the following day—not when everything that afternoon went so horribly, irreparably wrong. The next time he saw her, instead, was some weeks later—after the accident. After David's death. After he'd finally arisen from his sickbed, recovered enough to walk but with a fierce limp as a souvenir of that ill-fated race.

And after she'd become another man's wife.

Chapter One

London, May 1818

Sophie did not recommend widowhood as a rule, but there were undoubtedly certain advantages. She could come and go as she pleased, for example, without any man to fuss over her whereabouts. She could spend an entire day reading, or playing piano, or painting. (She had not, in fact, ever spent an entire day doing any of these things.) She could slip a tot of brandy into her afternoon tea without suffering a man's disapproving gaze. (She absolutely *had* done this, on more than one occasion.) And she could eat a leisurely breakfast, presented with a mouthwatering array of baked-good bounty, without a single other person to interrupt the peaceful solitude of her breakfast room.

Or, rather, she *imagined* this last thing was possible; her sisters, however, made certain that this option was almost never presented to her.

"Sophie!"

Sophie glanced up from the newspaper she was idly perusing over a cup of tea, resisting the urge to roll her eyes heavenward at the sight of not one, nor two, but *three* of her sisters beaming at her from the doorway of the room. Behind them, Grimball, her long-suffering butler, managed to bleat a frantic, "Mrs. Brown-Montague! Mrs. Lancashire! Mrs. Covington!"

Harriet, Sophie's youngest sister—by a mere sixteen minutes—turned a radiant smile on him. "Thank you, Grimball, but I do not think we need announcing! We are *family*."

"Why does that sound like a threat?" Sophie murmured, rising to embrace her sisters in turn.

"Sophie, sarcasm does not suit you," scolded Betsy, Harriet's twin. She caught sight of the platter piled high with croissants on the sideboard. "Ah! I see that Mrs. Villeneuve has made croissants! How convenient, when they are my *particular* favorite!" She gave them a look of such lascivious appreciation that Sophie felt rather protective of the virtue of a platter of baked goods.

"Mmm, yes," Sophie agreed, resuming her seat as Harriet, Betsy, and Alexandra fell upon the bounty on offer. "It could not *possibly* be that it is a Monday, and Mrs. Villeneuve is in the habit of making croissants every Monday—a fact of which you are perfectly well aware?"

"No," Betsy said brightly, placing two croissants on a plate and eyeing a third. "I think it is a mere happy coincidence—the eyes of fate smiling upon us on this joyous day of sisterly reunion!"

"Betsy," Harriet said severely, "have you been reading novels again?"

"Writing them, actually," Betsy said, and Sophie and Harriet both blinked; before they could pursue this most intriguing line of inquiry, Betsy fell into raptures at the sight of a particularly enticing apple tart and was temporarily deaf to any further queries.

"How was Cornwall?" asked Alexandra—Sophie's middle sister, who had been widowed within a year of Sophie. She had selected a more reasonable quantity of pastries and was now settling herself in a chair directly opposite Sophie.

"Lovely. I think my hair still smells of salt." Sophie had recently returned from a fortnight at a house party hosted by Viscount Penvale and his new viscountess.

"It's been an age since I went to the seaside," Alexandra said a bit wistfully.

"Perhaps we should take a holiday together, once the Season is over," Sophie said, taking a sip of tea and watching her sister scrutinize the jam options before her. "We could go to Brighton and go sea bathing," she added, merely to annoy Alexandra; Alex hated to be cold and was generally reluctant to dip more than a toe into the frigid English waters.

"I think a nice walk along the shore would suffice, thank you," Alexandra said, spreading raspberry jam upon a piece of toast. "Besides, I don't know what I shall have planned for the summer."

Sophie frowned, and opened her mouth to inquire further—she did not recall her sister having previously mentioned any potential plans for after the Season concluded—but before she could do so, Alexandra continued, "I want to hear more about the house party." She took a bite of toast and directed a look of innocent inquiry at Sophie—one that had Sophie instantly on guard. "Was there any interesting company?"

At the sideboard, Harriet and Betsy broke off their murmured discussion and turned inquisitive gazes upon Sophie.

"Violet and Audley were there," Sophie said serenely, reaching for a butter knife with calm deliberation. "And Emily and Belfry announced that they're expecting a baby."

Betsy—who was herself expecting, and therefore a bit more emotional than usual—was unable to suppress a soft, misty, *"Oh!"* at this news. Harriet turned a disgusted look upon her twin, and Betsy added, a touch defensively, "Well, just *think* how beautiful their baby will be! Those eyes!"

"All babies have blue eyes," Harriet informed her sister, with the wisdom of a woman who had herself produced just such a creature the previous autumn, and Betsy sighed.

"Yes, I know, but—"

"Any *other* company of note?" Alexandra asked, a bit louder than necessary, exchanging an exasperated glance with Sophie; they were both accustomed to the trial of attempting to hold a conversation while in the twins' company. "Any . . . gentlemen?"

"Several," Sophie said. She broke off a piece of the croissant on her plate. She had her doubts as to the veracity of her cook's French heritage—she had an accent that was prone to rather alarming wobbles at the slightest provocation—but there was no denying that the woman had a way with bread products. "Our numbers were even."

"Any *unmarried* gentlemen?" Alexandra persisted; Sophie glanced up and met Alex's gaze. A brief, silent battle of wills was conducted. Sophie sighed resignedly; her sister, sensing victory was within her reach, leaned forward in her seat.

"Lord Weston was there," Sophie said shortly, a fact her sister clearly already knew—proof that the *ton*'s gossip mill was as efficient as ever.

"*Was* he?" Alexandra asked thoughtfully, tapping her chin.

"Alex." Sophie bit back a dozen things she wanted to say to her sister, beginning with the fact that it had been *seven years* since she had fancied herself in love with the Marquess of Weston, and spent a spring dreaming of the future they'd share—a dream that had proved too fragile to handle even the slightest bit of strain. And, since it had been, again, *seven years* since these events, she would very much appreciate being able to attend an event at which Lord Weston was also present without sparking a speculative fervor among her nearest and dearest.

She said none of this, however; as the eldest of five, she was well-practiced at resisting the urge to snap at her younger sisters. Instead, she merely waited for whatever torment would come next.

"Was he looking well?" Betsy asked, taking a bite of apple tart. She was blond-haired and pink in the face and rather round about the middle, given her pregnancy, and she had a dimple in her chin. She was darling, in other words, which was why it should not have been possible for an expression so closely akin to diabolical to cross her angelic face.

"I suppose." Sophie popped a piece of her croissant into her mouth.

"Did he seem to be in good spirits?" Harriet asked, sitting down next to her twin and reaching for the teapot. Where Betsy was blond and pink-cheeked, Harriet was dark-haired and less rosy, though she did sport deceptively charming dimples of her own. Sophie had always darkly considered the twins' dimples to be the human equivalent of the camouflage that predators in the wild used to lure unsuspecting prey to their demise.

"It was May in Cornwall—it's not physically possible to be in anything other than good spirits," Sophie said, a bit shortly.

"And yet you seem to be managing a rather impressive display of *bad* spirits at the moment," Alexandra said, her gaze on her sister shrewd. Sophie suppressed a sigh.

"Perhaps," Sophie said, laying down her butter knife, "it is because I am no longer *in* Cornwall—which, in addition to its sunny skies and ocean vistas, also has the advantage of being a week's journey away from the three of you."

"I am wounded!" Harriet cried, flinging a dramatic hand to her breast in a display that would have been a bit more convincing had it not also been accompanied by her attempt to simultaneously take a generous bite of croissant. "But," she added quickly, "as it happens, things have been ever so interesting *here*."

"Have they?" Sophie asked idly.

"They *have*," Harriet confirmed, casting a knowing glance at Alexandra, who suddenly seemed very busy stirring sugar into her tea—an interesting preoccupation for a woman who, to the best of Sophie's knowledge, did not actually take sugar in her tea. Sophie's attention sharpened on her sister. It was suddenly clear to her that this was the reason the twins, at least, were here this morning: They had news that they thought would interest their eldest sister, and they badly wanted to see her reaction.

"Define 'interesting,' would you?"

"Alex has a *beau*," Betsy said in theatrical tones.

Alexandra shot a withering glance at her sister, laying down her teaspoon. "You make me sound like I'm a blushing debutante who just made my curtsey to the queen. I don't believe widows have beaux."

"What shall we call him, then?" Harriet asked, a wicked gleam in her eye. "Your paramour?"

"Your inamorata?" Betsy suggested.

"I believe he would technically be her *inamorato*," said Harriet, who had recently decided that she was bored, and had therefore begun attempting to teach herself Italian.

"Lover?" Sophie offered—it was the obvious word they were all tiptoeing around, after all.

"He is my—my gentleman caller," Alexandra said primly, causing both twins to hoot with laughter.

Sophie suppressed a smile. "Indeed. And would you be so kind as to enlighten me as to the identity of this gentleman caller?" She could barely get the expression "gentleman caller" out with a straight face; she felt like a maiden aunt.

Alexandra sighed, putting on a show of exasperation, but a soft smile played at the corners of her mouth as she said, "The Earl of Blackford."

Sophie blinked. "Belfry's brother?"

"The very one."

"He's awfully handsome," Harriet said thoughtfully, "though I do think his brother is perhaps even *more* handsome."

"They both have those blue eyes," Betsy said with a wistful sigh; she considered it a great tragedy of her life that both she and Sophie—as well as their absent sister, Maria—had been blessed with golden hair, but without the accompanying blue eyes that one might expect, theirs being a middling shade of brown.

"I was not aware that you and Blackford were acquainted," Sophie said to Alexandra, ignoring Betsy and Harriet as they lapsed into a dreamy contemplation of the precise shade of the eyes of the Belfry brothers.

"We must have been introduced at some point, but I'd never exchanged more than a few words with him, until we were both guests in the same box at a performance of *The Talk of the Ton.*" This was a new production at the Belfry, the somewhat-scandalous theater owned by Blackford's younger brother, Julian; the show was unique in that it featured only female performers, and was a somewhat ruthless—albeit amusing—skewering of the *ton.* Shows had been sold out for weeks.

"We struck up a conversation," Alexandra continued, "and . . . well, we rather hit it off. He's escorted me to a few balls and dinner parties—we go riding on the Row. . . ." She spoke all of this very nonchalantly, but there was a telltale hint of color in her cheeks and a softness about her as she spoke of him that told Sophie that this was not a mere lark, nor the beginning of a simple affair. And yet . . . something about her voice, some slight note of restraint, gave Sophie pause.

Sophie took a sip of tea, giving herself time to think. Blackford was, from everything she had observed, a true gentleman—she had met him at several events that Emily and Belfry had hosted. Alexandra was not the type to rush into love at a moment's notice, so Sophie had few concerns about the match—but what *did* concern her, at the moment, was her sister's rather strange demeanor as she relayed this information. To be sure, her face lit up and her voice softened upon uttering Blackford's name, but there was something oddly constrained in her manner as she informed Sophie of this development. Alexandra was the quietest and most demure of Sophie's sisters, particularly compared to the boisterous twins; and yet, recalling Alexandra's courtship with her late husband, Sophie couldn't help but think that something seemed to be troubling her sister now, by comparison. Was it guilt at finding happiness again after being widowed, or was there some other concern at play?

"Alex," Sophie said carefully, "are you in love?"

All at once, something in Alexandra's face shifted—whatever softness had been there seemed to vanish, and her features were at once schooled into a look of bland unconcern that was bafflingly at odds with the expression she'd worn just moments before.

"I wouldn't go that far," Alexandra said with a wave of her hand. She lifted her teacup to her mouth; Sophie was aware that Harriet and Betsy were watching both of them quite closely. "We barely know each other."

Sophie glanced at the twins, in time to see Harriet frown, and Betsy open her mouth to protest; this was enough to confirm for Sophie that this was not at all in line with what Alexandra had told them previously.

"I like Blackford, Alex—if he makes you happy, then I think this would be a wonderful match." Sophie kept her voice as gentle as possible, feeling as though she were approaching an easily spooked horse. She liked all of her sisters' husbands—even Maria, the second-eldest, had married Edgar Grovecourt, a man who, while perhaps a bit priggish for Sophie's taste, was fundamentally decent. And in the past, her approval had always seemed important to her younger sisters—a hurdle any suitor needed to clear.

But Alexandra appeared unmoved by this offering on Sophie's part; instead, she waved a hand airily once more, and Sophie was tempted to swat it out of the air; something about the studied casualness of this gesture irritated her. "Let's not get ahead of ourselves—I don't know that I'm going to *marry* him."

Sophie frowned. "Why not, if your feelings are mutual?" She paused, then added more gently, "Is this about Colin?" Colin had been Alexandra's first husband—a younger son who'd bought a commission in the army and died at Waterloo barely a year after he and Alexandra had wed. Alexandra had been devastated by his death three years earlier; coming as it had within a year of Sophie's husband's death, their widowhood had brought the sisters even closer.

Alexandra's face softened at the sound of her late husband's name. "No," she said, a tinge of sadness in her voice. "I loved Colin—I still miss him every day—but I know he would want me to remarry, if I found someone I wished to spend my life with."

Sophie reached across the table and placed her hand on

Alexandra's. "Still, it would be entirely normal if you were to feel some guilt about falling in love again—and I'm certain Blackford would not wish to rush you into anything, if you did not yet feel ready to remarry."

Alexandra turned her hand palm up so that she might give Sophie's a quick squeeze. "I know," she said, her gaze on Sophie affectionate, before shaking her head as if to clear it. She then added, in a more businesslike tone, "I'm just not entirely certain that Blackford is that man, though he—" Here, she broke off abruptly, as though she'd been about to disclose something she'd rather not share.

"*Has* he asked you?" Sophie was beginning to have grave concerns about the wisdom of attending country house parties in the future, if one month away from town was sufficient to see her sister receiving marriage proposals, of all things. Clearly she should not allow herself to be removed from their presence for so long—they might be adults, but they still needed her guidance, as this conversation proved.

"Not yet," Alexandra said cagily; seeing Sophie's gaze boring into her, she sighed and relented. "He might have . . . hinted."

"And what do you intend to say to him, when he *does* ask?" Sophie pressed.

"I'm not certain." Alexandra's tone was carefully light, in a way that seemed artificial. "I'm very fond of my life the way it is now, you know—I mean to say, I wouldn't be able to pop over here for breakfast half so often if I were married to an earl and living in some mansion in Grosvenor Square."

Sophie frowned; while she had, in some ways, come to appreciate the independence that her widowhood had offered her, she had never got the impression that Alexandra fully embraced it. She had been deeply in love with her husband, and stunned by his sudden death— and, too, she was four years younger than Sophie, and had found it something of a shock to leave her parents' home at nineteen only to find herself a widow little over a year later. Once her official mourning period had ended, she had never, so far as Sophie was aware, displayed much interest in flirting with the many eligible gentlemen who had looked her way, and she had certainly never done something so bold as embark on an affair.

Something that Sophie herself had done the previous summer. And while Alexandra had certainly not been disapproving—unlike their sister Maria, who had made more than one snide comment once the gossip had reached her ears—she had seemed more than a little bit mystified by the proceedings. And so, for Alexandra now to be seriously contemplating refusing an offer of marriage—from a future marquess and, more importantly, a man she was obviously very fond of, despite her odd attempts to downplay the affection that so clearly existed between them—struck Sophie as somehow . . . *wrong*.

Alexandra, meanwhile, had taken this opportunity to engage the twins in conversation on other matters—the Northdale ball was in a few days' time, and Harriet offered a lengthy monologue about the neckline of the new rose silk gown that she was debuting—but Sophie was only half-listening, chiming in when a response was clearly expected, but otherwise preoccupied by her thoughts.

Her mind was stuck on one offhand sentence Alexandra had uttered: *I wouldn't be able to pop over here for breakfast half so often if I were married to an earl.*

And the more she thought about it, the more a niggling suspicion began to grow—and grow.

Alexandra wouldn't refuse an offer of marriage for *her*, would she?

Surely, despite their closeness—despite the fact that they saw each other nearly daily, dined together multiple evenings a week, went for long walks in the park together, shared their deepest thoughts and fears . . .

Surely Alex wouldn't turn down Blackford's proposal, for all of that?

Would she?

Sophie watched her sister. Given Alexandra's strange behavior at breakfast, Sophie had little faith that she'd get an honest answer from her, were she to ask directly.

She meant to find an answer—though she wasn't entirely certain what she intended to do about it—and that meant she needed to have a conversation with the Earl of Blackford.

Soon.

So it looked like she would, indeed, be going to the Northdale ball.

"I've never been so pleased to be back in civilization in all my life." This was uttered in tones of deep satisfaction by Diana, who was nursing a glass of champagne and surveying the crowded ballroom with a sharp eye.

"I do not think Cornwall is entirely removed from civilization," Sophie said, taking a sip from the champagne flute in her own hand. "And besides, I rather thought you were enjoying yourself."

"She was," put in Lord Willingham. "She just doesn't want to admit that her brother was right and she was wrong."

Diana cut a narrow look at her husband. "I wasn't *wrong*. I merely had concerns about Penvale relocating to a remote clifftop with a woman he'd barely exchanged two words with."

"I like Jane," Sophie said mildly, in regards to Penvale's new viscountess. "I think she's very amusing."

"As do I," Willingham—Jeremy, to his friends—said. "Anyone who can irritate Diana so thoroughly earns my stamp of approval." He reached out and clinked his own glass against Sophie's, and they exchanged a grin.

"How lovely to see you two so chummy," Diana said, watching this exchange. "Does it remind you of other, more intimate moments?"

Both Sophie and Jeremy choked on their champagne, which had undoubtedly been Diana's aim; she was perfectly well aware of—and entirely unbothered by—the fact that Jeremy and Sophie had had a brief affair the previous summer, before Diana and Jeremy had fallen in love. (Or, in Sophie's personal opinion, before Diana and Jeremy had *admitted* that they'd fallen in love.)

"Diana, what have you done to poor Jeremy and Sophie?" asked Emily, materializing at Sophie's side, her blue eyes wide and concerned. She was wearing a gown of yellow silk and looked, as ever, utterly luminous. Her husband hovered protectively at her elbow.

"Just reminiscing fondly about old times," Diana said with a serene smile.

"Quite," Sophie said, recovering her power of speech now that most of the champagne seemed to have exited her windpipe.

"How . . . nice," Emily said, a bit uncertainly.

"Isn't it?" Diana asked cheerfully. She wound her arm through Jeremy's and turned to Emily's husband, Julian. "Belfry, is that your brother over there? I saw him at a dinner party the other evening and . . ."

Diana's words faded into the background as Sophie wheeled around quickly, looking in the direction Diana had indicated. And, indeed, just a few feet away she saw the Earl of Blackford deep in conversation with Lord James Audley and his wife, Violet. This was too perfect an opportunity to pass up.

"If you'll excuse me," she said abruptly.

"Sophie!" Violet cried as she approached. "You look lovely tonight, wherever did you find the fabric for that gown?"

Sophie glanced down; when she had ended her mourning and half-mourning periods, she had commissioned a new wardrobe for herself—one a bit more daring, a bit more colorful than what she'd worn during her marriage. Fitz wouldn't have minded any of these gowns, precisely, but Sophie had spent the duration of her marriage acutely aware of the reasons she'd wed—of the four younger sisters who needed to make successful matches of their own. The entire point of her marriage had been to ease their way, so she'd always done her best not to call attention to herself, to float beneath the level of *ton* gossip.

But she was no longer a wife. And all of her sisters had been happily wed—until Alexandra's widowhood, of course. To Sophie's mind, she had accomplished what she'd set out to do, and therefore, upon reentering society, she thought that she might do something that *she* wanted to do, for a change. She'd taken considerable delight in commissioning a wardrobe that was precisely what she wished. The gown she wore tonight was a deep-purple silk, with small pearls encrusting the cap sleeves.

"I shall give you the name of my modiste," she promised Violet, and then turned to the man standing next to her. "Lord Blackford."

Blackford, always a gentleman, bowed over her hand. "Lady Fitzwilliam. You are looking lovely this evening. I believe you are recently returned from Cornwall? The seaside clearly agrees with you."

"Thank you," Sophie said, offering him a smile. "Did my sister inform you of my recent travels, then?"

"She did indeed."

"How lovely that you two have grown so close in my absence," Sophie said. "I have been so eager for Alexandra to find happiness again."

Blackford blinked at this remark, which possessed all the subtlety of a hammer. "An admirable sentiment from a sister, I'm sure."

"Yes." Sophie heaved a weary sigh. "It is exhausting, you know, having four younger sisters. One does so often find that they will not behave precisely as one would wish. One might even find them being maddeningly stubborn for no apparent reason. It is *most* irritating, as I'm certain you can appreciate."

Blackford raised a brow, and Sophie's smile widened a touch. "Lady Fitzwilliam, I do believe I hear a waltz starting—I don't suppose I dare hope that you still have this dance free on your dance card?"

"I do," Sophie lied cheerfully, with only the slightest apologetic flicker of the eyes in the direction of Audley, to whom she'd *actually* promised this dance. "How positively fortuitous," she added demurely, and allowed Blackford to lead her to the dance floor with a quick wave of the fingers in the direction of Violet and Audley, who watched this exchange with great interest.

"Why," said Blackford, as they took their places amid the other couples, "do I feel as though I was just carefully maneuvered?"

"I couldn't say, I'm sure," Sophie said innocently. "So, have you spent much time with Alexandra?" If they only had the duration of one waltz, she couldn't afford to waste time on pleasantries.

"A fair amount."

"How often do you see her? Weekly? Daily?" She paused delicately. "Nightly?"

To his credit, Blackford took this in stride. "Shall I save us both time and come right out and tell you that I'd like to marry your sister?" Blackford's voice was amused, and a smile played at the corners of his mouth. Harriet and Betsy were right—he *was* quite handsome, with dark hair and vivid blue eyes. She had never heard much about him in the way of gossip—she knew that he'd once been the lover of the widowed Viscountess Dewbury, before she'd gone on to marry her second husband, but beyond that Sophie had merely heard that he always paid his debts on time, and was generally considered an upstanding sort of chap. He was in line to inherit his father's title, but she believed he and his father were close, and he doubtless hoped that day was still a long way off.

In short, nothing she had ever heard of the man had given her the slightest pause as to his suitability for her sister—which was why she was so perplexed by Alexandra's reaction at the breakfast table a few mornings earlier.

"I am happy to hear it," she said cautiously.

"Lady Fitzwilliam, may I be frank?"

"By all means."

"Well, then I think I ought to inform you that I do not believe your sister will marry me whilst you are still unwed."

"I'm a widow," Sophie said automatically.

"But one who has not yet remarried," Blackford said gently. "And I would never presume to encourage a lady to remarry who does not wish to do so—I gather the widowed state has certain advantages. But I believe that your sister fears for your happiness, and is reluctant to find happiness of her own if she feels that she is . . . well, leaving you behind, I suppose."

Blackford looked distinctly uncomfortable—no doubt the poor man was worried he'd cause her to have a fit of the vapors, or some other swooningly female reaction—but Sophie was not offended. Rather, she was feeling quite grim—she'd been hoping that her suspicion at breakfast would prove to be unfounded.

Sisters! Would they never do what she wished them to?

"I am not lonely, Lord Blackford," she said carefully. "I like my life very much."

And it was true: She *did* like her life. Was it all that she had once imagined? Well, no. But it was perfectly satisfactory all the same.

"I am certain you do, Lady Fitzwilliam," he said, almost gently—and it was this gentleness that, for the first time, allowed the slightest painful pang to reach her chest. It was absurd and ridiculous, but she suddenly felt a bit like weeping over this entire foolish mess Alexandra had created. "And please know that I do not confide this to you out of some desire to persuade you to any course of action. But I thought, if perhaps you could speak to Alex . . . ?"

There was a hopeful note in his voice on this last query, and Sophie nearly smiled to hear it. The thought that this man—heir to one of the oldest estates in England, to an ancient title, rich in family and friends and in every gift a man could receive from birth—should still sound so desperately eager to marry her sister delighted Sophie. And the notion that Alexandra would attempt to ruin both their happiness for Sophie's sake was very near unbearable. To her astonishment, she realized that she was growing the slightest bit *angry*.

And, all at once, she was very, very determined to see Alexandra and Blackford wed, no matter what it took.

"I should be happy to speak to her," she said. Speak. Knock her sister about the head with a serving spoon. Whichever suited, really. "I know we would all be delighted to welcome you to the family—my sisters are quite taken with you."

"Well, I'm only interested in marrying just the one," Blackford said, with a quirk of the mouth that made Sophie like him all the more.

Which meant that Sophie needed to speak to her sister. She did not relish the prospect; something about Alexandra's demeanor at the breakfast table intimated that her sister might choose this exceptionally inconvenient moment to decide to be exceedingly stubborn. It was a family trait that tended to rear its head at the precise moments that one might wish it *wouldn't*.

And then, as the waltz came to an end, and she sank into a curtsey before Blackford, her gaze alighted on a familiar pair of broad shoulders. She had caught sight of them out of the corner of her eye while she and Blackford had been dancing, and had determinedly ignored them; their owner was not a man she allowed her thoughts—or eyes—to linger on.

Anymore.

At that precise moment, he turned, his green eyes scanning the room. They landed on her for a split second, catching and holding, and Sophie inhaled sharply.

He looked away first.

She took a second, steadying breath.

And then, with the suddenness of a thunderclap, she knew *precisely* how she could convince Alexandra to marry Blackford.

If she could somehow find someone to aid her—and she very much feared that there was only one particular someone who would do.

So she would have to persuade him.

Chapter Two

Seven years earlier

Sophie fell in love with a man with perfect shoulders and too many names.

"John Percival George Horatius Arthur Audley," she repeated, a questioning note in her voice. "Have I got them all?"

West tilted his head. "You've missed a St. John in there some-where," he said after a moment's consideration. "After Horatius."

"But your Christian name is *John*," she protested, barely suppressing her laughter. "What do you need a St. John for as well?"

"It's a family name," he said, all wounded ducal—or, more accurately, *future* ducal—dignity, but he was betrayed by a telltale twitch at the corner of his mouth.

Sophie loved that twitch.

She'd seen it first on the night they met, at a musicale that could be charitably called "interpretive." It was early in the Season—Sophie's third—and her mother had deemed the evening's entertainment un-missable, so eager was she for her eldest daughter to see and be seen by all the prospective matches sure to be present. (Sophie, for her part, could not possibly understand why a gentleman would choose to subject himself to a musicale if he had the option to spend his evening getting foxed at his club instead; she raised this point with her mother, who pinched her nose and said, "*Sophia*" in pained tones, which she tended to resort to only if Sophie alluded to intoxicating spirits, chamber pots, or any portion of the anatomy north of the shin.)

Sophie was not enormously fond of musicales in general—she found that she had only so much patience for sitting in an uncomfortable gown listening to music at an hour that produced the effect of a lullaby—but they were usually tolerable. That evening's event, however, had been hosted by Viscountess Holyoak, who seemed convinced that her two unwed daughters were violin prodigies, and who only later that year—too late to be of use to any of the unfortunate attendees that evening—would come to be known as increasingly hard of hearing.

Sophie's mother had abandoned her almost immediately upon arrival, spotting a friend in the far corner whom she wished to greet. Sophie had found a seat in the third-to-last row—not so close to the back of the room that it would seem like a deliberate attempt to escape on her part, but far enough back that if she allowed her eyes to drift shut briefly with her head firmly upright, no one was likely to notice. It was a relief to be here without Maria; her younger sister was in her first Season, and Sophie felt a vague sense of obligation whenever they attended an event together. It was up to her to set a good example—to help Maria navigate the treacherous waters of the *ton*. If Maria were here, Sophie would not have allowed her eyes to flicker shut for even a moment. And she *certainly* would never have contemplated escape.

But Maria was not with her, and barely five minutes into the evening's entertainment, Sophie determined that—for the sake of her own sanity—she could not remain in this room for the next hour. She had never before attended a performance at which the musicians' defi-nition of "Mozart" and Mozart's own definition of "Mozart" differed so wildly; she spared a longing glance for the candles burning in sconces along the wall, wondering if she could fashion their wax into earplugs, but abandoned this in favor of the simplest option:

Flight.

She slipped out of her seat, making a whispered inquiry of a liver-ied footman as to the location of the ladies' retiring room, and escaped gratefully into the silence of the hall.

Except it was not silent, not truly—Lady Holyoak's music room must have the thinnest walls known to man, Sophie thought ruefully; she had thought merely to flee into the hall for a minute (or ten), but now she set off in the direction the footman had indicated. After all, a lady could take positively *ages* in the retiring room, and no one would ask her a single question about it.

She rounded the series of corners the footman had described and found the room she sought, but then paused—at the end of the hallway was a set of French doors leading to some sort of terrace, and they had been left ever-so-slightly ajar. A telltale wisp of smoke curled past the glass, indicating that whoever had opened them was still there. Sophie supposed it was some servant or other, taking a minute to escape from their duties, and thought she should likely leave them in peace; her curiosity got the better of her, however, and she took several hesitant steps in that direction—

Just in time to nearly run headfirst into the man who opened the doors at that moment, dropping a cheroot and grinding it beneath his heel before he lifted his foot to step inside.

Both stopped in their tracks, startled.

Sophie recognized him instantly—there could hardly be a single eligible young lady of the *ton* whose mama had not made her excruciatingly aware of the existence of the Marquess of Weston. He was tall and broad-shouldered—good God, those shoulders—and athletic in build, which was displayed to excellent effect by the fact that he was tailored within an inch of his life. Everything he wore, from the snowy-white cravat at his throat to his gleaming black shoes, screamed of money and good taste. He was handsome, too, and not merely in the way of those aristocrats who relied on tailoring and a devoted valet to lend the impression of good looks to a man of average appearance. No, Lord Weston had thick, nearly black hair that was combed back from his face, the slightest hint of a curl smoothed into submission, and eyes of a vivid, arresting green. Everything about his face seemed to have been designed with the utmost care, from the sharp blades of his cheekbones to the dark slash of his eyebrows, lending him a rather stern expression.

One of those eyebrows was now lifted in arrogant inquiry.

"I beg your pardon," he said a bit stiffly; he and Sophie had never been introduced, though they'd certainly attended the same events a number of times, and she'd seen him from a distance. She wondered if he even knew her name.

She should, she knew, make some excuse and beat a hasty retreat—the daughter of an upstart viscount who'd married into a family who made their fortune in *trade*, of all things, could not possibly have anything to say to the heir to one of the oldest ducal titles in England. And yet, something about the lift of that single, arrogant eyebrow made her stop thinking entirely, and so the first words out of her mouth to one of the most eligible bachelors in England were:

"You do not seem like the sort of man to smoke a cheroot."

The brow inched higher.

"That's a rather bold assumption to make, considering we've never spoken." He made a show of peering around, as if in search of a chaperone, then glanced back at her with a shrug. "As I do not see your mother anywhere nearby, perhaps we might forgo the formality of introductions? I find myself quite desperate to know what sort of man you *do* think I am, if not a cheroot-smoker."

Sophie pressed her lips together to suppress a smile; she had not expected him to be amusing. "I am Sophie Wexham," she said, the words sounding strange on her lips—she'd never introduced *herself*, she realized, as there was always someone there to do it for her. Polite society was rather predicated on this rule.

"I know."

It was her turn to lift a brow. "You do?"

"Almost everyone seems to know who I am, so I make a point of trying to learn who others are, too." She gave him a skeptical look, not entirely convinced by this rather pretty proclamation of his concern for his fellow man. He sighed, then admitted, "I saw you at the Mottram ball last week, and I asked my friend Willingham who you were."

A thrill should not have coursed through Sophie at this, but it did nonetheless. She had no business having *thrills* over men like the Marquess of Weston.

"I am Weston, by the way," he added as an afterthought.

Sophie waved a dismissive hand. "As you so charmingly mentioned, *everyone* knows who you are."

Then, for the first time, she witnessed the telltale twitch at the corners of his mouth—the sign that he was amused, but wouldn't let himself show it. "I believe I said *almost* everyone." He dusted an imaginary speck of dust off his sleeve. "I wouldn't want to presume that every pretty young lady I meet is already aware of my existence."

"Are you trying to charm me?" Sophie asked suspiciously.

Another twitch. "Perhaps. Is it working?"

She suppressed a smile of her own. "Perhaps."

Belatedly, he seemed to realize that they were still standing in the doorway, the door slightly ajar behind him. He stepped fully inside and clicked the door shut, then gave her an assessing look. "Shouldn't you be enjoying the sweet tones of the Misses Durand serenading you with . . ." He floundered.

"Mozart," Sophie supplied helpfully. "Left before they even started playing, did you?"

"Lady Holyoak was a friend of my mother, and I like to pay her the respect of accepting her invitations, but . . ." He trailed off, and Sophie could tell his gentlemanly instincts were at war with his truthful ones. "Well, I heard the young ladies play last year," he finished diplomatically.

"I cannot imagine they have improved." Sophie paused, struck by a troubling possibility. "Unless they *have*, in which case I truly pity anyone in attendance at last year's musicale."

"It was indeed harrowing," he admitted. "So I thought it might be better if someone found me smoking, rather than just cowering on a terrace with my hands over my ears." He grimaced. "I always forget quite how much I dislike cheroots."

"So I was right, then," Sophie said smugly. "You're *not* the sort of man who smokes cheroots."

"Guilty as charged." He was watching her with an odd gleam in his eyes—one that was close to a smile, somehow, even if his mouth was not cooperating. "Shall I escort you back so that we might suffer together?"

Sophie sighed. "I suppose—my mother will no doubt notice my

absence eventually. Although, if listening to those violins is the price I must pay to find an eligible husband, I think I'm perfectly happy to remain unwed, even if all of my younger sisters *do* marry before me, as has been Mama's latest dire prediction."

Lord Weston offered her his arm, and she took it; it was reassuringly firm under her hand, and she caught the faintest scent of sandalwood, no doubt from his soap. She determinedly tried to ignore it—who cared about nicely scented marquesses with strong arms? Not she. Obviously!

"How many Seasons have you had?" he asked curiously, glancing down at her. Sophie was of average height, and he had at least seven or eight inches on her. She felt a bit exasperated with herself at the discovery that she, like most other women on earth, appeared to have a bit of a weakness for a tall, dark, and handsome man.

How frightfully *clichéd*.

"This will be my third," she said, suppressing a sigh. "I've four younger sisters, and the next one just made her debut, so my mother feels strongly that I ought to . . . set a good example, if you will."

"By settling down with some dull fellow with a crumbling pile in Sussex, I suppose?" They were walking at an inordinately slow pace, so as to delay for as long as possible the aural horrors that awaited them.

"No," Sophie said slowly, thinking it might be simpler if her mother were as strictly mercenary as that—it would certainly be easier to resent her, if Sophie did not know that she truly only wanted her daughter's happiness. (But a crumbling pile—or a fully intact one—would not go amiss.) "My parents . . . well . . ." She trailed off, then cast a furtive glance up and down the hallway, confirming they were still alone. "They're in *love*."

"Ah," West said, nodding. "Your father's one of the footmen, then?

Bold of him and your mother to continue the affair, even after a child was produced, but rather touching, in its own way."

Sophie glanced up at him, saw the insistent tugging at the corners of his mouth, and burst out laughing.

Later, she would think helplessly that that was probably the moment she fell in love with him.

"My birth was entirely legitimate, thank you very much," Sophie said, still chortling. "But my parents' marriage was a matter of practicality—my father's family had a newly granted title, but no fortune to speak of, whilst my mother's family had plenty of the latter to share—and then they had the absolute gall to fall sickeningly in love, went on to have five children, and have spent the past two decades staring rapturously across the breakfast table at each other. So they want me to marry, but they also want me to marry someone I *like*, which just makes it that much more difficult."

"Because you dislike everyone you've ever met." His tone was serious, but she glanced up and caught that gleam in his eye. The Marquess of Weston had a sense of humor! This, on top of his cheekbones and his scent and his height, was frankly beginning to strike Sophie as a bit unjust.

"Because it's an awful lot of pressure!" She resisted the urge to stamp her foot. "It will break their hearts if they think I've married because they want me to, and then I end up miserable and they have to watch me drift about sadly in an unhappy marriage for the rest of my days."

"So let me be certain I understand this," he said slowly. "You're worried you'll disappoint your parents by not marrying—and you're also worried you'll disappoint them by not marrying happily enough?"

"*And*," she added, "I'm worried that I need to make a decent enough match to make my family seem at least somewhat palatable to the *ton*, so that my sisters can make good matches, too."

"Why are they unpalatable?" he asked, frowning, and Sophie experienced a brief, powerful desire that she, too, could be a wealthy, titled man, one who did not spend his days with a mother filling his ears with talk of matrimony, who did not feel acutely conscious of the need to marry upward, to secure his spot among the rest of the aristocracy. One who didn't file away every piece of information ever heard about any other member of their class.

"My father's title is quite new," she said, instead of vocalizing any of those thoughts. "It only dates back to his father, so his family is already not considered terribly high in the instep, and then my father made the unforgivable error of marrying a Landsdowne."

West frowned. "As in, the shipping company?"

"The very one. We reek of trade."

The words were a test, she realized—one she hadn't entirely intended to set for him, and yet which proved irresistible once the opportunity arose. How would this man, with a lineage far more ancient than that of the king, respond to this revelation of her own roots?

He made a great show of sniffing the air around him. "Odd. I don't smell anything."

And then he smiled at her.

And her heart went *thump, thump.*

And in the days—and weeks—and years to come, with all that would pass between them, with a Season of courtship, his accident and her marriage, the surreptitious glances across ballrooms, the fleeting pressure of his hand on hers in polite greeting at this event or another—

She would never quite manage to forget the way her heart felt, that first night they met, when she was basking in the bright, unexpected glow of his smile. Despite the pain this memory would cause her, she could never bring herself to wish it away.

Chapter Three

"Is that really necessary?"

There were many sounds that West was fond of: The pounding of galloping hooves. A piano playing a complicated concerto. Once—but not at all recently—a woman's sighs in his ear.

His father's voice, in his own home, before the hour of noon, was not one of them.

West pushed up his helmet, offered Hawthorne a grimace, and lowered his foil. "Father," he said, politely bowing his head as he turned.

"West. If you feel up to fencing, then would Angelo's not suit better than your valet?" Hawthorne was not merely his valet, but one of his closest friends—a fact that his father, as fixated on status as he was, would never acknowledge.

"Hawthorne is a better opponent than any I've yet found at Angelo's," West said, which was not entirely true—Hawthorne was damned handy with a sword, but he'd never had any proper training, and doubtless there were opponents at the fencing academy who could beat him without undue difficulty. West, however, had no interest in fencing at Angelo's, not when he was slow and clumsy where once he'd been quick-footed, capable of beating most men he knew. Hawthorne, bless him, never gave him the slightest ounce of pity, even as West's movements were halting, his footwork appalling.

He really shouldn't be fencing at all; he knew there would be hell to pay later, as there always was when he attempted anything that involved him setting aside his cane for any duration of time. But it made his mind go temporarily, blissfully blank—and, occasionally, this was too powerful a temptation to resist.

How kind of his father to appear just in time to ruin all of that blissful blankness.

The Duke of Dovington was an imposing man, for all that he was nearing seventy; his hair was entirely gray, but still thick upon his head, and his dark eyes were as sharp and intelligent as ever. West and his brother both took after their father in appearance; staring at the duke was rather like gazing into a mirror showing West what he'd look like decades in the future.

He hoped, however, he'd manage to be a bit less of a complete and utter ass.

With this bit of warm familial regard in mind, he handed Hawthorne his foil and crossed the room, gritting his teeth against the pain in his leg as he walked. His cane was leaning carefully against one wall, and West took the time to shrug back into his waistcoat and jacket before reaching for it, acutely conscious of his father's eyes on him all the while. His father, being a duke, was accustomed to everyone he deigned to speak to springing into action to meet his every need, and West was not above allowing himself the small pleasure of forcing him to wait.

"Do you have something you wish to discuss?" he asked, his tone blandly polite as he turned to face his father.

"Yes. Perhaps we might step into your study?" The duke was

dressed for riding—he and West's brother, James, shared a fondness for morning rides in Hyde Park, though West was fairly certain that both of them took some pains to ensure that they rarely encountered each other on these rides—and there was a trace of impatience in his voice, as if he could not believe that he had to take time out of his busy day of wafting around on a cloud of ducal superiority to pay his son a visit.

"I think the library will do," West said pleasantly as they left the ballroom and entered the first-floor hallway, inclining his head at a door to his left.

Sparing a brief regret for the hope that, by the time he reached the age of two-and-thirty, he would be above pettily trying to thwart his father in matters of little importance—clearly, this was not going to happen—he opened the door, allowing his father to precede him into the room.

The library was one of West's favorite rooms in his London residence; it was situated toward the back of the house, meaning there was little noise from the street here, and the walls were papered in a dark green that reminded him of a gown—

He broke off that thought abruptly, before his mind could even finish formulating it.

He broke off any thoughts that led to *her*.

He made his way toward a stuffed leather armchair near the fireplace, where a small fire burned, and gestured at the chair opposite in silent invitation.

"Shall I ring for tea?" West asked politely.

"I did not come here to drink tea with you," his father said, which was precisely what West had expected he would say. "I came because I caught wind of some disturbing gossip that I wish to discuss."

West had a decent guess what this gossip was about, but he certainly wasn't going to tell his father that.

"I understand," the duke continued, "that you are recently returned from Cornwall."

"Indeed." West leaned back in his chair, contemplating ringing for tea despite his father's rejection of his offer—*he* was feeling rather thirsty, after that fencing session. "You may have noticed we did not have our weekly dinner at White's for several weeks running?"

His father flicked an impatient glance at him; he did not approve of anything in West that hinted even slightly at sarcasm, or at any sense of humor at all. It was his opinion that heirs to dukedoms did not *need* a sense of humor—one could hire someone to laugh at one's jokes when appropriate, after all, so one needn't worry about actually being *amusing*.

"I was informed that Lady Fitzwilliam Bridewell was also in attendance."

West went still at the name, though he was at least grateful that his father had got to the point quickly.

"She was," he said quietly. "And I believe I informed you once in the past that I should not like to hear her name cross your lips again."

His father regarded him, assessing, for a long moment; West met his gaze directly, something he had always made a point of doing, ever since he was a small boy being called into his father's study to be reprimanded for some offense or other.

"I played cards with the Duke of Altborough the other night," his father said at last.

West blinked at this non sequitur. "I was unaware Altborough was in town—I thought he was in poor health."

"He was, but apparently is feeling improved now that the weather has warmed. Did you know he has three daughters?"

West allowed a beat of silence and then another. "I do not think I knew the precise number, but yes, I know he has daughters."

The duke allowed his gaze to wander around the room. "They're all unmarried—well, one's a widow. Out of mourning, though. The other two are still unwed—the youngest just made her curtsey to the queen this spring."

"A bit young for my taste," West said; for all that he knew plenty of men who thought nothing of taking a wife decades younger than themselves, he found the idea of attempting to woo a naïve eighteen-year-old distasteful.

The duke waved a dismissive hand. "The other two are older, then. Perhaps the widow might be more to your liking?" He allowed one single, precise second of silence before adding, "It seems you've a weakness for them."

West leveled a steady gaze at his father. "Why this sudden fixation upon my marital prospects? I thought you'd despaired of that long ago."

West had ensured that he had, in fact. Once he'd learned how his father had thwarted his first—and only—attempt at marriage, he had felt little guilt in allowing his father to believe that there was no point in attempting to arrange one for him.

"Yes," his father said, regarding him thoughtfully in a way that West liked not one bit. "Because of your accident. And its tragic repercussions." There was a note of wry skepticism to his voice that set West further on edge; all of his conversations with his father felt like high-stakes chess games, and this one seemed to be veering more sharply in that direction than usual.

"Yes," West said slowly. "As we've discussed."

"Hmmm." The duke drummed his fingers on the arm of his chair. "I believe it was Dr. Worth who told you that you could never hope to father children, in the wake of your injury?"

"Yes," West said, a bit tersely.

"How interesting, then, that I recently spoke to Dr. Worth, and he knew nothing of this supposed condition." His father sat back in his chair and gazed steadily at West, awaiting his next move.

West decided, after a split second of contemplation, to brazen it out. "Perhaps his memory is failing him in his old age." He spared a silent thought of apology for Dr. Worth, who had been his doctor since he was a boy but who *was*, in truth, growing rather elderly.

"Perhaps," his father allowed. "However, he seemed to think—how did he phrase it?—that there was no reason a broken leg and a scratch should have any effect whatsoever on your ability to produce any number of heirs."

West pressed his lips together, allowing several satisfying curses to circle inside his head without uttering a single one. "It was a bit more than a scratch," he said mildly—it had, in fact, been a deep, thoroughly nasty wound that had become infected—but, unfortunately, Dr. Worth was not otherwise incorrect.

"Of course." His father nodded. "Now, perhaps *my* memory is failing me as I age"—his mouth quirked in amusement, as if the mere suggestion that he'd lost even a fraction of his mental faculties was so ludicrous as to be laughable—"but whilst I cannot recall what precise words you used, some years ago, I remember receiving the distinct impression that you would be unable to father any heirs, and so there was little point in worrying about a wife for you." He waved a hand. "Doubtless, I misunderstood—I cannot imagine that you would deliberately mislead me, after all."

The duke smiled a humorless smile, then continued. "Now that I've realized *my* mistake"—he paused again, allowing the emphasis on that word to sink in—"it of course stands to reason that it is high time you were considering marriage."

The words landed like a thrown gauntlet.

"Perhaps I am not yet interested in marriage."

This was entirely the incorrect thing to say—this much was immediately obvious to West. He was thirty-one years old and he was first in line to a dukedom; he did not have the luxury of waiting to marry until he at last took an interest in the institution. He was expected to produce an heir, after all, and the fact that his father—thanks to West himself—had not believed this to be a possibility was the only reason he'd been granted a reprieve these past several years.

His father, however, did not argue with him. Instead, he gazed around the room, allowing a taut silence to stretch between them; finally he said, almost idly, "I've been thinking of selling Rosemere."

West felt it like a blow to the stomach, as it had no doubt been intended; he pressed his lips together tightly to prevent any pained exhalation of breath. "Oh?" he managed after a moment.

"Yes. It's turned quite a profit these past few years, you know—it would no doubt fetch a handsome price."

West did know—he was directly responsible for its prosperity. Rosemere was one of the few unentailed properties that the dukedom owned, and one that his father had gifted to him, upon his twenty-first birthday. His mother had brought the property, which belonged to her family, to her marriage as part of her dowry; West had few, vague memories of the mother who had died when he was only four years old, but he remembered with peculiar, vivid clarity how much she had loved Rosemere. He had a memory of her laughing as she cut roses from the garden, the sound bright and free, and he felt the strangest lump in his throat whenever he recalled it.

His father, however, had never felt the same—it was a small holding, nothing compared to the grander entailed estates, and he had never paid it much attention. That the duke did not see Rosemere's value was no small part of the reason that West loved it so much—a sentiment he had endeavored to hide from his father. He had seen, after all, what his father did to things—people—that West loved. But apparently, he had not hidden it well enough.

"I know you've spent a fair amount of time there over the years," his father continued, "but it really seems the sort of home that ought to be for a . . . family." He shrugged; that shrug, along with every single element of this discussion, was carefully choreographed. "And since you've no intention of marrying . . ."

He did not need to make the threat more explicit. West understood perfectly well.

His father rubbed his hands together. "I should be off—I've a busy day."

Intimidating underlings, making servants cry, et cetera, West thought darkly.

"Do let me know if you'd like an introduction to one of Altborough's daughters," his father added, rising from his chair.

West rose with him, his gaze lantding longingly on the sideboard against the far wall. Was it too early for a drink?

The clock chose that moment to chime the eleven o'clock hour.

Eleven was only an hour from noon. And noon was not really so very early, after all. Was it?

"I look forward to discussing this further with you at dinner this week," his father called on his way out.

No, West decided. Today, noon was not early at all.

He was nearly finished with his second brandy when Lady Fitzwilliam Bridewell appeared in the library.

West blinked at her, then at his butler, Briar, who was bowing himself out of the room wearing an expression of unmistakable curiosity. He glanced at the glass in his hand. This *was* his second, wasn't it? He hadn't lost count at some point, and actually consumed an amount of spirits that would lead to hallucinations?

Lady Fitzwilliam's gaze followed his and her eyes widened slightly. Belatedly, he realized that—hallucination or not—she was still a lady, and he was instantly on his feet, gritting his teeth slightly against a wince as the sudden motion jarred his bad leg, which was still protesting the morning's exercise. Fortunately, the two(?) glasses of brandy had gone a long way toward silencing its louder objections.

"Lady Fitzwilliam."

"West."

She was always Lady Fitzwilliam to him now, even in his thoughts. He didn't allow himself the pleasure of thinking of her as anything else. He liked, however—too much, far too much—the fact that, at some point in the past year, she had once again taken to addressing him by his nickname. Everyone called him West, it was true; to do otherwise would have drawn more attention to them in company. But this did not diminish the small jolt of pleasure he got every time he heard her say his name.

"You are at my house," he said. "Alone."

"And you are drinking," she said. "At . . ." Her gaze flicked to the clock on the mantel. "Noon."

West resisted the urge to follow her gaze to confirm the time. Was it still only noon? He'd lost track of time at some point while drinking the second(?) brandy, which was a rather more generous pour than the first.

"I've had a trying morning."

"Ah." She did not inquire further; they no longer had the sort of relationship that would permit such an intimacy. Although apparently they had the sort of relationship that would permit an unmarried woman to call on an unmarried gentleman at his home, unescorted, and—well, no. There was no sort of relationship that permitted *that*.

"I have been rather distracted this morning. Did I forget an engagement we had?" This was so implausible as to be laughable, and the slight curve at the corner of her mouth confirmed that she knew this as well as he did. That hint of a smile was like a punch to the chest. She was not dressed with particular care—she wore a simple green walking gown, a bonnet in her hand that she had apparently removed upon being admitted to the house. Her golden hair gleamed in the firelight of the library. She was still—was always—the most beautiful thing he had ever seen.

"No, I—I'm here today with a proposal." She paused, then seemed to reconsider the wisdom of *that* particular word, given to whom she spoke, and the seven years of history that stretched between them. "A proposition," she corrected, and then a hint of color stole into her cheeks—a rarity for a woman who was not prone to blushes. "Apparently there is no word I can use that will not seem ill-advised the moment it leaves my mouth," she said with an exasperated sigh.

"Would you like to sit down?" he asked, gesturing at the armchair opposite him, the one that his father had vacated scarcely more than an hour before.

She seemed about to refuse, and then her gaze flicked to his leg, and she said, "Yes, of course." There was no hint of pity in her face or her voice as she crossed the room to sit, and West followed suit with some relief at the feeling of weight being lifted from his protesting leg. He wondered a moment later, however, if this had not been a mistake—if perhaps a bit of pain was worth suffering—because she was suddenly much, much closer to him than she had been a few moments before. And he organized much of his life with the unstated but determined goal of avoiding being in close proximity to her if possible.

Lately, unfortunately, it had not been possible—and he had an uneasy feeling that, whatever her reason for calling on him today was, it was going to make that goal even less attainable.

She took a breath, as if steeling herself.

"My sister has formed an attachment," she announced, without further preamble.

"I presume you mean Mrs. Brown-Montague—otherwise, this seems like not quite the sort of confession I ought to be hearing."

She cast him a narrow look; he kept his face carefully blank, but after a moment an amused gleam lit her eyes, and he knew she could tell that he was teasing. Still, after all this time, she could always tell.

"Yes, it's Alexandra," she said. "She and the Earl of Blackford have fallen in love, it would seem, and she's refusing to marry him because she's worried about me."

He frowned. "Why is she worried about you?" he asked. "Is something amiss?" His tone was neutral; he knew all too well that she would not welcome any concern from him.

"She fears that if she remarries, she'll be leaving me all by myself again," she said, her glance skittering off his as she spoke. She shifted in her seat, and his gaze sharpened on her—Lady Fitzwilliam was one of the most self-assured women he'd ever met, and not prone to fidgeting. "Which is absurd, obviously," she added hastily. "It's not as though she and I share a home. I already live alone; nothing would change about my life if she and Blackford were to wed." There was something defensive in both her tone and her posture as she spoke these words, and he could see how much this conversation was costing her—admitting to *him*, of all people, that the younger sisters she had always focused so much of her energy on protecting might regard her as someone in need of protection, too.

"And you have not been able to convince her of this?"

She pressed her lips together. "She is being . . . difficult, when I have tried to broach the subject with her. I spoke to Blackford, who confirmed my suspicions. He thinks I just need to speak to her again, reassure her, but . . ."

"You're unconvinced?"

"She can be quite stubborn, occasionally," Lady Fitzwilliam said, and it took considerable effort for West to refrain from pointing out that this was a trait that seemed to run in the Wexham family.

"How does this concern me, then?" he asked, keeping his tone polite enough to soften the bluntness of the question. He and Blackford were friendly, but if she wished for him to speak to Blackford, he thought it might strike the other man as decidedly odd—and he couldn't imagine what good he could possibly do anyway. Nor, for that matter, why she thought to come to *him*, of all people, with this worry. Theirs had not been a relationship, of late, that invited the sharing of confidences. Or of anything else.

She took a breath, and then looked directly at him. "I was hoping that you might ask me to marry you."

Chapter Four

Seven years earlier

Sophie was not overly contrary by nature, but she was not certain how much more of her mother's giddy delight she could handle. After two and a half Seasons of increasing despair that her daughter would ever make a happy match, she now seemed to be relishing every moment of Sophie's courtship. Sophie herself had no complaints about said courtship, but she was occasionally possessed of the wild, absurd thought that it would be rather satisfying if West were a disreputable, fortune-hunting rake instead of a marquess of impeccable reputation, just to see her mother's reaction.

Then, as if on cue:

"Is West calling today, darling?" Lady Wexham trilled down the breakfast table, interrupting Sophie's thoughts. Sophie suppressed a sigh by taking a healthy sip of tea. Next to her, Harriet's spine straightened, her head turning eagerly; the twins were fourteen, and—in their minds—heartbreakingly far from their own debuts, and so they were living vicariously through Sophie's spring of romantic intrigue.

"Of course he is," Maria said with an eye roll. "He calls *every day.*"

Her words were softened by the teasing grin she directed at her sister; Maria seemed rather fond of West.

"I think it's sweet," Alexandra said with a soft smile; her debut was still a couple of years away and, unlike the twins, she was not overly eager to make her curtsey. She was in the habit of cheerfully waving Sophie and Maria off to whatever their evening's entertainment was with a sketchpad or novel in hand, clearly relishing the prospect of a quiet night at home. (Or, rather, as quiet as it was possible for an evening at the Wexham home to be, given that it was inhabited by Harriet and Betsy.)

"We are going to an exhibition at the Royal Academy," Sophie reminded her mother patiently, ignoring all of her sisters. "You agreed to chaperone us for this outing, don't you recall?"

"Oh, of course," her mother said vaguely, not sounding remotely concerned about her solemn duty to protect the virtue of her eldest child; West had charmed her so thoroughly that she clearly did not think she need worry about any ungentlemanly behavior from that quarter. So far, this assumption had proved correct—which Sophie was beginning to find a bit disappointing. She didn't wish to be ruined, of course, and she knew that West was far too honorable to take too many liberties, but surely a kiss or two was not too much to hope for? She knew that she *ought* not to hope for any such thing until a betrothal, but, well . . .

She'd been so frightfully well-behaved her entire life, and particularly these past few years. Surely it wouldn't hurt to be a little bit naughty, just once?

These thoughts had not left her mind by the time West called for her and her mother that afternoon; he presented himself at their door in a green jacket and waistcoat that perfectly matched his eyes, sweeping his top hat off for a polite bow over Lady Wexham's hand, and then Sophie's.

"You both look lovely today," he said, but his eyes were on Sophie as he spoke, and she smiled at him, resisting the urge to blush.

This moment was interrupted unceremoniously by Harriet and Betsy colliding into Sophie's back, nearly sending her toppling to the floor; West reached out and seized her elbow to steady her.

"Girls!" Lady Wexham suddenly sounded precisely as exhausted as one might expect of a woman with five daughters, all still living at home. "I believe I sent you upstairs for your music lesson a quarter of an hour ago, and I know from the sounds emanating from the music room that you have not improved sufficiently to cut your lesson short."

"We told Mr. Cumberland that we needed to visit the retiring room," Harriet informed her mother cheerfully. "He looked positively *mortified* and didn't ask any further questions."

"I'm certain he didn't," Lady Wexham muttered; the twins' music master was a young, exceedingly polite gentleman who, while apparently a virtuoso on the pianoforte, was quite plainly mildly terrified of his pupils. Sophie could not entirely blame him.

"I felt rather bad, embarrassing him," Betsy said a touch wistfully. "He does have such soulful eyes, you know; I should hate to cause him undue agony." Betsy was the more romantic of the twins, as proved by the disgusted snort Harriet offered in response.

Sophie cast a quick glance at West, still standing politely in the entryway, watching this frankly deranged scene unfold. He caught her eye and winked at her, then stepped forward and said gravely, "Miss Harriet. Miss Elisabeth. What an unexpected pleasure." He bowed over their hands, just as elegantly as he would any lady of the *ton*; Betsy blushed a bright red, while Harriet smiled coyly at West in a way that made Sophie think grimly that they were going to have to keep quite a careful eye on her in a few years. Not, she supposed, that that was anything out of the ordinary; since the twins were six years her junior, she'd been keeping an eye on them from the time they were old enough to walk, never quite trusting that their nannies and governesses were up to the task of keeping them in check. (This had proved, on more than one occasion, to be a well-founded concern on Sophie's part.)

"West, Maria says she does not think Mama will be a terribly effective chaperone," Harriet said briskly, and Sophie contemplated suffocating herself—or her sister; she wasn't picky at the moment—with her bonnet.

"Harriet!" Maria's horrified voice wafted down the stairs from whichever landing she was lurking on to eavesdrop.

"It's true!" Harriet called, tilting her head back so that her voice would carry up the stairs. "You said that Mama would be perfectly happy to allow West to compromise Sophie behind a piece of statuary if it would hasten a wedding!"

"*Harriet Catherine Wexham.*" Lady Wexham actually reached out and clapped her hand over her daughter's mouth.

Betsy leaned forward confidingly; Sophie felt a sense of great doom. "Mama would never allow you to compromise Sophie behind a piece of statuary," she said to West, wide-eyed and earnest. A muffled protestation on Harriet's part was, mercifully, unintelligible. "They're not private enough. If I were you, I would try to sneak her out to a garden somewhere instead." She paused, thoughtful. "Gardens are much more secluded, and *very* romantic, too." She gave a happy little sigh, then beamed at West as though she'd just shared a treasured family secret.

"Thank you, Miss Elisabeth," West said, straight-faced. "I shall take that under advisement—I am, as it happens, very fond of gardens myself." He gave her a brief, cheeky grin, then turned to Sophie and offered his arm. "Shall we? I believe there is art to view and virtue to be compromised."

And, choking on her own laughter, Sophie allowed him to escort her out the door.

While the Wexham daughters undoubtedly had a bit of a talent for exaggeration, their impression of their mother's attentiveness as a chaperone was not entirely inaccurate. And West, for one, was quite grateful for this.

It had been three weeks since the night he'd met Sophie at that horrifying musicale, and he felt . . . feverish. He called on her every afternoon, bringing flowers to her mother and charming her sisters, until he was at last permitted to take Sophie on a walk around the square, or perhaps a drive in the park. They danced twice at every ball; they talked for hours, about everything and nothing. He'd never met anyone whom he found so endlessly fascinating, and he wasn't even certain as to why—she was a well-bred English lady, with the limited experiences that that implied. And yet, he loved her mind—she was sharply observant, often piping up with a sly comment or clever joke that caught him off guard, surprising a laugh out of him. He'd never laughed so much in his life, he didn't think, as he had the past three weeks.

"Do you think the artist was having an affair with the subject of this painting?"

West blinked, drawn from his thoughts by the matter-of-fact question from the golden-haired, bonneted, *allegedly* innocent young lady at his side. He paused to consider the painting, and instantly understood why she'd asked the question: There was a certain air of intimacy to the portrait that was absent from most portraits of members of their class. More to the point, however:

"What do *you* know of affairs?" He slid a sideways glance toward her; of course she wasn't blushing. She rarely did. He found himself occasionally making comments, innuendos, specifically for the purpose of seeing if he could make her cheeks turn pink, because she looked lovely when she blushed, and he liked the knowledge that he was the cause.

He liked *everything* about her, full stop. He'd never felt this way about anyone in his entire life; David had teased him about it ("So much for sowing your wild oats—are you truly intending to marry at the age of twenty-four?"), and James had seemed perplexed but delighted ("She's very pretty, and I like her a great deal, but I didn't think you interested in marriage"). Even Hawthorne, his valet—when he wasn't preoccupied with his increasingly heated rivalry with the butler—had begun to twit him for his increased attentiveness to the state of his attire ("Do you think to woo this lady with impressive cravat knots?"). It felt as though his entire life had been turned on its ear on that evening three weeks ago. And he, who liked things to be orderly, for everything to go according to a carefully laid plan, found that this complete unsettlement of his existence was . . .

Well, it was bloody wonderful. What on earth?

"Nothing from my own household, I assure you," Sophie said, in answer to his question. "Mama and Papa are almost nauseatingly happy, as I've told you. But one does hear rumors."

"Does one? I must make more of an effort to converse with the latest crop of debutantes."

Sophie swatted him on the arm. "Not from *debutantes*, of course.

But the young widows are . . . quite merry. And not always mindful of who else might be in the retiring room when they are gossiping among themselves."

West had only the vaguest notion of the mysteries that occurred within the confines of the ladies' retiring room, and was too afraid to inquire further.

Sophie turned to face him fully. "Have *you* ever had an affair with a married lady?" Her tone was thoughtful, inquisitive, and her gaze on him was steady; West, absurdly, felt awkward, as if *he* were the virgin in this conversation.

He cleared his throat, and glanced around them; the summer exhibition at the Royal Academy was, predictably, quite crowded, but there was no one in their immediate vicinity who might overhear this conversation and spread the word that the Marquess of Weston had taken to corrupting young ladies. He'd made a halfhearted attempt to cultivate a reputation as a rake, upon arriving in town a few years earlier after leaving Oxford, but had never had the stomach for it, to David's disgust. How irritating if he should inadvertently become known for corrupting innocents, all because he'd taken it into his head to court a supposedly well-behaved viscount's daughter.

"I have not," he said in an undertone, taking her by the elbow to draw her closer, leaning his head down so that he wouldn't be overheard. "I don't—well—" He felt awkward at what he was about to admit, though he wasn't certain why he should feel embarrassed. "I've enjoyed . . . *friendships* . . . with widows before. But never a lady whose husband was still living. It seems unsporting."

Something in Sophie's face softened as she gazed up at him. "Unsporting," she repeated, the appearance of a dimple signaling the smile she was attempting to hide.

"That makes it sound like I'm discussing cricket, doesn't it?" He shook his head. "I don't have much recollection of my parents' marriage—my mother died when I was quite young—but I've always thought that if a lady was willing to entrust me with her body and fortune and, well, her *life*, then the least I could do would be honor our wedding vows, and ensure that she was as happy as I was capable of making her." Something that he was not entirely certain had been the case with his own parents' marriage; he had vague memories of a melancholy mother, one who adored her sons but who never seemed terribly . . . joyful. Not that he knew for certain, of course; his memories were the fuzzy ones of a young boy, and this was certainly not a topic he'd ever raised with his father.

Sophie regarded him steadily, then reached out with a gloved hand to take his, squeezing it. "I think you would make a lady very happy," she said softly, her gaze never leaving his, her hand feeling small and precious within his grasp.

"Do you?" he asked, offering her a half-smile.

She smiled back at him. "Do you think we could find a piece of statuary or a garden?"

His smile widened. "None appear to be immediately at hand," he said slowly. "But if you'd permit me to escort you to the retiring room, I feel certain we can find an empty hallway that would serve."

He tucked her hand into his elbow and, as he escorted Sophie from the room, gave thanks that Maria was right, and Lady Wexham was really not a very good chaperone at all.

Chapter Five

West had not realized his hearing would begin failing him at the age of one-and-thirty.

Admittedly, he thought he'd understood every word Lady Fitzwilliam had uttered up until this point perfectly well, but clearly some sort of alarming hearing loss had befallen him. Or, an even more disturbing prospect: Perhaps he had lost his mind. Did people now speak perfectly reasonable sentences to him, only for him to interpret them as bits of utter lunacy?

Because surely there had to be some explanation for the fact that Sophie Wexham had just asked him to marry her.

God, he'd even relapsed to the point of calling her by her maiden name in his thoughts—things were well and truly dire. Because he never allowed himself to think of her as such—not since he'd awoken after his curricle accident seven years ago, to the news that the young lady to whom he planned to propose had gone and married one of his school friends while he'd been lying in his sickbed with a badly broken leg and out of his mind with fever.

She was always—during the years of her marriage, and in the four years since she'd been widowed—Lady Fitzwilliam, both in voice and thought. Anything else felt far too risky.

"I beg your pardon?" The words were stiff.

"I'd like us to become engaged," Lady Fitzwilliam—*not* Sophie—said, her voice quiet, reasonable. "Not in truth, naturally, but merely for the rest of the Season, or perhaps a little longer—however long it takes Alexandra to see that I'm happy, accept Blackford's proposal, and get married."

"And you think that she won't be made a bit suspicious by this sudden turn of events?"

Lady Fitzwilliam avoided his eyes. "Alex has always thought that you and I—that is to say—" She blew out a frustrated breath. "She believed that we might one day be wed, and so I think that she would likely view such an announcement as . . ."

"As us coming to our senses at last?"

"Essentially, yes."

West was silent for a long moment, allowing his gaze to wander away from her toward the dancing flames in the fireplace. He was grateful for the faint hiss and pop of the fire, as it prevented him from listening to the sound of her breathing. He needed to *think*—and he found this peculiarly difficult to do when he was in her company.

"It would all be for show," Lady Fitzwilliam assured him, rushing to fill the silence. "It's obvious that, given—well, given events of the past, any marriage between us would be completely impossible. . . ."

She was still speaking, but West had ceased listening.

Impossible.

She was right—of course she was right. He knew that, understood it logically. There was too much history there, too much hurt. They'd thought to marry once, and where had it left them? With West shattered by grief from the loss of his best friend *and* the woman he'd been in love with, and with Lady Fitzwilliam married to another man, one he'd thought to call a friend. West and Lady Fitzwilliam, together, clearly left nothing but pain and destruction in their wake; there could be no future for them.

And yet, until this moment, and the sharp pain that gripped him at hearing her utter this assurance so calmly, with such quiet certainty, he hadn't realized how desperately he wanted just that.

He wanted to marry her.

Still, after all this time, he wanted it so badly that it was like a physical pain within him. He'd suppressed it, these past seven years, not allowed his mind to dwell on her—had gone to considerable lengths to avoid any situation that would put them in the same room. But then she'd had that damned affair with Jeremy, of all people, last summer—and ever since, she'd crept slowly but steadily back into his life. And now he'd been forced to acknowledge something that had been lingering at the corners of his mind all along:

He. Still. Wanted. To. Marry. Her.

He was an *idiot*.

Which meant that the logical, correct thing to do—the course of action that would prevent any further heartache on his part—would be to tell her, in no uncertain terms, that he would not participate in her ruse. Surely she could find another way to ensure her sister's happiness, one that did not involve lying to everyone they knew. One that did not involve him pretending the very thing that he still wished for above all else—that she had previously told him, quite clearly, she was unwilling to offer.

He opened his mouth to do just that—and then he paused.

And his conversation with his father earlier that morning suddenly came to mind, the threat that was hanging over him like a dark cloud: Marry or lose Rosemere.

And West, who was not a naturally devious man, felt a thrill of positively devious delight course through him.

Lady Fitzwilliam frowned. "Why do you look . . . like that?"

He leaned forward, bracing his elbows on his knees, and looked directly at her. "Because I think that a betrothal sounds like a perfectly *splendid* idea."

The Risedale ball had quickly become one of Sophie's favorite events each Season; the Earl and Countess of Risedale had a large home in St. James's—just around the corner from West's—and the countess had, upon her marriage a couple of years earlier, taken it upon herself to oversee an extensive renovation of the ballroom, which now resembled nothing so much as an orangery. There was a wall lined with windows overlooking the extensive terraced gardens, and the ceiling, too, was made of glass; ordinarily, Sophie imagined, one would be able to look up and see the dark sky above, but tonight, with the room filled with candles, a magnificent chandelier suspended from one of the iron supporting bars, the light from within was reflected back at her in the glass, the outside world invisible.

An appropriate metaphor for the *ton*, come to think of it.

She and West had agreed that there was little purpose in postponing their ruse, and the Risedale ball was a perfect opportunity to commence it; the Countess of Risedale was Blackford's sister, meaning he and Alexandra were certain to attend. Sophie had hesitated briefly, wondering if Alexandra would suspect something if she seemed to fall too readily into West's arms, but quickly discarded this concern. People, she had found, were quite eager to see what they wished; like it or not, Sophie's reunion with West was precisely what Alexandra wished to see. She wouldn't prove difficult to convince.

Therefore, a mere three days after her visit to West's home, she found herself standing in a ballroom, making idle conversation with Violet, and attempting to convince herself that she *wasn't* looking for him out of the corner of her eye.

"Is something wrong?" Violet asked, after Sophie had started for the third time in as many minutes; she kept catching glimpses of tall, dark-haired, broad-shouldered men and thinking, for a split second, that they were West, until her body almost immediately seemed to realize its mistake, even before her eyes could confirm it.

"Nothing," Sophie said brightly, taking a larger-than-planned gulp of champagne from the flute in her hand; she coughed, then coughed again, trying to catch her breath. Someone appeared next to her, pressing a monogrammed handkerchief into her hand.

Glancing up through watering eyes, she found that it was James Audley, West's brother.

"Are you all right?" Audley asked, mildly concerned. "Haven't caught some deadly illness, have you?" He turned to regard his wife.

"Why are you looking at me?" Violet demanded.

"Because I believe you are the expert on life-threatening diseases among our set. If you will recall, you had quite a scare last summer." Audley uttered this solemnly, but there was a telltale twinkle in his eye.

"I'm fine," Sophie said at last, her coughing subsiding. "Champagne is dangerous, apparently."

"So is your sister," Audley said darkly.

"Which one?"

"Harriet." He took a sip of his own champagne. "She cornered me to make all sorts of inquiries about a horse she's thinking of buying. She seemed to want something fast."

"That does sound like Harriet," Sophie said, suppressing a smile.

"And intimidating," he added. "I believe her exact words were, 'I want Hyacinth Montmorency to quiver in her boots when she sees me on horseback.'"

Sophie lost the battle with her smile. "She and Miss Montmorency have been friends since they were girls."

Audley blinked. "Friends? She described her like a foe on the battlefield."

"Yes," Sophie agreed. "They have a bit of a . . . healthy rivalry. Hyacinth is still unwed and Harriet is a bit jealous."

Audley frowned. "Shouldn't it be the other way around?"

"Oh, no," Sophie assured him. "Harriet considers it a great achievement to be a single woman of means. She was thoroughly disgusted with herself when she fell in love with George and married at the very respectable age of nineteen." She paused, then added thoughtfully, "Also, she's always been envious that Hyacinth has a much more interesting 'H' name than she does."

By this point, Audley looked frankly mystified. Violet patted her husband's arm in a vaguely condescending way, and said, "It's too complex for a man to understand, James; don't fret too much."

Audley's expression shifted from confused to appalled. "You make me sound like a fussing child."

"I believe I, too, have made that comparison before," came a familiar voice from behind them, and they turned; Jeremy had materialized in their midst. He clutched a glass of champagne in one hand and was craning his neck around as if in search of someone. "Haven't seen Diana, have you?" he asked.

"That way," Violet said, nodding to her left. "She was dancing with Lord Henry Cavendish."

"Cavendish," Jeremy pronounced darkly; Sophie wasn't entirely certain she blamed him, given Cavendish's reputation. (Although, in the interest of fairness, said reputation wasn't much worse than Jeremy's had been before his marriage.)

"He *was* looking quite handsome this evening," Violet added mischievously, and Jeremy rolled his eyes.

"His trousers were very tight-fitting," Sophie said, all innocence; Jeremy scowled at her, but before he could say anything else, Violet called brightly, "West!"

Sophie took a deep breath, then glanced down at her half-empty glass of champagne, taking a small sip as West joined their loose circle and greeted everyone in turn. There was an infinitesimal pause before he said, "Lady Fitzwilliam," and she turned to offer him her hand. She wished she didn't still feel a bit like a flustered schoolgirl in his presence, though she was fairly certain she was able to hide it well.

"West," she said calmly, very aware of Violet, Audley, and Jeremy's eyes all fixed on this unremarkable exchange of polite greetings.

"I enjoyed running into you at Hatchards yesterday," West replied; they had decided that they ought to allude to some sort of precipitating incident that had occurred out of sight of their friends, so that this sudden thawing of relations between two people who had gone to considerable lengths to avoid being alone together would not seem *too* strange and unlikely.

"As did I," she said, taking another sip of champagne. "Did you find the book you were looking for?"

"I did." He inclined his head. "I inquired at the counter, and they had another copy tucked away in the back room."

"I'm so glad." Sophie didn't dare look at their friends as she spoke; doubtless they were watching this exchange with some degree of curiosity as to why West and Sophie were conducting a conversation that sounded as though it had been scripted for two matrons swapping pleasantries in the village shop. She met West's gaze, and while his expression was all polite inquiry, there was a trace of amusement lurking in his eyes. She was not certain someone who did not know him well would have been able to spot it, even though she had not counted herself as such a person in a very long time. It was what she had loved about him, once: his serious demeanor, and the sense of humor he hid beneath it.

She drained her glass of champagne.

"May I fetch you another drink?" he said, taking this as the cue it was.

"Oh, I can do it myself," she assured him. "If you would be so kind as to escort me to the refreshment tables, though . . ." She gazed at him coyly through her lashes.

"I would be honored," he said, and offered her his arm. She turned to flutter her fingers in a wave at Violet, Audley, and Jeremy, who were all witnessing this little tableau with expressions ranging from incandescent hope and joy (Violet) to utter confusion (Audley) to amusement (Jeremy).

As soon as Sophie was certain they were out of earshot, she murmured, "Have you seen Alexandra?"

West tilted his head toward the dance floor. "She's waltzing with Blackford at the moment." His arm was stiff under Sophie's hand, his gait slightly uneven, but his back was straight and tall, his jaw closely shaven, his cravat tied in an elaborate knot so precise that she wondered idly if his valet had used a ruler to ensure that it was perfectly even.

Nothing but the best would suffice for the Marquess of Weston, of course.

"Do you think you should ask me to dance?" She glanced sideways in time to see his hesitation.

"I don't dance often. Ever since my ... accident"—she noticed the faint hesitation before he uttered the word—"I'm a bit awkward at it." And he, naturally, could not bear to be awkward at anything, she thought.

Sophie did not care to linger on the memory of what it had once felt like to waltz with him, his hand at her waist, their bodies pressed close.

"If it will hurt your leg—" she began, a bit hesitant, but he interrupted immediately.

"Plenty of things I do hurt my leg. That is not my concern." His voice was curt, and she determinedly did not look at him as they continued their slow progress toward the refreshment tables. She tried not to think about the accident that had led to his injury, unable to suppress the thought of the life she might have lived, had West and Willingham not raced that day. It was painful to consider, like staring directly at the sun; she came at the thought from sneaky angles occasionally, when she was feeling particularly morose, then just as quickly retreated when she grew overwhelmed by the mere act of considering some alternate reality in which Willingham lived, in which West had not been injured, in which she and West ...

"I would not wish to ruin a waltz you might enjoy with some other, more surefooted partner," he continued, interrupting this thought before she could allow it to take hold. He paused, cast her a consider-ing glance, and then added in a low voice, "No matter how appealing the prospect of waltzing with you might be."

Sophie glanced at him, startled; his tone had not softened, and he was looking away from her, his gaze taking in their surroundings, but that had sounded an awful lot like . . .

Flirting.

She did not know what to *do* with a West who was flirting with her. It had been seven years since she'd flirted with him; a lifetime ago. He, certainly, seemed like an entirely different man than the one she'd once exchanged sly smiles with across crowded rooms. The West she had known back then had been serious, yes, but still young—still certain that the world would arrange itself to his liking. Still amused by the *ton*, delighted by the joy of flirting with a pretty girl. The West she knew—or, rather, *didn't* know—now was someone else entirely. Sterner—sadder, she sometimes thought. Careful with his words, careful not to reveal too much of his thoughts. For *this* man to flirt with her was . . . well, she supposed it was expected, for the sake of their ruse, but she found herself peculiarly flustered by it.

"Perhaps at the next ball, then," she said lightly. "I think we've al-ready given our friends plenty to discuss." She suppressed a wild desire to laugh at the memory of their confused expressions. How odd it felt, to walk like this with him, no one else to act as a buffer between them. It was not the only time they had been alone in the past seven years—there had been a memorable afternoon four Junes ago, one that she did not allow her thoughts to dwell on; there had been, too, a handful of occasions in the past year, as they'd found themselves increasingly drawn into each other's orbits. A quick walk along a garden path at a country house. A tense, mostly silent escort through the doors of

Belfry's theater. A murmured exchange in a hallway in a manor house overlooking the sea.

Each of these instances stood out, bright as a jewel, in her memory. None of them had felt *easy*, however, and she realized that tonight she felt lighter, somehow, than she had done on any of those occasions. The roles they had to play for their scheme allowed them a bit of liberation, and Sophie was unexpectedly grateful for it.

They had reached the refreshment table, and Sophie allowed him to fill a glass with lemonade for her; much as she wanted another glass of champagne, to ease whatever the rest of the evening would bring, she thought it best not to drink too much when she was going to be in close proximity to him.

He turned, handing her the lemonade, and their fingers brushed.

Her eyes caught his and held. She'd forgotten about the particular darker shade of green his eyes took on in the evenings, in candlelight—a shade mossier and less clear than the vivid hue they were in daylight. A curl from his carefully combed hair threatened to break ranks and tumble onto his forehead, and she was possessed of a nearly irresistible desire to reach up and brush it back into place.

But that was dangerous—too dangerous.

Because while she was not fool enough to deny the attraction that still crackled between them, she knew that they could not act upon it—not when any sort of future between them was impossible.

Did he still want her? She'd never considered herself a vain creature, and yet she felt utterly certain that he did, if for no other reason than her unwillingness to believe that a desire this strong could hover in the air between two people without it being experienced on both ends. She knew there was plenty of unrequited love—and lust—in the world, but that was not what this was. She was certain.

She took a sip of lemonade and gave him her best attempt at a pleased smile, but he did not appear to be fooled. He opened his mouth as if to say something, but then his gaze flicked somewhere over her shoulder and caught there. "Your sister's coming."

"Which one?"

"Alexandra."

Indeed, Sophie belatedly registered that the waltz had ended, and the orchestra had struck up a quadrille instead. She took a casual sip of her lemonade, not turning to watch Alexandra approach.

"Laugh as if I've just said something amusing," she murmured to West.

"Do you really think that your sister will be convinced by the sight of me cackling like a lunatic?"

Sophie let out an annoyed sigh, though he had a point—he was not, perhaps, the world's most jovial man. So instead, she let out a high-pitched giggle.

West gave her an exceedingly skeptical look. "If your aim is to convince your sister that we have rekindled a long-lost love, it would perhaps be best if I were not grimacing in acute horror whilst she approaches."

"You were unwilling to laugh, so I had to! The least you could do is appear mildly amused, as if we have shared some secret joke. I understand that anything beyond moderate amusement would be more feeling than the famed Marquess of Weston is capable of expressing, but I thought you might be able to stretch your muscles at least this far."

West shot her a look. "If you think the noise you just uttered is what one emits when one is amused, then I shall make a mental note never to make you laugh again in your life."

"I don't think there's much risk of that," Sophie muttered; that eyebrow went up again, in irritation this time. Before he could reply, Alexandra's voice broke into their discussion.

"Sophie! And West! How . . . unexpected!"

Sophie turned to see Alexandra, on Blackford's arm, surveying herself and West with naked interest that she wasn't even attempting to disguise.

"Mrs. Brown-Montague." West stepped forward to bow over Alexandra's hand and shake hands with Blackford, any sign of his irritation of only moments before already erased.

"How nice to see the two of you together," Alexandra said, looking eagerly back and forth between them.

"We were just reminiscing about . . ." Sophie faltered.

"Cornwall," West reminded her. "We both recently attended a house party in Cornwall hosted by Lord Penvale."

"*Yes*," Alexandra said, with an undue amount of emphasis. "How *interesting* that you were both in attendance."

"As we are both friends of Penvale's, I do not actually believe it is so terribly interesting." Sophie smiled sweetly at her sister. "It seems more in the line of how invitations generally work."

"And friendships," West added.

"I believe my brother and sister-in-law were there as well," Blackford said after a momentary pause; he was giving Alexandra a mildly confused look, but seemed to think that someone should attempt to salvage this conversation.

"Oh, the *newlyweds*," Alexandra said dramatically.

"Well," Blackford said reasonably, "it has actually been the better part of nine months since they wed—"

"And now she is expecting a baby! How delightful!" Alexandra said, clasping her hands together more rapturously than the imminent arrival of a single baby perhaps merited.

"Babies are, indeed, delightful," Sophie agreed, amused, before deciding that the best strategy at this juncture would be to extricate herself from this exceedingly bizarre conversation, which had by now more or less served its purpose. "It has been so lovely running into both of you—"

"But I fear my friends are awaiting our return," West added smoothly, inclining his head in the direction of his brother and sister-in-law, who—from what Sophie could tell from a distance—had been joined by some of their other friends, all of whom were doing a dreadful job of pretending not to be watching West and Sophie from across the room.

"Of course, of course," Alexandra said brightly. "And I'm sure you two have much to . . . discuss . . . between yourselves?" Sophie suspected she would be the recipient of a breakfast visit the following morning.

"Indeed," Sophie agreed, and she and West turned to continue their progress around the room.

"I believe I am sweating," West observed after a moment. "Does your sister normally have that effect on men?"

"You'd have to ask Blackford. I'm not certain I'm cut out for this either—I feel like a horse who's just raced at Ascot."

This surprised a laugh out of West—a real laugh, one that she had not heard from him in a long, long time. She had forgotten how much his face lit up when he laughed, how much younger he looked.

Their eyes caught and held, and she felt it again—that spark between them, evident from the very first night they'd met. It was the reason none of the men she'd flirted with in the years since her widowhood—even Jeremy, with whom she'd had an *affair* last summer—had come close to matching the West of her memories.

She experienced a pang of longing as they made their way back toward their friends, but she fixed a serene smile upon her face and did what she had become quite skilled at doing: She ignored it.

Chapter Six

West had not courted anyone in seven years, and he had forgotten quite how much *work* was involved.

"My lord." West glanced up from the letter he was scrutinizing at his desk to see Briar, his butler, standing in the doorway to his study. "The gardener wishes to know if you would like to send Lady Fitzwilliam roses again, or if you would like a mixed bouquet this time."

West set down his letter with a sigh. "What did we send yesterday—roses?"

Briar's expression was impressively bland as he replied, "Indeed, my lord. Perhaps you noticed my use of the word 'again,' to imply that roses would be a repetition of a previous action?"

West shot Briar a look; for a man who had not yet achieved the age of forty, he was remarkably skilled at conveying an air of haughty butler-y disdain. West suspected it was *because* of his age, in fact; to be the butler to a future duke was a lofty position, and what Briar lacked in age, he seemed determined to make up for in arrogance.

"Perhaps let's send something different today, then," West said.

Briar nodded, then hesitated. "Are you aware that Hawthorne has been composing poems and signing your name to them, to be sent along with the flowers?" His tone was a conflicted combination of disapproval and reluctant amusement.

West grimaced. "Yes. It seems to amuse him, so I left him to it." He was not entirely certain this was wise, but he also didn't want Hawthorne to ask him too many questions about his sudden, joyful reunion with Lady Fitzwilliam, so this had seemed an innocuous enough way to distract him.

"Whatever you think is best, my lord," Briar said, his tone indicating that he clearly thought this was not, in fact, best. "I do hope Lady Fitzwilliam has a sense of humor."

"She does," West said absently, returning to the letter before him, only belatedly realizing the ease with which this assurance rose to his lips—as if he still *knew* Lady Fitzwilliam at all.

Briar offered a very correct bow and vanished to convey West's message to the gardener, who had been kept busier for the past week than he had in the entire duration of his employment with West. West had been sending bouquets to Lady Fitzwilliam daily, the hope being that her sisters and friends would call upon her and make note of the hothouse's worth of flowers in her sitting room. He'd also taken her out in his phaeton a couple of times, to Gunter's for ices, and shopping on Bond Street, all in the hope that they might be seen together. It had all been very . . . civilized.

The first outing—on horseback in Hyde Park, the day after the Risedale ball—had been decidedly awkward; for all that they'd been seeing more of each other, it had not fully prepared them for the reality of being alone together, mimicking what they had once been in truth. They had both looked determinedly ahead rather than at each other, their halting attempts at conversation frequently interrupted by passing acquaintances. They had discussed the weather, how much they'd enjoyed Penvale's house party in Cornwall, her sisters . . . everything other than themselves, and their history, and anything approaching how they felt about any of said history.

Things had continued along a similar course for the past week—a bit of the initial awkwardness had dissipated, but their conversation remained light, superficial; the point of these excursions was to be seen together, not to actually say anything of weight to each other. In that regard, their aim was being served perfectly: they'd encountered numerous friends and acquaintances while out and about, and West hadn't missed the light of interest that had sparked in more than one set of eyes once they'd been spotted together. It was foolish of him to find this all vaguely dissatisfying.

It was just that, after years of thinking of her—and also, pointedly, *not* thinking of her, somehow at the same time—it was decidedly strange to find himself so frequently in her company, and for this to so little resemble what time in her company had once been like. But he had been different, all those years ago—and so had she.

A clock chimed, recalling West from his thoughts and causing him to take note of the hour. Speaking of his soon-to-be fiancée (they planned to announce their betrothal that very evening), he realized that he was due to escort her to Hatchards in a quarter of an hour; Emily had just celebrated her birthday, and Lady Fitzwilliam wished to buy a book for her.

He sighed, and reached for his cane.

An hour later, West was beginning to think that a man should never agree to accompany a woman to a bookshop.

"What about this one?" he asked, waving a book in Lady Fitzwilliam's direction; she was standing a few feet away, scrutinizing the first page of what had to be the fiftieth book she'd picked up since they entered the shop half an hour earlier. She glanced up and squinted, trying to make out the letters embossed on the leather cover. He held it closer, and she shook her head.

"No, she's read that one—I heard her discussing it with Jane whilst we were at Trethwick Abbey."

West carefully replaced the volume on the shelf, and walked closer to Lady Fitzwilliam. "What's this one, then?"

"I'm not certain," she said, her tone a bit distracted as she skimmed the first few pages of the book in her hand. "It's been published anonymously—it seems to be about a gentleman by the name of Frankenstein." She flipped through a few more pages, then snapped the book shut. "It's newly published, at least; I worry Jane will already have loaned Emily a number of more popular books, and I don't want to get her something she's already read."

Emily, it transpired, was feeling somewhat weary as her pregnancy progressed, and was spending less time at her husband's theater and more time at home; she'd taken a fancy to Gothic novels—strongly encouraged by Jane, who was an avid reader—and her friends planned to surprise her with a basketful of books to occupy her during her confinement, which she would enter by the end of the summer.

"I think this one will do," Lady Fitzwilliam said decisively, and slipped past West to make her way to the counter, where her purchase was carefully wrapped in brown paper. West took her parcel in his free hand and offered her the same arm, which she took, and they emerged from the shop into bright afternoon sunlight. Piccadilly was bustling, and West tugged Lady Fitzwilliam closer to his side as they approached his barouche, where his driver patiently awaited them. He helped her in, then leaned back to instruct his driver to take them through the park on their way home—it seemed a shame to waste perfectly good sunshine, particularly when the vagaries of English weather only allowed so many such days in any given summer.

This done, he turned back to face her. She was wearing a white gown with a pattern of roses done in green, and her face was shielded from the sun by a bonnet with a matching green ribbon. She tilted her head back to look at him, and he realized that, on their previous trips to the park, they'd been side by side—either on horseback, or perched atop his phaeton. He was not used to having to stare at her face as they rode. Her cheeks were a bit pink, undoubtedly from the warmth of the day, and a single strand of blond hair had come loose, clinging to her temple beneath her bonnet. His hand twitched with the desire to reach out and tuck it behind her ear.

Instead, he attempted polite conversation—another of their meaningless chats that touched on none of the things he truly wished to say to her. "Lady Fitzwilliam," he began, then broke off at seeing a peculiar expression cross her face. "Is something wrong?"

She hesitated for a moment, then said, "You ought to call me Sophie. If we are to convince everyone that we are courting, that is. I think we might dispense with the formality."

Sophie. The name he had once spoken so freely, which now felt like a dangerous intimacy.

"All right." He inclined his head, casting around for a topic of conversation. "Evidently Blackford's sister told Emily she'd seen us out in the phaeton the other day." Emily had then shared this news with Violet, who had conveyed it to West—with all manner of inquisitive looks and significant pauses—at dinner the night before.

"Did she?" Sophie sounded satisfied. "I suppose our plan to be seen together is working, then." She hesitated, and West frowned, wondering what she was considering. "I was surprised, when you took me out in your phaeton," she said, after a silence had stretched between them for several moments longer than was polite.

He met her eyes. "Oh?"

"I wasn't sure if—I didn't know if you enjoyed—after Willingham—" She broke off, looking uncomfortable, but she didn't break his gaze, and he admired her courage in asking the question (or, at least, attempting to); few people mentioned his accident to him directly, and he never raised the topic in conversation himself. The memories were still painful, even as they'd grown less sharp and jagged at the edges with time.

"There's a reason I bought a phaeton, rather than another curricle," he said. He'd not been in a curricle since that afternoon—he doubted he'd ever climb into one again. Despite their reputation for a certain appealing danger, phaetons were safer than curricles—not that he'd be racing, in any case.

She nodded, and cast her eyes down at her lap, where her hands, carefully encased in white lace gloves, were gripping her paper-wrapped book. "I've realized," she said haltingly, "that I never told you how— how sorry I was. About the accident, I mean. About Willingham."

"But not about your marriage?" he asked, the words coming out a bit sharper than he intended, and Sophie flinched; after a moment he took a slow breath, then pinched the bridge of his nose. More quietly, he said, "I apologize. When would you have had the chance to offer your sympathy, anyway? I seem to remember us taking considerable pains to avoid speaking to each other."

It was true: In the first couple of years of Sophie's marriage, he had avoided so much as being in the same ballroom as her. Over time, he could manage to nod politely at her from a distance, to offer a word of greeting if they crossed paths directly and to do otherwise would have been rude, but at first . . .

Well, the West of seven—six—even five years ago had not been a man he was entirely proud of.

"You're right," she said, looking back up at him now, her brown eyes somber. "But that is not an excuse. And I want you to know how sad I was to learn of his death—to think how much pain it must have caused you." She glanced sideways as they rolled into the park.

He swallowed past an unexpected lump in his throat; he was accustomed to living with this grief and guilt, but not to speaking of it. "I still miss him, every day," he said quietly.

Her brow creased. "I never would have thought otherwise," she said, reaching out as if to grasp his hand, then thinking better of it, allowing her hand to drift back to her own lap. "I believe Jeremy knows it, too."

Jeremy's name sat between them, like a gauntlet thrown; West and Sophie had never discussed him, or the events of the previous summer. It had hurt, when West first learned of the affair; now, however, with Jeremy happily married, their liaison having been short-lived, Sophie never having displayed the slightest bit of discomfort in his presence, West could tell that there had been no great feeling involved on either side.

Why, then, did a flicker of jealousy still course through him at the thought of her kissing another man—of her going to bed with him, and having the lazy, meandering conversations that arose in the wake of lovemaking?

He held her gaze steadily as he fought against this feeling, and instead tried to focus on her words, which he knew had been intended as a gift. "Jeremy and I have only spoken of the accident once." It had been about a year afterward; they'd both been the worse for drink, though not so much so that he thought it likely Jeremy had forgotten. "He said he didn't blame me." He could not prevent a wry twist of his mouth at these words, something Sophie noted with a frown.

"Why should he?" she asked. "No one forced Willingham to get into that curricle—he'd been boasting to anyone who'd listen how fast it was. If you hadn't challenged him to a race, no doubt someone else would have."

"Or perhaps not. It was a stupid and reckless thing to do, you know—perhaps no one else would have been so foolish."

She set her parcel aside, leaning forward in her seat. "'Stupid' and 'reckless' are not words I would usually use to describe you."

Without thinking, he reached out to tip her bonnet back slightly, giving him a clearer view of her face. "Well, I was upset that evening," he said. "I don't know that I was acting at all how I usually would."

She went still; he frowned, reviewing the words he'd just spoken, wondering what had unsettled her.

"You were upset," she said, very deliberately, "because I told you about your father's threats to me—and my sister?"

Oh. *Damn* it.

"Sophie," he said, quietly and with great care, "you are not responsible for anything my father said to you—or for anything to do with how that made me feel. I'd have been more upset, later, if I'd learned you'd kept that from me."

"Perhaps if I hadn't told you about his threats that night, though, you wouldn't have challenged Willingham," she pressed, her face stricken.

"And if I'd spoken to my father more firmly in the first place, he never would have threatened you," he said firmly. He wondered if she could hear the regret that laced every word. "Besides," he added, "it's as you said—Willingham was an idiot about that curricle. He'd have found someone else to race." Perhaps, if he could convince her of this, he'd eventually manage to convince himself, too.

She held his gaze for a long moment, even as they rattled through the park, other riders and carriages flashing past with the occasional greeting from their occupants. West ignored this, though, all of his attention focused on the woman in front of him. Her expression eased somewhat, but she still looked troubled.

"I think there is plenty of blame to be shared, if we wish to continue down this route," she said after a moment with a slightly forced laugh, and it had the desired effect of shattering the odd tension between them. "It is in the past, I suppose, and there's no use dwelling on it."

West, who had leaned toward her, reclined back in his seat, exhaling slowly. He did not wish her to feel guilty for anything to do with his accident—but why, then, did he equally dislike this feigned lightness to her voice, her attempt to dismiss the history between them? Was it because it served as a reminder that, to her, their history was just that—the past, and nothing more?

This was not a question he could ask her, of course.

Without breaking eye contact, he said after a moment, "Is the plan still to announce our betrothal at dinner tonight?"

And Sophie, after a slight hesitation—an acknowledgment of all that had been said, and all that hadn't, and the weight of the words that had been spoken—nodded. "I've been thinking, though—we'll need to tell them when we plan to hold the wedding."

West went still. "The wedding."

Sophie blinked. "Yes. As we are betrothed—or we will be, as of this evening? They'll likely want to know all of our plans."

West frowned, considering. "I don't think we need to worry about that—they'll be so caught up in wishing us happy, they won't think to ask about something as frivolous as the wedding."

Sophie smiled sweetly at him. "If I needed proof that you've not spent much time with women in the years we've been apart, you have very kindly just provided it."

"Have you been paying attention to my romantic exploits, then?"

She faltered. "Of course not," she said quickly. "It's none of my concern, whom you spend time with."

He nodded. "Just as it's none of *my* concern that you went to bed with Jeremy for the better part of the Season last year, I presume?" Sophie's eyes widened, and he immediately wished the words unsaid. "I'm sorry," he said stiffly. "That was abominably rude."

"It did seem rather out of character," she agreed, then froze, like someone giving evidence at an inquest who belatedly realized they'd said something incriminating. "Not," she added, "that I presume to know your character."

Anymore.

The word hovered between them, unspoken but somehow thunderously loud as they rattled through Cumberland Gate and back into Mayfair.

Whatever streak of madness had provoked him to speak so bluntly apparently still had him in its grip, for he leaned forward, braced his elbows on his knees, looked evenly at her, and said, "If you do not know my character, then no one does."

A long, heavy silence fell before she found her voice at last. "You'll call for me at seven, then?"

And West, not trusting himself to say anything else, merely nodded.

West had been prepared for many reactions to his announcement of his betrothal that evening, but he had not been prepared for the weeping.

He was standing at the dinner table of Lord Julian Belfry and his wife, Emily; he had just informed the assembled group that Sophie had done him the immense honor of agreeing to be his wife; he had proposed a toast; and now, Emily was weeping.

This was, he supposed, not entirely surprising, given that she was expecting a baby; expectant mothers were prone to wild fits of emotion, he understood (mercifully not from firsthand experience). Still, it was rather disconcerting.

He had no further time to contemplate this, however, because—

"West!" His sister-in-law was out of her seat in a flash, and the next thing West knew her arms were around his neck so tightly that he became somewhat concerned for the amount of air flowing to his lungs.

"Violet, let the man breathe," James said after a minute or so of this, and Violet drew back enough for West to see that his brother was grinning like an idiot. James seized him by the shoulder and gave him a rough, back-slapping sort of hug, and West blinked back a strange rush of emotion.

It's not real, he reminded himself.

Across the table, Sophie was simultaneously having her hand wrung by her sister Alexandra and being heartily congratulated by Penvale and Jane. Penvale's sister Diana, meanwhile, was expounding to anyone who would listen—at the moment, merely her husband—that she had known this all along, that the seeds for this union had been planted when *she* had forced West and Sophie to go on a walk together the previous summer at Jeremy's country estate.

"Didn't they go on a walk in *spite* of your machinations, rather than because of them?" Jeremy pointed out. "Weren't you trying to convince me to go on a walk with Sophie instead?"

"I haven't the faintest notion of what you are referring to," she informed him, and then became conveniently deaf to her husband's voice, joining Jane in her well-wishes.

"How did this come about?" Violet asked, clasping her hands like an eager child; she had allowed James to tug her back down into her seat, though she continued to regard West and Sophie as though they were the products of a particularly cherished dream come to life.

West shrugged, as if it were not a terribly interesting story at all, and one that certainly did not involve feigning a romantic attachment in order to trick two of the people in this very room into marrying. "We were able to spend some time together, whilst we were in Cornwall," he said, with a nod at Penvale and Jane.

Jane brightened at this. "Was it when she hit a cricket ball into your—" She broke off, frowning, appearing to belatedly realize that this was not, perhaps, the most appropriate dinner table conversation.

Jeremy and James both suffered simultaneous, conveniently timed coughing fits.

"I doubt West's—er—delicate cricket injury was the specific

inciting incident for this romance," Penvale informed his wife solemnly, his mouth fighting a losing battle against a smile.

"I don't know," Jeremy said thoughtfully, having recovered enough to speak. "It might be an appropriate metaphor for marr—good *God*." He broke off abruptly, his face having gone pale. Next to him, Diana removed her hand from beneath the table and smiled serenely.

West felt a pang, as he did from time to time in Jeremy's company, when the fierceness with which he missed David caught him by surprise. Jeremy resembled his brother, and they were only two years apart in age; Jeremy was now older than David had ever been. It was a melancholy, unsettling thought.

His gaze flicked across the table, and he saw Sophie regarding him with a faint frown—something of his thoughts must have, somehow, shown on his face. With some effort, he pushed them aside.

"In any case," he said, raising his voice slightly to be heard over the general laughter in the room, "we've decided to marry." It felt a bit anticlimactic, stated so plainly, and he wondered if he should have phrased it in a more grandiose fashion. That was decidedly not his style, however, and would likely cause his brother and friends to conclude he'd suffered some sort of head injury.

"Sophie, what did Mama and Papa say?" Alexandra asked.

"I haven't told them yet—West only proposed this evening, you see," Sophie said, with a quick glance at West to ensure that he had heard and would therefore be sticking to this story.

"I am planning to speak to Lord Wexham tomorrow," West added.

Sophie dropped her fork. "*Are you?*"

He frowned at her. "I know that, as you are a widow, we don't need his permission, but I thought to discuss the matter with him, all the same."

"West, you should come to the picnic with us on Sunday," Alexandra said, before Sophie could offer any sort of protest.

West looked inquiringly at Sophie.

"During the spring and summer, when the weather's fine, my parents like to take the boat down to their Richmond estate and have a picnic every Sunday." A brief hesitation. "You . . . you could come with us, this week."

"*Could?*" Alexandra asked. "He simply must! Oh, Mama will be so delighted—are you going to tell her tomorrow, then, when you go to dinner? She will be beside herself, you know she always thought—"

"Yes, well, she can express her delight to West in person on Sunday," Sophie said hastily.

Alexandra cast a quick glance at Blackford that West could not decipher.

"Perhaps we could host a dinner to celebrate?" Violet suggested. "And we could invite all of your sisters, Sophie?"

"Even better—why not a betrothal ball?" Emily asked. "Wouldn't that be lovely? None of us had betrothal balls." This last was uttered a bit glumly.

Her husband looked at her askance. "I'm sorry," he said mildly. "Whilst I was busy riding to Canterbury and back to procure a special license so that I might marry you in an idyllic pastoral setting, far from your parents' meddling, was I remiss in not summoning half of London to a cow pasture—"

"I beg your pardon?" asked Jeremy, who had been the one to provide said idyllic pastoral setting for Belfry and Emily's wedding.

"—so that they might all dress in their finery and wish us happy?"

"No, of course not," Emily said, pressing a reassuring hand on Belfry's arm. Something in his expression softened as he gazed down at her. "But now that one of us is getting married properly, with a proper engagement—"

"*We* had a proper engagement!" Jeremy pointed out, gesturing to Diana, sounding more and more indignant by the moment. "I had to wear a bloody *waistcoat* to my wedding, if you will recall!"

"Who could forget?" James muttered.

"I just want *one of us* to have a proper betrothal ball!" Emily burst out, half-rising from her seat; this was so out of character for her that it successfully shocked everyone assembled into a momentary silence. "If none of you object?" she added sweetly, looking angelic as ever.

"I'm certain our mama will be delighted to host one," Alexandra assured Emily, clearly deciding that it was best not to argue with the inexplicable wishes of expectant mothers. The rest of the party appeared relieved when Emily resumed her seat with a pleased smile.

"She loves nothing more than an excuse to play hostess, and I'm certain Sophie and West wouldn't *dream* of disappointing her," Alexandra added, turning an inquiring gaze upon the couple in question. "Right?"

West flicked a glance across the table at Sophie, who rolled her eyes heavenward but gave a slight nod.

"Indeed we would not," he said to Alexandra. "We would be honored, in fact."

What he was actually thinking, however, was:

For a feigned betrothal, this was already starting to feel alarmingly real.

Chapter Seven

Sophie, not wishing to leave anything to chance, appeared in her parents' breakfast room at nine o'clock the following morning.

"Darling," her mother said, glancing up in surprise from a letter in her hand, "has someone died?" Across the table from Lady Wexham, her husband lowered his newspaper. Not waiting for a response, Lady Wexham continued, "Is one of the children ill? Is Betsy well? Did Harriet challenge someone to a duel?"

"I—what?"

Lady Wexham set down her letter. "I don't know! I simply wished to offer all the most likely possibilities!"

Sophie dropped a kiss atop first her father's head, then her mother's. "Everyone is fine. Am I not permitted to join my parents for breakfast?"

"Not at this hour," her mother said, looking equal parts relieved and suspicious. "Besides, I thought you were fixated on your cook's breakfast pastries."

"I can barely manage to eat one before the twins descend," Sophie said. "Dining here seems quite restful by comparison." She reached forward to pour herself a cup of tea. She did not think West would call so early, but she wanted to beat him to the punch. During the carriage ride home the evening before, he had not been remotely repentant for having surprised her with his plan to seek her father's blessing, so she had decided to steal a march on him.

Sophie rose and drifted toward the sideboard, considering the options—noticeably lacking in any pastries, as usual, she noted with a sigh—before piling her plate with eggs, conscious of her parents' eyes on her all the while. Back at the table, she set about briskly buttering a few slices of toast, spooning eggs atop one before taking a bite. She polished off one slice, then another, before taking a sip of tea, setting down her cup with a gentle *clink* of china, fixing her mother with a determined look, and saying, "Mama, I've something I wish to tell you."

"I assumed you did not appear here solely out of a desire to break-fast with your parents," Lady Wexham said. She had not resumed her perusal of her letter, but had instead spent the past few minutes regarding her daughter as one might look on a mystifying creature at the zoo.

"Yes, well," Sophie said, a bit sheepish, "what I wanted to—" She broke off at a faint sound. Was that the front door opening? She glanced at the clock. Seven past nine. Surely not—

But, yes, she was now fairly certain she heard footsteps approaching.

She turned her attention back to her mildly perplexed parents. "What I wanted to tell you is, I've agreed—"

At the sound of a throat clearing, she glanced over her shoulder to see that her parents' butler had entered the room.

"Yes, Mournday?" her mother asked.

"The Marquess of Weston is here to see you, my lord," Mournday said, looking toward her father. "He apologizes for the impolite hour, but I showed him to your study, as he said it was urgent."

Sophie huffed out an irritated breath.

"Thank you, Mournday," her father said with a faint frown; as soon as the butler had retreated, both parents turned inquiring gazes upon Sophie.

She offered them a faint smile. "Do you feel like planning a wedding, Mama?"

West was mildly embarrassed to realize that he was, of all things, *nervous*.

He stood in Lord Wexham's study, his hands resting on his cane without taking much of his weight, gazing at the portrait of the Wexham daughters that had pride of place above the fireplace. The sight of this portrait made him feel vaguely fond of a man who would so proudly display his daughters in a room that was ostensibly for business; he stepped closer, his eyes drawn magnetically toward the eldest daughter. Sophie looked younger, but not shockingly so; he guessed this portrait had been done at some point in the past five years, based on the appearance of the twins, who looked approximately of debuting age. Sophie was smiling softly, her expression inscrutable; he realized, with a jolt of surprise, that that complicated, opaque expression had become familiar to him, over the past seven years. She had never been terribly emotional, but she'd been easier to read when she was younger, her expressions less guarded.

He wondered how much he was to blame for the change in her.

Hearing footsteps, he turned in time to see Lord Wexham walk into the room, pause, and shut the door behind him. Sophie's father was, judging by appearances, a few years younger than West's father; tallish, but not imposing, with sandy hair that had largely turned to gray, and a face marked by laugh lines. He gave the impression of a man who was entirely content with the circumstances of his life; West had always liked him a great deal.

At the moment, Wexham was looking at him with an expression best described as a cross between irritation and amusement.

"Weston." Wexham extended his hand, which West shook.

"Lord Wexham. Thank you for seeing me so early."

"It appears to be a trend this morning," Wexham said, sounding faintly amused. Seeing West's inquiring glance, he added dryly, "My daughter is currently sitting at my breakfast table."

West did not have to ask which daughter he meant.

"Sit down," Wexham said, gesturing at one of the chairs opposite his desk, behind which he seated himself. He braced his elbows on the dark mahogany surface, pressed his fingertips together, and surveyed West evenly. He did not say anything else, and, after a moment, West took this as an invitation to speak.

"Sophie has agreed to marry me," he said, because he could hardly say *Sophie has asked me to pretend I've asked her to marry me* instead.

"Has she?" Wexham drummed his fingertips together once, twice. "Are you asking my permission? A bit belated, if she's already said yes, I think?" His tone was mild, but his gaze was sharp.

"Sophie is an adult, sir, and knows her own mind. We do not need your permission to marry . . . but we would appreciate your blessing." West was excruciatingly uncomfortable as he spoke, the words feeling like a mockery of the conversation he'd hoped to have with Wexham seven years earlier—one that had never occurred.

Silence met these words, one that lengthened without Wexham displaying any inclination to break it. He continued to gaze at West, his brown eyes so similar to those of his daughter, his expression thoughtful.

"This is the second time someone has asked to marry Sophie, as you well know," he said. He leaned back in his seat, resting his elbows on the arms of his chair. His gaze wandered up to the ceiling as he spoke. "And both times, it's come as a surprise. Bridewell's father was a school chum of mine—did you know that?" He glanced down in time to see West shake his head. "I'd always liked Fitz, but you could have knocked me over with a feather when he asked to marry my daughter—I wasn't even aware they were acquainted. But he assured me they'd come to some sort of understanding—Sophie herself was waiting outside the study door for the entire conversation. I've never been interested in dictating my daughters' matrimonial choices, as long as they weren't attempting to marry complete bounders, so I said yes." His gaze dropped back to West's now, razor sharp. "But he was not the man I'd been expecting—hoping—to have that conversation with." He paused a moment, presumably to ensure that West took his meaning.

"I do not know what passed between you and Sophie, seven years ago. I presume it was some idiocy to do with young love and too many emotions; I wonder now if I should have said no to poor Fitz when he asked for her hand—forced her to wait a bit, so that you might have mended whatever it was that had gone wrong between you." He sighed, shaking his head. "I love my wife a great deal, Weston; I do not think Fitz and Sophie were unhappy, precisely, but it gave me pain to see her in a marriage that did not seem as happy as mine has been."

"You and Lady Wexham have been very fortunate, sir," West said quietly. One only needed to look at the many examples of unhappy marriages that surrounded them in the *ton* to understand just how fortunate. He wondered idly if Sophie was aware of how clearly her father had seen her marriage—she, who was so fixated on ensuring that no one in her family had any cause to fret over her.

"We have," Wexham agreed. "A fact I reflect on nearly every day. My other daughters seem similarly fortunate." Another pause. "I would wish that for Sophie, too. And I am more pleased than I can say that you two have worked things out at last."

He stood, and West did as well, automatically reaching across the desk to take the hand Wexham was offering him. "I merely wish for her to be happy, West. And I know that you can make her so."

If only, West thought—as they left the study and returned to the breakfast room, where he was greeted by a tearful embrace from Lady Wexham, and an exasperated look from his supposed fiancée—he could convince Sophie of that.

Chapter Eight

Sophie almost—but not quite—felt bad for West.

It was Sunday, as fine an early June afternoon as one might have ordered from a catalogue of English delights. She and West had just arrived at the riverfront, having glided over the cobblestoned streets lined with dirty warehouses in the peaceful, quiet splendor of a well-sprung carriage with West's gleaming crest on the door.

No sooner had they made their careful way onto the yacht that would transport them to Richmond, however, than her family descended.

"West!" Betsy cried joyfully as soon as she spotted him. "When Sophie told us your news—"

"Have you decided on a date?" Harriet interjected eagerly. "She was muttering some nonsense about a long engagement, when obviously—"

"Have you finished terrifying the poor man yet?" her father asked jovially, making his way into the fray. "It will be good to have a son at last—"

"You have *three sons-in-law already*," Maria said through gritted teeth, and for once Sophie felt entirely in sympathy with her sister, considering that all three gentlemen were present on this very boat.

"Ah, but young Weston was meant to be the first!" her father said, and Sophie shut her eyes, mortified. She did love her family, but she was beginning to wonder if she would love them more if she lived in Italy, perhaps.

"I did always think you and Sophie would have the most beautiful babies!" her mother added, near tears, causing Sophie to reconsider her previous thought. Italy would still be too close. Perhaps the North Pole would suffice.

"It is a pleasure to see you again so soon, Lady Wexham," West said calmly, as polite as ever in the face of her family's frankly unhinged behavior, and Sophie's embarrassment faded on a wave of unexpected fondness. There was something so dreadfully comforting about West, she thought—a man who could be trusted to steer a steady course no matter what storm of wildly inappropriate comments he had to weather. She did not *want* to find him comforting—not when there wasn't any future for them—and she futilely attempted to will away the feeling.

"You must call me Mama!" her mother said, all aflutter, and Sophie contemplated flinging herself into the Thames.

"That is very kind of you," West replied, nothing in his tone indicating what Sophie knew to be perfectly true: that he would address her mother so informally only were he to sustain some sort of head injury. Perhaps not even then, come to think of it—she could just imagine him, concussed and suffering from a bout of amnesia, laid up in bed, still strictly and rigorously polite in his forms of address to every person who visited him in his sickbed.

She didn't like to think of him in a sickbed, she realized; it reminded her of when he *had* been confined to bed once before—when she had been young and in love and terribly sad and afraid, and she'd not been allowed to see him.

It had felt as though her heart were splitting open, then. And even now, the memory dragged up complicated feelings, ones she'd just as happily ignore.

By the time they had made their leisurely way several miles west down the Thames and alighted at the Wexhams' riverfront manor in Richmond, West had been made to dandle one of Maria's twin babies on his knee, consulted about potential names for *Betsy's* baby, quizzed quite rigorously by Alexandra on the subject of Lord Byron (whom West evidently knew personally, and by whom he was not remotely impressed), and even received a grudging nod of approval from Maria when he happily joined her in a discussion of abolition, of which they were both supporters.

Sophie tried very hard not to notice any of this, uncomfortably aware that they were essentially lying to her family. She'd thought this would be easier, for some reason. Perhaps, she thought, watching West solemnly offer his index finger for Harriet's baby, Cecily, to shake, her discomfort stemmed from the fact that this all skirted dangerously close to the future she *had* envisioned for herself, once upon a time. A future that she had done her best to put out of her mind for the past seven years.

It was a beautiful spring day, and they arrived in Richmond to find that a number of blankets had been spread on the lawns stretching down to the river, along with picnic baskets overflowing with sandwiches, savory pies, heaping platters of strawberries, cakes, and bottles of wine; they disembarked from the boat and made their way up the steps that ascended the sloping lawn toward the feast on offer. It felt natural, somehow, for Sophie to fall into step next to West, who, without making it obvious he was doing so, had carefully allowed the rest of the party to precede him.

"I'm sorry not to offer you my arm—but if I topple over, I fear I'd take you with me." His voice was wry, self-deprecating, amused—but underneath there was a note of bitterness that Sophie disliked.

She thought, momentarily, of making a joke in turn, of assuring him that she was clumsy enough to be the likelier candidate to send them tumbling. But no sooner had the thought crossed her mind than she sensed that this would not be the correct thing to say at all; instead she replied, "You needn't apologize for such things, you know."

His gaze was fixed carefully on the steps as they slowly ascended, and a quick glance sideways showed that his jaw was tight. "I am not bothered by my leg, most of the time. On days when it is particularly damp and it is aching something fierce, or when I have gone on too long a ride or danced one too many waltzes or fenced for too long with Hawthorne, it pains me, but most days, it is a regular sort of ache, a pain I have grown accustomed to. I barely even notice my cane these days—the weight of it in my hand feels natural to me. And I am not such a fool, nor so proud, that I am resentful of the thing that helps me walk nearly as quickly as I once did before my accident." He paused, but Sophie said nothing in response, sensing that he was just now working himself up to whatever it was he really wanted to say.

"But when I am with you, I find myself bothered by all the ways that I have changed. I'm bothered that I am not the man you once knew. I'm bothered that the pain in my leg reminds me of our past—of all that went wrong between us. And I'm bothered that I am bothered, because I have always prided myself on my ability not to let much of anything bother me at all."

She did turn to look at him now, coming to a quick halt. He stopped as well, but continued to face forward, a muscle ticking in his jaw. He might claim not to let much bother him, but she did not think this was entirely true; rather, he'd been trained since birth to suppress the things that *did* bother him, to the point that he could pretend they did not exist at all. He'd had this habit when she had first known him, all those years ago, and from what she could tell, it had only worsened with time. She did not tell him this, however—did not know how to do so. Instead, she told him something else that was also entirely true.

"You are every bit the man I once knew," she said softly; his face did not move as she spoke, but she saw him swallow. "I don't—" She paused, exhaled in frustration. She had, all at once, both too much and too little to say to him, and the words would not come. "I do not know all that you feel—what you must have felt, in the wake of your accident. But it seems to me far stranger that you would *not* resent the pain in your leg, and all that it reminds you of."

Willingham's death.

Her marriage.

She realized, with a guilty start, that she had spent these past years avoiding the thought of what the pain of those initial weeks and months must have been like for him. She had been mired in misery, too, but hers was of a different nature than his—and at least she fully understood the circumstances that had led to it.

At least she had not lost her best friend, in addition to the person she'd hoped to marry. To dwell too long on what those early months must have been like for him would have been to allow guilt to consume her—even as she knew, stubbornly, that she had done the right thing. That she had protected not just Maria's happiness, but ultimately West's own. Even if it had not felt like it at the time.

Nor now, whispered a traitorous little voice in Sophie's mind.

When he spoke at last, his voice was quiet, a bit more hoarse than normal. "I do not like to think of the days I lay in that bed, thinking of David—thinking of . . ."

Thinking of you.

The words hovered between them, unspoken but understood.

"They were the darkest days of my life, and sometimes, when I look at you—when I walk alongside you, as if nothing has changed—" He broke off, inhaling sharply. "I think of the two people I cared for more than anyone else, before that accident, and the fact that I lost them both, in no small part due to my own foolishness, and I can barely stand to look at myself in the mirror." There was raw pain etched into every word he spoke, so much that Sophie felt the echo of it deep within her, and had to swallow against a sudden lump in her throat. Her eyes prickled, but she would not cry—not before him.

She'd long since stopped allowing herself to cry over this man.

That he should lay the blame at his own feet was suddenly intolerable to her. She blamed the duke—she blamed the emotions, the impetuousness of youth—but she did not blame *West*. And suddenly, it felt very important that he should know this.

"I know that our past . . . is what it is," she said, very carefully, "but I think you should know that you are not to blame for what occurred between us—you are not responsible for your father's actions." She hesitated, then added, before she could think better of it, "And I do not think David, were he alive today, would wish you to blame yourself for your accident." She paused, then finished softly, "There's plenty of blame to go around."

He reached out a slow hand—slow enough to give her plenty of time to pull away, should she wish—and tilted her chin up slightly, so that their gazes met. "If that is true, then I would say the same to you. I blame my father for threatening you—but you were very young. I do not blame you for being intimidated by a duke, and for marrying someone else instead. Someone whose family would not try to frighten you away." His tone was bitter, but he held her gaze, the silence taut between them. For a moment, Sophie considered correcting him—telling him the full story, what precisely his father had threatened. If he believed that she merely hadn't thought him worth facing his father's hostility . . . well, she found this close to unbearable.

She drew a deep breath—

"Sophie! Why are you dawdling?" called Betsy from the top of the steps, and Sophie and West blinked, the heavy silence broken.

He took a step, as if to continue up the stairs, but she reached out and laid a hand on his arm to stop him. And then—quickly, without considering the words, or their wisdom—she said, "I think you should know that—no matter what impression I may have given to the contrary—I have never changed the opinion that I formed of you the first night we met."

"And what was that?" he asked, the words shocking in their roughness, coming from West, who always spoke with such urbane polish.

"That you were the best man I'd ever met," she said. And without another word, she turned to continue up the sloping lawn to where her family waited.

West had never known it was possible for a picnic, of all things, to be such a joy and such a torment, all at once. Sophie's family was largely as he'd remembered them, though her sisters—especially the twins—had all grown terribly mature in the years since he'd last been a regular caller at the Wexham family home.

Sort of.

"West, duck!" Harriet shrieked, and he obeyed, a projectile flying past overhead.

"Is that . . . a loaf of bread?" he asked as Betsy caught it and cackled gleefully.

"It is," Sophie confirmed from her seat beside him; they were sharing the same blanket, along with Alexandra and Blackford, who had spent much of the past couple of hours mooning at each other so blatantly that West was tempted to ask them if they'd mind finding a blanket of their own for some privacy.

"It's Pass the Bread!" Alexandra said brightly, sipping a glass of wine in a leisurely fashion.

"I beg your pardon?"

Sophie sighed, but a quick glance in her direction revealed the telltale dimple in her cheek that appeared when she was trying not to smile. "It's a game they invented when they were children, whenever we'd picnic outdoors; they had a food fight at the dining room table once, when they were about eight—we always dined as a family, even when we were young—and my mother made the mistake of telling them that one did not hurl loaves of bread at one's sister when one was indoors."

West immediately saw the logical outcome of Lady Wexham's unfortunately worded dictate. "Meaning that hurling bread out of doors was perfectly acceptable?"

"That is certainly how they interpreted it," Sophie said. "And Mama has always said that she wanted to raise daughters who were intelligent and capable of making logical arguments. We thought they might outgrow it, but apparently . . ."

"Watch it!" Alexandra shrieked, flinging herself to the blanket;

Blackford was not fast enough, however, and crumbs flew as he was whacked in the head by a flying loaf. The impact gave a surprisingly dense *thunk*.

"Good God," he muttered, rubbing at his head; without missing a beat, he seized the projectile in question and chucked it as hard as he could in the direction of Harriet who caught it handily.

"Oh, I do like him, Alex!" she called merrily, brandishing the bread in the air.

"Well, that is rather fortunate, then," her sister replied, "as I've actually a bit of news I wish to share."

Harriet dropped her loaf of bread; a quick glance to one of the other blankets revealed that Lady Wexham was literally aquiver with anticipation.

"Robert and I"—Alexandra paused dramatically; Lady Wexham seemed in real danger of toppling forward onto her face—"are going to have a baby!" she finished, flinging a theatrical hand to her stomach.

"*What?*" Lady Wexham shrieked; next to her, Maria clapped her hands to her mouth in horror, then reached over and covered the ears of her infant daughter, which seemed a bit unnecessary to West, given young Charlotte's age and general ability (or lack thereof) to comprehend spoken English in any of its complexities.

"Now, Blackford," Lord Wexham began, "I only want for my daughter to be happy, but I can't help thinking this isn't the way to do things at all—a bit out of order, I must say."

"Lord Wexham," Blackford began; he had flushed a bright scarlet, and looked as though he wished the grass would open up beneath him and swallow him whole. "I can assure you—"

"Now, Papa," Alexandra said, cutting off Blackford before he could say anything further, "there's no need to come over all missish, you know. It's not as though I'm an innocent debutante—I'm a widow! One can hardly expect me to resist temptation when it presents itself in so appealing a guise." She cast a rapturous look at Blackford, who had been reduced to mere sputtering.

"Surely you're going to marry him though, Alex," Betsy said in a hushed voice, looking mildly appalled; next to her, Covington, her husband, seemed to be trying very hard not to laugh. A quick glance sideways at Sophie confirmed a similar impulse on her part; she was gazing at Alexandra, West realized, and appeared to be having some sort of silent conversation with her sister.

That was when West caught on.

"Marriage," Alexandra said slowly, tapping her chin. "An interesting idea, Betsy, and one that I had not yet considered—thank you so much for suggesting it!" By this point, Blackford seemed to have lost the power of speech entirely, Maria was gaping like a horrified fish as Grovecourt patted her consolingly on the shoulder, and Lady Wexham appeared to be shedding actual tears into her handkerchief.

"Alex," Sophie said, finally seeming to decide that enough was enough—a judgment with which West rather agreed—"do you think you could stop tormenting Mama and that poor fiancé of yours?"

Alexandra flashed her elder sister a brilliant smile. "Since you asked so nicely, Soph, I suppose I could be convinced."

Lord Wexham looked at his middle daughter hopefully. "Does that mean—?"

Alexandra sighed dramatically. "Yes, Papa, I was having you on, of course our news is that we're engaged—Mama, for heaven's sake, stop *crying*, or I shall refuse to marry Robert out of pure spite."

"Assuming he still wishes to marry *you*, after what you have put him through for the last two minutes," West said, and Alexandra grinned at him. Blackford, for his part, at least seemed to be breathing normally again.

"Lord and Lady Wexham," he said, practically stumbling over his words in his eagerness to get them out, "I assure you that Alexandra was merely joking, and that everything about our betrothal has been entirely proper—"

"Now, now, darling Blackford," said Lady Wexham, who by this point had dried her tears with her handkerchief and was giving her future son-in-law a watery smile, "so long as there *is* a betrothal to speak of, I find myself much less concerned with what you two may get up to in the back of a carriage."

"*Mama!*" howled three of her daughters in unison.

"Welcome to the family, Blackford," said Lancashire, Harriet's husband, with the weary air of a man who has been involved in a long military campaign, welcoming a fresh-faced new recruit. "And Godspeed to you."

"*Speaking* of welcoming new members to the family . . ." Alexandra said, and she cast West a Significant Look. He immediately went still, not liking this Significant Look one bit. Violet was also exceedingly fond of Significant Looks, and he'd learned that they almost never boded well.

"Yes?" he ventured cautiously.

"Well," she said, drawing out the word, "I just thought that if West and Sophie are to be married, *and* Robert and I are to be married—"

"A double wedding!" Harriet shrieked.

"Precisely!" Alexandra said brightly.

Next to West, Sophie let out the faintest groan, likely audible only to him.

"Alex!" Lady Wexham's handkerchief was now waving in the air like some sort of flag, so enthusiastically was she flapping her hands. "I can almost forgive you your wretched trick, my love, because this is a positively *brilliant* idea!"

"I thought so, Mama," Alexandra said, a trace smugly. Her gaze sharpened on Sophie. "What do you think, Sophie?" She clasped a hand to her breast. "Two sisters, struck by tragedy in their first marriages, both finding love once more, stepping forward into their futures side by side, in the very same church!" West was surprised a band of trumpet players did not materialize to accompany the moving picture she painted.

"Er," Sophie said, casting him a look of vague horror.

Seeing that she was floundering, West stepped into the breach. "What an intriguing idea," he said, as diplomatically as he could manage.

"Does that mean you agree?" Alexandra looked at him eagerly. Considering that Alexandra's eventual marriage was the goal of this ruse they'd concocted, he didn't want to risk ruining the entire damned thing, even though a double wedding was decidedly *not* what he'd agreed to, in his initial conversation with Sophie. He was beginning to think they should have discussed this a bit more.

"I don't know—"

"But, West!" Alexandra said, wringing her hands. "What could be more joyous than two sisters celebrating a second chance at love, together?" She batted her eyelashes.

West cast Sophie a helpless look.

"We'll consider it, Alex," Sophie said, rescuing him. "But in the meantime," she added hastily, raising her wineglass, "perhaps a toast?"

West clutched his own wineglass the way a drowning man might grab a life raft, and joined the rest of the group in a hearty round of congratulations.

Internally, however, he continued to wonder: What, precisely, had he and Sophie got themselves into?

As the afternoon progressed, he had increasing cause to ponder this question; the conversation, mercifully, turned to other topics, and for a while he was spared from doing much more than nodding encouragingly and having a lengthy discussion with one of Sophie's brothers-in-law about cricket. (He saw Sophie making a determined effort not to laugh at one point, no doubt recalling the moment she had nearly maimed him during their most recent attempt at a cricket match in Cornwall, and he cast a dark look in her direction, which she pointedly ignored.)

He might have known this respite would not last; eventually, the group broke up, with Sophie, a couple of her sisters, and all the gentlemen except West and Lord Wexham engaging in a spirited game of pall-mall. West would ordinarily have joined in, but the sloping lawns at Riverton Hall were deceptively uneven, as he'd noted on the walk up the steps from the dock, and he thought it might be wise to spare his leg.

Sophie had cast him a brief, concerned look, but he waved her on and she was mollified enough to scamper after the twins to help them set the course. It was her natural tendency to fret, he knew; as the eldest of five sisters, she'd spent much of her life doing just that. It was part of the reason he was not married to her, in fact—and to have her fretting over *him* made some sort of dark, complicated feeling rise up in his chest, one that he did not fully understand and did not care to examine too closely.

Lord and Lady Wexham, meanwhile, were regarding their daughters and their husbands with expressions of mingled fondness and mild concern. (The latter was, in West's opinion, somewhat justified, considering that at the moment Harriet was setting up a pall-mall stake in a location that offered a decent chance of a player tumbling into the river.) Maria, however, settled herself next to him with an inquisitive look on her face that warned him that whatever was about to come out of her mouth might not be a question he wished to answer.

"Are you actually going to marry my sister this time?" she asked, without the merest hint of a pleasantry to soften the blow of the question. This should not have been surprising, based on everything Sophie had ever told him about her closest-in-age sister, and he paused before responding, studying her thoughtfully. She and Sophie bore the strongest resemblance of any of the Wexham daughters; both had similar shades of blond hair and nearly identical brown eyes, though Sophie's face was softer and Maria's a bit more angular, giving her the appearance of being the elder sister, despite being two years Sophie's junior.

"As this is the first time we've been betrothed," he said mildly, "I don't think 'this time' is an entirely fair choice of words."

Her gaze on him was sharp. "You might not have been officially betrothed, years ago, but everyone expected you to wed. And then you . . . didn't."

"Indeed." His voice was ever-so-slightly more curt than he generally permitted himself to sound; as far as he was aware, Maria had no idea that his father had threatened her reputation, should he and Sophie wed, so it was not fair to take out his irritation on her. But she had certainly known at the time that her actions that spring had been risky and foolish, for all that she'd only been eighteen. "I will certainly endeavor in the future not to inconvenience anyone with a life-threatening injury and resulting infection, lest your sister take it into her head to run off and marry someone else in the interim."

He regretted the words almost immediately; he did not need the speculative gleam in Maria's eyes to tell him that he'd said too much.

"Do you mean to tell me that it was *Sophie's* idea to marry Bridewell, then?" There was a note of barely concealed eagerness to Maria's voice that West imagined a Bow Street Runner might experience upon stumbling across a particularly good lead in the hunt for a criminal; he remained uncertain as to whether he or Sophie was the criminal in this metaphor. This was why he disapproved of metaphors.

He opened his mouth, then hesitated. What had Sophie told her sisters? He didn't wish to betray any revelations she wouldn't be comfortable with, but . . .

But, had the entire Wexham family considered him to be a villain for the past seven years? The thought bothered him more than he would have expected, like a loose thread on a sleeve that he couldn't prevent himself from tugging at.

"If you'd like to know why your sister married Bridewell," he said mildly, "I think you should ask her yourself."

Maria peered at him more closely. "Do *you* know why?"

"More or less." Never from Sophie herself, though—a fact that vexed him more with each passing hour spent in her company.

Damn it, he'd thought he could do this—could put the past behind them. Could do her this favor, seize the opportunity to teach his father a lesson while he was at it. Could listen to her laugh, feel the warmth of her hand in the crook of his elbow, converse with her, without allowing his every conscious thought to become fixated on her—on them—on the history they shared, and how it had all gone so terribly wrong.

But he was beginning to think he'd made a mistake.

Before Maria could ask anything further, there was a great shout of laughter and he and Maria turned their heads to see Harriet and Betsy clutching each other, giggling helplessly as their husbands attempted to fish the ball out of the reeds in the shallow water at the riverbank.

Sophie glanced over in West's direction, a look of resigned amusement on her face, and her eyes caught his for a moment—and in that moment, there was an expression of such intimacy, such knowledge, that West knew a second of uncanny certainty that this was what marriage to Sophie would have been like, that alternate life that usually felt so distant and yet which, in this moment, felt eerily close, as if only the thinnest of veils separated it from his true existence.

She felt, looking at him like that, like his fiancée in truth, not merely as a ruse. And he did not know what to do with the hopeless longing that he felt in that moment.

Something must have shown on his face, for Maria said, "Ah. Well, whatever happened between you and Sophie in the past, it's clearly mended now."

And West wished, so very, very badly, that this were true.

It was in the carriage, on the way home, that he broached the question.

"Does your family not know the truth of what happened between us?"

Sophie had been reclining lazily against the luxuriously upholstered seat, gazing idly out the window at the winding streets of London they were traversing; the bridge of her nose and her cheeks were a bit rosy, and her hair was beginning to escape from its neat coiffure, a couple of loose curls framing her face in a haphazard fashion. She looked relaxed and happy.

As soon as the words were out of his mouth, however, her demeanor changed in an instant. She straightened in her seat, all traces of ease in her expression immediately absent.

"The truth," she repeated slowly, her brown eyes fixed upon his face with a look in them that he could not quite decipher. "What truth would that be, precisely?"

"Well, your sister seems to be under the impression that *I* am the reason we did not wed."

"Which sister?"

"Maria."

"Ah. I thought you two looked rather cozy, whilst we were playing pall-mall."

"'Cozy' is not precisely the word I would have used to describe our conversation. Did you tell your family that I jilted you?" The question came out a bit more blunt than he'd intended.

"As we were not betrothed, it would be impossible for you to have jilted me," she said coolly. "And as for my family, all I told them at the time was that things could not possibly work between us, which was why I was marrying Fitz instead. I think they assumed it had something to do with your accident—perhaps you no longer wished to marry me, after all that had happened. Or perhaps I feared being your nursemaid." She paused. "I wasn't terribly concerned about what they believed, or whether it would make them think poorly of me—or you. I . . . wasn't concerned about many things, at the time." Her voice was soft, laced faintly with a remembered pain. "But I never gave them any details, so anything they may have surmised was not based on information they gained from me, I assure you."

This response, West thought, was notable for omitting as much as it answered. In between every two words were two dozen others that remained unspoken, and he was left not feeling any more enlightened than he had to begin with. All at once, he began to feel rather . . . *angry*. West was never angry; men in his position did not have the luxury of losing their tempers, of succumbing to emotions. Or at least, they shouldn't, and West had always held a particular amount of scorn for powerful men who used anger to intimidate those around them into doing their bidding.

But he, apparently, had his limits—and perhaps it should come as no surprise that Sophie would be the one to bring him to said limits.

"They're not aware, then, that you essentially acted as a martyr for Maria?" His voice was careful, even, but there was the slightest edge to it—and a quick flash of temper in Sophie's eyes let him know that she'd heard it. "That you took it upon yourself to sacrifice your own happiness for hers?"

She inhaled sharply. "It was more complicated than that."

"Was it? I recall our discussion at that ball with unfortunate clarity."

She pressed her lips together. "There's more to it that you don't understand."

"Ah. And I suppose it would be too much to hope that you explain it to me, then?"

Her gaze flicked to his, and held. "I believe you already know the basics—Fitz told you."

West felt a pang at the name, as he always did. He and Bridewell had known each other since they were children, and had always rubbed along well together. West *liked* Bridewell; he was the younger son of a marquess with more pedigree than fortune, and his expectations in life had always been considerably different from West's, but even in adulthood, they had shared a drink or a hand of cards at White's whenever Bridewell was home on leave from the army.

The betrayal of this man—one West had considered a true friend—in marrying the only woman with whom West had ever seriously considered matrimony . . . it had cut deep. They had only discussed it once, late one evening at White's, several months after West had recovered sufficiently from his accident to reappear in society once more. His leg had been paining him something fierce, as it was then still weak and unaccustomed to use. He, too, had been mired in grief and anger—there was the loss of Sophie, but also the loss of David. He'd never forget—though he very much wished he could—the morning he awoke in his sickbed to find his brother there, ashen-faced. It was James who'd broken the news to him of David's death, and he barely remembered the days that followed, the dark well of sorrow he'd descended into, robbed of the two people closest to him. That, combined with the lingering pain in his leg, meant that he'd grown very fond of a brandy (or three) in the evenings, to take the edge off; he had certainly partaken of quite a few on the evening in question, when he'd run into Bridewell at their club.

The conversation had been short, awkward; West, in pain, the worse for a few drinks, and not feeling at all charitably disposed toward Bridewell, had been uninterested in talking, and unwilling to hear what Bridewell wanted to say.

"He told me that my father spoke to you after the accident," West said, looking steadily at her. "Convinced you that we shouldn't marry. Renewed the threat against your sister—the threat, if memory serves, I *told* you I'd speak to him about. Had I been given the chance." His voice was cutting, but she did not flinch.

"That is true," she said simply. "But what Fitz didn't tell you—because I swore him to secrecy—is that I wasn't just trying to spare Maria. I was trying to spare *you*."

"Spare me," he repeated flatly. "Spare me from the knowledge that I was too much bother, you mean? That my title—my family—all of it, was too much? That you didn't trust me to make things right—to make you happy, without sacrificing your sister's reputation?"

"To spare you *pain*, you idiot," she said sharply, and something within him rejoiced to see her with color in her cheeks, her eyes sparking with temper. At least she was looking at him. At least she was discussing this with him, at last.

"Yes," he said, his words dripping with sarcasm, "God forbid I experience any *pain*, after all, not when my best friend—" He broke off, lest his voice crack; he avoided speaking David's name, in case doing so summoned any of the memories that he'd tried so hard to suppress: The reckless speed of their curricles. The precarious moment that their wheels had collided, sending them both toppling off-balance. The terrific noise of the crash. The shooting, searing agony of his leg. His howls of pain. And the terrible, eerie silence from David's curricle.

Sophie looked at him for a long moment, something in her gaze softening, but she did not speak, did not make any move to reach out to him, somehow sensing that he would not welcome it—that he could not bear to be comforted, not in these moments when his guilt was so enormous that he felt he'd drown in it.

But then, Sophie's words from earlier echoed in his mind: *I do not think David would wish you to blame yourself.*

And he thought of his friend—his laughing, reckless, loyal best friend, who he had loved so fiercely, and who he knew had loved him just as fiercely in return, even if they'd never once said as much.

And he began to believe, for the first time, that she was right.

This knowledge did not erase his guilt—nothing, he suspected, would ever do that—but it made it feel . . . smaller, somehow. Less all-consuming.

He knew that others would have told him the same thing, had the subject arisen—but it never did. He went to great pains, in fact, to avoid discussing it with anyone, and he did not know how to feel about the fact that he felt comfortable doing so with her, of all people. He exhaled a slow, uneven breath.

"Your father was going to make our marriage a misery," she said gently, at last. "He informed me as much, when I tried to visit you."

He felt her words like a blow. "When you tried to visit me," he repeated slowly, and his gaze fixed on hers with an unblinking intensity that other women would have quailed from, but which she faced steadily. "You didn't visit me," he said, but even he could hear the questioning note in his own voice, the barely concealed yearning, and thought it must be obvious to her how badly he wanted this to be true, what she was telling him. "They told me you didn't." Even as he spoke, he realized how absurd this was; had he truly believed this of her? He'd been under the impression, based on how Fitz had framed the story, that his father had paid a call on her—ridiculous, now that he thought about it for three seconds. But at the time, mired in grief and pain, having lost both his best friend and the woman he'd planned to marry in the span of mere days, he hadn't been thinking clearly.

"I did," she said simply. "And that is when your father made his move."

West gazed at her for a long moment.

"Tell me," he said at last.

And so she did.

Chapter Nine

Seven years earlier

Sophie would always remember that particular morning at the breakfast table, because she had never seen her parents' faces so grim. The Wexham household was one of laughter and joy, overall; there were quarrels, as was to be expected in a home full of five daughters, but these were mended readily enough, and did not tend to cause lasting damage. Which was why, when she entered the breakfast room after a second consecutive night of interrupted sleep, her thoughts occupied by her conversation with the Duke of Dovington at the Haverford ball, the sight of her parents' solemn, pale faces had stopped her in her tracks.

She did not recall precisely what words they had used to inform her of the news; her memories of that conversation would always be fragmented. *Curricle accident. Willingham was killed. West was badly injured.* All that she would recall afterward was the plunging swoop of her stomach, the sinking feeling within her chest. It felt as though a weight had settled there, one that she could not dislodge.

Her father had told her he was sending a note to the Duke of Dovington in the hope of further news, and her mother had pressed her to her chest with a strength that Sophie found smothering, but Sophie herself had said nothing, merely nodded. She did not miss the worried glance her parents exchanged as she made her way out of the room.

She drifted along, in the days that followed, like a ghost; she could not settle to any task, and was filled with enough restless energy that even sitting still came to feel like a hardship. Her father had received a brief reply from the duke, informing him that his son was gripped with a worryingly high fever, but there had been no further word, nor any invitation to visit—not that Sophie had expected one, given the duke's feelings about her presence in his son's life.

Her mind was occupied with thoughts of West lying in bed, feverish, insensible, with only his cold, stern father to watch over him. She thought, too, of Willingham—the laughing, golden man she'd seen only days earlier—and could not reconcile her memories of him with the knowledge that he was dead. When she thought of what this knowledge would do to West, if—*when*—he awakened, she felt a howl of misery clawing its way up from her chest and lodging in her throat; she felt as if she were choking on it.

By the fourth day, she could not bear it any longer.

It was easy enough, as it turned out, to dress quietly, to sneak down the servants' stairs and make her way to the mews. The family coachman had always been fond of her, and it was relatively simple to convince him to take her out in the carriage, once she threatened to set off on foot alone and hail a hack. Particularly after she told him her destination, and something in his face softened—the servants, after all, were hardly unaware of the concerns that gripped the family upstairs.

The Duke of Dovington lived in an imposing mansion in Berkeley Square; Sophie had ridden past it before, but had never had cause to knock at the door. This morning, it was answered by the most regal-looking butler she'd ever seen; for all that it was a thoroughly indecent hour of the morning, he did not have a single hair out of place.

"I was hoping for news of West—of Lord Weston, I mean," she said, hating how uncertain her voice sounded. She stiffened her spine, took a breath, and added, "I am aware this is a difficult time for the family, but if you would please give my card to the duke"—she extended the engraved calling card she had carefully tucked into her reticule half an hour before—"and inform him that I do not intend to leave until I have spoken to him, I'd very much appreciate it."

After a lengthy pause the butler stepped back, allowing her to stand in the entrance hall while he withdrew, presumably to inform his employer of a shockingly improper young lady refusing to remove herself from the property. There was a long enough delay that Sophie began to wonder if she really was going to have to refuse to leave—and to wish, not for the first time, that West's brother were in town; Lord James was at a house party in the countryside, and was presumably making his way back to London with great haste, but had not yet arrived—when the steady click of footsteps on the marble stairs drew her attention upward, and she watched as the Duke of Dovington descended toward her.

Even now, at this hour, with his eldest son lying horribly ill, he looked entirely ducal, his attire immaculate. There were dark circles under his eyes, however—the only sign that his nights had recently been as sleepless as Sophie's own.

"Miss Wexham," he said; there was a slightly frayed edge to his voice that betrayed his exhaustion. "This is unexpected."

"I realize that this is a bit unorthodox, but I've been desperate for any news of West," she said; she clasped her hands tightly before her, only in this instant realizing that, so hasty had she been in dressing without her maid, she had neglected to put on gloves. The duke's eyes dropped to her bare hands, then flicked back up to her face, but whatever disapproval he was experiencing was at least not visible in his expression.

He inclined his head to the right. "Let's step into my study."

Sophie felt as though a pit had formed in her stomach at these words, and she trailed the duke through the door he indicated, scarcely taking notice of her surroundings. Had West taken a turn for the worse? Had he . . .

But she could not form the word—could not breathe life into it, even in her thoughts. Something of her anxiety must have shown on her face, much as she was attempting to maintain a cool demeanor before this man she did not like, nor trust, because he said, as soon as the door closed behind him, "The fever broke in the night."

Sophie felt weak with relief; she reached out to grip the arm of a leather chair, suddenly feeling a bit uncertain as to her legs' ability to support her.

"The physician left an hour or so ago," the duke continued. "West has not yet awoken, but we hope he will do so today. Dr. Worth said to give him as much time to sleep as he needs, so we are not attempting to wake him."

"May I see him?" Sophie blurted out; she felt oddly as though she might burst into tears, but could not bear the thought of doing so before the duke.

Predictably, he shook his head. "I'll not have him disturbed."

A flash of irritation cut through her overpowering, giddy relief. "I don't intend to disturb him—I just want to *see* him."

An arch of the brow—a gesture eerily reminiscent of his son. "Do you think that I am lying to you, Miss Wexham? That my son is dead, and I am attempting to conceal the fact? Or that I have some other sinister purpose in mind?"

"Of course not," Sophie said impatiently, though come to think of it, she wasn't entirely certain she'd put any of that past the duke, based on all her interactions with the man thus far. "It's just that I'm very—very *fond* of West, and I've been so worried—"

"Yes. Well." The duke cleared his throat. "In fact, Miss Wexham, I am glad you called this morning, unexpected as it was. I'd been hoping to follow up on our conversation of a few evenings past."

For a moment, distracted as Sophie was by thoughts of West's well-being, she didn't realize what the duke meant; that night at the Haverford ball felt like a lifetime ago, even though it had been less than a week. All at once, however, the memories returned, his threatening words echoing in her mind:

You have younger sisters, do you not, Miss Wexham?

She went very, very still. Then, feigning coolness, she asked, "What about it, Your Grace?"

"Well," the duke said conversationally, "I thought I had made my position, as it pertains to you and my son, perfectly clear—but your presence here this morning would indicate otherwise. So perhaps I ought to speak a bit more plainly."

"Yes," she agreed, her heart thudding in her chest. "Perhaps you ought."

"Very well. If you do not wish me to put it about that I personally witnessed Miss Maria Wexham in the company of the Marquess of Sandworth slipping away from a ballroom, not a chaperone in sight, just a few weeks ago, then I'd very much appreciate it if you took yourself far, far away from my son."

Sophie met his eyes, even as a chill crept through her. Sandworth was a reprobate—fifteen years older than Maria, handsome and suave, but lacking in much of a moral compass, from what Sophie had heard. West, who was usually fairly measured in his speech, had made it clear that he was not fond of the man—and that was *before* he and Sophie had discovered Sandworth and Maria pressed together in a shadowy corner of Vauxhall Gardens a fortnight earlier. Sophie had, at the time, been terrified that someone had noticed Maria and Sandworth sneaking away together, but after a week passed and no whisper of gossip emerged, she had begun to relax, thinking they'd escaped unscathed.

Sandworth was a dreadful snob—his family line was nearly as old as West's, and she knew that he'd never marry Maria, a fact he'd made perfectly clear when he all but laughed in West's face at the suggestion, that night at Vauxhall. (This had been a particularly bold reaction on Sandworth's part, considering that West had had him by the throat, pressed against a hedge.)

Maria, of course, was young and foolish and overly fixated on titles, and had not been interested in Sophie's warnings, after she'd seen them dancing together at a ball a week or so before the night in question. Quite probably the very same ball where the duke had witnessed this, Sophie thought grimly. Maria had evidently held romantic visions of making a spectacular match with Sandworth, but his reaction—and hasty retreat, without so much as a glance in her direction—that evening at Vauxhall had disabused her of these notions.

The Wexham parents had been horribly angry, when West had grimly deposited their shamefaced daughter back into their keeping; the quarrel that evening, upon arriving home, had been enough to rouse all three younger sisters from their beds to eavesdrop shamelessly on the landing. Maria had spent the next two days locked in her room, pleading a headache and refusing all of Sophie's attempts to speak to her; eventually, she had resumed her normal activities when Lady Wexham had begun to talk of calling for a doctor, concerned about Maria's health. Maria had been a bit standoffish toward Sophie ever since; Sophie knew her sister was embarrassed about having so badly misjudged Sandworth, and decided to give her space, merely relieved that they had avoided catastrophe, and that her sister's reputation remained intact.

Now, though, all of this effort on Sophie's part could be ruined, if the duke so much as breathed a word of this. He would do it—she did not doubt it for a moment. He was a duke, a man accustomed to getting precisely what he wanted. And what he wanted right now was for his son to marry someone considerably more eligible than the daughter of an upstart viscount.

"Do you not think West would object to this, once he found out?" she asked, deciding to brazen it out. "Do you not think he would take issue with you ruining the reputation of the sister of the woman he wishes to marry?"

There: the faintest flicker of uncertainty in the duke's gaze, though it was quickly masked. He *wasn't* certain, she realized—he was fearful of the bond she shared with his son, of whatever power she had over him. Perhaps now he would retreat, would concede that West's life was his to do with as he wished, would resign himself to her presence.

But no—she should have known better than *that*.

He inclined his head. "A fair point, Miss Wexham." A delicate pause. "Have you considered, then, what West himself would sacrifice, were you to wed?"

"I think you'll find that other members of the *ton* might view a great love match with a more benevolent eye than you do, Your Grace.

And anyone who disapproves of me would not risk incurring the wrath of a future duke by being anything less than polite to me."

"Unless," the duke said, "they knew they would incur the wrath of a *current* duke by so much as speaking to you in public." He offered a thin smile.

"And do you think that West will want anything to do with you, if you make my life such a misery?"

"No, I don't suppose he will," the duke conceded. "Perhaps he might even think to live quietly in the countryside, away from the gossiping *ton*, hosting his friends who are too loyal to shun him—or you." There was a brief pause, one that felt decidedly menacing—an impression that was confirmed a moment later when the duke added, "Although, it would be unfortunate that he would no longer have Rosemere to retreat to."

Sophie frowned. Rosemere, she knew, was the country estate that had been West's mother's particular favorite—the one that had been in his charge, these past few years. He'd spoken of taking Sophie to visit. "Rosemere belongs to West."

The duke shook his head. "No, it does not. Rosemere belongs to *me*—it is part and parcel of the dukedom, and has been so ever since his mother brought it to our marriage as part of her dowry. I have handed it over into West's keeping, knowing his fondness for it, the fact that it was his mother's favorite . . ." The duke trailed off, as if to allow Sophie to appreciate the value that West placed on Rosemere—not that she needed any reminding. She'd heard him speak of it often enough, heard the genuine affection in his voice as he described his time there, the work he was doing, the relationships he had built with his tenants. She knew how much effort he'd dedicated to it, in the years since he'd left Oxford.

He loved that house, and its surrounding land, just as his mother had.

"It's unentailed, you know," the duke said. "Since it's not part of the original entailment, and was only recently acquired. It would be easy enough to sell."

"You wouldn't," Sophie said softly, but she knew he would—this was a clear indication that he would do *anything* to prevent West from marrying her.

"I would," the duke confirmed. "My son is young, Miss Wexham. He does not know his own mind. He does not know what—*who*—he truly wants. And if I have to make him unhappy to teach him this lesson, I will." He walked toward her steadily. "Walk away now—find some other gentleman in search of a hefty dowry, a bit less concerned about your family's history. But leave my son alone, or I shall make him—and you—regret it every day henceforth."

"Have you let West know any of this?" she asked.

"No." The duke's voice was curt. "Because my son is stubborn, and he fancies himself in love, and I know perfectly well that he'd try to call my bluff, to tell me that these are sacrifices he's willing to make. For *love*." The duke's voice positively dripped with scorn on this last word, and Sophie knew a moment of piercing sympathy for the late duchess.

"But if *you* love my son, Miss Wexham . . . well, I ask you, how much do you wish him to suffer, for your sake?"

He walked past her to the door, opening it and standing back to allow her to pass. He offered her a short bow in the entryway, and then made his way back upstairs without another word, confident in the knowledge that he had already said enough.

Later that afternoon, word circulated around London that the young Marquess of Weston was out of immediate danger, though he remained bedridden—an impromptu toast to his good health was offered at a ball in progress that evening.

Sophie was not in attendance.

In the days that followed, she kept to herself; a letter to her, from West, written in the hand of his valet, went unopened and unanswered. She needed time—time to *think*. Time to plan. Time to work out how she was going to extract herself from a near-engagement. How she would convince West that she didn't love him, that it had all been an enormous mistake, when everything within her was crying out to the contrary.

In the end, the solution presented itself rather neatly. It was on a ride in the park a couple of days after her meeting with the duke that she stumbled across Lord Fitzwilliam Bridewell, looking positively despondent, regarding a lady departing on horseback with a look of lovesick anguish that Sophie knew well.

They struck up a conversation as they rode on a slow loop around the park that afternoon; she learned of his circumstances (thrown over for his lack of prospects by the earl's daughter he fancied himself in love with; in rather desperate need of a dowry) and she told him of hers (in rather desperate need of a husband, if only to save West from himself; possessing a very handsome dowry of her own).

It was easy enough to come to an accord; he was initially hesitant, given that he was an old friend of West's, but she was able to persuade him that a marriage between herself and West would lead to nothing but unhappiness for the latter, given the duke's threats. Fitz, ultimately, was not difficult to convince; he was so heartbroken by the rejection of the lady he'd spent all Season chasing, and so alarmed by his father's recent threat to cut his allowance, that he could see quite clearly the advantage of a cordial, entirely loveless union with Sophie.

The betrothal was announced within the week, to the great puzzlement of everyone except the couple themselves. Banns were called, and they were married within a month; by the time West at last was well enough to be seen in public again, Sophie was another man's wife.

It was only on her wedding night, after her new husband had retreated to his own bedroom and Sophie lay alone in a large bed in the bedchamber adjoining his, staring into the darkness, that she at last allowed herself to weep.

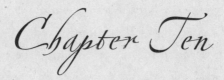

Chapter Ten

By the time Sophie finished speaking, the carriage had stopped no fewer than three times; each time, West had knocked his cane on the roof, signaling to his coachman to keep circling, and finally had a quick word with the man. Other than that, however, he did not interrupt as Sophie told him the truth of what had occurred seven years earlier between herself and the duke.

At last, she fell silent; at almost the same time, the carriage came to a halt once more. She glanced out the window, then blinked in surprise—she had not been paying the slightest attention to where they were bound, so wrapped up had she been in her own tale, and only now realized that they were outside West's home, rather than her own.

She looked at him inquiringly.

"Would you like to come inside?"

"I'm surprised your notions of propriety would allow such a thing." She meant her tone to sound light, but it came out more charged than she had intended.

"You've already called on me at home once. My virtue is now hopelessly compromised."

He handed her down from the carriage and ushered her into the house, hesitating for only the briefest second, apparently to consider the best room. Study? Drawing room? Sophie amused herself by imagining his mental calculations—the drawing room was more spacious, with more comfortable seating, but did the number of upholstered surfaces offering the opportunity to recline horizontally lend a certain illicit tawdriness to the proceedings? The study was more proper, more staid, but a desk chair was certainly not as comfortable as a settee, particularly after a long day of travel by carriage and boat; his leg must be paining him by now.

This being West, however, she knew without a doubt which consideration would win out.

"Briar, we'll be in the study," he told the butler, ushering her down the hallway with the faintest press of his hand at the small of her back.

"Ha," she muttered. "I owe myself a shilling."

"I beg your pardon?" He closed the door behind them.

"I knew you would choose the study, rather than the drawing room."

He leaned back against the door, watching her as she made a slow circuit of the room. It was neat as a pin; his desk was clear of mess, featuring nothing more than a tidy stack of papers, a pen and inkwell, and a few books set to one side, their spines perfectly aligned.

His gaze on her felt heavy, and her neck prickled under his regard. She resolutely ignored this—she knew all too well that he was not interested in a liaison with her. And *he* likely understood better now why she considered marriage to be out of the question.

"How, precisely, did you know that?"

She drew a book off the shelf, squinting down at it; it was one of the account books for Rosemere from two years prior. The spine was cracked, the leather rubbed buttery soft, not a speck of dust visible on the pages; clearly, this was a volume he consulted often. She swallowed against a sudden lump in her throat, and carefully replaced it on the shelf before turning to him.

"Because a study is more proper, obviously. Less conducive to amorous activity."

"Any room can be conducive to amorous activity, Sophie." His voice was low, like a caress.

Her eyes shot to his, and, for the second time in the past five minutes, she felt a blush rising in her cheeks; he met her gaze evenly, unblinking.

"I shall keep that in mind, thank you," she managed, feeling oddly disconcerted. She knew—thanks to a conversation, some years earlier, that she still remembered with unfortunate clarity—that he was not interested in an affair. How dare he now make her blush?

But then, he'd always been able to do so, seemingly without even trying. She'd proved oddly resistant to blushing in the face of other men's flirtations—she'd spent two months in Jeremy's bed without a single rosy cheek, to the best of her recollection—but West was the exception, as he was to so many things. She'd spent the better part of the past seven years attempting to train her body out of this reaction to his presence.

She took a seat in one of the chairs before the desk, in hope that he might sit as well, but he did not move for a long moment, merely continued to lean against the door, surveying her. He'd loosened his cravat; she caught sight of the tiniest hint of skin at his throat. At last, he pushed off from the door and made his way toward her; instead of settling behind his desk, however, he took a seat in the chair next to hers. Without the barrier of the desk between them, the room felt considerably more intimate.

Any room can be conducive to amorous activity, Sophie.

West's thoughts clearly lay along different lines, however, because after a moment he said, "My father and I quarreled, you know."

"Oh? When was this?"

"After that run-in with Bridewell seven years ago. I showed up at his front door at midnight, the worse for drink—he was not amused, as you might guess."

"Indeed." Sophie hated to think of West like this—younger, full of grief and pain and heartbreak, drowning his sorrows in brandy.

"I told him that I knew he had something to do with frightening you off—that he was the reason I couldn't have a happy marriage."

"Did he deny it?" Sophie asked evenly.

"He did not," West said, leaning back slightly in his chair, his jaw flexing. "I think that might have made me almost as angry as the fact that he'd interfered in the first place—the fact that he admitted it so brazenly. That he didn't feel ashamed, or even apologetic. He merely told me that I'd be grateful to him later."

"Were you?" The words rushed out before she could consider them; she immediately wished them unsaid, and yet also wished, quite badly, to know his response.

He turned his head slowly to face her; there was a bit of pink in his cheeks from a long afternoon in the sun, and his dark hair was mussed from the breeze on the river.

"Not for a single second."

He held her gaze in a moment that stretched taut between them. She wished to reach out and touch him, to rest her palm against the sharp lines of his face, to let him relax into her touch, just once.

Instead, she carefully knotted her hands together in her lap.

"I did, however, have my revenge," he added conversationally, breaking the tension that built with each moment the silence between them lengthened.

"Did you?"

"I may have led him to believe that my accident had left me incapable of having children." He said this easily, cheerfully, and she proceeded to choke on air at this revelation.

"Are you all right?" he asked solicitously as she coughed and gasped for air. Before she could recover, there was a knock at the door; it opened a moment later, revealing someone bearing a tea tray. Two someones, in fact—not maids, however, but . . .

"Hawthorne. Briar." West's voice was dryly amused. "This is . . . unorthodox."

Briar, she recognized as West's butler. He was perhaps in his late thirties, dark-haired, with a stern brow. The other man was shortish and wiry, with hair of a dark blond and a shrewd, intelligent face; after a moment, she registered the name.

"You're West's valet!" she said delightedly; she had memories of West mentioning him, years earlier, when they'd been courting. From what she recalled, they were from the same village in Kent, and had known each other for years.

Hawthorne swept her a surprisingly gallant bow as Briar carefully set down the tea tray. "Does my reputation precede me, my lady? How thrilling." He batted his eyelashes at her; Sophie suppressed a laugh. She had the distinct impression that Briar, next to him, was resisting the urge to offer a very un-butler-like eye roll only with great difficulty.

"How *do* you get his cravats knotted so precisely?" she inquired curiously. "They keep his chin tilted at such an attractive angle."

"I contemplate how much I'd occasionally like to strangle him, and channel that fervent energy into my craft instead," Hawthorne said, straight-faced.

Sophie laughed, while Briar—evidently deciding that things had gone quite far enough—reached out to clamp a firm hand upon Hawthorne's arm. "We thought you might want some refreshment, my lady," he said, very politely.

"And none of the maids were available to perform their duties?" West asked skeptically.

"I wouldn't wish them to become overly excited at the sight of a lady of gentle breeding," Briar said.

"Of course," West agreed. "Odd, though, that that's never been a concern on the numerous occasions Violet has come to call."

Hawthorne grinned. "I caught him attempting to eavesdrop at the door, and told him to fetch a tea tray and preserve some of his dignity."

"A Trojan horse, if you will," Sophie agreed cheerfully; Briar looked mortified.

"Without the bloodshed, I would hope," West said. He paused, then leveled a glance at his staff. "Was there anything else, gentlemen?"

"Of course not," Briar said, beating a hasty retreat, his hand still with a firm grip on Hawthorne's forearm. "We'll leave you to it, my lord." He caught sight of the complicated, extremely suggestive eyebrow waggle that Hawthorne was offering West, and more or less shoved him bodily from the room.

Sophie turned to West as soon as the door clicked shut. "Very *friendly* staff you have here."

West cleared his throat, looking a bit embarrassed—a rarity for him, and one that Sophie took a moment to savor as a small pleasure.

"They are most intrigued by our betrothal." He lifted a milk jug in her direction. "Do you still take your tea black?"

"A splash of brandy would not go amiss, if you have it," she said boldly, and was rewarded with a lift of that arrogant brow but no further commentary as he stood, rounded the desk, and opened a drawer, extracting a decanter that was three-quarters full. He added a splash of brandy to her tea, then looked at her inquiringly; she tilted her head to the side, and he added another splash. There was a moment of brief consideration, and then he added a splash to his own cup as well.

She leaned forward to gently tap her cup against his. "Cheers." There was silence for a moment as they both sipped their tea.

"My father is why I agreed to this betrothal, you know," West said.

Sophie, who'd had her teacup raised halfway to her mouth, lowered it again, a chill coursing through her. "What do you mean?"

"When I . . . misled him as to my reproductive capabilities, shall we say . . . he stopped fussing about me finding a suitable bride, and focused all his energy on James, since he was now the one on whose shoulders the future of the dukedom lay." A bitter note crept into his voice. "I had cause to regret that later."

"As well you should," Sophie agreed; the duke's meddling had led both to Violet and James's marriage *and* to their subsequent estrangement, though they'd now sorted things out once and for all, and seemed very happy.

"Recently, however, he has learned that I was not being entirely honest with him, and so he came to see me the other day—the same day you did, in fact. He implied that he should be happy to sell Rosemere, since I—lacking a wife and children—had little need for a country estate."

Sophie felt a rush of anger at these words, at the realization that it had been *seven years*, and the duke didn't even have the decency to come up with a better way to threaten his son, and those who loved him. It was just a *house*. It was a pile of stones in *Derbyshire*, for heaven's sake! She was irrationally angry—with West, for caring so much about a stupid house; with West's mother, for loving the house in the first place; with herself, for feeling angry at all, as well as helpless and frustrated and a dozen other things she didn't know how to put a name to.

And, most of all, with the duke. She dearly hoped she ran into the Duke of Dovington in the very near future, because at the moment, she thought she could quite happily murder him. And while murdering dukes was undoubtedly a hanging offense, she was beginning to wonder if perhaps she couldn't get away with it—who, after all, would miss him?

"Nice to see his tactics haven't changed the slightest bit in the past seven years," she said coolly.

"It's my fault," West said, rubbing a rueful hand over his face. "I made the mistake of letting him know how much I loved that property—how much it meant to me. Not in words, of course—"

"Of course not," said Sophie, amused in spite of herself.

"—but I didn't hide it well enough. And now he sees it as nothing more than a weakness to exploit."

Sophie thought of her own father—he was not a perfect man, but he loved his daughters fiercely, and wanted only the best for them, wished for their happiness above all else. So, too, did her mother; for all that she had been irritatingly obsessed with finding a husband for Sophie, during her years on the marriage mart, she knew that her mother had wanted her to find love, not merely an impressive title.

"You deserve better than a father who sees everything you love as an advantage to seize," she told West softly. He glanced down into his teacup, and she frowned; did no one else tell him this? "You're a good man, West," she said, the words simple but true. "And your father knows it, and takes advantage of it, because he's an ass."

This surprised a chuckle out of him; the sound of his laugh always seemed like a precious gift, so rare was it. He glanced back up at her, an expression in those vivid eyes that she couldn't quite decipher.

"You deserved better, too," he said. "What my father did to you—the way he sought to manipulate you—" A note of bitterness crept into his voice, and it made something in Sophie's chest ache to hear it. "You care for your sisters—you cared for me—and my father knew this, and took advantage of it. And you did not deserve this."

"It wasn't your fault," she said, realizing that the expression she'd seen in his eyes a moment before was *guilt*. In being honest with him, had she merely given him another thing to feel guilty about? Would things between them always be this way, laced with pain and guilt and thoughts of what might have been? Moments like this made her feel even more convinced that there was no future for them—not when they were still so mired in the past. Not, too, when his mention of fatherhood—his duty to provide an heir—only reminded her of another obstacle to any future they might share. An obstacle that she did not feel ready to divulge, on the heels of so many other confessions this afternoon.

"Thank you," he said, gazing steadily at her, and then cleared his throat, dispelling the weight of the moment. "He did not make it clear that he had any particular candidate in mind for matrimony, so I thought perhaps our feigned betrothal could teach him a lesson—teach him to back off. No doubt he'll be so relieved when we—when it is revealed that we are not to wed, after all . . ." He shifted in his seat as he spoke, about as close as this man ever came to fidgeting; he was not looking her in the eye. "I suspect he'll be so relieved that he'll stop caring overmuch about whom I marry."

A thought occurred to Sophie now—one that perhaps ought to have struck her much earlier, before she involved West in this hare-brained scheme to begin with. "Did you . . . have someone in mind? For marriage, I mean?" She tried to ignore the current of dread forming within her as she awaited his reply; she hadn't heard a rumor of him courting any young ladies, but he was of an age when men of his station began to consider marriage, and he certainly had to be one of the most eligible bachelors of the *ton*—perhaps even more so because of his accident. The slight air of tragedy that had clung to him ever since seemed to have only increased his appeal, even if it made matchmaking mamas a bit cautious. But if he were to make it clear that he was ready to marry at last—well, he'd be beating them off with his cane.

She did not care to dwell on how little she liked that prospect.

"I did not." There was not a single ounce of uncertainty in his words.

She opened her mouth. Shut it again. Everything about the past hour—everything they'd revealed to each other—was reason enough that she should stand up and walk out of this room. Go home, where it was safe—where she wouldn't tell him something she shouldn't. Where she wouldn't ask him any more questions she didn't want the answers to.

Instead, she locked gazes with him, and said, "But you'll need an heir."

That arrogant lifting of a single brow—did they teach this gesture in duke school? she wondered grumpily.

"I believe I technically already have one," he said, adding blandly,

"Is it not wonderful to be blessed with the soothing balm of sibling affection?"

Sophie laughed in spite of herself. "Is that your plan? Let Audley and Violet worry about providing an heir to the title, and you can go about—what? Raking your way about town?"

This did not actually sound remotely like him, but she was bluffing her way through this entire exchange, feigning a comfort and bravado that she did not feel. It was the only way she knew how to speak to him of this.

"Yes," West said dryly. "That is indeed perfectly in line with how I have spent the past seven years." He took a sip of his tea, then leaned forward to place the cup—still half-full—carefully on the edge of his desk, and shifted slightly in his seat so that he was facing her more directly.

"I've no interest in marrying whatever debutante fresh from the schoolroom my father thinks has the bluest blood and the best hips for childbearing. I've a brother, who is happily married—and if he should not produce a son, for whatever reason, I've plenty of cousins. Went to Oxford with the next in line after James, in fact. He cheats at cards, but is otherwise a decent sort." This was uttered reluctantly, Sophie noted with amusement; she was fairly certain West would rather lose the use of his good leg than cheat at cards.

"The point is, I don't give a damn what my father hopes for my future anymore—and would very much like him to take his nose out of my affairs."

She regarded him thoughtfully, considering the questions she wished to ask him, the other half of this conversation that she wished, suddenly quite desperately, to have with him.

The words stuck in her throat, however; somehow, despite all that they'd revealed to each other this evening, she could not bring herself to risk anything further. "It seems to me, then," she said, "that if we are to teach your father a lesson, we need to make certain that he is forced to watch us be the happiest betrothed couple on earth."

"Did you have something in mind?"

"I believe I do," Sophie said, leaning forward in her seat. "I think that we need to make a bit of a scene." And she felt something close to a smile tugging at the corners of her mouth. She was, all at once, determined to enjoy herself—to enjoy this ruse, this pantomime of the life she might have lived. She could parade before the duke as his future daughter-in-law, even if she would never hold that role in truth. She told herself that she still felt as certain of this fact as she had seven years earlier. And four years ago, too—the last time she had had cause to consider the prospect of becoming the Marchioness of Weston.

And she ignored the beginnings of the faintest whispers of doubt, lurking at the corner of her mind, and asking, *What if?*

Chapter Eleven

Four years earlier

Sophie would not have said that a graveyard was the ideal spot to commence an affair, but she supposed there must have been stranger settings for such developments. Not that she knew from personal experience—one of the wearying things about being a lady of gentle breeding, the daughter of a peer of the realm, et cetera, was that she had always been uninterestingly well-behaved.

The June sun cast the quiet, grassy graveyard in dappled shadows, and Sophie felt perspiration bead at the back of her neck beneath the heavy black fabric of her dress; she spared a passing mournful thought for the closet full of fetching summer frocks that would not be worn this year, cast aside for the array of mourning gowns that had appeared in her dressing room within days of Fitz's death. She was wearing a particularly elaborate hat-and-veil concoction this afternoon and, with a surreptitious glance around, Sophie lifted the veil to allow a hint of a breeze to waft across her face.

It was as she was doing so that she caught sight of a flicker of movement out of the corner of her eye. She turned her head sharply; her body seemed to recognize him before her eyes did, some tingle of awareness creeping up her spine, raising gooseflesh on her arms. She hated that, even after three years, he still had this effect on her.

She tilted her head back to take him in: those vivid, arresting eyes; cheekbones that appeared to have been carved by a sculptor. He was clad in the finest of everything, immaculately tailored, boots shined to a gleam. He leaned upon his cane slightly as he gazed down at her.

"Lady Fitzwilliam."

"Lord Weston."

His mouth pressed down slightly at the edges at the sound of his title on her lips; he'd told her to call him West on the night they'd met. The use of his title felt strange.

"I wished to offer my condolences."

"I—yes. Thank you. I received your note."

The note in question had been written in his own hand, instantly recognizable to her even though it had been years since she'd received any correspondence from him. It had been as formal and stilted as his speech today; she'd read it twice, then filed it carefully away in the drawer in her desk where she kept the rest of the letters of condolence she'd received, like some grim treasure trove she could revisit whenever she was feeling particularly maudlin.

She felt vaguely disgusted with herself—if this was the effect widowhood was going to have on her, she could not in all honesty recommend the state to anyone else. One would have thought this went without saying, except that Sophie had seen a number of women who seemed suspiciously cheerful after their husbands' deaths. No doubt *those* women were not keeping a drawerful of ghastly souvenirs in their sitting rooms.

While she was occupied by these thoughts, an odd, strained silence had fallen. West—no matter what she called him aloud, in her mind he would always be West—looked as though he wasn't quite certain how to proceed. This was itself a novelty; this was as close to uncomfortable as she'd ever seen him.

After another few moments, he said, "I did not come here to seek you out—I wouldn't wish to intrude on your privacy, whilst you are grieving."

She felt these words like a sharp pinch, as she did every time someone alluded to her supposed grief. And she *was* grieving—she'd liked Fitz, and they'd rubbed along tolerably together, even though it had become apparent within a month of their marriage how poorly matched they were. But, while she was certainly sorry that he was dead—in battle mere days before the war's end; the entire thing was a horrible waste—she was also not grieving the way a wife properly should. Perhaps not even the way West himself was—despite the fact that he and Fitz had had precious little to say to each other for the past three years, they had known each other since boyhood, and she was certain that his loss stung.

"You are not intruding," she said, forcing herself to meet his eyes, to let him see whatever he would in hers. "I merely wished to get out of the house, but my maid had a fit at the thought of me going riding in widow's weeds. This seemed one of the only acceptable places to go, if I did not wish to be judged for enjoying myself too much."

West flicked a glance around the small churchyard, full of weathered headstones; the one before them was fresh marble. There were no other visitors, merely a collection of headstones and grass spotted with a few persistent wildflowers. "I suppose a graveyard is judged suitably somber," he said. "Little chance of you lifting your skirts and dancing a jig atop one of the graves, after all."

"I would bet ready money that most graveyards have seen that more than once," she replied, and there was a faint twitching at the corner of his mouth, a ghost that recalled past conversations when she'd had the knack of offering just the right sly retort to slide under that stern exterior and surprise a hint of a smile out of him.

"But not from you?" The question was quiet, and there was a trace of uncertainty to it, uncharacteristic from this man who always seemed so terribly certain of everything. Behind the question, she heard all the other, unspoken, questions:

Were you happy with him?

Do you regret his death?

And then, quietest of all:

Do you regret your marriage?

And she could answer none of these—not honestly, at least. Not with the full truth. Not when there was no point to it, even now.

So instead, she simply said, "No. Not I."

West turned to look at the simple headstone before them, his eyes tracing the freshly carved words: *Fitzwilliam Charles Bridewell, 2 February 1787–10 April 1814. Beloved son, brother, and husband.*

Certainly true on two counts—and true . . . enough, on the third. Even if it did not feel that way to Sophie, standing in her widow's weeds, feeling as though she were performing a display of grief that she was not fully experiencing.

A silence fell between them, and Sophie felt a small pang of loss for the ease they'd once had—the words that had fallen, eager and quick, tumbling over each other in their rush to spill out of her mouth. She had been so young then; she had not learned to be cautious, to watch what she said—or, rather, she *had*, but not with him. And he, who had learned that lesson young—too young—had let down his guard with her, and this had made her feel powerful, invincible, as though there were nothing on earth that she could not accomplish.

But now, there was too much history between them—a not insignificant amount of it centered on the man whose name they now gazed at, carved into marble.

"When we were boys, he told me that he was missing a toe because a sheep bit it off," West said, breaking the silence.

This was so unexpected that it startled a laugh out of Sophie. "You can't be serious."

"I am. I knew he had to be lying, but I spent weeks trying to catch him without his shoes on so I could check for myself." Sophie sneaked a glance at him, and saw that his gaze was still fixed on the headstone; in profile, the angles of his face were even more perfectly chiseled than they appeared head-on, and she suppressed a sigh. Men simply should not be *allowed* to look like this, she thought.

"And?"

"And eventually I caught him unawares and sat on him until I could tug his shoe off and count his toes for myself."

Sophie could barely imagine the man standing next to her doing such a thing—having ever been so young, so mischievous.

"And then," he added, "my father caught me at it—Fitz was visiting Brook Vale Park on a holiday from Eton—and he thrashed me. Apparently it wasn't very ducal."

This was uttered in a matter-of-fact tone, but Sophie nearly flinched as if she'd taken a blow. West's father was the reason she had so much difficulty in imagining a version of West that was so carefree. So young. The Duke of Dovington had done his best to ensure that his firstborn and heir was a carefree boy for as little time as possible, and then had continued to attempt to arrange all the details of his life like chess pieces.

Sophie knew this better than anyone, after all.

"All this is to say," West said, turning to face her directly now, and her breath caught in her throat at the intensity of his gaze, "that for a very long time, he was a good friend of mine, and I'm more sorry than I can say that he is dead."

"Thank you," she said softly, and—because solitude, apparently, did not suit her, and had addled her head, or at least that was the only explanation she was willing to entertain for the utterly inexplicable thing she did next—

She reached out and took his hand.

And he went very, very still. His gaze dropped to her hand, engulfed in his larger one.

And then his gaze lifted back to hers. And caught. And held.

And Sophie was suddenly reminded why she had spent the past three years not allowing herself to so much as glance across a ballroom at him—because once she met his eyes, what happened next was inevitable.

Watching a woman brush her hair had never been a particular, specific fantasy of West's, but he could watch Sophie at her dressing table for the rest of the night, he thought. Quite happily.

She was running a silver hairbrush through her long golden waves, wrapped in a luxurious dressing gown that she'd donned over her chemise. He hated seeing her in her black dress—hated the loss it reminded him of; hated the knowledge that she'd be wearing black for another year.

He buttoned his waistcoat, his eyes still fixed on the slim hand that moved the brush methodically through the hair that he had mussed with his own fingers not an hour before. Reaching for his coat, he took a breath—uncertainty did not come naturally to him, but he'd never had to ask a woman he wished to marry how he might go about courting her while she was still mourning the husband she'd thrown him over for.

He settled on a simple, "How do you wish to proceed?"

Sophie's hand slowed, and she carefully set her brush down on her dressing table. She turned to him with a questioning look. "Very discreetly, obviously."

"Yes," he said slowly. "But I meant more—are we going to tell anyone? Or just wait until you are out of mourning, and surprise them?"

She frowned. "It's hardly the sort of thing I'd like to confess to my parents over Sunday night dinner."

It was West's turn to frown. "I thought they might be pleased."

Sophie's eyebrows shot toward her hairline. "That their daughter, who was widowed only a couple of months ago, is conducting an affair with the unmarried heir to a dukedom?"

West's frown deepened, uncertain if she was jesting. "No," he said carefully. "That their daughter is being *courted* by the unmarried heir to a dukedom—a man she was once rather fond of, if memory serves." He tried to keep the edge out of his voice—something with which he usually had little difficulty—but he didn't quite manage it.

Sophie inhaled a single, sharp breath, and somehow he knew that he was not going to like whatever came next.

"Courting," she repeated. "West, you—you can't *court* me. This can't—we can't—" She waved her hands, seeming at a loss for words—a rarity from a woman who had always, from the very first night he'd met her, when she was only twenty, seemed almost astonishingly self-possessed.

"You are a widow now," he said evenly, and some dark part of him took a petty pleasure in the sight of her slight flinch at the word "widow." Perhaps it was the same part of him that thought nothing—or, at least, not enough—of taking to bed the widow of a man who'd once been a friend, before he was even cold in his grave. He could add it to the list—considerably longer now than it was a few years earlier—of things with which he had to reckon when he glanced in the mirror each morning. "Once your mourning period is over, there will be nothing standing between us—unless . . ." He trailed off, unable to continue. Unless this had meant nothing to her—when it had meant *everything* to him, as everything about her always had. That had always been the trouble; he, who so carefully controlled his emotions where others were concerned, seemed curiously unable to do so with her alone.

"That changes nothing of our past," she said. "That changes nothing about the reasons we could not marry then. Unless your father has recently had a touching change of heart and . . . well, of his entire philosophy of life?"

The words were bitter—not that he could blame her.

"I have told you before, and it is still true, that it does not matter to me if my father approves of this match." He spoke each word very carefully, stepping toward her with slow intent.

She rose, even as a flush crept up her neck—a sure sign that she was growing angry. "Perhaps it does not matter to *you*, but it very much matters to *me*."

"What is the trouble?" he asked, frustrated. "Your sisters are all married—he cannot destroy their prospects anymore. There is no reason we could not wed."

Sophie cut her glance away from him, an odd expression flickering across her face. She did not answer him directly, instead saying, "I thought we'd already been through all this—I thought we could be sensible! There is clearly a lingering . . ." She faltered briefly, scrabbling for a delicate way to describe the way the very air between them always seemed to come alive the second they set foot in the same room. The way he could barely catch a hint of her perfume before he wanted to press her against the nearest wall, every gentlemanly impulse that usually governed his behavior instantly forgotten.

He waited, bitterly amused.

". . . attraction," she said carefully after a moment, lifting her chin, "between us, and I thought we could be adults about it—a discreet affair—"

He leaned forward. "I do not want, and have not ever wanted, to conduct an *affair* with you."

She held his eyes, her gaze defiant. "It is all I will ever offer you—because we are never going to marry." She presented the words like a thrown gauntlet, with color high in her cheeks.

He took a step back. Turned, very deliberately, and retrieved his cravat from the bedpost where he'd knotted it not so many minutes before, it being put to a far more interesting use than its usual role of guarding the scandalous few inches of skin at his throat from innocent feminine eyes. Clutched it in his fist. And then turned, slowly, back to her, and said, "Then I do not think we have anything left to discuss." He offered her the shortest bow that courtesy would allow. "Lady Fitzwilliam."

She crossed her arms across her chest. "Lord Weston."

And then he turned and left her bedroom, descending the back stairs to the kitchen, where he could make his exit unobserved by the prying eyes of the *ton*.

It was only once he'd emerged into the mews behind her house that he allowed himself a single, soft expletive. He slapped his palm, once, against the brick wall before him, allowing his forehead to briefly rest against his forearm, his eyes fluttering shut against the memory of the words he and Sophie had just exchanged.

And then he opened his eyes, straightened, placed his hat atop his head, and headed toward the street with slow, measured steps to hail a hack—the Marquess of Weston once more, the man he was in Sophie's company tucked carefully away.

Chapter Twelve

"Are you certain this doesn't bother your leg?" Sophie asked for the second time.

West shook his head. "No more than anything else does."

Sophie pressed her lips together, clearly biting back whatever it was she actually wished to say. Instead, she merely offered, "That does not *precisely* answer my question."

He glanced sideways at her, weighing his words. Nothing about the first thirty-one years of his life had made him feel easy with admitting to even a hint of weakness—but this was Sophie. He had been comfortable unburdening himself to her . . . once. And the past week had done nothing more than remind him of all that he missed from those days. "If we ride too long, it will be sore later," he conceded. "But I can tolerate it for a short distance—it's certainly not any worse than my weekly fencing sessions with Hawthorne."

He expected her to debate him further—to take issue with the fencing, at least, which he was perfectly well aware no doctor would have advised—but she merely shook her head and said, "All right." Catching his surprised look, she added, "If you think I'm going to waste my time arguing with a man who turns noble suffering into high art, you must have taken leave of your senses entirely."

"Noble suffering?"

Sophie nodded, her gaze fixed on their surroundings—they were on Rotten Row at five o'clock, meaning it was positively teeming with aristocrats. It put one in mind of rats on a ship. "You have been raised with the knowledge that you are one day to possess enormous wealth and responsibility, and so you seem to have decided at some point that making a mild martyr of yourself is the best way to offer some sort of atonement for the privilege you inherited on the day you were born."

She ignored his indignant sputtering and offered a cheerful wave to Lady Wheezle, who was out walking one of her alarmingly small dogs and who gave Sophie a mildly suspicious look at this display of enthusiasm. This look quickly melted into one of intrigued delight upon seeing West at her side; he offered her a more restrained nod of the head in greeting as they rode past.

"What do you think she does with the other dogs?" he asked Sophie in a low voice. "She only ever walks one at a time, but she must have half a dozen."

"How on earth can you tell? They all look the same—like potatoes with wigs."

West could not suppress an amused snort, and Sophie cast him a sideways glance, a smile creeping across her own face.

"They're different colors," he informed her. "There's a black one, and a tan one, and a white one, and a sort of off-white one—"

"I did not realize that you paid Lady Wheezle sufficient attention to be able to describe her dogs in such detail. She's a widow, you know. If you are seeking a new inamorata, once our ruse comes to an end."

West gave her an appalled look. "She must be at least seventy."

Sophie sniffed. "That merely means she's experienced. I like to think that when I'm seventy, I could catch the eye of a dashing young nobleman if I set my mind to it."

"I've no doubt," he said with complete sincerity, but this felt dangerously like flirting, something he did not trust himself to do with her—not when merely being at her side was sufficient to drive all thoughts of every other woman he'd ever kissed out of his mind. It would have been a lovely state of affairs, had they *actually* been betrothed.

"Violet and Audley," Sophie said in an undertone, interrupting West's thoughts. He glanced up; his brother and sister-in-law were approaching them on horseback. Violet in particular looked downright delighted when she caught sight of them.

"West! Sophie!" she called.

"Violet," West said. "James."

"We were just out for a ride," Sophie said, smiling radiantly as she tried to nudge her horse closer to West's. He reached out a hand to seize her by the elbow and steady her when her attempts at nudging threatened to dislodge her from her sidesaddle entirely.

"Yes," James said slowly, looking at Sophie with some perplexity. "We can see that."

"It's a nice day for it," West added inanely.

Now Violet was looking at them strangely, too, but appeared determined to ignore the fact that West and Sophie seemed to have been replaced by two people who had never had an interesting conversation in their lives. "We ran into your father a few minutes ago, West," she told him. "He was in a bit of a temper. I don't suppose . . ." She trailed off, before adding delicately, "I don't suppose he was very pleased to be informed of your betrothal in a *note*." She seemed to be torn between disapproval and amusement.

"No," he agreed. "I don't suppose he was. But if I were to list the number of things he has done over the years that *I* have not appreciated, we'd still be standing here at midnight, so I expect he shall learn to manage his disappointment."

Now James, Violet, *and* Sophie were all regarding him rather strangely.

"West, are you feeling all right?" James asked, real concern evident in his voice.

"*Dearest,*" Sophie said through a smile, "I thought you were going to inform him yourself."

"And so I did, my . . ." He trailed off; the word that had sprung naturally to his tongue was not one he could ever utter to her again. She was not his love—she was not his *anything*, not anymore. Not in truth, at least. His father had seen to that, seven years earlier. "Potato," he finished weakly, Lady Wheezle's root-vegetable-like dogs apparently still on his mind.

James's eyebrows were approaching his hairline. "Your potato," he repeated, sounding as though he was approximately five seconds away from summoning a doctor.

"You know how it is," Sophie said quickly, never once allowing her smile to slip, though there was now a telltale, slightly hysterical twitching occurring at the corners of her mouth. "When one has been reunited with a long-lost love, it all feels fresh and new again, nicknames just . . . materialize."

"Nicknames involving . . . vegetables?" James asked.

"Now, James, need I remind you that I have made references to aubergines *several* times recently?" Violet put in innocently. "Vegetables are truly the height of romance."

West and Sophie both blinked. West leaned forward slightly in his saddle, to confirm that his brother was indeed blushing.

"I do not think this is the time for that, Violet," James said—West was mildly impressed that he was able to speak at all through so tightly clenched a jaw.

"In any case," Sophie said, mercifully interrupting this thoroughly disturbing turn the conversation had taken, "my . . . potato and I are very happy. I am *so* sorry to hear the duke does not share in our joy. Perhaps we should go discuss it with him directly?" She reached out to lace her fingers through West's, a gesture that likely looked more affectionate than it felt, considering she was gripping his hand so tightly that he thought he was likely to lose feeling in it at any moment.

Violet and James both looked mildly perplexed by this suggestion—it was not often that one of their set announced an intention to speak with the Duke of Dovington willingly—but West could hardly explain to them that they were attempting to rub an entirely feigned betrothal in his father's face. Instead, he merely said, "Perhaps," raising Sophie's hand to his lips for a kiss; this, it was immediately obvious, was a mistake. The kiss was fleeting, but the smell of her skin was so familiar to him that he was instantly awash in memories—of the feeling of her lips against his, the taste of her skin, the silky weight of her hair in his hands.

He dropped her hand as if he'd been burned.

Sophie did not look at him as she said brightly, "Well, we'll be off! Lovely to see you!"

West kicked his horse into a trot, not daring to turn around as he and Sophie rode away. If he had to guess, however, he would wager that both James and Violet were watching their retreating backs with utter confusion.

"That went well," Sophie said, her voice positively dripping with sarcasm.

"It was a rehearsal," he said a bit stiffly, his eyes still on the path ahead. "We'll do better next time, when we see my father."

"*Will* we?" she asked skeptically. "You compared me to a root vegetable!"

"I was put on the spot."

"You were not! If you cannot even come up with a moderately sane term of endearment without excessive consideration, then I think perhaps this plan might be doomed to failure."

"Might I remind you," he said, jerking the reins with more strength than he intended, causing his horse to come to a shuddering halt, "that this was *your* idea?"

"Which *you* agreed to!" she hissed, reining in her horse as well. "If you don't think you can play the role convincingly, you should have just told me so from the outset rather than allowing me to waste time and energy on this ruse instead of coming up with some other option."

"As if I've just been having a delightful time of it." He was growing more irritated by the moment, and took a deep breath, trying to master his temper. This was not a task with which he ordinarily had much difficulty—that was something he'd always prided himself on. But she did have a peculiar way of irking him that no one else had ever quite managed.

"No one forced you to do this, you know."

"Perhaps *you* might have noticed that I have a peculiar difficulty in saying no to you," he shot back.

"Odd, then, that you had no trouble whatsoever rejecting me four years ago."

He could tell from the look on her face that she hadn't meant to say this—that it had spilled out in the heat of the moment. The gentlemanly thing to do would be to ignore it, to try to steer this conversation onto more stable ground.

Instead, what he said was:

"Odd, as I seem to recall it a bit differently. I all but asked you to marry me, and you could barely control your eagerness to inform me of all the reasons that would never happen."

"Reasons that I would think you understood better now, given that I explained them to you not two days ago," she said through gritted teeth. She must have dug her heel into her horse's side, for it reared slightly—Sophie could have steadied it herself, but before she had the chance to do so his arm shot out, grasping her reins, bringing the horse back under control. Under his hand, one of Sophie's hands still gripped the reins; he could feel the warmth of her skin through her glove.

She looked up at him and exhaled a slow, shuddering breath.

And it was at precisely this moment that he heard his father's voice hailing him, less welcome at this instant than it had possibly ever been in West's entire life.

"West."

He wrenched his gaze away from Sophie's face to see his father approaching on horseback. His father loved horses and he rode beautifully, his seat as impeccable as it must have been thirty years prior. West loosened his grip on Sophie's hand as the duke approached, but did not drop it.

"Father." He inclined his head toward the duke. "I believe you remember Lady Fitzwilliam?"

Sophie, for her part, offered the duke a serene smile. She was wearing a riding habit of forest green, and a matching hat was set atop her gleaming golden hair, which was combed into an elaborate braided knot at the back of her head. Her spine was straight and she'd loosened her grip on the reins so that they rested easily in her hands—she might not be a natural horsewoman, but as the daughter of a viscount, she'd been taught to ride and had a good seat. She looked every inch a future duchess, and West knew it would not matter to his father one whit. The thought was enough to send a dangerous current of anger coursing through him; he'd been fighting against that anger for seven years, and was growing less interested by the day in suppressing it, now that he knew the full truth of what had happened all those years ago.

"Indeed." The duke glanced from West to Sophie and back again. "I was intrigued to receive a note from you, West."

"Yes." West's tone was careless, even as his grip on Sophie's hand tightened slightly. "I thought you'd want to know about recent developments. I was so inspired by our discussion last week that I thought it best to take your advice to heart immediately."

"I see." A muscle in his father's jaw was ticking; West realized that he was perilously close to enjoying himself, and so pressed onward.

"Yes. I'm certain you didn't *really* mean to threaten me, but I started thinking about what you said, and all at once, I realized that Rosemere badly needed a mistress—and, eventually, the pitter-patter of small feet." He managed to utter the words "pitter-patter" with a straight face, but it was a very near thing. He did not dare look at Sophie, but detected a slight stiffening in her posture out of the corner of his eye at these words.

"And so you wasted no time in seeing to this matter."

"Exactly." West offered his father a thin smile, which the duke did not return.

"We are, naturally, so thrilled," Sophie chimed in, offering the duke a smile of such sickly sweetness that West was surprised not to see bees buzzing about her. "My sister is also newly betrothed—to the Earl of Blackford, perhaps you've heard?—and we are discussing a *double wedding*." These last words were uttered so rapturously that West half-expected to see tears glistening in her eyes as she spoke. "Would that not be lovely, Your Grace?"

His father looked as though he'd just swallowed nails. "It would be . . . an event," he managed.

"*The* event," Sophie corrected. "Of the entire Season, I expect! I mean to say—two of the *ton*'s most eligible bachelors, long causing despair to matchmaking mamas who eyed them like the fattest calves at the county fair, finally settling down to matrimony, both in love matches with daughters of a mere *viscount*."

She offered the duke another sickening smile, and West realized that—while she was undoubtedly enjoying herself a great deal in the moment—she was also very, very angry. It was a relief, this realization; he wanted her to be angry. She *deserved* to be angry. And, perhaps, if she was angry . . .

Then she was still as pained by what had happened all those years ago as he was.

She had explained the full history to him in even tones, not allowing emotion to creep into her voice, almost as if it were a show she'd seen at the theater, those involved mere players upon a stage. But this thin, constant edge of anger that laced her voice now—this proved that she was not unmoved.

That perhaps she still cared for him, beyond the obvious attraction that crackled between them like sparks.

He could not suppress the quick surge of hope that rushed through him at this thought.

"Truly an inspiring tale, Lady Fitzwilliam," the duke said. "No doubt the revolutionaries in France would have cheered at this story of peasant triumph."

West glanced sideways at Sophie, whose smile faltered slightly at this, because—he was nearly certain—she was trying not to laugh.

"Quite," she said primly. "No guillotines in your future, Your Grace! What a relief!" She offered a tinkling little laugh. And then, West witnessed one of the most astonishing things he'd ever seen in his entire thirty-one years of existence:

His father's lips twitched. As if he were *amused*.

Naturally, he quickly wrestled them back under control. But Sophie was not yet done. "And I'm certain my parents will wish to host a betrothal ball, for Alexandra and me—you *must* attend. I'm sure Papa would be *delighted* to see you."

"Of course." The duke was watching Sophie consideringly now, like a man who had gone into battle thinking his opponent armed with knives, only to be confronted with a cannon. "I shall be awaiting my post each day with bated breath." His gaze flicked to West. "West. You will join me for dinner at my club on Sunday night as usual?"

West inclined his head. "I wouldn't dream of missing it, Father."

"Indeed. You have, after all, been so obedient of late." The duke gathered his reins in his hands, and nodded at them. "Good afternoon."

And then he kicked his horse into a trot, and was gone.

"You know," Sophie said thoughtfully, "I really rather enjoyed that."

Chapter Thirteen

West was fond of his brother, but when, the night of his encounter with James and Violet in Hyde Park, West recalled that he'd invited James over for an evening of cards and brandy, he could not deny a certain sense of foreboding. By the time James arrived, West and Hawthorne were already settled in the library, brandies in hand; James appeared, announced by Briar, and barely so much as blinked at the sight of West drinking with his valet.

"Do you know, I think Briar might actually have grown a single gray hair at last," James said as soon as the door had shut behind the butler, who spared a censorious look for the reclining Hawthorne (one that Hawthorne ignored).

"He's older than I am," West said patiently, accustomed at this point to his friends' oft-repeated jokes on the subject of his butler's age.

"Barely." James moved to the sideboard uninvited. He flicked a glance over his shoulder at Hawthorne. "Does he disapprove of you?"

Hawthorne offered a lazy shrug, taking a sip of brandy. "Probably. He seems to disapprove of most things." A quick, private smile flashed across his face.

James raised an eyebrow at this, but refrained from comment as he crossed to seat himself next to West, setting his half-full tumbler on the card table. James was perfectly aware of the reasons that Hawthorne—who had grown up on the estate of the ducal seat in Kent, the son of the stable master—had wished so badly to flee the village of his youth, and why he'd leapt at the opportunity to serve as his childhood friend's valet.

West, who had his own suspicions as to how, precisely, his valet and butler might or might not be entertaining themselves, carefully did not look at his brother. So long as the household was running smoothly, he had little cause for complaint.

"Interesting you should mention entertainment, Hawthorne," James said, taking a leisurely sip of his brandy and ignoring the cards West had dealt him. "Violet and I were fortunate enough to have some *entertainment* of our own this afternoon, when we ran into West and his betrothed on Rotten Row."

West cleared his throat. "Yes. Well. We were delighted to see you."

Both James's and Hawthorne's eyebrows lifted at that.

"It was a nice day for a ride," West offered.

The eyebrows inched higher.

"I think I may have had a touch of sunstroke?" he suggested feebly.

"That would go a long way toward explaining it," James agreed cheerfully.

Hawthorne was beginning to look mildly put out. "What on earth did I miss whilst I was spending my afternoon polishing his lordship's riding boots?"

"I was *wearing* my riding boots," West said testily. "And don't think I didn't notice that my jacket for this evening hadn't been pressed."

"Appalling," Hawthorne agreed, reclining in his seat with the insouciance of a man who was comfortable in the knowledge that his employer was also one of his best friends. West's father had disapproved of this arrangement from the start, and at moments like this, West could almost think that his father had a point.

Almost.

"West and Lady Fitzwilliam went for a ride in the park and gave a convincing performance as a pair of children acting in a pantomime of how they think an affianced couple should behave," James informed Hawthorne.

Hawthorne leveled his dark-brown gaze on West. "Fascinating." He drew the word out into an improbable number of syllables.

"Isn't it just," James agreed. "Violet and I were discussing it and she could not help but observe that something seemed decidedly odd about the entire exchange."

"And so she ordered you to interrogate me?" West asked.

"Not in so many words." James took a sip of his drink, and settled more comfortably in his chair. "She merely asked if I might be amenable to taking advantage of the invitation my beloved brother had already extended, and perhaps conduct a . . . subtle investigation."

"If this is your idea of a subtle investigation, then I do not think you've a bright future as a private inquiry agent," West said darkly.

James's smile was satisfied. "Which is why I thought instead to simply ask you what in the name of hell is going on."

"A question *I* have also been wishing to ask," Hawthorne said, raising his glass in a toast. He adopted an expression of angelic innocence. "But, naturally, I would never presume to question his lordship's personal affairs."

"Oh?" West inquired. "When did you have this admirable change of principle, Hawthorne?"

James let out a chuckle at that, and Hawthorne offered West a cheeky grin. West rested his elbows on the card table, rubbing at his temples. Did he feel the beginning of a headache coming on? Was this a common side effect of acquiring fraudulent fiancées and then engaging in elaborate displays of soon-to-be-marital affection in front of one's family and friends?

Despite his best attempts at bad humor, however, he found that he couldn't quite manage it. And furthermore, he realized in a rush, he badly wanted to tell someone the truth. He hadn't appreciated what a burden this ruse had become, until he was faced with the prospect of dispelling it.

He opened his mouth, then shut it again, considering how best to explain the tangle he found himself in. And so he decided to tell the truth.

"Sophie asked me to help her feign an engagement so that her sister would agree to marry Blackford."

Whatever James and Hawthorne had been expecting, it clearly hadn't been this; they both sat wearing identical expressions of slack-jawed astonishment.

At last, James muttered a curse under his breath. "Violet is going to be unbearably smug about this."

"She *knew*?"

"Not the specifics." James waved a dismissive hand. "But she was convinced that all was not right."

"Well, you may return home and congratulate Violet on being a keen observer of the human condition."

James looked appalled. "I'll do nothing of the sort; that would merely encourage her. Oh, I won't lie to her," he added, seeing West's stern look, "but I'm certainly not going to *compliment* her. I'll have my hands full enough trying to prevent her from hatching some deranged plan to ensure that you and Sophie actually get married after all."

"Well, Sophie did tell Father that we were having a double wedding," West said. "So I suppose we'll see whether her desire to force him to attend outweighs her desire to never, under any circumstances, marry me."

Hawthorne frowned. "She told you that?"

"She told me that with explicit clarity the last time we discussed it—four years ago. She has not given me any reason to believe her feelings have changed in the interim."

James nearly fell out of his chair. "You asked Sophie to *marry* you only *four years ago?*"

West frowned now, too. He disapproved of such liberal employment of italics; it was borderline hysterical. "Our paths crossed soon after her husband's death. We . . . talked," he said delicately, which James and Hawthorne—being no fools—naturally immediately understood to mean something entirely other than "talking." Their eyebrows performed another round of irritating in-unison lifting, which West ignored. "I, foolishly, thought that now that she was widowed, our path was clear and we could wed, once she was out of mourning. She felt otherwise."

A silence fell that felt expectant, somehow. West looked from his brother to his valet, both of whom were regarding him almost incredulously.

"What?" he asked, a bit defensively.

"That's *it?*" James sounded flabbergasted, which was truly saying something, given that his brother was not a man in the habit of expressing strong emotions. They'd both been trained well by their father.

"I believe when a lady informs you that she will—and I quote—*never* marry you, the gentlemanly thing to do is to retreat."

"West," James said patiently, "did she tell you *why* she would never marry you?"

"We didn't get that far in our conversation."

"Of course you didn't," James muttered. "Is this a family curse? Did some ancestor of ours offend a witch at some point, generations ago? Though 'inability to communicate' seems like an oddly specific curse."

West was unamused. "I think I liked you better before you reconciled with Violet," he said darkly. "You didn't joke then."

"I'm only half-joking now," James shot back. "For God's sake, you've been in love with Sophie for years, and you didn't even think to ask her *why* she was so dead set against marrying you?"

"It doesn't matter, because I know now," West said coldly. "I thought I understood the full scope of things then, but it turns out I was wrong." He informed James and Hawthorne in as few words as possible about the duke's intervention—first in threatening Maria, then in threatening him.

"Well," Hawthorne said, "I can't say I blame her. Are you certain you're worth all this?"

West cast him a dark look. "She's close to her family—and they've been nothing but kind to me. I do not think she can fathom marrying me, if it would mean a permanent rupture with my father, my losing Rosemere . . . and I don't know how to make her understand that she is worth more than all of that to me."

"Well," James said, "I don't know that I'm in a position to be offering much in the way of romantic advice, given, er, recent events"—West fought the urge to smile at this—"but it seems to me that this farce you've found yourself enmeshed in is actually a perfect opportunity."

West frowned. "What do you mean?"

"Everyone in the *ton* thinks you're engaged. You'll have to spend an awful lot of time together. This is the perfect opportunity to court her—convince her that it's worth it. That *you're* worth it. That *you* can be her family, even if Father will not accept her."

"I want her to want to marry me, James. I don't want to have to pressure her into it."

"Then don't. Simply make her see that she means more to you than anything else on earth—because she does, doesn't she?" He paused, and glanced at West. Whatever he saw in only the most cursory glance at West's face was enough to answer his question, which in turn left West feeling oddly naked.

"Or . . ." Hawthorne said slowly, and West suppressed a sigh; he was not accustomed to finding himself in the role of the man receiving romantic advice from his friends, and he did not think he enjoyed it. "You could ask her."

"Have you been listening for the past ten minutes?" West asked, irritated. "I *did* ask her—or as good as—and she gave me an unequivocal no."

"Not to *marry* you, for Christ's sake." It was Hawthorne's turn to sound vaguely exasperated. "You toffs and your fixation on marriage, it's unhealthy."

West had no reply to this, considering that Hawthorne had his own, very valid reasons for being skeptical of the institution of marriage, and the rules surrounding it.

"I meant," Hawthorne continued, "that if, last time, she felt that you weren't taking her concerns seriously . . . perhaps, this time, you should ask her how you two could make this work between you. An affair—marriage—whatever it is you want. You could be her partner, rather than her protector. Work it out together."

Hawthorne fell silent now, looking mildly embarrassed to have offered this little speech, full of uncharacteristic sincerity as it was.

James, for his part, looked impressed. "When did valets get so wise?"

"When they had to spend all their time learning how to tie cravat knots, and therefore had a fair amount of extra mental energy to expend," Hawthorne shot back.

"I'll think about this, thank you," West said, feeling strangely overwhelmed. This was a novel sensation for him; because of the position he had been born to, he was accustomed to people turning to him for counsel, to the heavy weight of responsibility he had borne on his shoulders since a young age. He spent hours with his secretary each week, sorting through correspondence, all from people who were certain that they had a problem that only the Marquess of Weston would be able to solve. And it would only get worse—exponentially so, he knew—once his father died and he assumed the title. There would be votes in Parliament—a dizzying portfolio of ducal properties to manage—men of importance seeking his opinion. This had never daunted him; it was his birthright.

But *this*? Seeking to convince Sophie, once and for all, that he was a good bet—that he was worth whatever unpleasantness his father heaped upon them, should they wed? Trying to create a future for them, rather than simply mourning the life they hadn't led together these past seven years? This felt more intimidating than any task he had ever approached.

He wished that David were here; he missed his friend often, though over the years he'd grown used to his absence, and was no longer in the habit of turning multiple times a day, looking over his shoulder for a man who would never be standing there again. But

David, for all his recklessness, his rakish behavior, his refusal ever to take anything *too* seriously, had been an uncommonly good listener—and, too, he had seen West clearly, in a way that others often didn't. To most of the world, West was the heir to a duke, stern and powerful, a man to be admired; to David, however, he'd been the boy he'd met at the age of ten who had a horror of frogs (particularly when hidden in his boots). David never hesitated to take him down a peg, when he deserved it—to tell him when he was making a mistake.

He would give anything to have a friend like that with him now; for all that James and Hawthorne were closer to him than any other people in the world, he was still the elder brother of one, the employer of the other. With David, he'd been close to an equal—and his friend had never been in the slightest bit awed by him.

But David was not here—and that was another weight that rested on his shoulders, and would for the rest of his life.

"Are you feeling noble and gloomy and martyred about something?" Hawthorne's voice broke into his thoughts.

"He is," James informed him. "I can always tell. He's got his Long-Suffering Tragic Duke expression on."

West blinked. "I beg your pardon?"

"Violet calls it that," James said, having the grace to at least look a trifle sheepish. "I seem to have picked up the habit. It's not inaccurate, you know."

West paused; considered these words. Contemplated the satisfaction of chucking a vase at his brother's head versus the fuss Briar would kick up about having to scrub bloodstains out of an Aubusson rug. And instead said, his voice utterly pleasant, "James?"

"Yes?"

"Please bugger off."

Chapter Fourteen

Sophie was at Hookham's circulating library, half-listening to Violet and Jane as they debated at length the merits of two volumes of poetry Violet was attempting to decide between, when she heard her name uttered by perhaps her least-favorite voice in all of London.

All of England, even. The world? Given that Sophie had never left the country, for her this was one and the same.

"Lady Fitzwilliam."

She wheeled around and discovered that her ears had not deceived her: the Duke of Dovington was, indeed, standing a few feet away, regarding her with a mixture of hostility and curiosity. Sophie was all at once acutely conscious of every single thing about her personal appearance, and was glad that she happened to be wearing a newish gown of sky-blue silk embroidered with small white flowers—not terribly formal, as it had not seemed necessary for a simple afternoon outing to the library, but she was wearing a new pair of gloves and the ribbons on her hat matched her gown and, all in all, she thought she looked perfectly presentable. Even to a duke.

Even to *this* duke.

She gritted her teeth, and dropped into a curtsey. Violet, sensing some disturbance, turned, and her face went slightly pale at the sight of her father-in-law. She and Jane curtsied as well, though Sophie noted with some amusement that Violet's was perhaps a trifle shallower than it should have been.

The duke acknowledged his daughter-in-law with a short nod. "Lady James."

"Have you met Lady Penvale yet, Your Grace?" Sophie asked. "She is fairly newly arrived in town."

"I have not," the duke said, offering a slight inclination of the head in Jane's direction. "Best wishes for your marriage." It was not uttered with much warmth, but it was slightly less dismissive than Sophie might have expected from him, considering that Jane's family was of considerably more humble origins than her husband's—or even Sophie's, for that matter. Of course, Jane had not had the audacity to attempt to marry one of the duke's sons. He could afford to be polite to *her*.

"Thank you," Jane said faintly, looking entirely out of her depth to be conversing with a duke; Sophie knew that she felt a bit like a fish out of water amid Penvale's more elevated circle. This was likely doing nothing to make her feel more comfortable—but then, one did not expect to bump into a duke at a lending library! Didn't he have servants to fetch books for him? Couldn't he *buy* any books he wanted? This thought crept into Sophie's mind along with a sudden rush of dark suspicion—it *was* odd that he was here. Had he somehow sought her out? It seemed too peculiar and unexpected a coincidence that he should suddenly happen to be here—a place she could not imagine that he frequented—at the exact same hour that she was.

"Lady Fitzwilliam, would you be so kind as to spare me a moment of your time—perhaps outside?" the duke inquired.

Sophie and Violet exchanged startled glances; Sophie had no

doubt that, were she to announce that she had no interest in conversing with the duke, Violet would drag her out of the library without another word, but Sophie thought it might be best to hear the duke out. And, in spite of herself, she was curious.

"Certainly." She pressed the books she'd been holding—a couple of Gothic novels that Jane had enthusiastically recommended—into Violet's hands, and followed the duke through the winding shelves of Hookham's and outside into the bright June sunshine. The duke nodded at the impressive carriage stopped before them on Bond Street, the ducal crest prominently placed.

"We might have a bit of privacy in there."

Sophie had a wild thought that West would be very irritated if his father kidnapped his alleged fiancée, but that was her only thought before an impeccably liveried footman was handing her into the carriage, the duke on her heels. The door shut firmly behind him, and Sophie sat opposite the duke in silence for a moment, trying not to notice how exceptionally comfortable the cushioned bench in this carriage was. West's carriage was the most luxurious she had ever ridden in, but his father's was something else entirely, as though there were a special design reserved only for dukes. There might well be, she reflected with amusement. After all, when one had pockets as deep as the Duke of Dovington's, there was little that was out of reach.

"I cannot express how surprised I am to find myself, once again, contemplating the possibility of you becoming my son's wife," the duke said after a moment. He was gazing steadily at Sophie; he resembled both of his sons quite strongly, though his eyes were brown, not green. She wondered idly if they got their eyes from their mother; she realized that she'd never seen a portrait of the late duchess.

"And you've come to offer your felicitations?" Sophie asked

sweetly, all innocent surprise. "That is *very* kind of you, Your Grace—particularly when we just saw each other in the park!"

The duke's mouth did not budge a centimeter, but there was a slight deepening in the lines at the corners of his eyes that indicated that perhaps—just *perhaps*—he was amused.

"Something along those lines," he said, very dry. "I trust your memory has not begun to fail you at the advanced age of—how old are you, precisely?"

"I am shocked you ever convinced a woman to marry you, if you traipse about inquiring as to ladies' ages on a routine basis," she shot back.

"The ducal title does go a long way toward smoothing any rough edges in my manners."

Sophie permitted herself a brief internal eye roll; this man, like his son, *had* no rough edges—everything about him was polished. Born to the highest echelons of society, he had never, not for one single moment, questioned his right to belong there. He had never questioned *anything* about his life, or his beliefs, which was why he had felt perfectly comfortable preventing the marriage of one of his sons, and neatly arranging the marriage of the other (unbeknownst, at least initially, to both bride and groom in that particular union). He moved about the world, *his* world, like a queen on a chessboard, and arranged the pieces around him like pawns until it all lined up as he wished.

"I'm younger than both of your sons," she said evenly. "What is your point?"

"In that case, I cannot imagine that your memory has begun failing you so badly that you have neglected to recall a conversation you and I had cause to share at an uncivilized hour of the morning seven years ago."

Sophie took a deep breath; she knew that the duke was attempting to stoke her temper, but she was determined not to lose her composure. She did not care what he thought of her for her own sake—she knew that her family was too common for him, that in his eyes the daughter of a viscount with a title as new as her father's would never be fit for the heir to an ancient family, and she was entirely unbothered by this fact—but she had a moment of fierce determination not to make anything about West's life, and his relationship with his father, more difficult than it already was. She did not want the duke's approval for herself, but for him.

"Your son is an adult perfectly capable of making up his own mind," she said. "I suggest that if you have an issue with his choice of bride, you take it up with him."

"I tried to, all those years ago," he said. "He was uninterested in my opinion. He was young and foolish and wasn't thinking clearly."

"He is one-and-thirty now," she said, idly examining her gloves, feigning an ease that she did not remotely feel. "Perhaps he will be more open to hearing your thoughts."

The duke's single, skeptical "hmm" informed her how likely he thought this turn of events to be. "He is peculiarly stubborn where you are concerned," he said, sounding vaguely put out at this mystifying weakness on his son's part. "I do not believe he will listen to reason, which is why I must turn to you instead, in the hopes that you will." His tone turned brisk, businesslike. "My promise to you of seven years ago stands: If you marry my son, then the day after the wedding I will be in my solicitor's office, arranging for the sale of Rosemere."

"You would make him miserable, then," Sophie said, "solely to punish him for disregarding your wishes?"

"There is nothing I would not do to protect the good name of my family, Lady Fitzwilliam." He lifted his walking stick—one that, unlike West's, was purely ornamental—and tapped the roof of the carriage; a moment later, the door was opened by a footman. "Thank you for your time," the duke added, nodding at the door, a clear dismissal. "I hope I've given you much to think on."

Sophie gritted her teeth and offered him her most charming smile. "It is always so nice to spend time with family . . . *Papa*."

She took her time slowly exiting the carriage—all the better to relish the look of horror that she had caused to flicker across the duke's face—and made her way back into Hookham's, searching for her friends. She found Violet and Jane engaged in a whispered debate, one that they broke off as soon as they caught sight of her, twin expressions of relief crossing their faces.

"Is everything all right?" Sophie asked cautiously.

"We were debating the merits of storming the duke's carriage to liberate you," Violet said matter-of-factly. "Honestly, I think doing so might have caused him to stop acknowledging my existence whatsoever, and I can't tell you what an improvement that would be."

"No liberation necessary," Sophie said, gesturing at her unimprisoned self. "He merely wanted to discuss my betrothal."

"I'll bet he did," Violet said darkly, with a grim edge to her voice born of long experience with all the ways the Duke of Dovington could make his sons' lives a misery. "You're not going to let him scare you off, are you?" she added, a certain canny light suddenly evident in her gaze that Sophie did not entirely understand.

"Of course not," she said a bit carelessly, distracted as she was by an entirely unfamiliar trickle of anger that was slowly making its way through her. How *dare* this man try to *once again* threaten her—threaten West! She imagined the look on his face as he sat in the back of a church, watching her exchange wedding vows with his son, and she liked it quite a bit.

Too much, given that she was not *actually* going to marry West, and it felt far too dangerous a thing to contemplate, rather like Icarus flying too close to the sun. In truth, she realized in a rush, the prospect of marrying West—of loving him, of trusting him with her heart, of risking further heartbreak for him . . .

It frightened her.

And she did not like that. It made her feel rather . . . ashamed.

And she, who had been so frustrated by the realization that West was allowing his father to govern his behavior, suddenly felt less certain. Because her behavior was governed by fear—and she found little to admire in that, either.

And she did not know how to mend this, for either of them.

She blew out a breath in frustration, and smiled brightly at Violet and Jane. "Shall we go sign out our books?"

If either of them found her sudden change of topic odd, they did not say anything, turning to make their way to the counter. Sophie trailed after them, her thoughts churning.

Chapter Fifteen

"I do believe if her bodice was half an inch lower, I'd need to cover your eyes," Penvale said to Jane.

Sophie glanced around, wondering to whom he was referring, but after only a split second she spotted the likely offender: a lady whose neckline was adventurous to the point of being gravitationally implausible. She bit her lip to prevent a smile.

"Why should you need to cover *my* eyes?" Jane asked her husband waspishly. "I believe, of the two of us, *I* am the one possessed of the anatomy that would be on display. Perhaps it is your maidenly gaze that *I* should be protecting."

"Maidenly?" Penvale objected. "If my memory serves—"

"I see Belfry's attempts to civilize his theater have been only partially successful," West said hastily, managing to head off whatever the inappropriate conclusion to Penvale's sentence would have been, though this did nothing to dispel the heated gaze husband and wife were sharing. (Admittedly, some of that heat was born of irritation. But not all.)

"I don't think he's that interested in civilizing it," Sophie said thoughtfully, allowing West to take her elbow and steer her past an earl who was weaving drunkenly on the arm of another gentleman;

something about the proprietary way his companion gripped his arm made her think that this was not merely the act of a man ensuring that his foxed friend didn't topple over. She had no time to contemplate this, however, because they had arrived at Belfry's private box—the best in the theater, naturally—and were greeted by an assortment of their friends within.

"I see we're the late arrivals," Sophie said cheerfully, twining her arm more securely through West's as she smiled around at the assembled couples. Alexandra, looking very pretty in a square-necked gown of champagne-colored satin, was standing close enough to Blackford that he must have a very fascinating view directly down her bodice— one that he was taking full advantage of, if his constantly dropping gaze was anything to judge by. They were deep in conversation with Violet and James, one that seemed to be hastily broken off as soon as Sophie and West entered the box. Also assembled were Diana and Jeremy, Emily and Belfry, and Harriet and her husband, George Lancashire.

"I thought Betsy was coming, too?" Sophie asked her sister, as Harriet came to press a quick kiss to her cheek.

"She was," Harriet confirmed. "But evidently she's feeling poorly today." She grimaced. "Having a baby is not a remotely enjoyable process, you know."

"Except for one bit," Belfry drawled, approaching with Emily on his arm in time to hear this. His wife poked him in the side, blushing rosily. She was beginning to look a bit round herself, Sophie thought, though she knew that Emily still had a few months before she planned to enter her confinement.

"How is the wedding planning going?" Emily asked, still looking rather pink in the face; her husband evidently noticed this as well, as his arm curved around her waist and he pressed a quick kiss to the top of her head.

"It would be going *better*," Harriet interjected, before Sophie or West had the chance to utter a single word, "if Sophie would let *me* take charge of matters."

"I simply cannot fathom why I might be hesitant," Sophie said dryly; Harriet's wedding two years earlier had been nothing short of a spectacle.

"Neither can I," Harriet said, conveniently deaf to Sophie's sarcasm. "Especially with it being a double wedding, we need to settle on a date, send invitations—"

"Oh!" Emily clasped her hands. "A double wedding! How lovely!" Her face fell. "Oh, but I hope it's not too late in the summer, otherwise I might not be able to attend." Her hand gestured vaguely in the direction of her abdomen.

"Isn't the baby due in October?" Sophie asked, frowning.

"Yes," Emily said slowly, "but you never know! It might take it into its head to put in an early appearance and disrupt everything—I shouldn't be surprised, considering who its father is," she added, with a half-affectionate, half-exasperated glance at her husband, who looked unrepentant. His arm was still tight around her waist.

"Well," Sophie said, "I'm certain that won't be a problem—"

"Then you'll have the wedding this summer?" Emily asked brightly, the appearance of a dejected mother-to-be that she'd worn a moment earlier suddenly mysteriously absent. "Sooner, rather than later?"

"I—well—" Sophie looked helplessly up at West, with whom she was still arm in arm. "I don't think we've decided upon a firm date—"

"Well, naturally," Harriet said reasonably. "You'd need to ask Alexandra and Blackford." She turned. "Alex!" She waved her hand, beckoning, and Alexandra was at her side within seconds. "We were just discussing your wedding!" Harriet said eagerly. "It would be easier to properly plan if you were to set a date."

Alexandra flicked a glance at Sophie, who attempted to communicate with her own gaze: *Please stop this madness.*

"How right you are," Alexandra said smoothly, and Sophie reflected that perhaps she ought to brush up on her nonverbal communication. It clearly was not working as well as it once had. "We"—she cast a rapturous look over her shoulder at Blackford, who appeared momentarily blinded by it—"are, naturally, eager not to delay too long. Right, darling?"

"I'd procure a special license tomorrow, if you'd let me," he confirmed, offering his betrothed an affectionate look.

"Which I won't," Alexandra agreed. "We must have a proper wedding! Shall I send a note to the rector at St. George's tomorrow, inquiring about a date in . . . oh, I don't know—early July?"

"Early July," Sophie repeated, casting an increasingly desperate look up at West. *He*, at least, did not seem to have any difficulty deciphering it.

"That's very . . . soon," he offered.

"Precisely!" Alexandra beamed at him. "We don't want to wait any longer than necessary to commence our happily-ever-afters, do we?"

"Our—what?" Sophie asked.

"Like something out of a fairy tale, don't you think? Riding off into the sunset on a white horse—darling, do you own a white horse?" Alexandra asked; seeing her fiancé's shake of the head, she added, "Well, if you could see to acquiring one in the next month—you, too, West—that would be most appreciated."

"You intend for us to depart our wedding on horseback?" Sophie asked, growing more alarmed by the moment.

"On *white* horses," Alexandra corrected. "So much more romantic! Like princesses being rescued by knights in shining armor."

"How . . . charming," Sophie managed, wondering if Alexandra had taken leave of her senses entirely.

"I'm glad you agree!" Alexandra said.

At this moment, the orchestra began tuning, which was a mercy in multiple ways: not only did it stop Alexandra from spouting more appalling details of her vision for their wedding, it also saved Sophie from having to attempt to keep her facial expression from slipping into outright horror. She'd never been so grateful to take a seat— strategically selecting one as far from both of her sisters as possible at the far end of the box, where she and West might manage a whispered exchange with some semblance of privacy.

As soon as the music commenced, giving her a bit of cover, she turned to West, whose eyes were fixed on the stage with an expression of such careful neutrality that she was certain that he was internally whimpering.

"What are we going to do?" she hissed, glancing past West to where Diana and Jeremy were—mercifully—more engaged in exchanging flirtatious glances than in paying the slightest bit of attention to what their companions might be discussing.

"Head to Tattersall's, apparently. It would seem I need a new horse."

"You are not buying a white horse, West! We're not *actually getting married!*"

"Yes," he said, a bit acerbically. "Thank you ever so much for the reminder—I was likely to forget otherwise." There was the slightest edge to his voice.

She decided to ignore this. "How are we going to get out of this? We can't let up the ruse until Alexandra and Blackford are safely wed—but how can we see them married without doing the same ourselves?"

"This was *your* idea, you know," he said in an undertone. "Did you not consider such a complication, when hatching this scheme?"

"Did I consider that my previously rational sister might completely lose her senses and start insisting on some sort of double wedding straight from a fever dream? No, I did not."

"Shall I take myself off in my phaeton?" he inquired politely. "Stage another accident? It did successfully prevent our wedding once before, after all." And *that* was a definite edge—he wasn't even trying to conceal it. She bit her tongue against the first half-dozen irate replies she felt like offering him, and took a deep breath.

"Since it seems your memory is failing you a bit, at your advanced age," she said evenly, "I will take it upon myself to remind you that seven years ago, we were not engaged. I did not jilt you, because you'd never asked me to be your wife in the first place. I was at perfect liberty to marry someone else, if he offered."

"As you proved only too willing to do."

"For reasons that I have now explained to you." Her own voice was growing sharp now—enough so that Diana ceased running her hand in an alarming direction up Jeremy's leg to cast a surprised glance in their direction. Sophie offered a syrupy smile in return—she might have overdone it, if Diana's astonished blink was anything to judge by—and squeezed West's arm until he, too, offered what he seemed to believe was a smile, but which was in actuality closer to a pained grimace.

"If you could attempt to look less like a hostage, that would be appreciated," Sophie murmured, as soon as Diana turned back to Jeremy. They fell silent as the orchestra's opening number came to a close and the actors below began speaking; several minutes later, however, when the lead actress had burst into a particularly energetic song-and-dance number and Sophie thought she could again speak without being overheard, she said, "I had the most charming conversation with your father the day before yesterday."

This had the expected effect: West's arm went rigid where it rested next to hers, and his jaw looked so tight that she wondered vaguely if she should be concerned about him breaking a tooth.

"Where did you have this conversation?" he asked in a low voice, turning at last to fully face her. The candlelight of the theater did nothing to soften the sharp angles of his jaw and cheekbones. Although it was late evening, his jaw was as cleanly shaven as it was in the morning, and the elaborate knot of his cravat kept his chin at just such an angle that one was left with the impression that he was looking down his nose at whomever he was conversing with. Nothing about this man spoke of softness, or affection; the simmering anger in his voice as he addressed her now made him seem very ducal—and very dangerous.

In an undertone, she quickly summarized her encounter with the duke at Hookham's, watching his jaw clench tighter and tighter with each sentence.

"I'll speak to him," he said at once, the moment she'd fallen silent. "I apologize. He had no right to approach you like this. I'll see that he doesn't do it again."

"I thought it was rather complimentary, actually," Sophie said airily. "He sees me as a threat—evidently our ruse is working."

"Not on everyone," West said tersely; when she cast him a surprised glance, he sighed, rubbing a hand over his face. He looked tired, she thought; the lines that bracketed his eyes, usually faint, looked a bit deeper than usual. She wondered if he'd been sleeping—and, if not, what the cause was.

But then, how he passed his nights was none of her concern.

"James and Violet were evidently a bit perplexed by our performance on Rotten Row the other day," he admitted in an undertone.

"I can't imagine why."

"Yes, thank you, I'm aware that I'm rubbish at this—that point has been well made, my potato. But . . ." He trailed off, looking the slightest bit shifty. Sophie was instantly on alert; in the seven years she'd known this man, she had never once, for a single moment, seen him look *shifty*. She hadn't thought him constitutionally capable of it.

"What did you do?" she demanded in a whisper, alarmed.

"I might have admitted to James and Hawthorne that we're not actually engaged."

"*You did what!*"

"He was already suspicious," West said in a low voice, leaning closer to her as he spoke; this close, she could smell the sandalwood of his soap, and the scent of his skin—so familiar that it caused a ghost of a memory to arise, unbidden, of his arms around her, his lips on her throat in the corner of a London mansion a lifetime ago. "I decided to take him into my confidence."

"And I expect he told Violet," Sophie murmured grimly, the memory of Violet's peculiar gleam as she'd looked at Sophie that day at Hookham's making more sense now.

"I would not, ordinarily, make such a decision without asking you," he said, his voice having grown even quieter—enough so that Sophie found herself leaning in toward him, the better to hear above the noise of the actors on the stage below, and the music that accompanied them. He paused, and added, "Ours may not be a betrothal in truth, but it still seems only fair to treat our arrangement with the same respect that I would, were we actually engaged. And I would not make any decision of import without consulting you."

His tone was even, but Sophie felt the words like a blow; her gaze locked on to his, and whatever expression was on her face caused something worried to flit across his, evident in the wrinkling of his brow as he gazed back at her.

I would not make any decision of import without consulting you.

But *she* had, seven years ago—was that what he was implying?

It was nothing more than the truth—but a truth that she felt like a knife nonetheless.

She cleared her throat. "I had my reasons for making a decision about my future, all those years ago, and I had my reasons to not *consult* you, too."

The wrinkle in his forehead deepened. "I was not—I did not—" He blew out a breath, frustrated; it was odd and uncomfortable to watch him struggle for words, he who always seemed so in command of himself. "I did not intend that as a slight, Sophie. I intended—hell." He broke off, shaking his head, and then leaned even closer, so that his mouth hovered near her ear and she felt the warmth of his breath on her skin. His hand nudged hers, where it rested on the armrest of her chair, the merest glancing contact, through the fabric of her gloves, sufficient to raise the fine hairs on her arm.

"I intended to show you that what happened seven years ago is in the past, and that we might chart a different course. Now."

Sophie did rear back at this, eyes wide as she regarded him. There was nothing in his face to suggest he was jesting, or sharing a private joke with her. He was not, after all, a man prone to much in the way of laughter.

He'd laughed with her, though. Before. That was one of the many things she'd fallen in love with—the glimmers of a sense of humor in this man who presented such a stern face to others. But if West at age twenty-four had seemed stern on occasion, it was nothing compared to the man seated next to her now. The West she had once known had been so *young*—not yet scarred by his accident, his friend's death. By her perceived betrayal. It gave her a pang, the realization that she bore some of the responsibility for the man he'd grown into. This was a man she admired fiercely—and still wanted quite helplessly, no matter that her common sense urged her otherwise—but the West she had once known knew how to laugh, even if it was not as frequent as she would have wished.

This West, though . . .

Even a fortnight earlier, she would have said that she could not imagine the man before her laughing—but now she knew better. Now she knew that she still had the power to pull a reluctant laugh from him, seemingly against his will. And now—dangerously—she knew that she still found this power as thrilling as she had at the age of twenty.

"You cannot think that we have any sort of future together," she managed, her voice still soft enough not to carry, even as she wanted nothing more than to lock them both within a private room and—

Well, she wasn't entirely certain what she'd do with him, once she had him there. Shout at him, probably.

Or kiss him.

Or both.

"You have said something along those lines to me before," he said. "And I cannot help but think that, whilst I would give up much for you, I will not give up the right to know my own mind. Not even to you."

And Sophie, astonishingly, felt something like shame burn within her.

He, however, looked entirely unruffled by this exchange, and leaned back in his seat, putting some much-needed space between them; Sophie found it alarmingly difficult to speak when he was so close to her.

"In any case," he said calmly, as if they'd been exchanging nothing more interesting than bland pleasantries about the weather, "it occurs to me that if Violet and James have grown suspicious of our behavior, then we run the risk of others becoming so as well."

"Well," she managed, her thoughts still in a tangle, "if you would see fit to stop comparing me to root vegetables, we might stand a better chance of convincing them."

He didn't laugh, but the lines at the corners of his eyes deepened as he looked at her, and she found she couldn't look away. It reminded her at once of the numerous occasions during that first spring when they'd been courting, when he'd catch her eye across a crowded room, or from the opposite end of a dinner table, and they'd share some unspoken joke, communicating solely through a quirk of the mouth or the raising of an eyebrow. It had felt like they held an entire private universe between them.

She had known, even then, that she was lucky to have found this with someone; it was only now, seven years later, with the bitterness of experience, that she knew precisely *how* lucky.

She could not afford to allow her thoughts to drift along these lines. She needed to remind him of what she was prepared to offer—an offer that she knew he would not take.

"There's one way to ensure that we're a bit more convincing, you know," she said quietly, tilting her head and leaning forward once more so that her words landed softly on the sliver of exposed skin just beneath his ear.

"Oh?" he murmured, gazing down at her, his gaze inscrutable. "And what did you have in mind?" This was a bit more flirtatious than she'd expected by way of a response—but if he thought to bluff, she'd put that attempt to rest.

"What I offered you four years ago," she said quietly. She reached out a hand and very deliberately traced one finger down his forearm.

"Four years ago, you informed me you'd never marry me." His voice was careful, even.

"But, if you will recall, I was more than willing to come to some other sort of arrangement," she said, just as carefully. "You were the one who was unwilling, in that regard . . . so I eventually found entertainment . . . elsewhere." Her gaze flicked toward Jeremy, who was entirely oblivious to this conversation, as he was at the moment occupied in whispering something—doubtless inappropriate—in his wife's ear.

"You really think," West said, his voice still low and even, "that we could go to bed together, and walk away again?"

"I've confidence in my own ability to resist temptation," Sophie said lightly.

"Then I don't have much confidence in your memory," he said. "Because I have relived that night—afternoon—we spent together hundreds of times in the past four years, and I don't think either of us could walk away again. I think we'd ruin each other."

"I'm a widow. You can't ruin me."

His gaze on her was steady. "I didn't mean your reputation." A brief, heavy pause. "I meant that I'd ruin you for anyone else."

A slow, simmering heat seemed to have taken up residence in Sophie's stomach; she was acutely conscious of her pulse making its presence known in a way it normally did not. She knew she was playing with fire, and yet she could not bring herself to stop. Not when she'd been so very good—had resisted temptation for so very long.

"If you'd like to test that theory," she said, even more quietly, "you know where to find me."

And then she was leaning back in her seat, the spell broken, her attention fixed again—or, more accurately, for the first time all evening—on the actors on the stage below her.

She did not think he'd say yes—could not imagine that the West she knew now, the man he'd become, would be amenable to such an arrangement, not when he'd once spoken so firmly against it.

But she was conscious of every breath, every move that he made beside her. She heard the slow, ever-so-slightly unsteady exhale he let out after a few long moments had passed. She heard him shift in his seat. And she felt once again the nudge of his finger against hers, where their hands rested between them, the brief, deliberate contact like a lick of flame on her skin, even through the fabric of her glove.

And she wondered, for the briefest of moments, if perhaps, this time, she was wrong.

Chapter Sixteen

One year earlier

"You are looking quite well tonight, Soph."

Sophie was not certain compliments counted when they came from one's little sister—but, in this instance, she knew that Harriet was correct.

"Thank you." She took a sip of ratafia, idly gazing around the room. It was a pleasantly cool early May evening outdoors, which was a relief, because the ballroom was—as the hostess would no doubt be crowing about the next day—a dreadful crush. Sophie had never entirely understood why this was a state to be desired; she, personally, reserved a fair bit of resentment for the inevitable trickle of perspiration that would creep slowly down her spine during these events, impossible for her to reach and wipe away.

Fortunately, her gown tonight was a midnight blue that would disguise any telltale perspiration—and which looked quite fetching on her, she knew. She'd commissioned an entirely new wardrobe from her modiste this year, one that was a bit more daring than she was accustomed to. But it had been three years since she'd been widowed— three years since that one, perhaps ill-advised afternoon with a certain marquess—and she had grown to realize that she was feeling a bit . . . *bored*.

So she'd put on a new dress with a plunging neckline, and had Fox, her lady's maid, dress her hair with more than usual care that evening, and as she stood there with Harriet, scanning the room for familiar faces, she told herself that there was absolutely not any one particular gentleman who she was hoping might take note of this fact.

Until he walked in the door.

West looked handsome this evening, as always; his hair was combed neatly back from his face, and his green eyes glittered in the candlelight. She did wish that he would do her the courtesy of not always looking so enticing every time she saw him, but that alone would require him to think of her as often as she thought of him.

The first time she had seen him last Season, at the first event she'd attended since her husband's death, they'd caught sight of each other across the room at the Royal Academy, where they were both attending an art exhibition. Their eyes had locked for a split second, he'd offered her a polite nod, and then he'd moved on to continue speaking to a group of his Oxford friends and their wives.

She'd felt as though she'd been kicked in the stomach, and was furious with herself for feeling that way. *She* was the one, after all, who had told him that they could never marry—a reality that she could not deny when she spotted the Duke of Dovington a minute or two later, surveying the room like a predator taking note of the location of all of its prey.

Occasionally, she thought she felt West's eyes on her at these events, after they'd moved past each other—but whenever she turned, he was deep in conversation with someone else, or sometimes nowhere to be seen at all.

Which meant she was imagining it, like some sort of lovesick fool.

Tonight, however, she was determined not to be that lovesick fool any longer. She was twenty-six years old, and she was tired of allowing a short-lived love affair at the age of twenty to occupy so much of her thoughts. If he had moved on, then so would she; therefore, she proceeded to dance, chat, and flirt her way around the room over the course of the next couple of hours. Truth be told, she had forgotten how exhausting *ton* events were; she had never considered herself much of a bluestocking, but the years since she'd been widowed had taught her of the joy that could be found in a quiet evening in her drawing room or library, curled up before the fire with a book on her lap. She found herself thinking of that vision of domestic coziness almost longingly as she finished dancing a rather energetic reel and tried very hard to ignore that dreaded trickle of perspiration on her back.

She slipped off the ballroom floor, fanning herself, and was just considering attempting to beat a path through the crowd to the refreshment table when she turned—

And nearly ran headfirst into West.

"Oh!" Sophie reared back like a spooked horse.

"I beg your pardon." His words came out stilted, almost accusatory. She felt a flash of annoyance. From above his elaborately knotted cravat, he seemed to be looking down his nose at everyone present, which did not improve her temper.

"I didn't see you—I'm sorry." She sounded stiff, even to her own ears; she didn't know how to speak to him anymore.

The thought was sharp, like a razor sliding against her skin.

"It was my fault," he replied, gentlemanly as ever. "I'll just allow you to—" He stepped back, as if to allow her to pass; she was about to do so when suddenly, so quickly she nearly missed it, his eyes dropped to her neckline.

A spark raced down her spine at the sight. His eyes dropped to her décolletage once more. This time, they caught there—not for so long that it felt lecherous, but long enough that she felt a strange surge of awareness of her own power. He might be a marquess—might be the heir to one of the most powerful men in England—but now, in this moment, he was in *her* thrall.

A moment later, his brain seemed to catch up to his eyes, and he wrenched them north again. The polite thing to do would be to pretend she had not noticed. But instead, she looked him directly in the eye.

And raised both eyebrows.

And then—then! The faintest trace of color appeared in his cheeks.

She had made the Marquess of Weston *blush*.

She felt nearly giddy as their eyes locked, he looking embarrassed and frustrated and a dozen other terribly human emotions that she was not accustomed to seeing him permit himself. Or at least not permit himself to show.

He cleared his throat, offered a brief nod, and walked away.

Her jaw dropped, though she quickly wrenched it shut—surely, surely things had not progressed to so dire a state that she was to start gaping like a fish in a crowded ballroom. This was the single rudest thing she had ever seen West do—not just to her, but to anyone, with the exception of the unfortunate Marquess of Sandworth, whom he'd held by the throat against a hedge that fateful night that they'd discovered him in Maria's company. West was always exquisitely, excruciatingly polite; even in the six years since their aborted courtship, he still always had a courteous nod or bow for her.

But this!

A slow smile began to creep across her face as she considered the matter. In the past two minutes, she had caused West to gape openly at her décolletage, and then left him so agitated that he'd forgotten his manners completely and turned his back on a lady without a word of farewell.

He was *flustered.*

He still wanted her.

He wouldn't do anything about it—this was proven by the way he had all but fled from the sight of her breasts (an intriguing event in and of itself; she had not been aware that her rather modest bosom possessed this sort of power!). But the true question was: What was *she* going to do about it?

"Lady Fitzwilliam, can I possibly be the luckiest man in Christendom, to have discovered you alone and not surrounded by a pack of admirers?"

She glanced up, startled; Jeremy, the current Marquess of Willingham, was standing before her. He had the exact same shade of golden hair that his elder brother had had, she thought sadly.

Jeremy had a reputation as something of a rake, a reputation bolstered in the years since he'd assumed the title after his brother's death. They had spoken occasionally, danced every now and then, but Sophie tended to avoid him—he was too close to West. Best to keep herself far away.

But tonight, she was not feeling at all cautious.

"Lord Willingham." She offered him a slow, flirtatious smile. "You've caught me whilst I was attempting an escape from this crush."

A slightly pained expression crossed his face. "Please—Jeremy. My friends call me Jeremy." The slightly strained note in his voice made her think this was not a simple matter of preference for his given name, but she did not question it, and his expression eased nearly as quickly as it had tightened, that lazy, appreciative gleam reappearing in his eye as he gazed at her.

"And are we to be friends, then?" she asked coyly, and he blinked, then gave her a slow, seductive smile.

"I can think of nothing that would make me happier," he said. "Is your next dance taken?" He projected an air of boyish hope that did not fool Sophie for one moment, though it did amuse her. And it was nice, she thought, to converse with a gentleman and not feel an emotion stronger than amusement.

And a bit of attraction, too, she thought, glancing at Jeremy from beneath her lashes as she consulted her dance card.

"I appear to have promised this dance to Lord Risedale," she said.

"Risedale is currently making sickening cow eyes at his wife over there"—he jerked his head to the left—"and no doubt will not be too put out if he cannot find you to claim his dance."

This was likely true; Risedale and his new countess were known to be a love match, and while Sophie actually liked the earl quite a bit—he was a perfect gentleman, and also a genuinely interesting conversationalist, a skill that was in short supply among many of his peers—she did not think she needed to feel too guilty at skipping their dance.

"Did you have a suggestion as to what I ought to do instead, if I am not to dance this set?" she asked. She considered carefully, and then batted her eyelashes at him.

His gaze flicked to her neckline.

Men, she thought, were awfully predictable.

"I find myself desiring a bit of air, and wondered if you, too, might like a chance to cool off—you look flushed." His tone was all solicitous inquiry, and his gaze was all wicked knowing.

Sophie hesitated for only the briefest second, before taking Jeremy's proffered arm. She did not allow her eyes to drift to either side as he escorted her onto the terrace—but later, after a quarter of an hour of rather heated kissing and a murmured invitation in Jeremy's ear, as she returned to the ballroom, hoping her hair wasn't too badly mussed, she glanced to the left, and locked eyes with West.

She counted it as a small victory when he looked away first.

Chapter Seventeen

God save him from musicales.

"Stop grimacing," Sophie said under her breath from the seat next to him.

West cast her a mildly exasperated look. "I'm hardly *grimacing.*" He thought he'd perfected the look of polite interest he was currently directing toward the front of Lady Worthington's music room, where several of the countess's nieces—Violet's cousins—were sawing away at the violin.

Sawing was probably a bit unfair; it was just that, having repeatedly experienced the trauma of Lady Holyoak's musicales—he felt honor-bound to put in a brief appearance every couple of years or so, once the memory of the last one he'd attended had faded enough to make him think this was a remotely good idea—he rather thought that something within his ears had gone slightly wrong, because he was no longer capable of enjoying the sound of a string instrument. Even when he heard one played by a skilled practitioner, he was on edge, as though the screeching were about to commence at any moment.

Sophie rested a hand on his arm, then immediately removed it. "Why is your arm so tense?" she hissed. "You're behaving as though you're about to face the guillotine."

"A tempting prospect," he murmured; at that moment, the young ladies finished playing, and he joined in the enthusiastic applause. He suspected, gauging from the looks of genuine appreciation on the faces of people around him, that the ladies had actually been quite good, but he was unable to confirm this with any degree of certainty from his own experience.

The room filled with chatter as everyone rose from their seats; he spotted Violet and James near the front of the room. They were speaking with the youngest of her cousins, who appeared to be barely out of the schoolroom and seemed a bit overawed by the experience. He reached for his walking stick, then glanced down at Sophie and offered her his arm.

"Care to get some air?"

They skirted the edges of the chattering crowd as they made their way toward the French doors set against one wall, leading out to the terrace.

It was a warm evening, and the scent of roses wafting up from Lady Worthington's extensive gardens engulfed them as soon as they stepped through the doors. The music room was ablaze with light, which spilled out onto the deserted terrace; Sophie dropped his arm, and drifted slowly from the doors, past the first set of windows, until she found a pocket of shadows. She was wearing a pink gown that barely hugged her shoulders, her hair piled high atop her head. As West followed her, his gaze lingered on the creamy skin of her shoulders, on the single golden curl resting tantalizingly against the side of her neck. She leaned carefully against the wall and tilted her head up to gaze consideringly at the sky; West, however, could not tear his eyes from her face.

"Do you miss the stars, when you are in town?"

He blinked. It was a romantic, fanciful sort of question from a woman not given to those tendencies. "I suppose so," he said, after a moment's thought. "But more than that, I think I miss the way the darkness feels less ominous in the countryside."

She turned her head sideways to look at him. "What do you mean?"

"There's less light, so you become accustomed to the darkness, if you need to go anywhere after sunset. The shadows seem darker in London, since they're right at the edges of all that light."

"That was dangerously close to metaphor for a man who I believe once told me he didn't believe in such a device." There was a hint of a smile playing at her lips, and everything about this conversation was making West feel acutely conscious of the darkness, of her proximity, of the warmth of her skin that he could feel under his palm, if he simply extended his hand.

"I *believe* in it," he objected mildly. "I just think it should be applied sparingly."

Her mouth curved into a proper smile, and he looked away, swallowing. The sight of her smile was like a physical blow.

She reached out a gloved hand, to take his hand again. "You know," she said, "if we're worried about our ruse not being convincing enough, all we need do is spend another ten minutes out here."

"Perhaps we can muss your hair a bit, before we go back indoors," West suggested. "To lend the proceedings a bit of . . ." He considered.

"Licentious credibility?" Sophie suggested.

"Something like that."

"Or . . ." The word was long, slow, drawn-out. It contained an improbable number of syllables for its two letters.

"Or?"

"Or," Sophie repeated, and she tilted her head back slightly, so that her gaze on him was heavy-lidded and lazy, "we could do something compromising . . . in truth."

Something about her manner suggested that she was throwing down a gauntlet—one she did not expect West to pick up. She was offering him nothing more than what she'd offered four years earlier. And, he realized, she thought she knew him well enough to predict how he'd respond—that he'd step back, demur.

What would she do, he wondered, if he did the opposite?

If he reminded her of just how *good* they were together?

He reached out and very deliberately leaned his cane against the wall.

Sophie's eyes tracked this movement, then flicked back to his.

He took a step toward her, and then another one, until there were only a few scant inches of space between them. He reached out, and rested one arm on the wall above her head. She tipped her head back farther to meet his eyes, and he saw her swallow.

He allowed himself one single, satisfied second to revel in the sight, and then he ducked his head and pressed his lips to hers.

It should have felt strange, and new, and unfamiliar, kissing her again after all this time, and yet, in that first instant, the overpowering sensation that hit him was one of homecoming. His body seemed to recognize hers, and a thousand memories crashed into him as he reached out to cup her jaw, tilting her head to a better angle so that he could kiss her properly. There was the softness of her skin under his hand, and the electric feeling of her hand sliding across his shoulders, into the short hairs at the nape of his neck.

He pulled back after a moment, resting his forehead against hers, and she opened her eyes, blinking up at him.

"What is it?" she asked, the slightest breathless edge to her voice.

"It's still us," he said, his tone dangerously near marveling, and no sooner were the words out of his mouth than he registered how foolish and inane they must have sounded to her, but something complicated was playing across her face, and nothing about her expression indicated that she found him foolish.

Instead, she merely said, "It's still us," and tugged his head down to hers.

Where there had been the slightest bit of tentativeness, of hesitation to their last kiss, none was now present: This was all hot, fast certainty. Her nails were digging into his shoulders sharp enough to cause a bolt of pleasure to arrow directly south, and his tongue teased open her lips, slipping into her mouth and tangling with hers. He stepped closer, so close that her breasts were brushing his chest, and he dropped his arm from the wall above her head to wrap around her waist instead, tugging her more firmly against him. She pushed back after a moment, and he made as if to step back, break the kiss, but she seized his jacket without removing her mouth from his, turning them so that it was now his back at the wall, thudding against it with surprising force, and she was leaning against him, all of her soft curves pressing against him, her leg reaching out to twine around one of his as one of his hands drifted toward her breasts—

"I *knew* you needed a chaperone!"

Sophie drew back with a start, and West loosened his grip on her enough to put some space between them, but kept a hand at her waist as they turned to peer down the length of the terrace, where Alexandra, Violet, and—heaven help them—Harriet were standing. All three wore expressions of varying degrees of amusement, though there was something a bit inscrutable about Alexandra's; it was Harriet, however, who had spoken, and there was a note of barely concealed glee in her voice now.

"Betsy is going to be so distraught to have missed this—she went to the retiring room a few minutes ago—you know how ladies in a *certain condition* are," she added, her tone heavy with meaning. "But Alex said that you'd come out here a few minutes ago, and I, naturally, was *horrified* that an unmarried couple was allowed to escape onto a darkened terrace, without someone to protect their virtue."

"How considerate of you," Sophie said. "Particularly given that I once found you and George behind a set of drapes in my very own library, before you were wed."

"A youthful indiscretion," Harriet said, waving an airy hand. "I am a *mother* now, Sophie. I have *maternal instincts*."

"Doesn't Cecily have colic?" Sophie asked skeptically.

"Indeed," Harriet said brightly. "Which is why George is at home with her this evening! It is so useful when gentlemen know their place is in the home," she added fondly.

"In any case," Alexandra said, casting her younger sister a look of half-affection, half-exasperation, "Harriet was quite insistent that we follow you out here, convinced we would find you doing something compromising. And she was correct." There was a note of faint surprise in her voice, which seemed strange to West—should not they expect to find an affianced couple doing something mildly scandalous? He was distracted from this thought by the sight of Violet, who looked as though she was trying very hard to fight back a smile. Violet, who—he remembered in a flash—was now aware that his and Sophie's betrothal was feigned, thanks to James.

He met her gaze, and the look in her eyes informed him in no uncertain terms that his brother would be hearing about this incident in approximately three minutes.

He glanced down at Sophie. "Shall we go back indoors, dearest?" he asked her, very dryly.

"Indeed," she said lightly, allowing him to take her hand. She reached for his cane and, as she handed it to him, added in a murmur quiet enough that only he could hear, "I believe that will have made our ruse considerably more convincing, don't you think?"

Ruse. If she thought that was a ruse—that that kiss had been nothing more than a ploy to make their act convincing, to pull the wool over her sisters' eyes—then West was tempted to ask her if she'd experienced the same past five minutes that he had. Nothing—*nothing*—about that kiss had felt like a ruse, or like acting, to him.

But then he heard it: the slightest, shakiest exhale as his fingers brushed hers, taking possession of his cane. And he knew, in that instant, that she was no less affected than he had been.

And if she thought she could kiss him like that, and then still insist that they had no future together, that this feeling that burned between them was something to be ignored . . .

Well, he would simply have to prove to her otherwise.

"It is very charming for a man to take it into his head to host a dinner party, do you not think?" Violet asked brightly from within the cozy confines of her carriage.

James cast her a vaguely inquiring look, resembling, Sophie thought, nothing so much as a man who was half-afraid to hear whatever was about to come out of his wife's mouth, but who had learned from long experience that it was always best to make at least a show of interest.

This was evidently all the encouragement Violet needed. "I mean to say—West has no wife!" She smiled dazzlingly at Sophie. "No one to serve as hostess! And yet he is hosting a dinner! It is rather as if a horse had taken it into its head to walk on two legs instead of four."

This was apparently too great a slight to his sex for James to let pass. "How marvelous that a creature of such inferior intellect should manage such a feat."

Violet turned innocent eyes upon her husband. "Oh, are you *offended*, darling? Is it terribly exhausting, having someone behave as though the smallest achievement on the part of a member of your sex is so astonishing as to be barely credible? How dreadfully tiresome that must be! I cannot imagine what that must be like, of course."

"Thank you, Violet, I believe you've made your point," James said. "Though why *I* should be the one to receive this little monologue, when—last I checked—I have not done anything lately to incur your wrath, is beyond me."

"I have not had anyone to monologue at in a self-righteous fashion on the inequities women face for at least a week," Violet explained cheerfully. "I like to ensure that I don't fall out of practice."

"You're in top form," Sophie assured her.

"Ah, look, we've arrived!" James said, sounding as relieved as a man escaping the gallows, though Sophie did not miss the quick kiss he pressed to the top of Violet's head before hopping out of the carriage and waiting to hand them down.

In short order, they had joined the throng in West's drawing room, where everyone had assembled before dinner. It was a decent-sized crowd, thanks to the web of complicated family and friendship ties at work, and their party rounded out to an even twenty for dinner—an ambitious enough task for a seasoned hostess, much less for a bachelor. But West seemed entirely at ease as Sophie made her way to his side, where he lifted her hand to his mouth for a brief kiss. This dinner party was intended to be a celebration of their betrothal for only their closest friends and relations, separate from the more elaborate ball her mother was planning in her and Alexandra's honor.

"Darling," West said, offering her his arm, "I was just telling your sister here about Alexandra's plans for the wedding. With the horses," he added, dry as toast.

The sister in question was Maria; her husband was deep in conversation with Harriet's and Betsy's husbands, but Maria was focused entirely on West, wearing an expression of mild horror.

"Sophie," she said, "you cannot possibly plan to leave your wedding ceremony on horseback."

Sophie smiled serenely. "It was Alex's idea—if you've a complaint, I suggest you inform her."

Maria snorted, which itself was indicative of her distress—her fussy sister would ordinarily never allow such a noise to pass her lips, lest someone think her common. Maria had a great abhorrence of all things common—this might be why she seemed fond of West, come to think of it. No one in possession of their senses could ever mistake him for a man with even a nodding acquaintance with common.

"Since when have you been willing to acquiesce to a harebrained scheme, just because Alexandra suggested it?" Maria asked suspiciously.

Sophie bit back a sigh; the less than two years that separated herself and Maria had felt like a large gulf when they were girls, and

Sophie had felt protective toward her anxious younger sister, but as they'd grown, and Maria had learned to hide her anxiety behind a mask of propriety and occasional judgment, it had grown more difficult for Sophie to muster up those same feelings of protective affection that had once come so naturally to her.

The fact that Maria herself had played a role in Sophie's hasty marriage to Bridewell was something, too, that Sophie had failed to entirely put out of her mind. This was not exactly fair, considering Maria herself remained entirely unaware of the threats the duke had made about her reputation; Sophie had been careful not to breathe a word of it, knowing that her sister would feel partly responsible. At the time, considering their parents' fury surrounding the entire flirtation with Sandworth, Sophie rather thought Maria had been punished enough, without adding an extra layer of guilt to her woes. The fact remained, however, that Sophie had limited patience for being lectured about *bad ideas* by someone whose own lapse in judgment had proved to have such devastating, unintended consequences.

"It's her wedding, too, Maria," Sophie said shortly. "If she wants to leave on horseback, she's perfectly within her rights to do so."

"But why do *you* need to?" Maria pressed—a question that Sophie had not paused to consider previously. "Why are you having a double wedding at all? If you want different things for your weddings, doesn't it make more sense to have separate ceremonies?"

"What a sensible idea," West said, taking a healthy sip of his brandy. Sophie tried—and failed—not to look at the casual grip of his fingers on the glass, which summoned a memory of those same fingers brushing the underside of her breast a few nights earlier, just before Harriet had seen fit to interrupt them.

"I don't understand why Alexandra wants a big wedding at all," Maria said. "She already had one with her first husband."

"She wants to celebrate finding love again," Sophie said, feeling defensive. "I suppose that's understandable."

"But don't you recall how she complained about it the first time?" Maria asked. "She hated all the pomp and fuss—said if she could do it over again, she'd elope to Gretna Green."

"She was only joking—she doesn't wish to kill Mama," Sophie said, though now that Maria mentioned it, Sophie did recall some of Alexandra's complaints, which she'd previously forgotten. Her rather shy sister had found all the attention overwhelming—entirely at odds with the woman who now had visions of a dramatic departure on horseback. It did seem a bit odd, but . . . "Besides, people are allowed to change their minds, Maria."

Maria frowned suspiciously at this, clearly of the opinion that anyone so flighty as to change their mind should be regarded as untrustworthy at best, dangerous at worst.

Further conversation on the topic was forestalled by the ringing of the dinner bell, and the usual bit of scampering as everyone attempted to work out precedence for entering the dining room, though it seemed a bit silly, dining as they were solely among close friends. Eventually they were all settled around the table and the conversation was occupied for a while with discussions of plans for the end of the Season, when Jeremy would be hosting his annual hunting party at his estate in Wiltshire, an event that had taken on a less ribald, considerably more domestic flavor now that he'd married.

All too soon, however, conversation turned once more to Sophie's alleged wedding.

"Have you decided what you're going to wear?" Betsy asked, spearing a bite of roast duck with considerable gusto.

"If you need a waistcoat, West, Jeremy could loan you the one he wore for *our* wedding," Diana offered slyly.

"A tempting offer," West said, straight-faced—Jeremy had lost a bet to Diana and had been forced to wear what Sophie thought was quite possibly the most horrifying waistcoat known to mankind to his wedding, though it must be admitted that he had done so quite cheerfully.

"Oh!" Alexandra clasped her hands eagerly. "Sophie, we should buy new gowns! Perhaps we ought to go to the modiste together!"

"I have plenty of gowns," Sophie said hastily. "I don't think it's necessary—"

"But not one you ordered *specifically* for your wedding!" Alexandra said severely.

"I did not wear a new gown for my wedding," Emily said, with a soft smile in her husband's direction, "and I did not find the day lacking—oh!" She broke off, glancing down under the table. "Violet, did you just kick me?" Her voice was full of wounded betrayal.

"Why on earth would I do that?" Violet asked innocently, sipping from her wineglass. "But, Sophie, Alexandra is right—you should have a new gown!"

"If I am to be departing the ceremony on horseback," Sophie said sweetly, "then would a new gown not be unwise? Much better to wear something older that I wouldn't mind getting dirty if the horse kicks up a bit of mud, I should think."

"It is not so difficult to remove mud from a gown!" Alexandra said airily, before faltering slightly. "Er, is it?"

A brief, uncertain silence fell.

"In any case," Alexandra continued, seeing that no one had an answer for her, "I insist! New gowns for us both! I shall collect you tomorrow and we shall be off to a new modiste I've been meaning to visit."

"Mmmm," Sophie said, with as much enthusiasm as she was capable of mustering. She was acutely aware of Violet watching her like a hawk, and she plastered a more eager smile on her face. "I shall be anticipating it as I would anticipate . . . er . . ."

"Our wedding?" West suggested, very dryly.

"Precisely," Sophie agreed feebly.

"Sophie, are you quite all right?" Betsy asked. "You look a bit unwell."

"No doubt it is merely a touch of lovesickness," Alexandra said breezily. "I'm sure it will subside."

"Audley," Blackford said, clearing his throat, "I heard you're planning a visit to Oxfordshire to take a look at Risedale's stables."

Sophie shot Blackford a grateful look as talk turned to James and the Earl of Risedale's scheme for building out his stables into some sort of profitable enterprise, and she relaxed slightly as the attention of the room shifted away from her. She took a healthy sip of wine, and glanced up to see West's gaze on her.

He frowned in silent inquiry. *Is anything wrong?*

She shook her head with a small smile, and turned to Penvale, who was seated next to her, and who had been silently taking in the events of the past five minutes with a mildly nonplussed expression.

"I see it's your turn to attempt to carry on a romance whilst ignoring the interference of our friends," he said. "A solemn rite of passage for us all, you know."

"Indeed." Sophie took another healthy sip of wine, wishing briefly that it was something stronger.

"Cheer up," Penvale said bracingly. "Once you've married and made a show of suitable matrimonial bliss, their attention moves on and you are allowed to become the smug married friend dispensing unwanted advice instead. It's much more fun, I promise."

Sophie laughed, lifting her glass to his in a toast, but couldn't help thinking that it might not prove so simple in her case—because matrimonial bliss was not going to be the outcome.

Chapter Eighteen

By the time the dinner party broke up, it was past eleven; the meal had been followed by a rousing, somewhat inappropriate game of charades in the library—Jane, in particular, had proved surprisingly adept at imitating a seagull, to Penvale's mystifying horror—which had been fueled by several glasses of port and sherry. At last, however, only West, Sophie, Violet, and James were left, Violet being helped into her wrap by James, who was admonishing her to be careful not to take a chill "for the sake of your delicate lungs" with an entirely straight face.

West took a deep breath. He'd made up his mind—and he trusted James and Violet to be discreet—but still . . .

"I have something I wish to discuss with Sophie," he said carefully, flicking only the slightest glance in her direction as he spoke. "I can send her home in my carriage afterward."

"All right," Violet said, borderline gleeful, and wasted no time in seizing James by the arm and practically dragging him from the house, barely giving poor Briar enough time to bow them out the front door before they'd gone.

"You're very quick, Briar!" Violet called admiringly over her shoulder. "It is helpful to have a butler with such youthful legs!"

Briar's face was carefully blank as he shut the door behind them;

he turned to West, said simply, "I can't decide if that was an insult or not," and bowed himself out of sight.

"Briar will be much more at ease once he is old and gray, I think," Sophie said, a note of amusement in her voice.

West turned to look at her, then inclined his head in the direction of the library, from which they'd just come. "Would you like to speak privately?"

Sophie walked toward him slowly; she was wearing a gown of red velvet that sat tantalizingly low on her décolletage, and her cheeks were a bit flushed from sherry and laughter. Her golden hair was piled high atop her head, a few curls having been allowed to frame her face, and he curled his fingers against his palm to resist the urge to reach out and tuck one of those curls behind her ear.

"All right," she said simply, coming to a halt when she was close enough that she had to tilt her head back to meet his eyes. "Or . . . we could go upstairs?"

She looked at him directly as she said it, the faintest hint of a challenge in the words. She was testing him, he realized. She wanted to see how far he was willing to take this.

He lifted a brow at her, then offered her his arm. He saw the faintest hint of surprise register on her face before she took it, and he led them up the stairs.

The *click* of the door as he shut it behind them sounded loud in the silence between them as they entered his suite of rooms. It was a warm evening, and there was no fire in the grate; lamps were lit about the sitting room, encasing them in a rosy glow, and Sophie wandered around slowly, coming to a halt before one of the large windows overlooking the back garden.

Slowly, she began to remove her gloves; West, standing on the opposite side of the room, could not have torn his eyes from the motion of her hands if his life depended on it.

She glanced over her shoulder. "I take it you wanted to speak to me about my . . . proposal?" Her eyes crinkled slightly at the corners. "Otherwise, we've shocked Violet and James for absolutely no reason, if this is a conversation that could have waited until morning."

He began to take slow, measured steps toward her, the *thunk* of his cane muffled by the thick carpet. "I don't believe Violet and James are very easily shocked. He did compromise her on a balcony on the very night they met, after all."

Sophie turned back to the window, leaning down to drop her gloves on the armchair situated before it. "True." Her voice was amused. "Perhaps that's what I ought to have done, the night we met."

"Compromised me?" He was only a few feet away from her now, and he paused to appreciate the straight line of her back, the slight curves hinted at beneath her dress.

Still, she did not turn, though she must have been aware of his proximity. "Yes. Ruined the reputation of the upstanding Marquess of Weston, turned you into a despoiler of virgins—we'd have been engaged before your father could have taken it into his mind to have an opinion on the matter."

"I was a bit less upstanding back then, if you'll recall." He'd had a brief phase of wild-oat-sowing prior to meeting her, an attempt to relieve the pressures of his position.

She cast him a saucy glance over her shoulder. "I *do* recall, thank you. Who would have thought that the alcove behind a potted fern could be so terribly . . . educational?"

He recalled the interlude in question with almost painful clarity. It was the first time he'd got a hand beneath her skirts; looking back on it, it had been terribly risky, but they'd been young, and as good as engaged, even if he hadn't officially asked her yet.

If only he'd asked her.

He'd been a fool.

He shook his head to clear it.

She turned now, and the suddenness of the movement did not give him time to carefully school his features into the more neutral expression he usually tried to adopt in her presence. One that would not frighten her—not make her realize that he felt the same way about her now as he had seven years earlier.

Except . . .

He was growing weary of pretending.

Sophie's gaze skittered off of him, and she began a deliberate perusal of the sitting room. He watched her take it in: the polished mahogany furniture; the blue wall hangings; the stack of books on one of the end tables; the open door behind him that led to his bedroom.

"Shall we have something to drink?" she asked, her gaze having alighted on the sideboard beneath an ornate gilt mirror. Without awaiting his reply, she made a beeline for the decanter of brandy and the bottles of wine arrayed there; in the mirror, he could see the faint furrowing of her brow as she reached for one of the bottles, scrutinizing the label. "Perhaps a glass of claret?" she tossed over her shoulder, waving the bottle in question.

"If you wish," he said, approaching her slowly; she turned at the sound of his footsteps, bottle still in hand. He watched her for a moment, then cleared his throat. "What are you doing?"

"I am opening it for you," Sophie said, her hands busy.

"I am not certain that is, in fact, what you are doing." Sophie, for all that she was generally a lady for whom the word "competent" seemed to have been invented, was struggling with a corkscrew—this was clearly a task with which she had limited experience.

"Did you want any help with that?" he asked after another moment.

"No," Sophie snapped.

"All right," he agreed politely.

The struggle continued; Sophie was growing slightly red in the face. A strand of golden hair had fallen into her face, and she blew an irritated breath at it.

"I know it would be impolite for me to sit," he said after another long few moments, "but my leg is beginning to ache—"

"For heaven's sake!" She thrust the bottle at him; he mentally congratulated himself for successfully guessing that mentioning his leg would end this farce. He accepted the bottle from her and, in a few twists of the corkscrew, had it open.

He filled two glasses, set the bottle down, and raised his glass to her. "Cheers," he offered.

She clinked her glass against his, still thoroughly out of sorts. "I'm even more irritated now that I've learned that you look very attractive whilst opening wine bottles." She took a seat in one of the armchairs before the empty fireplace, and he sat in the chair opposite hers.

"I have often thought that brandishing a corkscrew is indeed the surest way to woo a woman," he murmured. She rolled her eyes, and he nearly smiled.

"I can tell you are trying not to smile," she informed him. "And I wish you wouldn't."

"Smile?"

"No, try not to. You have a very nice smile, you know. On the rare occasion it makes an appearance."

"I smile when the situation merits it," he said, taking a sip of wine. He'd been saving this particular claret for a special occasion—which, upon reflection, he supposed this evening qualified as.

"As if it's a particularly fetching coat you only wear for the nicest events," she said, and *she* was smiling, and if his smile was nice, or however she found it, hers was radiant. He looked back down into his glass.

A brief silence descended upon them; she was gazing into the empty grate, evidently deep in thought, which gave him the opportunity to look his fill. For so many years, he'd had to take her in in hasty, furtive gulps: a quick glance across a crowded ballroom, or down a dinner table, careful that no one should observe him doing so. It felt almost dizzyingly luxurious to look at her for as long as he pleased.

"I enjoyed dinner tonight," she said absently, taking another sip of wine. "With your brother—and my sisters—and all their friends. It was . . . nice." She sounded mildly surprised by this realization, that the display of domestic harmony they'd put on tonight had been enjoyable. He was tempted to push at this, but instead broached another topic he'd considered often, these past weeks—and months.

"You have become closer with them. With Violet's friends, I mean. I recall you used to only be close to your sisters."

He remembered something she had told him once, years earlier: *Why should I need other friends, when I've four sisters? Who could possibly be better company than them?*

He remembered the pang her words had caused; he'd grown up in a household with a dead mother, a controlling father, and a single younger brother who seemed to resent him half the time. He could not imagine calling a large, loving family like the Wexhams his own. But he'd gone off to school, and made friends with David Overington, the future Marquess of Willingham. They'd met at Eton, and continued on to Oxford together, and he had found the joy that came of belonging, of having another person on whom one could rely.

The thought of David sent a pang through him. But he realized with a start that over the course of this past year—since he'd repaired his relationship with his brother, become closer to his brother's friends, too—the pain of David's absence had lessened, like an old wound that was slowly healing.

"I've discovered there's something to be said for being intimate with someone who didn't know you when you were in leading strings," Sophie said now, drawing West back from his own maudlin thoughts. "And, besides, my sisters are adults now. They've all married and are starting families of their own. They don't . . . need me. Anymore."

He set down his wineglass and leaned forward, bracing his elbows on his knees, leveling his gaze directly at her. "Sophie. Your sisters will always need you."

"But it's not the same." She took another sip of wine. "After I—after I married Fitz, I turned my attention to them. Now *they* needed to marry well. *They* needed to be happy. I chaperoned them for events—I hosted balls for Alex and the twins, the years they debuted—I gave them advice when they had suitors. And all along, I thought, if I could ensure that all of them were happy in their marriages, then it wouldn't matter that I—"

She broke off, as if suddenly realizing what she was saying. What she'd been *about* to say.

He waited.

"That I wasn't happy in mine."

She spoke each word very carefully, very deliberately, without ever allowing her gaze to waver from his—so that he'd know that she meant it. That the words hadn't slipped out by accident.

He'd known, on some level, that this was true. He was not a vain man, but he flattered himself that Sophie hadn't gone from loving him to marrying another man without more than a moment's regret; he'd known that her marriage to Bridewell must have hurt, in both the same and an entirely different way to the manner in which it had hurt him.

But she had never admitted it to him, until now.

And he knew, somehow, that he must proceed very, very carefully.

"Did they—*do* they—know that?" He deliberately leaned back in his seat, as if the topic didn't matter very much to him at all, as if he were approaching a particularly shy cat. For years, all he had wanted— more than to kiss her, or hold her, or make love to her—was simply to *talk* to her. She was his favorite person to talk to.

She was, he feared, still his favorite person, period.

She gave a sort of half-shrug, one that seemed *helpless*, somehow, even though that was nearly the last word he'd ever use to describe her.

"I don't know—somewhat, I think. They were very puzzled when I married Fitz. Particularly with you being so ill—they thought me heartless. Maria and I quarreled about it, and we've never fully recovered from that quarrel, I don't think."

"Because you let a future duke slip through your fingers?" he asked, thinking of Sophie's status-obsessed younger sister.

"Because she knew that I was in love with you," Sophie said quietly, and gazed down into her drink for a long moment. "I mean, yes, she also thought I was a fool to throw away the chance to be a duchess someday—she *is* Maria, after all—but more important to her was the fact that I loved you, and I was marrying someone else. She thought it monstrously unfair to Fitz, for all that I tried to tell her that he didn't love me, either. Maria is surprisingly romantic. She didn't know the truth of what happened with the duke—she still doesn't—because I knew she'd feel guilty. But since I couldn't inform anyone of why I'd done what I'd done, they . . . disapproved."

"And then, once I'd been married awhile and hadn't had a baby, they started to worry about that, too—I think that was what made them finally forgive my impetuous marriage. They felt so sorry for me that they managed to get over their disapproval, I suppose."

Something in her tone confused him; it was somehow wry, almost guilty.

"And you didn't want their pity?" He was hazarding a wild guess, feeling his way along in the dark. It made him uncomfortable; he was unaccustomed to speaking without being entirely sure of what he was saying. Future dukes did not speak unless they were sure. Future dukes were *always* sure.

But that was the magic of Sophie, he thought—it had been seven years ago, and he felt it again now:

With her, he did not need to be certain. She did not think any less of him for this.

"I did not think I deserved it," she said, very quietly, and she lifted her eyes to meet his. "Fitz and I . . . ours was not a particularly passionate marriage. We entered it heartbroken, both of us, and he soon developed interests that lay elsewhere, and made sure I was aware that I could do the same—but he liked the idea of children, and we were both lonely, and it was convenient enough, having another warm body on the opposite side of the connecting door. So we—we went to bed together. Often enough, over the years, that it began to seem odd to us both, when there was no resulting child. It bothered him." Her gaze on him was steady. "But it never bothered me."

West was silent for a long moment, taking in what she had just told him. He had never heard anyone, male or female, express such a thought. In his experience, couples who were unable to have children were to be pitied; the wife was always to blame, though he'd personally always found this assumption on the part of most men of his acquaintance to be based on some rather flawed logic. But whether a child was something to be desired was never in question—and anyone unable to produce one must feel the loss quite deeply.

He had never, not once, considered that anyone might feel otherwise. But then, he was a marquess, would be a duke someday; children were, in his world, not so much beloved additions to the family as necessary acquisitions, like a new horse or a particularly fine carriage. He'd never once, in the whole of his life, paused to consider whether he *wanted* them.

"You do not want children, then?" he asked, finding his voice, his mind still full of these thoughts.

"I had never thought to want or not want them," she said. "It's not as if I'd have much of a choice in the matter, once I was wed—that is what a wife is for, is it not? Providing heirs?"

He nearly flinched at the last word. *Heirs.* Most men would wish for a wife to provide them with children, it was true, but he could not help but think her word choice had been deliberate. After all, how many men had to worry as much about their future legacy as he did? As another man's wife—as Bridewell's, for instance—she would not feel the weight of this so heavily. He suddenly appreciated what a bold and presumptuous thing it had been, expecting her to marry him.

"But then, when no children appeared, I realized that I didn't . . . mind. And as I thought about it more, I realized that I'd never looked at other women's babies and longed for one of my own. I love my nieces and nephew, but I have never felt a pang of loss that my marriage did not produce a baby of my own.

"So you see, West, it's just as well that we never wed—you can't possibly have a duchess who can't produce an heir. But you also needn't worry that I'll fall pregnant from any . . . recreational activities, shall we say, that we might choose to engage in."

She was still meeting his eyes very steadily, but he felt certain that this was in some sense an act; she was stating this boldly to shock him, to put him off, to see how he'd react.

He paused a moment, to gauge his own emotions: How *did* he feel about this? He wasn't entirely sure; but he knew, with utmost certainty, that when he'd wanted to marry Sophie seven years ago—when he'd spent all those years since longing for her—it was not because he wanted her to supply him with an heir and a spare.

He'd wanted her for herself, because she made him happy.

Everything else was . . . well, everything else was negotiable.

"How do you know that you're barren, and it wasn't Bridewell who was the problem?" he asked now, the thought belatedly occurring to him.

She rolled her eyes. "Isn't it always the woman who is at fault?"

"I am no doctor," he said carefully, "but it seems to me that there are two sets of organs involved in the act, and it seems just as likely it could be the husband as the wife."

"Would you be willing to risk it, though?"

He rose from his seat then, and approached her with slow, deliberate steps; he leaned down and braced his hands on the arms of her chair, bringing his face close to hers.

"Need I remind you that, until recently, my father was under the impression that *I* could not have children?"

She frowned. "I know, but—well, you just told him that to irk him. It wasn't true."

"I told him that," he said very deliberately, "so he'd abandon any hopes of me marrying and providing him with an heir, when I'd no desire to do so."

Not unless it was with you.

He did not speak the words aloud, but they hovered between them, understood.

She swallowed. "You would have changed your mind eventually— you *will* change your mind," she corrected. "You can't mean to be a monk."

"If I have done so for the past four years—and then close enough for the three before that—then I don't have any notion of what I mean to do," he said evenly.

Her frown deepened. "But then—" Her eyes widened.

He waited, ignoring the ache crawling up his leg.

"You have not—that one night—"

"Afternoon, really," he said. "But yes." He hesitated. "There were— during the years that you were married, once I recovered, there were other women. Not frequently, but when I . . . I couldn't bear it." He'd closed his eyes, and tried not to picture her face. "But after that afternoon . . . there's been no one."

"But *why?*"

"Because," he said simply, "you had ruined me."

And then he leaned down and kissed her.

There was less hesitation in this kiss than there had been a few nights earlier, on Lady Worthington's terrace; their bodies remembered each other now, and fell back into the rhythm that had once come so naturally to them: his hand cupping her cheek, their tongues tangling together, her fingers curling around his neck. Time seemed to slow, and all he was aware of was the feeling of her warm body pressed against his, the silkiness of her hair in his hands.

Another feeling, however, was slowly beginning to crowd in around the edges, an arc of pain lancing up through his leg as he rested more of his weight upon it. It had been a long day, and he'd gone riding that afternoon, and his leg was letting him know in no uncertain terms that it did not appreciate this treatment.

"Is something wrong?" Sophie asked, pulling away from him in response to some infinitesimal signal from his body. She was flushed and utterly lovely, her golden hair mussed and slipping out of its coiffure.

"No," he said, and reached out to pull her up out of her seat. She tugged him by the cravat and drew his mouth down to hers.

This time, she controlled the kiss, and he was happy to let her; he, who had to be in control in so many other aspects of his life, who kept himself so perfectly contained at all times, was pleased enough to relinquish that control here, where there was no one else to see. Her hands were at his cravat still, hastily unknotting it, and soon she had it loose and the warmth of her hand was at his throat, leaving goose bumps in its wake. He shrugged out of his coat, and then her hands were at the buttons on his waistcoat and he was sliding it off a moment later, and then she was unbuttoning his shirt, and her fingers were greedy on his skin, the muscles of his abdomen tensing under her whisper-soft touch.

They stumbled drunkenly backward, West drawing her with him through the doorway that connected to his bedroom. It was darker in here, fewer lamps burning, and the low light made her eyes look like dark pools, drinking him in as she broke their kiss and surveyed him for a long moment.

She stepped back, her gaze on him hungry, and he felt himself grow harder under her scrutiny.

"Why do you look . . . like *that?*" she asked, gesturing at him in indignation. She sounded almost annoyed, and also appreciative, all at once.

"I started an exercise regimen, when I was recovering from my accident," he said. "In an attempt to regain my strength. I found I liked the way it helped me . . . stop thinking." Of David, and his death, and his own terrible, overpowering grief and guilt; of Sophie, at first, when all he'd wanted to do was think of her, and doing so was a constant agony; and then, later, when his longing for her had become less all-consuming, he'd come to appreciate the way his mind went blank of *everything* when he was physically exhausted. It was a relief, when he could allow the rest of the world to fade away, even for a little while.

But there were other ways to do that.

Ways that he'd once loved—once made a very frequent habit of.

Ways that had lost their appeal, once he'd lost her.

Until now.

He shrugged off his shirt and walked toward her; when he concentrated, he could control his limp, make it nearly unnoticeable, even if doing so caused him an added degree of pain. Now, however, his limp was heavy, but nothing in her face indicated that she minded it. That she was thinking of the man—nearly a boy—she'd once loved. Instead, appreciation for the man before her was written in every line of her face.

"Now your shoes," she said, crossing her arms across her chest, regarding him with some anticipation.

He sat on the edge of the bed, and tugged at his shoes; a quick glance at Sophie confirmed that she was watching this display with some appreciation.

"Now your trousers."

"Are you planning on joining me at any point?"

Her gaze narrowed. "Eventually."

Something about that look on her face, and the curtness that crept into her tone when she ordered him about, sent more blood rushing south, and he fairly flung off his trousers and smalls and a moment later he was sitting before her, entirely nude. He rose to his feet and took a step toward her, but she held up a hand to stay him.

"Sophie—"

"Wait," she said slowly, a smile playing at her lips, and there was nothing in her expression but open appreciation, and lust, and *need*.

She made a slow circuit around him, and he grew, if possible, even harder under this scrutiny. She came to a halt directly before him, so close that he could have reached out and seized her with the slightest movement of his arm, but he remained still, allowing her to look her fill. There was color in her cheeks, and her chest was rising and falling more rapidly than usual. Her gaze dropped to his leg, and he instinctively reached out a hand to cover the ugly scar that crisscrossed one thigh, where a jagged piece of wood had gouged him badly in the crash, then froze mid-motion, and allowed his hand to drop.

She reached out a hand instead, her fingers tracing the angry scars on his thigh; they had faded with time, but would never vanish.

Her gaze flicked up to his. "Does this hurt?"

His mouth twisted into a wry smile. "No more than usual."

A lie, in some sense; his pain today was certainly worse than normal. But her cool hand on his skin eased him somehow, even though all she'd done was trace a gentle line along the map of his pain.

Her gaze lowered again, down to his shin, where the break had healed poorly, causing the limp that plagued him to this day, and her hand continued its progress, down nearly to his knee and then back up again—and then farther up, and farther. Her finger reached his inner thigh, and he closed his eyes.

"Sophie—"

Her hand curled around him, and he bit off her name on a groan. Her grip tightened, and he inhaled sharply; a moment later, it was gone, and he opened his eyes to protest—

In time to see her, gazing directly at him, lick across her palm with slow deliberation, and then return that hand to his length, giving him a slow, agonizing stroke.

"Jesus Christ."

"Mmm," she said, her eyes following the motion of her hand. "I do love when you *talk*."

"I talk all—bloody *hell*—all the time," he managed.

Her smile, smug as a cat who got the cream, widened. "Not like this." Another deliberate stroke. Her hand loosened and she stepped back, then sank to her knees. He reached out and gripped the bedpost just before she engulfed him in her mouth.

It was warmth, and heat, and gentle suction, but also there was a growing pain in his leg, an agony mixing with the pleasure in ways that at first almost heightened it, then slowly, surely became more of a distraction.

"Sophie—wait," he said, the words more of a gasp than anything else. She drew back, looking up at him in question.

"It's—I need to sit down. I don't think my leg can take this."

He'd long since stopped feeling much in the way of regret when it came to his bad leg; if occasionally he longed for the days when he could race his brother or friends across a field and beat whoever was foolish enough to agree to his challenge, he didn't dwell on this feeling, as it did little to serve him in the moment.

Now, however, he felt frustration bubbling up as Sophie shuffled backward on her knees, allowing him to gingerly sit on the edge of the bed. He so desperately wanted her, of all people, to see him as whole, unbroken. Not someone to be gentle with. Some of what he was feeling must have shown on his face—itself an alarming notion, given how he prided himself on never allowing any such thing to occur—because a frown creased hers.

"What's wrong?"

He shook his head. "Nothing—obviously," he added, gesturing at his lap, where his cock was making it quite plain that it objected to this interruption in the evening's entertainment. Her frown did not ease at this attempt at levity, however, and he sighed.

"I'm annoyed about my leg," he said honestly. "And I do not wish it to make things . . . that is, I do not wish you to worry about it, while we . . ."

"I can promise you, West, if you'd let me get back to what I was doing, I will not be thinking of anything except trying to make you spend, and how much I like doing so."

"Do you?" he asked, his voice hoarse but coherent, which he thought quite a feat after nearly swallowing his tongue.

"Shall I show you?" she asked, her voice coy, and he swallowed, a curt nod all that he could manage under the circumstances. And then she was on her feet again, turning her back and casting him a flirtatious look over her shoulder. "If you could just help me, perhaps . . . ?"

She lifted her arms and a moment later he was tugging the dress over her head. Then his fingers were on the laces of her corset, loosening them until that, too, was cast aside.

She turned then, revealing a chemise made of whisper-thin linen, nearly transparent in the lamplight, the silhouetted curves of breast and waist and hip a tantalizing promise through the fabric. A moment later, however, that barrier was gone, too, and she was standing before him, entirely naked, and if he'd thought his memories of her were accurate, he realized that he'd still, somehow, forgotten the absolute glory that was Sophie, all bare skin and golden hair—which, even now, she was removing the pins from, shaking out around her shoulders—and saucy gleam in her eyes.

He braced his hands behind him on the counterpane to disguise their trembling. "You are beautiful." It was not the most elegant or smooth of compliments, merely three simple words that felt as though they'd been wrenched from deep within him, but it was what he had thought every single time he had laid eyes on her for the past seven years, and he'd never been able to say it. Had gone out of his way to avoid saying much of anything at all to her. To speak those words now felt like a privilege he had not earned.

The rosiness in her cheeks deepened. "Thank you."

"Come here," he said, and she walked toward him slowly, her hips swaying, just enough for it to seem seductive rather than exaggerated.

"I thought I was giving the orders this evening," she said lightly, coming to a halt before him and reaching out a single finger to trace down his shaft. He jerked at her touch, biting off a curse before it could cross his lips.

"In that case," he said, looking directly into those beautiful brown eyes, "I'd very much like it if you told me to taste you."

"I—I think I'd like that, too," she said, a slightly breathless note to her voice that stoked some innate masculine pride that he did his best to ignore most of the time.

"Then come here," he said, pushing himself back a bit on the bed as she approached. When she was standing directly before him, he reached out and seized her by the waist; it took a bit of awkward maneuvering, but a few moments later she was on the bed, straddling him.

He leaned back and, with a firm grip on her thighs, urged her forward, until she was straddling his face.

"You might want to hold on to the bedpost," he said, and then, without a moment's further hesitation, buried his head between her thighs, and licked.

"*Jesus Christ*," she said, and then, "*God.*"

A few moments later, he came up for air. "Did you wish to pause these activities and attend a church service instead?"

"*No,*" she said, quite fervently, and then her hand was in his hair, tight enough to send a fresh rush of blood to his cock, and she was urging him back to his purpose. "Don't stop."

He had no intention of stopping, not when she was ordering him about in that commanding tone, and for some time he was conscious of nothing more than the taste and smell of her, and the small, urgent noises she was making in the back of her throat, mingled with an occasional burst of profanity that delighted him more than it probably should. His hands were tight on her thighs, keeping her firmly anchored in place, and he felt them beginning to tremble, her grip on his hair growing nearly painful, and a moment later she was cresting, and he saw her through it, keeping her pressed to his mouth, until she at last pushed herself away and collapsed limply on the bed next to him. He raised himself up on an elbow just as she reached an arm out to twine around his neck, pulling his mouth down to hers, the kiss messy and heated.

She rolled onto her side, flinging her leg over his hip, and—

"Are you sure?" he asked breathlessly, nearly out of his mind with wanting.

"Yes," she said, kissing him again, and then he was sliding into her, wet and slick, and then there was nothing but tightness and heat and mindless pleasure, the sound of her gasps in his ear. They were slow at first, finding their rhythm, but then after a minute they worked it out, her hips rising to meet his, his hand against the flat of her back, holding her tight to him. He closed his eyes and focused on nothing but the warmth of her, the softness of her skin pressed against and around him, the pleasure arcing down his spine as he moved within her. And then, all too soon, his thrusts grew erratic as he chased his release, and he slid his hand between them, pressing his thumb to a certain spot, and she shattered around him with a wordless cry, just in time for him to withdraw and spill on her stomach.

For a moment—a minute, five minutes, ten?—there was nothing except the sound of their heaving breaths.

"Good God," Sophie managed at last. "I'm not going to be able to walk tomorrow."

"That was the goal," he mumbled, the words not as cocksure as they might have been, given that he could not yet muster the strength to open his eyes. After another lengthy pause, he willed himself to a seated position, and then—though the thought was not appealing, given the jumbled state of his own mind and limbs—he rose, crossing to the basin against one wall where there was a cloth he could dampen and then hand to Sophie. She wiped at her stomach, a wry smile crossing her face as she did so.

"Gentlemanly of you, considering it likely wasn't necessary."

"We don't know that," he said mildly, settling beside her on the bed. "And I didn't want you to be forced into anything you're not willing to do." Like motherhood—or marriage to him, for that matter. He could not bear it if she married him solely because she was expecting a baby she wasn't even certain she wanted; he thought the pain of this knowledge would be even worse than the pain of losing her had been.

She flung the cloth aside, and scooted backward on the bed until she was reclining against the pillows, looking like a queen, for all that she wasn't wearing a stitch of clothing.

And West—who would later think that perhaps his brain had not been functioning quite normally, given the circumstances—said, without thinking twice, "That was worth the wait."

She went still, then slowly sat up, lovely and unashamed of her nudity—she scarcely even seemed to notice it, as all of her attention remained fixed upon him.

"West," she said carefully. "I wonder if we ought to have discussed this ahead of time—what this would mean to me. Versus what it would mean to *you*."

He felt the strangest desire to laugh, of all things. How many first-born sons of dukes had to worry about going to bed with women who were appalled by the notion of marrying them?

Instead, he merely said, "I've not asked anything of you, Sophie."

"But—for you to have given up other women for *four years*—"

"I didn't precisely *decide* to do so, you know," he said. "There were a number of women, over the years, who made their interest known."

Sophie huffed, leaning back against the pillows once more. "I don't doubt it."

His mouth curved up slightly at the corners. "Jealous?"

She crossed her arms and looked at the ceiling again. "Certainly not. You can bed every woman of the *ton*, for all I care."

"Of course," he agreed, stretching out beside her and tracing a single finger down her arm, leaving gooseflesh in his wake. "I kissed a couple of them—no one marriageable, but a couple of discreet widows. But whenever I closed my eyes, I saw your face."

She turned her head on the pillow to look at him. "West." It was soft, pained.

"I can't help it," he said. "I've tried to forget you—I've tried to move on—I've tried to convince myself that I'd be just as happy without you, eventually. But I can never quite manage it. I only want you—I've only ever wanted you."

"I want you, too," she said softly. "But not enough to toss everything else about my life into a blazing fire." She pushed herself up onto her elbows. Small frizzing tendrils of hair, mussed from his fingers, formed a golden halo around her head. "Your father was willing to ruin my sister's marriage prospects if I married you—he was willing to destroy the one thing you care about the most, that gives you a sense of purpose."

"Your sisters are all married now—quite happily, I believe—with one exception, and I know Blackford well enough to know that there's nothing my father could do to convince him not to marry Alexandra, at this point."

"But *you*," she pressed, sounding frustrated. "Even if my sisters are safe from him, *you* aren't. He could still sell Rosemere, could cast the tenants off the land, all for the sake of spiting you."

"I don't believe he will," West said levelly, even as the thought caused a sinking feeling in the pit of his stomach, one that had recurred ever since his father had first issued this threat. He *didn't* think his father would—it was ultimately pointless—but he disliked the possibility all the same. He was not a gambling man; he played low stakes at the card tables, when he played at all; he did not consider it his right, given the privilege he was born to, to risk the fortune that countless people depended on, in some way or another.

"But there's risk, all the same." Sophie said, as if reading his thoughts. "And I do not want you to risk that for me—I do not want a future with you, not if it means you've given up something so great, something you care for so much."

"I care for *you*," West said, frustration creeping into his voice to match the frustrated note in hers. "And I do not know why you value your own happiness so little—why you are so quick to give it up."

"Even if I weren't," she said evenly, "the fact that I cannot guarantee you an heir should be enough to make you see reason."

"*I don't care about a bloody heir.*" He pushed himself to a sitting position, and then rolled off the bed entirely, ignoring the sharp pain in his leg that resulted from moving too quickly. He leaned down and scooped up his smalls and trousers from the floor, pulling them on with a furious energy that coursed through his limbs. Sophie watched in silence. "I have a brother—I have cousins—I don't care who inherits the bloody title after me, not if caring means that I don't get to spend the rest of my life caring for *you*. When will you realize that you are worth it, to me? When will you stop putting your happiness last, behind everyone else's?"

"Easy enough to say, when one is to inherit a dukedom," she said coldly. He eased himself back down onto the bed and leaned forward, bracing his elbows on his knees.

"You knew my position the night we met," he said softly. "It did not bother you then."

"Perhaps I've changed my mind."

"Then if that's the case—if I cannot convince you that the man I am is worth all the bother that comes from the title I hold—then I do not know what else I can say to persuade you."

She rose, too, and reached for her chemise, pulling it over her head, hiding her bare skin from his view.

"Neither do I," she said softly, reaching for her corset, and after a long moment of silence, without another word, West leaned forward to help her with the laces.

Chapter Nineteen

Ten months earlier

He found her in the gallery of a country house in Wiltshire.

It was August—a sunny, sticky afternoon that lent itself to lazy conversations and restful sojourns in the shade. Sophie knew that at least some of the other members of their party—who had all, like herself, arrived within the past several hours—were strolling around the garden, or resting in the cool quiet of their rooms. She, however, had merely assured herself that her trunk had made its way to the guest room she'd be occupying for the next fortnight, left her bonnet on her bed, and then taken herself off on a walk around the house, her footsteps muffled by the expensive rugs that covered the floors.

She had considered carefully before accepting Jeremy's invitation to his annual shooting party; their liaison had ended on friendly terms, and over the course of the previous month she had become closer to Violet, who she knew planned to attend. She thought it would be rather nice to escape the heat of town for a few weeks in the country-side, in the company of friends she hoped to deepen her acquaintance with. And had she not said to Jeremy, when ending things, *I do hope that we might still be friends?* She had meant it, too; she liked Jeremy, for all that their short-lived affair had not been particularly earth-shattering.

(She very much feared that her expectations regarding lovemaking had been set far too high because of a single afternoon three years earlier.)

So here she was; but after a long day in a hot carriage, subjected to her lady's maid's unending chatter, she badly wished for five minutes to herself. Time alone was not a commodity she'd been lacking, these past three years, yet there were still occasions when she found herself craving the chance to gather her thoughts in peace.

Or perhaps, today, it was merely the knowledge of who would be awaiting her, once she eventually joined the group, that sent her on a slow, circuitous tour of the house. Whatever her motive, it was ultimately futile: It was as she was standing in the gallery, thoughtfully regarding a portrait of Jeremy and his elder brother as boys, their arms slung round each other's shoulders, that she heard footsteps, and the muffled *thunk* of a cane on carpet, and she knew whom she would find even before she turned to face him.

He came to an abrupt halt the moment he spotted her.

Sophie knotted her hands together, and inclined her head. "Lord Weston."

"Lady Fitzwilliam."

An awkward silence fell; West was looking around the room, seeming desperate for something to rest his eyes on that wasn't her face, and Sophie studied him. He wore a dark-blue jacket and riding boots; his cravat was a bit loose, and his hair mussed. He must have been out of doors, she thought; he had not yet transformed back into the immaculately groomed version of himself that would no doubt appear at the dinner table in a couple of hours' time.

After another long moment, he looked directly at her; there was a bit of color in his cheeks, presumably from the heat. It had been a long time since *she* had been the one to put color there.

"I apologize for disturbing you—I got a bit turned around, looking for my room. I'll just—"

He made as if to turn and leave, and Sophie was sorely tempted to let him; she did not know what to say to him anymore. Had not known for years now, in fact. She'd seen him at a Venetian breakfast a week earlier and they'd made polite, tortured conversation about the quality of the blackberries being served, for heaven's sake. But—they were to be here for a fortnight, inhabiting the same house. It was a very large house, but they could not avoid each other indefinitely.

She opened her mouth to say—well, she wasn't entirely certain what she intended to say. But before she had to work it out, he stopped mid-turn, blew out a frustrated breath, and took a step toward her.

"I want you to know," he said, his voice low but perfectly audible in the echoing silence of the room, "that I do not think James should have drawn you into his and Violet's problems. It was—it was badly done."

Sophie blinked, startled; this was not what she had been expecting from him. West's brother had, the month before, flirted with her a bit to make Violet jealous—but it had been harmless, and he'd apologized afterward. She still had the very courteous note he'd sent her tucked away in a desk drawer somewhere; only now did she pause to wonder if the man before her might have encouraged his brother to such an action.

She knew of no way to ask—not without making this conversation more intimate than she wished it to be. She and West could never be intimate in any way again.

"Your brother apologized, and there was no harm done," she said, a bit stiffly. "I certainly was eager enough to help Violet exact revenge."

He nodded. "Right. Well. I merely thought to . . . tell you. That it's not how he normally behaves."

She regarded him contemplatively for a moment. "He's an adult, West." His nickname felt strange on her tongue. "You don't need to apologize for him."

"Yes. Of course." She thought, for a second, that he wasn't going to say anything further—that he would leave the room on this stilted, awkward note. Instead, he tilted his head to the side and added, "Though I would think that you, of anyone, would understand a first-born's perhaps unreasonable concern for a younger sibling."

She sucked in a breath, but did not avert her eyes from his. "Is this how it is to be, then?" she asked softly. "We cannot exchange more than a few sentences without delving back into the past?"

He had the grace to look ashamed. "That was unnecessary," he said. "I'm sorry. I don't know what came over me."

She crossed her arms over her chest. "We're to be here for a fortnight, you know. We might at least attempt to be less uneasy in each other's company."

"Shall I ask you about the weather, and your journey here, and whether it is your first time visiting this county?" His voice was skeptical.

"It might be a nice start," she said shortly; he was not inspiring much desire in her, at the moment, to ease things between them. "If we can't discuss anything of import—anything *interesting*—then we might at least try small talk."

He looked at her for another long moment. "You and I have never made small talk, Lady Fitzwilliam."

It was true, Sophie realized; from the night they had first met, they had skipped the inconsequential, dull chatter that passed for polite conversation among the *ton*, and had plunged headfirst into a frankness and intimacy that had only halted with his accident and her marriage. They didn't know how to be polite acquaintances—they'd never been that to each other.

And now, it was all they could be. That, or nothing at all.

"We might as well attempt it," Sophie said, lifting her chin.

After another brief pause, he nodded. "All right." He inclined his head toward the door. "Might I escort you back to your room? Perhaps you can tell me how you are finding Elderwild so far—this is your first visit, is it not?"

"It is," Sophie agreed, and walked toward him until they were side by side, separated by a careful, safe couple of feet. In unison, they began to walk; at that moment, in a motion that seemed to be almost *compulsive*, against his will and better judgment, he flicked a quick glance over his shoulder, at the portrait Sophie had been looking at when he'd found her.

The portrait of Jeremy . . . and David.

He looked away again a moment later, fixing his glance steadily ahead, and Sophie continued to chatter mindlessly as they left the room, filling the silence between them with a lengthy monologue on her impressions of Jeremy's estate thus far. Only once, as they walked, did she dare allow her gaze to rest on his profile for a moment, and she quickly dropped it—but not before she'd seen the expression of pain written upon it.

She did not alter the casual babble pouring from her mouth almost unbidden, and he seemed content to listen in silence. But for a brief, sharp moment, she wished with a frightening fierceness that she might be able to say something—*anything*—to ease that pained expression on his face.

But while there was a time when she might have done such a thing, years earlier, those days seemed nothing but a distant memory to her now; the West and Sophie of then, and who they'd been to each other, had no bearing on the West and Sophie of today, who no longer had anything of import to say to each other.

It was a good reminder, she thought determinedly, whenever she found herself tempted by the green eyes and broad shoulders and sharp jawline and the hundred other pieces that combined to make the man—dangerously alluring to her still, after all this time—who now walked beside her.

Their past was not one that bore revisiting—and his pain was no longer her concern.

And if she told herself this often enough, perhaps one day she'd truly believe it.

Chapter Twenty

"*I still don't see why this is necessary,*" Sophie said as she was helped out of Violet's carriage by a footman and ushered into Madame Blanchet's shop.

"Sophie, you are getting *married,*" Alexandra said rapturously, sweeping past her through the doorway and into the modiste's small, elegant establishment. "Were you planning on showing up to St. George's wearing a pillowcase?"

"A valid concern," Sophie agreed solemnly, "if my entire house were to burn down. Otherwise, I thought I'd wear one of the dozens of suitable gowns I already own."

"If I'd known she was going to complain so bitterly, I would have left her at home," Alexandra said to Violet in a stage whisper.

Violet appeared to be enjoying herself thoroughly, though after a moment she did take pity on Sophie and reach over to offer her a consoling pat on the arm. "If it's any comfort," she said, "*I* had to pick out my trousseau in the company of my mother, and was then subjected immediately afterward to an attempt to explain the marital act that frankly was the stuff of nightmares, so I really think you're getting off rather easy." Violet's mother, the Countess of Worthington, was the sort of woman that Sophie would diplomatically describe as "difficult"

247

(and more honestly describe as "nearly insufferable"), so this did indeed make Sophie's own trials seem rather mild by comparison.

She gazed around the shop; Madame Blanchet was fairly new to London, having arrived only a couple of Seasons earlier, but her gowns had already been spotted on several countesses, a couple of marchionesses, and, once, a mistress of one of the royal dukes, which had put her services in considerable demand. The gowns in question—or at least the ones that Sophie had seen herself—tended to be a bit more elaborate (and ruffled) than Sophie's taste inclined toward, but she'd thought it wise not to put up too much of a fuss; it wasn't as if she'd be wearing the resulting gown, after all. Alexandra was the one *actually* getting married, and Sophie was happy for her to have whatever gown she wanted, designed by whomever she wished.

The shop was stuffed to the rafters with bolts of fabric and half-sewn gowns, and the woman in question was bearing down upon them at this very moment, attired in a simple but immaculately tailored gown of pink silk with a lace overlay.

"*Bonjour, mesdames!*" she trilled, the feather stuck somewhat haphazardly into her coiffure vibrating slightly as she spoke. "*Et bienvenue dans ma boutique!*"

"*Bonjour*, madame," Alexandra said. "I am Mrs. Brown-Montague—I believe you received my note?"

"*Oui, oui!*" Madame Blanchet clapped her hands together eagerly. "And I am so eager to help you create the perfect gown for your delightful nuptials—to an earl, *n'est-ce pas?*" A mercenary gleam came into the woman's eye as Alexandra nodded, but Sophie was more amused by the wild fluctuations of the modiste's French accent. This was not unexpected—the majority of so-called French modistes and maids in London had never come closer to France than perhaps casting a longing glance across the Channel from the safety of the Sussex shore—but Sophie was feeling a hint of the devil at her shoulder today, given her mood.

"*Bonjour, madame,*" she said solemnly. "*C'est un plaisir de vous rencontrer et j'ai hâte de bénéficier de votre experience.*"

Madame Blanchet's smile faltered only for a split second before she hitched it back into place. "*Oui . . . madame,*" she said weakly, and then immediately commenced asking Alexandra a very complicated series of questions about which precise *shade* of blue would best flatter her when riding away from the church atop a white horse.

Violet shot a sly sideways smile at Sophie, who smiled serenely back.

". . . but we should really be focusing on Sophie," Alexandra said a minute later, and Sophie felt a brief pang of alarm as she drifted over to her sister's side. "I was thinking that perhaps we could wear matching dresses!" She said this so brightly that it was clear that she hadn't the faintest notion that Sophie would disagree.

Sophie frowned at her sister. "I don't think that's nec—"

"If we're to stand up there together, saying our vows, don't you think it would look lovely if we were color-coordinated?" Alexandra asked. "I was thinking we could wear identical bonnets!" This was suggested in the tones one might use when promising a child a great treat, and Sophie attempted to look appropriately gratified, while privately wondering if perhaps her sister's brain had been addled by the sun. She and Blackford *had* been going on an awful lot of rides together, on fine afternoons; was a sudden fixation on matching wedding bonnets a sign of sunstroke?

"Mmmmm," Sophie said noncommittally.

"And then perhaps if I'm to wear blue, you could wear . . ."

Alexandra trailed off, tapping her chin thoughtfully with her index finger as she regarded Sophie consideringly.

"Pink?" Madame Blanchet suggested. "It would look lovely with her complexion"—she seemed to have adopted an even heavier accent, perhaps hoping that Sophie would assume she spoke some quaint regional dialect Sophie could not hope to understand—"and then the two of you would appear like—what are the flowers, the ones that bloom in the summer?"

"How helpfully specific," Violet murmured.

"Hydrangeas?" Alexandra supplied eagerly.

Madame Blanchet snapped her fingers. "*Exactement*! Perhaps you could both carry bouquets of the *hydrangeas*"—this word was pronounced with great care and an exaggerated attempt at a neutral English accent—"in the color of each other's dresses!"

"I'm not certain—"

"And then," Madame Blanchet forged ahead, ignoring Sophie's rather feeble attempt at interrupting, "we must discuss the ruffles." She said this rather as the Duke of Wellington must have called meetings about battlefield strategy to order.

"I do not think ruffles favor me very much, madame," Sophie said firmly. "I was hoping for something simpler—"

"But, *Sophie*." Alexandra turned a pleading gaze upon her. "It's our *wedding*. Surely you don't want to wear a gown that looks precisely like anything else you might wear!"

This was, in fact, precisely what Sophie would like to wear, had she been left to her own devices. (And had she *actually* been planning to be married.)

"Unless there's some reason that you don't want this wedding to feel like a special occasion?" Alexandra added, all wide-eyed hurt and confusion. "I know—I know—" Her lip began to quiver, always an alarming sign; Alexandra was not terribly weepy by nature, but when a certain mood took her, she could turn into a watering pot with terrifying alacrity. "I *know* it's not a *first* marriage for either of us—that we are no longer in the first bloom of youth—"

"You're three-and-twenty," Sophie said dryly; given that she was four years her sister's senior, she was beginning to feel downright haggard. (Though this sentiment might be directly attributable to this conversation.)

"—and I know that a second marriage ceremony is perhaps not as exciting as the sight of a virginal young bride tripping her way down the aisle at the end of a long, chaste courtship full of longing glances, but I was still hoping that we would find a way to make it feel special." Alexandra's eyes had turned downright misty at this point, and even Violet was giving Sophie a mildly reproachful look. "And I wanted to share it with *you*," Alexandra concluded, then fished in her sleeve for a handkerchief, which she pressed to her mouth as if overcome with emotion.

Sophie, feeling as though she'd just weathered a long military campaign, reached out and patted Alexandra on the arm. "You're right—I'm sorry." She turned a pained smile upon Madame Blanchet, who was regarding this exchange with a somber, funereal air, but who perked up immediately upon seeing Sophie's look of resigned acceptance. "Madame Blanchet, I defer to your expertise."

"*Très bien!*" the modiste said brightly. "Shall I show you the feathered bonnet I had in mind?"

"And perhaps a new gown for your betrothal ball would be in order, too, Sophie," Violet put in helpfully, and Sophie cast her a look of wounded betrayal.

Alexandra clasped her hands together in delight, and Sophie sighed.

There was a particular kind of torture that came in the form of being trapped in a closed carriage with a woman one had recently bedded, then quarreled with, and West was currently suffering as its victim.

Sophie had sent him a note the previous afternoon, notifying him that her sister had requested their presence at dinner at her house, which was how he found himself here, sitting opposite his supposed fiancée, an uncomfortable silence hovering between them. More than a week had passed since they'd quarreled; he'd seen her at a dinner party and a ball since then, but by unspoken agreement, they'd avoided spending much time alone together, until now, in his silent carriage.

He was not a stranger to these silences—in the past year, as his orbit and Sophie's had been drawn slowly closer by the tangled web of mutual friends and family that they shared, he'd found himself in her presence more often than he'd wished. But no—that wasn't entirely true, was it? He was growing tired of lying to himself about what, precisely, he wished where Sophie was concerned. But it had certainly been more often than was wise, and he'd grown used to the awkwardness and weight of the silence that had often descended on these occasions—a stroll through a garden on an estate in Wiltshire; a silent walk through the corridors of Belfry's theater, where they'd happened to arrive at precisely the same moment. Sophie was better at these moments than he was; for all that he'd been raised the son of a duke, trained to be nothing but gallant at all times, his instincts seemed to abandon him in these encounters, and he often found himself biting his tongue, uncertain what to say to her. She, however, always had a polite word about the weather, or a piece of news to share—anything to lighten the mood even a little.

Which was why it was so telling that she was not making the slightest effort to do so this evening. Instead, she was staring fixedly out the window as they rattled through Mayfair, her face looking strained in the light of the carriage's lamps.

At last, moments before they drew to a halt outside her sister's house, she glanced at him, her expression unreadable. "We'll still need to put on a good show for Alexandra."

He swallowed a wave of bitterness—he *had* agreed to this, after all. And any man of sense might have known that his heart would emerge a bit bruised—he could hardly lay the blame for that at her feet, not when this outcome had seemed all but predestined. "Of course," he said shortly, and reached for his cane as the door opened.

"West! Sophie!" Alexandra called gaily, as soon as they were ushered into the drawing room by a footman. "Won't you join us for a tipple before dinner?" She took a sip from a small glass of sherry, and Blackford, who was shaking West's hand, held a glass of brandy.

"We're a bit informal tonight, as it's only the four of us," Blackford said, bowing over Sophie's hand and inclining his head toward the sideboard along one wall. "Can I tempt you?"

West exchanged a quick glance with Sophie, who shrugged and nodded, and in short order she was sipping a sherry of her own, while West was enjoying a glass of quite excellent brandy.

"We'll be dining on the terrace," Alexandra explained, gesturing at the French doors that were flung open to admit a warm breeze, "since we're so few in numbers, and it's such a pleasant evening."

West thought that he and Sophie managed a fairly convincing

show as they sat with their drinks; Alexandra carried much of the conversation with a lengthy anecdote about Lady Wexham's increasingly elaborate ideas for the betrothal ball she'd be hosting the following week, and soon enough they were seated at a small table on the terrace, illuminated by candles and the clear light of a low-hanging moon.

Once the soup course had been brought out and the wineglasses filled, Alexandra lifted hers. "A toast, perhaps? To second chances." Her gaze was on her sister as she spoke, wide-eyed and innocent.

West carefully did not look at Sophie as he clinked glasses with the others; for her part, Sophie was quick to find another topic of conversation.

"This soup is *delicious*," she said quickly—a compliment that might have been more convincing, had she waited to actually taste said soup before offering it.

"I did not think you so fond of soup, Soph," Alexandra said, sounding amused.

"Well," Sophie said a bit weakly, "it's so . . . liquid."

West looked at her skeptically, which provoked a glare from her in response.

"It has been a long day," he said smoothly to Alexandra and Blackford. "We went riding on Rotten Row this afternoon"—a lie—"and it was terribly hot. We might have got a bit too much sun."

He could feel Sophie's glare, and reflected that she likely did not appreciate his implying that she was suffering from sunstroke, but he ignored her; until she stopped waxing rhapsodic about soup, he was perfectly happy to let the others think she was experiencing a temporary bout of sun-induced insanity. They were English, after all; they could not be expected to function under these conditions.

"Have you gone back to Madame Blanchet for another fitting,

Sophie?" Alexandra asked a minute later, her gaze on her sister still mildly concerned. "She did say she'd write when she had something for you to try on."

"Not yet," Sophie said cautiously taking a dainty spoonful of soup. "She wrote yesterday to invite me in for another visit, but I've yet to reply." She paused, her spoon halfway to her mouth. "But wait. Haven't *you* received a note? I can't think why I should have received one and not you."

Alexandra looked momentarily flustered, but recovered quickly. "Indeed!" she said, perhaps a bit too brightly. "She—er—rushed mine, at my request. I went in a few days ago for another fitting."

Sophie frowned. "Why should she rush yours and not mine? We're to be married on the same day."

"Er," Alexandra said, "she thought that I might be more challenging to fit. Due to a ... feminine complaint."

The entire table went silent, contemplating the implications of this. Alexandra blushed rosily, apparently belatedly realizing it, too.

"Not *that* sort of feminine complaint," she said hastily. "More of an issue of ... er ... unusual hip-to-waist ratio."

"Indeed?" Sophie sounded exceedingly skeptical. "I've never heard you complain of any such thing before."

"Well," Alexandra said, seeming to fully commit to this mildly unhinged explanation, "I didn't wish to mention it to you, but my last modiste noted—apparently dresses have been fitting me incorrectly for *years* and no one had thought to mention it." She offered a trembling lip by way of conveying her wounded dignity. "You cannot imagine how traumatizing it was to receive this information."

"About your ... hips." Sophie sounded unconvinced.

"About my hips," Alexandra confirmed.

"I do not believe this is a portion of your anatomy I am supposed to believe even exists," Blackford observed, to no one in particular.

Sophie and Alexandra appeared to take no notice of him, their eyes still fixed upon each other, some sort of silent conversation occurring.

"West has promised to take me on a wedding trip!" Sophie announced, without preamble.

West, who had a glass of claret halfway to his mouth, froze for a moment, then set said wineglass down carefully on the table. "I have?" he inquired mildly. Sophie looked at him sternly. "I *have*," he amended, offering Alexandra a bland smile. Sensing that a bit more was expected of him, he added, "The thought of seeing my beloved in the bright sunshine of—" He looked inquiringly at Sophie.

"Italy," Sophie reminded him.

"Italy," he agreed smoothly, "was too tempting a prospect to ignore." He was gripped by a sudden image of Sophie, sun-kissed and tousle-haired, sitting on a balcony in some warm Continental city, glancing invitingly over her shoulder at him, and he was pierced by a pang of longing.

"What a charming idea," Alexandra said brightly, her stare still unblinking upon Sophie. "So terribly *romantic*. You must tell me the itinerary you've planned, so that Blackford and I might take inspiration for *our* wedding trip."

Blackford blinked. "*Are* we going on a wedding trip?"

"We are now," Alexandra informed him. She looked back at her sister. "I don't suppose you recall the precise sites you plan to visit, on this entirely well-planned wedding trip?"

"I should have to consult my notes at home," Sophie said through gritted teeth.

"Naturally, naturally." Alexandra waved her hand. "I shall call on you tomorrow, then?"

"I did not think you such an avid traveler, Alexandra," Sophie said, watching her sister with a narrow-eyed expression.

"Funny," Alexandra said sharply. "I was just thinking the same thing of *you*."

Blackford was looking at West in silent inquiry, which West ignored. Mercifully, the next course arrived, disrupting whatever alarming, unspoken battle of wills Sophie and her sister were presently engaged in, and together Blackford and West were able to steer the conversation into less openly combative territory.

He wasted no time, however, on the carriage ride home.

"Would you care to explain to me precisely what you and your sister were doing at dinner?" he asked conversationally, the moment the carriage door had shut behind them.

Sophie turned to him indignantly. "She suspects something! Can't you tell?"

"Even if she does, I fail to see how concocting an elaborate Continental holiday was the best diversionary tactic."

"That is because you don't have sisters," Sophie said with a dismissive wave. "She was trying to *goad* me into admitting something! As if I would be so easily cowed! Younger sisters might think that they have certain tricks up their sleeves, but they should know better than to attempt to outwit an elder sister of superior wisdom and experience." She flicked an invisible speck of dust off her sleeve, looking quite pleased with herself.

"This is absurd." West crossed his arms over his chest, watching her narrowly. "Have you given any thought to how we are going to extract ourselves from this supposed betrothal, now that we've tangled ourselves up so deeply?"

"As a matter of fact, I thought we might stage an argument at the betrothal ball."

"The ball that your mother is going to considerable effort to host, and that your sister is evidently looking forward to with great anticipation, designed to celebrate what is supposed to be one of the happiest events of her life?"

Sophie leaned forward, frowning. "I'm not suggesting we quarrel on the ballroom floor in front of all the guests, but if we can arrange for Alexandra to stumble upon us mid-argument, later in the evening, then she won't be entirely surprised when we announce the end of our betrothal shortly after—but by that point, *she* will be too publicly committed to Blackford for her to call off *their* wedding."

"I see." He leaned back in his seat, still watching her carefully. "Have you—as part of your careful plan—considered what our supposed quarrel is to be about?"

She looked away now, her fingers worrying at the beading on her reticule. "I don't see why we couldn't use the truth of the issues between us, to some extent—the fact that your position, your family, make it impossible for us to marry."

"Ah." He paused briefly. "You wish to lie, then."

Her gaze shot back to his, startled. "It's not a lie!"

"No." His tone was firm. "It's the story you've concocted for yourself, in your head, because you've decided that I'm too much trouble to take on—but it's not *true*." He pressed his lips together. "I will suffer much for you, but I do have to draw the line at allowing you to believe a fiction—though you were perfectly content to allow me to do so, for the better part of seven years."

"I have *explained* to you why I could not marry you!"

"And I understand your reasons better now—but if you will not marry me now, I would like us to at *least* be clear on the reasons."

"You haven't—we haven't—" Sophie lifted her hands in frustration, and West relished the sight; he could not bear to discuss these matters with her if she appeared cool and unmoved. He was grateful for any sign that she was as moved as he was—even by anger, at the moment.

"If I thought there was the slightest chance that you would have me, I would be on my knees before you in an instant," he said quietly.

She blew out an exasperated breath. "This is ridiculous—you can't even pretend to be in love with me without us quarreling."

He lifted a brow. "I'm finding it's the pretending *not* to be in love with you that is the problem, actually."

That, at least, momentarily shocked her into silence. West, for his part, was darkly amused—had she really not known? Or had she merely not thought he would dare to say it?

At last, after a long moment, she sighed, her expression sad. "Love is not enough of a basis for a marriage, West—not if it comes at the cost of everything else one holds dear. I would not ask that of you—I would not wait to see if you came to regret it." Her voice was quiet, calm, but West knew her well enough still—always—to detect the note of sadness, of *longing* that ran beneath her words.

And suddenly, he understood.

He understood it *all*.

"You're frightened," he said, and she blinked, a faint crease forming between her eyebrows.

"I don't—"

"You're frightened that I wouldn't choose you, above everything else. Or that if I did, I would regret it."

A hint of color appeared in her cheeks—a telling sign in a woman who was not prone to blushes. West noted this, but did not linger on the thought; he was gripped with the giddy certainty of the truth of his words, his thoughts dwelling on the entire history of his courtship with Sophie, of all the heartbreak in their past—

And he felt nearly close to laughter. Because it all made sense, at last.

"Tell me what I have to do to prove to you that I mean it." He reached out and gripped her hand, the contact electric even through his glove and hers. "Tell me what I must do to prove to you that I wouldn't regret it—that you are *everything* to me."

"You can't!" she burst out. "This isn't *Romeo and Juliet*—I'm not going to drink poison just because the only man I've ever loved can't marry me! I *like* my life—and I think you like yours—and I don't want you to destroy everything you've worked for, that you care about, simply because you think we're the characters in some sort of romantic tragedy!"

The carriage drew to a halt, startling them both; they'd been so preoccupied by their argument that they hadn't realized they'd reached Sophie's house already. She gathered her reticule, waiting to alight, but just as the door creaked open and she prepared to rise, West reached out and gripped her elbow, drawing her startled gaze back to his.

"I do not think our story is a tragedy, Sophie," he said quietly, his eyes locked on hers. "I think it is a love story—a romance, like one of those novels by Miss Austen that Violet is always banging on about." He released her elbow, and leaned back in his seat as the carriage door opened fully, allowing Sophie to depart. "And I am going to prove it to you."

Chapter Twenty-One

The air was damp and the sky foreboding as West made his way to his father's house the next day. Clouds had begun to gather overhead before he left home, and by the time he arrived in Berkeley Square, the first raindrops had started to fall. West leaned a bit more heavily than usual on his cane as he ascended the front steps—damp weather always seemed to aggravate the pain in his leg—and he nodded at his father's butler, who informed him that His Grace was in the library.

"I'll show myself in, thank you, Jennings," West said, making his way up the stairs before the butler could protest. The library was just off the second-floor landing, and West offered a brief tap at the door in warning, but did not wait for a reply before he entered.

"West." The duke looked up in surprise from where he sat in an armchair, reading a letter. He folded the letter and set it aside on a side table as West approached, though West caught enough of a glimpse of the handwriting to suspect that it came from a woman. He'd never been privy to much of his father's personal life; once, years earlier, James had asked him idly if he thought their father had a mistress—it had been nearly two decades at that point since their mother's death, after all—and West had paused, startled, to contemplate. It was difficult to reconcile the stern, unyielding man who had raised him with the idea of a man who might be capable of great tenderness toward a woman. He'd always imagined his father employing a series of short-term mistresses he could set up in tidy little houses kept safely away from the rest of his life, but it was difficult to imagine any of *those* women sending him a letter.

There was so much about his father that he did not understand—because his father had ensured that this was the case.

"What brings you here this afternoon?" his father asked, watching him carefully. They had not spoken since Sophie had informed West of her meeting with the duke at Hookham's; West had even sent a note of excuse for their usual Sunday night dinners the past two weeks, claiming that he had other engagements. He'd half-expected his father to show up on his doorstep, demanding an explanation for his absence, and for his supposed betrothal, but his father seemed to be waiting him out.

"I was out with Lady Fitzwilliam," he said casually, "and happened to be passing your house on my way home."

"Ah."

West ignored the multiple open chairs near his father's, instead taking a slow, circuitous route around the room. The duke did not speak, apparently aware that he was engaged in a high-stakes chess game with his son, waiting to see what move West would make next.

"I was thinking, Father, about our discussion a few weeks ago." West came to a halt before the fireplace—empty today—and studied the portrait above the mantel: one that had been painted before James's birth, of the duke and his duchess and their toddler heir. Judging by the age West appeared to be, his mother would have been expecting James at the time, but the artist had carefully arranged the scene so that her pregnancy was not visible. The duke dandled West on his knee, and his wife had a hand on the duke's elbow, her expression serene.

West had often wondered how James felt whenever he entered this room, seeing a portrait given pride of place that did not even acknowledge his existence ... but West had never paused to consider how *he* felt.

His relationship with his father had always been a complex one: There was less of the tension that characterized the duke's dealings with James, particularly in recent years, but instead the weight of expectation, the knowledge that his father had devoted his life to his title, and that he expected West to do the same. Everything about this seemed encapsulated in that portrait above the mantel: the fact that he was in his father's arms, rather than his mother's; the fact, too, that his father did not hold him close, affectionately, but rather stiffly displayed him for the viewer's eye.

I have done my duty, he seemed to be saying.

And West knew that—in his father's eyes—he was failing to do his. Never mind the years of his childhood he'd spent following his father around his various estates, the hours upon hours he'd spent in his father's study, learning how to perform the role he'd been born to. Never mind that he'd excelled at school—first at Eton, then Oxford. Even his attempts at youthful high spirits and dalliance had been tame compared to those of his friends, the knowledge always lingering at the back of his mind that he was to be a duke someday, that other men would look up to him.

And then there had been the matter of choosing a wife.

He turned.

"Which discussion was this?" his father asked, his tone a master class in studied disinterest. "I have many conversations with many people over the course of a day, you know—I can't say that every single one lingers in my mind."

This was a lie. His father had an unusually good memory.

"I thought this one might have been a bit more memorable," West said pleasantly. "You seemed to be ... *threatening* me. If I did not marry." He shook his head, as if amused by his own foolishness. "I am sure I must have misunderstood, however. I cannot think that you would do such a thing to your son and heir." A pause, and then, his voice harder, he added, "Particularly not one whose happiness you have already destroyed once in the past."

His father's eyes locked upon him. "Is that what this is about, then?" he asked quietly. "Is this some sort of revenge?"

West inhaled slowly; he'd always been adept at keeping his temper where his father was concerned, even when it sorely tried his patience to do so. "Is my planning to marry the woman I've loved for the past seven years *revenge*, Father? No." He shook his head. "Though it is certainly very illustrative, in terms of your character, that you would think so."

The duke rose to his feet now, evidently deciding that this was not a conversation he wished to conduct at a disadvantage. "You are perfectly well aware that when I speculated as to the future of Rosemere," he said, "Lady Fitzwilliam was not the bride I had in mind for you."

"And *you* are perfectly well aware," West shot back, "that I am an adult with a mind of my own, capable of making my own decisions—and unwilling to allow you to arrange the details of my life to your liking."

"There is nothing stopping me from carrying out that threat," his father warned. "You have no claim to Rosemere." *Yet.* "The property is in my name and unentailed, and I am certain I could find a willing buyer—indeed, it will likely be easier to do so, now that you've devoted so much time and care to its upkeep."

"This is true," West agreed thoughtfully, and some small part of him rejoiced at the quick raising of his father's brows, a small tell—one that he ordinarily would have been careful to hide. West must truly have him rattled. "But it's equally true that there is nothing stopping me from marrying Lady Fitzwilliam—tomorrow, if I wished to."

"Called the banns, have you?" his father asked skeptically.

"Belfry was able to obtain a special license when he married Lady Emily, you know—evidently the Archbishop of Canterbury is an old family friend." West picked up a vase from the mantel, examined the maker's mark painted on its underside, and carefully set it down again. "It is useful to have connections, I find."

His father took several slow, measured steps toward him. "Do not attempt to bluff with me, West," he said softly. "Not when you've so much more to lose than I do."

In that moment, West felt nothing so much as an overwhelming sadness for his father—because he actually thought this was true. He thought that West had everything to lose, but seemed incapable of realizing that West had far, far more to gain.

Rosemere was important to him—it had once belonged to his mother, and he had spent years as its caretaker. The work had made him feel close to her, to a woman he barely remembered. And he cared for his tenants, had worked hard to ensure that they were treated fairly and protected. The thought of giving it up caused a sharp pain deep within him. But when compared to Sophie—

"I'll see about sending you the account books for Rosemere," he said, reaching out to shake his father's hand. "So that whoever the new owner is can see that it is well cared for."

"West." The duke sounded almost . . . uncertain. West was not sure that he'd ever heard his father sound this way. "She can't possibly be worth this."

West met his father's gaze directly. "The fact that you still think that, after all this time, proves to me that we've nothing further to discuss." He paused, then added, "I suppose you have received Lady Wexham's invitation to our betrothal ball?"

His father's voice was curt. "Indeed."

"I expect to see you there, then," West said, and turned without waiting for a reply. He could not prevent himself from slowing his steps a bit, hoping in vain that his father would call after him—but he did not allow himself to come to a stop, and he walked out the door with his head held high.

Sophie was leaving her solicitor's office after a meeting with him a couple of days later when she found West awaiting her outside, standing beside his phaeton.

She raised an eyebrow at him as she approached. "I do not recall that we had an engagement."

West extended a hand, which she took. "It's a fine day, and I thought I might persuade you to go on a drive with me in the park."

She looked around with exaggerated curiosity, seeking the carriage she'd arrived in.

West cleared his throat. "I might have taken the liberty of sending your driver home, after promising that I'd see you there safely."

"I shall be having a word with him," Sophie said, allowing him to help her climb up into the phaeton. "If he permits any ruffian off the street to announce himself my escort and relieve him of his duties, I think he needs a scolding."

"Yes," West agreed gravely, climbing up beside her. "I shall certainly support you in that endeavor, should I ever notice a ruffian attempting such a thing."

Sophie bit back a smile, then cast him a glance out of the corner of her eye. She hadn't seen him in a couple of days, he having been called out of town on a matter of business overnight; he looked in incredibly good spirits, and she could not suppress the smile that crossed her own face at the sight. He was so often stern and solemn that his good moods always proved infectious to her; no doubt they presented a picture of a blissfully joyous affianced couple to any members of the *ton* they might have unknowingly driven past.

The park was full of other riders and carriages, and their conversation was frequently interrupted over the next three-quarters of an hour by the numerous acquaintances they had to greet. When at last they pulled up before Sophie's house, however, she turned to face him full-on.

"Would you like to come in?" she asked.

His gaze flicked to the houses that surrounded hers; he was no doubt envisioning unseen eyes peering through the curtains down at them. "I wouldn't want to cause any gossip that might damage your reputation," he said, a faint crease appearing between his eyebrows. She wanted to reach out with her thumb and smooth away that crease.

"I think it is acceptable for a man to pay a call upon his fiancée for a few minutes," she said, smiling at him. She leaned forward and added in an undertone, "It just means that we'll have to be fast."

She wondered, for a moment, if he would take her up on this

offer—they had not gone to bed together since the night of his dinner party, and the quarrel that followed. Their discussion after dinner with Alexandra and Blackford a few days earlier had not resolved matters; if anything, it had left Sophie more confused than ever. Some reckless mood seemed to have West in its grip, however, and so in short order Sophie found herself pressed up against the door of her drawing room, being kissed within an inch of her life. Her hat had been tossed aside, her gloves discarded, and a sudden breath of cool air on her thighs made her realize that, while she'd been distracted by his mouth, he'd been inching her skirts up her legs. She hooked a leg around his hips, pulling him closer, feeling his hardness against her stomach. Her hands were in the short hairs at the nape of his neck, and she tore her mouth away from his to let out a shuddering gasp when she felt his fingers between her legs.

"Perhaps—the settee?" she said in his ear, and he allowed her to pull back enough to drag him by the hand across the room and shove him down before her on the emerald-green brocade settee. There was color in his cheeks, and his dark hair was mussed from her hands. His green eyes were darker than usual, and he was looking at her with naked want. He looked utterly delicious.

"Unbutton your breeches," she said, barely recognizing the commanding note in her voice, and his hands immediately went to the placket on his breeches. "Now touch yourself," she added, and he obeyed, stroking with a sure hand. She could wait no longer, however, and lifted her skirts into one hand as she climbed onto his lap, her knees straddling his thighs, took him in hand, and sank down onto him. A groan tore from his throat, a low, broken sound, and she pressed her face to his neck, tugging at his cravat to loosen it enough that she might inhale the scent of his skin. From there, it was a fast race to completion, no words exchanged between them other than breath-less gasps and moans. He slid his hand between them, stroking with his thumb, and she shattered around him; moments later, he withdrew and spilled onto her thigh.

For a minute or two, there was no sound but their breathing. West's arms were loose around her waist, her face still pressed to his neck. At some point, he began to stroke up and down the length of her back, his fingers running gently over the knobs of her spine. One hand toyed with a curl that had come loose from her coiffure.

"Are you aware," Sophie asked thoughtfully, when at last she'd recovered the power of speech, "that your butler and your valet are conducting an affair?"

She felt his mouth curve into a smile against her hair. "How did you work it out?"

"You know?"

"Of course I know—I live in the same house with them. How oblivious do you think I am?"

Sophie paused diplomatically; West very nearly spluttered. "It's not *you*, specifically," she reassured him as she attempted to extract herself from his lap, rather inelegantly. West pulled a handkerchief from his jacket pocket and handed it to her, which she quickly made use of. "It's, well . . . men don't tend to be very observant about these things," she explained as she fluffed her skirts around her and attempted to regain as much dignity as was possible when one had recently had the fingers of the man one was conversing with between one's legs.

"Well, perhaps I am a bit more observant than the average man, then," he said, a hint of smugness in his voice. "A fact that you may have, on recent occasions, had cause to appreciate."

Annoyingly, he was not wrong. He was the third man she'd gone to bed with, and she had not known it was possible for a man to pay such close *attention* to her in the act of love. She felt, when she was lying beneath him (or above him, as was more immediately relevant), as though he was paying attention to every movement, every sigh she uttered, making a careful note of what she liked. It was . . .

Well, it was rather nice, she thought primly.

"Perhaps," she allowed, with a slow hint of a saucy smile.

He cleared his throat. "In any case, yes, I'm aware—Hawthorne and I were friends in boyhood, you know."

Sophie nodded; he'd spoken of him on more than one occasion, when they'd been courting when they were younger.

"We were . . . well, we were as close as two boys of such vastly differing stations could be, and when it was time for me to go away to university, I took him with me as my valet. Village life had become a bit . . . untenable for him, by then. It's not an easy place to be, if you've a secret to keep."

"He told you?"

"I caught him," West said. "With the valet of one of the house-guests my father was hosting, when I was sixteen or so. I promised him I'd never tell anyone, and I was happy enough to take him with me—I needed a valet, and he needed an escape. And it was nice to have someone who knew me as *me*, rather than as a future duke, which I'd pretty quickly learned was how almost everyone else saw me."

"And Briar . . . ?"

"I needed a butler when I came down to London to set up my own residence, and he is Wooton's nephew," West said, naming James's butler, who had originally been employed by the duke. "So I took him on, even though he was young, because he was damned good, and it wasn't long before I became aware of a certain number of lingering looks in my household. It's no bother to me, so long as Hawthorne doesn't become so lovestruck he stops being able to tie my cravat or shine my shoes."

Sophie recalled noting, on her first visit to West's London residence, how small a household he maintained for a man in his position, and wondered if this was part of the reason—a certain amount of discretion would be desired. And then too, the thought struck her that things like this—small, private things about West that most of society was unaware of—had always represented, to her, the non-ducal side of him. Proof, in her mind, that they could be happy if only he were not to one day be a duke—did not have the responsibilities that went with his position. Now, however, it occurred to her how wonderful it would be, knowing that such a thoroughly *decent* man was a duke. How much better the lives of the people who relied upon him would be, once he inherited his title. And that *this*—his small kindnesses, and his weightier responsibilities, and his inherent decency—was all part and parcel of who he was, and why she . . .

Why she loved him.

"Dare I ask what on earth Briar and Hawthorne's relationship has to do with anything?" West asked, interrupting her thoughts.

Sophie did not pause to consider before answering with complete honesty. "I was trying to think of something to say that might distract you before you could ask me to marry you." She paused. "Also, I've been meaning to ask you about it, and haven't found a good time until now. It seemed . . . thematically appropriate." She gestured at their disordered clothing.

This surprised a laugh out of him—not a polite chuckle but a *real* laugh, one that lit up his face and that made her laugh in turn.

"I don't know why you are constantly accusing *me* of being on the verge of dropping down to one knee, when *you* are the one who recently asked me to act as your fiancé. Perhaps I should be the one who is skittish." There was a faint note of teasing in his voice, a lightness that was so rarely evident in his conversation, and it made Sophie's chest ache to hear. She had thought—had feared—that the weight of the guilt they shared, over all that had happened seven years earlier, would be an insurmountable obstacle to any future they might have had. Now, however, she realized how much lighter she had felt, these recent weeks, having someone to discuss those events with—someone who had experienced the same pain and guilt that she had. It gave her an inkling of what a future between them could be like—one in which they helped each other lay those ghosts to rest—and she liked the thought of it far too well.

She did not mind his sternness—she loved it, because it was so integral to who he was—but the small hint of a smile tugging at the corners of his mouth now was so terribly dear.

He was so terribly dear. To her. He always had been—which frightened her as much now as it had seven years ago, as she'd stood at the door of his father's house, waiting to hear whether he was alive or dead.

And, she realized in a rush, had he not accused her of this very thing—of fear—just a few days earlier? She had laughed it off as she made ready for bed that evening, offering Fox one-word answers about the evening as her thoughts had churned in her head.

"You're right," she said, and she still felt so startled by this realization that she didn't know what else to say—how to begin to confront the enormity of what she now knew to be true. How to proceed now that she'd acknowledged it.

He, however, was not privy to her thoughts—and indeed seemed wrapped up in his own. "You know, I have never wished to be wanted solely for my title, or my fortune," he said quietly. "But it's something I resigned myself to, long ago—the possibility that I might marry a woman who only wanted me for those things, who saw me less as a man than as a prize. And who am I to complain about such an arrangement, when it is no worse than what most women of the *ton* suffer when they make their debuts on the marriage mart? But," he added, and his gaze on her was piercing, "I found, to my surprise, that there is something I minded even more."

"Oh?" Her voice was hoarse.

"Being *not* wanted, on account of my title. By the only person I'd ever truly wanted—and who I knew wanted me. But just not badly enough." These last words were spoken even more quietly—so quietly that she had to lean forward in order to hear. She felt them like a knife slipped through her ribs.

"And I thought, after all this time, I'd resigned myself to it—to the reality of us. That there never would *be* an us. But these past few weeks have reminded me of what existed between us—what *still* exists." He stood and began to pace the length of the drawing room before her, his steps slow. "I do not know how to convince you that I do not care if you bear me no sons, or ten. I do not know how to convince you that you matter more to me than my father, or a house, or a piece of land—that I would weather any threat from him, if it meant that I could be with you. I do not know how to convince you that I would do whatever is within my power to protect your family—your sisters—from any damage he might do. All I can do is tell you that I have never lied to you—nor have I ever made a promise I have been unable to keep. And I promise you now, I am prepared to do whatever it takes to marry you."

His back was to her now, he facing the empty fireplace. Sophie was dimly aware of the sound of birds chirping outside, carriages rattling past in the square. It was as if she'd briefly forgotten the rest of the world existed, and now it was seeping back into the room.

He turned. "I paid my father a visit the day before yesterday, and informed him I'd have all of Rosemere's account books sent to him."

Sophie blinked. "You—what?"

"The account books," he repeated slowly. Evenly. "So that he might sell the property—or do whatever he damn well pleases with it. I'm not sacrificing you for a bloody *house*, Sophie—not when you already made that choice once."

She opened her mouth to protest, and he raised a hand to quiet her. "I understand—I do." He took a step toward her, and stopped, swallowing. "I just don't want to make the same choice again now."

Sophie rose and stepped toward him, weighing her words. She reached out a hand to him. "You were right, the other evening," she said quietly. "I was—I *am*—afraid." She took a deep breath. "I'm afraid you're willing to give up too much for me, and that you'd regret it someday. I'm afraid we'd marry, and you'd find yourself without the estate you've cared for all these years, without an heir to carry on the ducal line—with only . . ."

"You?" His voice was low, amused. His grip on her hand tightened. "There is no *only* when it comes to you, Sophie." He tugged on her hand, drawing her toward him. He stood, framed by sunlight against the window, so beautiful that it made her throat ache to look at him. "I have the rest of it now—I have Rosemere; if I wanted a young wife who could bear me ten children, I've no doubt I could find one this very evening. But I don't *care*, because I only want you—and I don't have you." He cast a wry glance at Sophie's hair, still mussed from their interlude on the settee. "Not in the way that matters, at least." He reached a hand out, slowly, to cup her cheek, his palm warm against her skin. "I love you, and the only future I want is one with you in it. Please tell me what I have to do to make you believe me."

Sophie closed her eyes against the intensity of his gaze, pressing her cheek into his hand. And she realized that she *did* believe him. He'd just shown her he was willing to give up the very thing she'd been so afraid of him sacrificing for her—and she realized, too, that it was not *her* decision to make. It was not her right to tell him what he should or shouldn't give up for her. She was so afraid of him regretting it, being unhappy, because she loved him—she *loved* him—but—

But now *she* was the one making him unhappy. His father would always be there—would always disapprove. Might or might not try to make his disapproval known in other ways; might or might not try to make their lives more difficult than they needed to be.

But in this moment, it was Sophie who was choosing unhappiness for them—and she didn't wish to do so for a single moment longer.

She opened her eyes. "I love you, too," she said softly, turning her head to press a soft kiss into his palm. She stepped forward, reaching up to rest her hands against his chest. "I love you, and I am tired of allowing your father to dictate how we live our lives, and I just want—I just want—I just want *us* to decide for ourselves!" She was, she noticed vaguely, growing rather angry. She was standing here, having just told her beloved that she loved him, and yet she was *still* thinking about his *bloody father* and it was—

Honestly, extremely annoying.

West looped an arm around her waist, pulling her closer to him, and Sophie tilted her head up for his kiss. "I never knew escorting a lady home from the solicitor could be so momentous an occasion," he murmured against her mouth, and tilted her head back to allow him access to her jaw, and the long line of her throat.

Sophie huffed out a laugh, closing her eyes against the sensation of the warmth of his mouth at her neck—

And then his words registered. And her eyes flew open. And a small smile began to tug at her mouth.

Because suddenly, she had a very, very good idea.

Chapter Twenty-Two

Sophie supposed, after twenty-seven years' acquaintance with the Viscountess Wexham, she should no longer be surprised by the extent to which her mother obsessed over every detail of a party. And surely the occasion of the engagement of not one, but *two* of her daughters would aggravate this existing tendency to a degree that bordered on absurd.

This was why, one week later, Sophie found herself standing in the ballroom of her parents' Mayfair home, listening to her mother opine at length about how many candles was *too* many candles.

"We want to look well-lit, not vulgar."

"Indeed," Sophie murmured, catching Alexandra's eye and suppressing a smile with some difficulty. "Given the other details of the wedding, *clearly* we don't wish to be seen as vulgar."

Alexandra narrowed her eyes at her. "Do you have a complaint to voice, Sophie?"

"Not at all," Sophie demurred, turning in a slow circle to admire the afternoon light spilling into the ballroom through the enormous windows. "I am merely looking forward to experiencing the wedding of your dreams."

"If you have some objection to raise, I'd be delighted to hear it,"

Alexandra said, lowering her voice slightly so that their mother—now debating, apparently with herself, whether potted plants encouraged licentiousness—would not overhear. "For if there is something about the plan for our wedding that is upsetting you, I'd naturally be *more* than happy to remedy it. It's your wedding, too, after all." She paused with deliberate care. "Isn't it?"

"Of course," Sophie agreed. She had been avoiding Alexandra this past week. She'd already suspected that her sister guessed some of what was afoot between her and West, and today's conversation merely served to confirm it. Maintaining a healthy distance seemed the safest option for all involved.

"I had the most interesting conversation with Maria recently," Sophie said idly. "She reminded me of how much you complained about the fuss of your first wedding." She paused deliberately. "I'm so overjoyed to see you've had such a change of heart in that regard."

She was rather curious to see how Alexandra would respond to *that*, but before her sister had a chance to do so, they were interrupted—their mother seemed to have belatedly noticed their lack of attention.

"Girls!" cried Lady Wexham, for all that the "girls" in question had both been married and widowed. "I need you to focus on what is important: How likely do you think it that someone loses their virtue behind a potted palm?" She paused to consider her own question. "Or do you think the fronds would get in the way of any lewd behavior?"

Sophie—and, from the looks of her, Alexandra, too—had not the slightest idea of how to respond to this query, but it did prove successful at driving her simmering quarrel with her sister out of mind.

For the moment.

It was the next day—the day of the betrothal ball, at last—and Sophie was seated in her library, enjoying a leisurely cup of afternoon tea while attempting to read the book Jane had loaned her, about a haunted house that did not actually appear to be remotely haunted, when Grimball opened the door and announced solemnly, "Mrs. Brown-Montague."

"Hello," Sophie said, glancing up in surprise as her sister sailed into the room. "What on earth are you doing here? I assumed you'd be tormenting your lady's maid by not being able to make up your mind which hairstyle you wanted for tonight."

"Ha," Alexandra said, sinking down next to Sophie on the settee beneath the window. Her dark hair was coiled at the back of her head, and she was dressed for riding. "I've been in the park with Harriet, actually, and thought I would stop by on the way home. I haven't much time—I've a footman waiting for me outside. But I wanted to discuss tonight with you."

Sophie set her book aside, a dark pang of foreboding in her chest at her sister's tone. "What about tonight?"

"It's very important to Mama, you know," Alexandra said briskly, and Sophie nearly rolled her eyes.

"I'm well aware, thank you. Or have you not noticed the multiple notes per day from her about everything from the number of candles to whether ratafia is still served in the best houses?"

Alexandra ignored this. "I would hate for Mama's memory of tonight to be tarnished in any way."

Sophie narrowed her eyes at her sister. "In what way, precisely?"

Alexandra took a deep breath. "If, for example, it should come to light that you were feigning a betrothal."

A brief silence fell. Sophie was a bit impressed; she had not thought her sister would come out and say it so bluntly, but clearly Alexandra had had enough of the elaborate farce that had been playing out for more than a month—and Sophie, for her part, was entirely in agreement with this sentiment.

"I suppose this is the part where I'm supposed to tell you that you're entirely mistaken and I've not the faintest notion what you're referring to."

"You could, I suppose, if you wished to be incredibly irritating. But I'd personally prefer it if you didn't, and if you told me the truth instead."

"The truth," Sophie repeated, considering her words carefully. "The truth is, I'm not engaged to West, and I *did* ask him to feign a betrothal, solely so that you'd agree to marry Blackford." It felt liberating to speak these words aloud; West had confessed to James, but she'd had no such opportunity, and admitting it made her feel like a weight was being lifted.

"I knew it," Alexandra said. She eyed her sister narrowly. "I didn't think you'd admit it so readily, though."

Sophie threw her hands up in the air. "What was the point in denying it, if you'd already worked it out? I promise not to spoil Mama's night, by the way—I can't believe you think I would."

"You were hardly behaving like yourself, this past month—if you didn't plan to go through with the wedding, then I presume you've some sort of plan for staging an elaborate quarrel with West, and how was I to know that you didn't plan to do so tonight?"

"Because you might credit me with a *bit* of common sense," Sophie said, a bit more acid in her tone than she intended, or than was perhaps fair, given that that had, until recently, been precisely her plan.

"Perhaps I shall start doing so when *you* credit me with being an adult capable of holding an intelligent conversation," Alexandra said with uncharacteristic sharpness. "You might have just spoken to me and avoided this entire unhinged scheme, you know. I presume you concocted this plan after waltzing with Blackford at the Northdale ball last month?"

"Indeed. Directly on the heels of one of the stranger breakfast conversations of my entire life," Sophie said, crossing her arms. "In which you acted like a criminal when I so much as dared to question you about your feelings. You can understand how I might have thought you wouldn't be receptive to a reasonable conversation."

"But you didn't even try." Alexandra's voice had lost its edge now, and there was a muted quality to it—one that was almost sad. Sophie felt a pang of guilt, which she tried to suppress. Why should she feel guilty for trying to ensure her sister's happiness?

"I was too busy trying to make sure that you didn't throw away a love match out of some misplaced sense of sisterly obligation."

"A misplaced sense of sisterly obligation—I'm not sure I could have said it better myself." Alexandra rose. "I'm not a child, Sophie. I've wed and been widowed and, I'll admit, I had a foolish moment there at breakfast that day, but you still could have tried to speak to me—to hash things out like adults. Instead you've drawn us all into a farce—let Mama and Papa think that you're planning a wedding when in fact you have no intention of being married at all. And what if I hadn't realized what you were about?" she added. "Did you intend to walk to the altar with me and only then inform me that you'd had a change of heart?"

Sophie felt something very close to shame burn within her; for all the occasional pangs of guilt that she'd experienced over the course of the past month, she hadn't properly considered just what impact breaking her supposed engagement would have on her family.

"I just wanted you to be happy," she said quietly, looking at her sister, whose own expression softened in turn.

"I know." Alexandra reached across to squeeze Sophie's hand. "But that's not your responsibility to ensure. And for heaven's sake, you didn't need to agree to every single idea I suggested about the wedding—if I hadn't already worked out that you were feigning your betrothal, I would have thought you'd sustained a head injury."

Sophie managed a smile at that; Alexandra reached for her gloves, which she'd discarded upon entering, and drew them on as she turned to depart. "I'll see you tonight, I suppose. You might do us all a favor and spare us the swooning over West, though."

She swept out of the room; Sophie wished to call after her—to apologize, dispel the slight strain that still lingered between them— but she remained silent. *This evening*, she promised herself. *This evening, it will all be right.*

It was a peculiarly tense carriage ride across Mayfair that evening, and West did not entirely understand why. Blackford had offered the use of his carriage, so that the two betrothed couples might arrive at the same time, and West and Sophie had accepted; West had been the last to join the group, and had found Sophie and Alexandra sitting in slightly strained silence upon his entrance. A frown at Blackford had yielded no information other than a shrug, and West had let the matter lie; he had a fair amount on his mind at the moment, after all.

As chance would have it, they arrived right on the heels of Diana, Jeremy, Penvale, and Jane, who had evidently come in one carriage as well.

"It took us *ages* to get here," Diana said, as soon as West and Sophie approached. "I thought I'd perish in the carriage. I didn't realize this was to be the event of the Season."

"My mother is an . . . enthusiastic hostess," Sophie said diplomatically. "I believe she even sent an invitation to the prince regent."

"Did she really?" Jane looked half-fascinated, half-horrified at this news.

"Hope springs eternal, et cetera," Alexandra said, joining them. She inclined her head. "Shall we?"

The Wexhams' house was blazing with light. Flickering torches lined the walkway up to the house, and the double doors were flung open, liveried footmen standing ready to greet each arrival. Lady Wexham had clearly spared no expense; as they stepped into the entryway, they were greeted with the sight and scent of dozens of exquisite bouquets of fresh flowers on every available surface and hanging from the walls in chained pots. Mingled with the flickering candlelight, the effect was near-magical, though West gave a shake of his head at the whimsical thought.

They proceeded into the ballroom in pairs, being announced in turn. The betrothed couples, by unspoken agreement, were left for last. Jane and Penvale directly preceded Alexandra and Blackford; Jane looked rather pale and uneasy, but Penvale glanced down at her with a private, reassuring smile that she met with one of her own. They passed into the ballroom; then West heard: "The Earl of Blackford and Mrs. Brown-Montague," and Blackford and Alexandra were gone, only a brief glance from Alexandra in Sophie's direction by way of farewell.

West glanced down at Sophie; while she was not overwhelmingly petite, height had always run in the Audley line, and the top of her head could fit neatly under his chin. From his vantage point, he could see the freshwater pearls studded throughout her hair; he also had a pleasing view directly down the front of her bodice—her gown was a radiant pink silk embroidered with white roses—and, as if sensing the direction of his thoughts, she glanced up at him with a smile of pure, wicked promise.

"Shall we give everyone a shock?" she murmured. "It's not too late to change your mind, you know."

"I'm ready," he said, then leaned forward and had a quick word with the Wexhams' butler, who was about to announce them. The butler blinked, his gaze flicking back and forth from West to Sophie and back again.

"But—I don't—"

"We're going to shake up this betrothal ball a bit, Mournday," Sophie said lightly, giving the butler a cheerful smile. "I promise you, we're not in jest."

"All right," Mournday said, still looking slightly dubious, and then turned back to the room at large—a room that West knew contained her family, and his, all of their friends, everyone who was anyone in the *ton*—and announced:

"The Marquess and Marchioness of Weston."

Chapter Twenty-Three

One week earlier

"*I thought finally coming to my senses with my tragic long-lost love* would involve a bit more sweeping romance, and a bit less time spent inside a solicitor's office."

Sophie shot West a look of tolerant affection as she stepped back, allowing him to open the door and usher her out onto Bond Street, where her solicitor's office was located. She employed the services of Edwards & Higgins, Esq., as her mother's family had done for decades now, and Mr. Edwards himself had been happy to make himself available to meet with her for the second time that day—particularly once he realized that she intended to bring a marquess with her to this meeting. He was a small, round man who had had the same shock of disorderly white hair for as long as Sophie could remember, and he had nodded with unquestioning delight when Sophie informed him that she'd taken it into her head to make a real estate acquisition.

"But with the utmost discretion," she'd informed Mr. Edwards in hushed tones. "It is a rather delicate matter." She trailed off with a significant look, while West nodded solemnly next to her, and Mr. Edwards did not ask any further questions; he merely looked eager to do their bidding, as he so often did, considering the exorbitant fee Sophie paid to retain his services.

That mission accomplished, she found herself blinking in the afternoon sunshine as West handed her up into his phaeton. It was a few hours since she'd left here after her prior meeting with Mr. Edwards; the events of the afternoon had progressed with such rapidity that they'd begun to take on a sort of dreamlike state of unreality. West loved her—she loved him—and they were finally, finally going to be married.

Except . . .

"I do not want to leave a wedding on horseback!" she burst out as soon as they were settled in the phaeton and West had taken the reins. "That nightmarish dress Alexandra convinced me to order from Madame Blanchet is the least practical frock for riding imaginable, no doubt I'll muddy it and then Fox will scold me, and in any case, what is wrong with a perfectly good carriage? This is madness."

West spurred the horses into motion and spared her a brief sideways glance. "I thought you suspected your sister of fabricating all of these mad wedding details in an attempt to force you to admit that we weren't really engaged."

"I did—I *do*—but that's no help to me, now that we actually *are* engaged." Sophie felt the blood drain from her face as she fully contemplated the horror that awaited her. "West, I do *not* want to wear that dress."

"Then wear a different dress," West said practically, and Sophie was sorely tempted to fling her reticule at his head. Men!

"It's not about the *dress*," she said, and was mildly satisfied to see a look of puzzlement cross his handsome face. His brow crinkled very charmingly when he was confused, and he was so rarely confused that it was not often that she was able to appreciate the sight. "It's about the entire wedding—a *double wedding,* for heaven's sake. What on earth was I thinking? Why did I agree to this?"

"Because you never had any intention of going through with it," West said reasonably.

"But now I want to!" Sophie said. "Oh, God, what am I going to do?"

West cleared his throat. "As it happens, I may have considered the likelihood of such a possibility."

Sophie, preoccupied by thoughts of herself wafting down the aisle of St. George's looking like some sort of iced, tiered cake, took a moment to register his words. Then she cast him a suspicious glance. "What do you mean?"

"Well. If you will recall, I had cause to leave town overnight briefly this week."

"Yes," Sophie said slowly.

"I had to visit the ducal seat in Kent, which is, you know, very close to Canterbury."

"Canterbury," Sophie repeated slowly, and then cottoned. "You obtained a special license!"

"Apparently the archbishop has some sort of long-standing quarrel with my father." West sounded smug. "I appealed to his better nature and sense of romance—and may have mentioned that my father would not be pleased by this marriage."

"I could kiss you," she informed him.

"Best not to shock Lady Wheezle," he said, nodding politely at the lady, who was just now being driven past in her barouche, a dog in her lap, eyeing them with naked curiosity beneath a towering hat.

Sophie, meanwhile, was considering the implications of this news.

"But . . . you had no notion that I'd agree to marry you—I'd told you multiple times that I wouldn't, in fact!"

"But," West said, "as I for some reason still need to remind you—I hadn't yet asked you. And I had a suspicion that if I ever had cause to ask you, it would be because I was confident you'd say yes."

"You *still* haven't asked me," Sophie pointed out, which was true; they'd been so caught up in—well, primarily in kissing, and then another round of hasty, perhaps overly athletic lovemaking on the settee—but eventually in discussing Sophie's plan, and their suddenly urgent need to visit her solicitor, that they'd not actually got around to the proposing part of the afternoon's schedule.

"You know, I've envisioned asking you to marry me countless times over the years," West said. They'd reached the edge of Hyde Park, and he pulled the phaeton over into a shady copse not far from the gates, where they were not immediately in the line of sight of anyone who might be passing. "It usually involved me down on one knee, making grandiose statements of undying love and affection, and then sweeping you into a waltz whilst a string quartet serenaded us by moonlight."

This was, more or less, akin to what Sophie's own youthful fancies had involved. She'd never been the type to envision her own betrothal as a girl, but once she'd met West, she'd found that she was not immune to such daydreams after all. She'd spent the past seven years trying her best to forget them. And now—

Now she realized that she didn't care if he asked her on one knee, or both, or by moonlight or in a thunderstorm or before the entire *ton* or before no one at all. She just cared that he asked her.

"I've imagined it a dozen different ways," he continued, carefully looping the reins and then reaching out to take her hands in his, "but in every single one of these fantasies, the only thing that really mattered was that you said yes." His green gaze on her was steady, unwavering, and so full of love that she felt a lump rising in her throat. "Sophie, will you marry me?"

And, after all that time—after all the years of words left unsaid between them, all the thousand things she'd wished to say to him during that time—in the end, she kept it simple.

"Yes."

And before the word was entirely out of her mouth, he was kissing her, and her arms were looping around his neck, and there was no need for any other words at all.

Violet and James were the only ones they took into their confidence.

"A wedding! By special license!" Violet said, for at least the fourth time that morning. It was two days later, and they were in Violet and James's drawing room, awaiting the arrival of the rector.

"This is quite thrilling, you know," Violet continued eagerly; she was wearing a gown of blue-and-white stripes and a matching bonnet, and appeared close to bouncing on her toes. "First Emily and Belfry, now you two . . . it's so much more romantic than a traditional church wedding, don't you think?" She tilted her head up toward her husband, who looked down at her with some bemusement.

"I thought our wedding was perfectly romantic, thank you," James informed her mildly.

"I'd hope so, considering the haste with which it took place," West said, and his brother grinned at him.

"Efficient," James corrected. "It was efficient."

"As is this one," Sophie said, and West glanced down at her, his throat tightening at the sight of her. Instead of the infamous ruffled monstrosity that she'd commissioned with her sister, she was attired in a gown he'd seen her wear before, one of green silk adorned with a pattern of white vines and leaves. Her hair was dressed simply, and she held a bouquet of white roses. There was nothing about the scene that suggested it was the wedding of a future duke.

It was perfect.

Initially, Sophie had taken some convincing—she'd been racked with guilt at the notion of leaving Alexandra to enjoy their elaborately planned wedding alone. West, however, had felt compelled to point out the obvious.

"Sophie," he'd said two evenings earlier, as she paced around her bedroom in a dressing gown; West had arrived after dark on horseback, sneaking up the back stairs from the mews. He'd waited seven years, and did not intend to wait even another two days to sleep beside her. "Do you think that *Alexandra* wants the wedding she is planning?"

Sophie paused in her pacing. "No," she said consideringly. "Maria's right—Alex didn't enjoy all the fuss surrounding her first wedding. She's undoubtedly doing all this just to spite me."

"Then perhaps you would be doing her a favor, by stealing a march on her and wedding in secret?" West suggested. "Then she and Blackford can change whatever plans they have made, and arrange a wedding more to their own liking."

Sophie's face had cleared at that, which was how they found themselves here, two days later, preparing to take their vows. They'd asked Violet and James to serve as their witnesses—a request that had been met with such incandescent joy by Violet that West had feared that she would twist his hand off entirely as she wrung it in a congratulatory fashion—but had decided to invite no one else. They did not wish word to reach the duke until the matter was settled—particularly not when they had a plan in place for him, the pieces already arranged. So it was to be a quiet, clandestine wedding—and West could hardly wait. It was a sunny afternoon, and the drawing room was lit with a rosy glow; Violet had outdone herself, filling the room with vases overflowing with roses and peonies, sweet peas and larkspur, and it was amid the scent of fresh flowers, with the windows flung open to admit a warm breeze, that West and Sophie spoke their vows at last. The rector looked mildly shocked when West pulled Sophie toward him for a kiss, and busied himself with his prayer book.

Afterward, they drank champagne and ate a sickening array of pastries that Sophie's French cook had sent over in honor of the occasion, and discussed what was to come next.

"I don't believe I've ever attended a betrothal ball for a couple who had secretly married ahead of time, and planned to create an enormous scene," Violet said thoughtfully, taking a bite of a madeleine. "I do wish other people would consider how much more entertaining it is to do things *this* way."

"Entertaining," West repeated with faint incredulity. "Convoluted and mad, I believe you mean."

Violet smiled. "That seems to be a requirement for any of our set to find love, West. Congratulations on joining the club."

West glanced down at Sophie, who was settled next to him on the settee, a champagne flute in hand, resting her golden head against his arm.

And he could not prevent the smile that broke across his face.

Chapter Twenty-Four

Sophie didn't know what reaction she had been expecting—but she did know that silence, somehow, felt wrong.

She held tightly on to West's arm as they descended the stairs into her parents' ballroom, enough of a hush having fallen over the assembled crowd that the faint *clunk* of West's cane on the stairs was more audible than it should have been.

As they walked, she looked for familiar faces among the guests, and didn't have to look far—Diana, Jeremy, Jane, and Penvale had evidently wasted little time in seeking out their friends. Her sisters and their husbands, West's brother and sister-in-law and all of their friends, were gathered near the edge of the stairs, watching their descent. The expressions on their faces ranged from confusion to amusement, as if West and Sophie had just played a grand joke on them all . . .

Until her eyes met James's. He raised an eyebrow at her, and she raised one in return as she and West stepped off the final step into the room.

"Would anyone care to explain what, precisely, is going on here?" This came from Diana, who rarely shied from bluntness.

"Yes, please!" added Harriet, looking somewhere between flabbergasted and ecstatic. "Sophie, you cannot mean to tell us that you have already married West! But—the double wedding!" She paused, adopting a crestfallen expression that she seemed to consider an appropriate show of grief for the loss of the great—now tragically unfulfilled—joy of the promised double wedding.

"Oh, heavens, you're right," Sophie said, clutching her chest dramatically. She turned to West. "Is it too late to annul the marriage?"

"Rather," he replied, extremely dryly.

She turned to Alexandra, who was watching the proceedings thoughtfully, not having spoken yet. "Do you think you might be able to face getting married without me?" Sophie asked, a bit hesitant after their conversation earlier that afternoon.

Alexandra smiled. "Considering that Blackford and I have been planning our own small wedding separately for the better part of the past month, I do think that we'll manage somehow."

Now it was Sophie's turn to gape. "You—but—"

"Oh, good lord," Penvale muttered, and Sophie turned to him, startled. He blinked, apparently not having intended to speak loudly enough for the rest of the group to hear him, but several heads had turned in his direction, and more were following suit. "Well," he said, a bit sheepishly, "aren't you all rather exhausted by this by now? It's been a *year* since Violet took it into her head to convince Audley she was at death's door, and since then we've had Audley threatening to send her to a Swiss mountaintop to commune with goats—"

"He did specifically mention the goats," Violet confirmed.

"—and then Diana attempting to force Jeremy to marry the most dreadful young lady I've encountered on the marriage mart—"

"She's not on the marriage mart anymore," Diana said confidingly to Emily. "Did you hear that her brother purchased her a cottage in Sussex?"

"—and then Emily was making frankly absurd threats to Belfry about wanting to appear onstage, and then my *own wife*"—he spared a dark look for Jane—"tried to haunt me out of my own home, and *now this,* whatever *this* actually turns out to be—no doubt *you*"—he gestured at Alexandra—"are about to inform West and Sophie that you were simply attempting to trick them into marrying, since anyone with eyes has been able to tell for *years* that they're still in love with each other!"

Alexandra blinked. "Well, yes, actually." She turned to Blackford. "That's about the shape of it, wouldn't you say?"

"I believe so," Blackford agreed affably.

"Exactly." Penvale was breathing rather heavily. "My point is, aren't you all weary of all of this by now?"

"Penvale," Violet said hesitantly, and then let out a slight cough; the glare he turned on her at this juncture was so fierce that she ceased immediately. "A joke, a joke!" she said hastily. "But," she added, her tone that of someone attempting to reason with a recalcitrant toddler, "whilst I would never blame you, I do think it worth pointing out that if *you* hadn't sent me that note informing me that James was on his deathbed—which he patently was not, I might add—then this entire series of events would never have been kicked into motion." She smiled brightly at him. "So, when you think of it like that, you're really the reason we're all here! Just think, if it weren't for you, Emily and Belfry might never have met!"

"It's true," Emily chimed in, beaming.

Penvale looked appalled. "I am getting a drink," he said, and walked away without another word.

Jane waved cheerfully after him before turning back to the rest of them and saying, rather eagerly, "Now that we've rid ourselves of him, would you please continue explaining what exactly is afoot here?"

"I should rather like to know that, too, Sophie darling!"

Sophie suppressed a sigh with some difficulty; the voice was that of her mother, and really she ought to be surprised that it had taken a full two minutes for Lady Wexham to make her way across the ballroom. Given the circumstances, Sophie would not have been shocked had her mother spontaneously sprouted wings and swooped down upon them within seconds.

West lowered his arm slightly—the one that Sophie was still gripping, perhaps a bit too tightly—but she realized a moment later that he was only doing so in order to take her hand in his.

"Lady Wexham," he said, nodding at her mother. "Lord Wexham," he added, looking over her mother's shoulder; her father approached, evidently attempting to appear foreboding but seeming rather delighted instead. "I am sorry that we have not been entirely honest with you for the past week—past month, really," he amended quickly.

Vaguely, from behind her, Sophie heard Mournday announce another arrival, and the inquisitive buzz that had slowly filled the room upon her arrival seemed to turn to the more natural hum of conversation. They were no longer the center of attention.

"However," West continued, and she turned her attention back to him—they hadn't worked out precisely how they would explain matters to her family, and she realized now that she wasn't sure what he was going to say. "I have loved your daughter for the past seven years, and when she came to me proposing a feigned betrothal—something she only did out of concern for her sister," he added, his gaze flicking to Alexandra—"I said yes, because I have never stopped loving her." He turned to Sophie now, looking down at her as he added softly, "Not for one single moment."

Sophie could not tear her eyes from his. It was still such a luxury, to be able to look at him as much as she wanted—she felt like someone emerging from the desert dying of thirst, now able to take deep gulps of water. For so many years, her glances at him had been swift, stolen snatches of time—looking in his direction when he was distracted in conversation, never allowing her gaze to linger for too long, lest someone else notice. Lest her expression say everything that she would not put into words—even to herself, as the years went by.

"And so," he said, looking back at her parents, her sisters, their assembled friends, "when we realized that our feelings were mutual— that we did not want to repeat the same mistakes of the past—we thought it only right to marry as quickly as possible, before anyone else could talk us out of it."

"And I suppose," came a stern voice from behind them, "that by 'anyone else,' you mean me?"

Sophie's shoulders went up before she even turned; she knew that voice all too well. But she would not allow its owner to dictate any- thing about her life anymore. She lifted her chin, tightened her grip on West's hand, and turned.

"Your Grace," she said, dropping into a shallow curtsey.

The Duke of Dovington was looking . . . decidedly odd. Not in ap- pearance—he looked much as he ever did in that regard, dressed with the utmost care in black and white evening attire, his cravat knotted elaborately. She supposed she should be honored he'd deigned to put in an appearance this evening at all and that he'd clearly dressed for the occasion; but then, blatant, obvious disrespect had never been his weapon of choice. He favored more subtle tools.

However, despite his immaculate appearance, there was something unsettled about him that Sophie could not recall seeing on any previous occasion. His eyes flicked back and forth between West and Sophie rapidly, and Sophie felt West's hand tighten on hers.

"Father." He inclined his head.

The duke tilted his head. "West." He turned to look at Sophie, a pause growing heavier with each passing second. "Lady Weston."

Sophie felt, rather than heard, the entire assembled group behind her exhale.

"I suppose you thought I was bluffing," the duke said conversationally, and Sophie bit the inside of her cheek to steady herself for a moment before responding.

"On the contrary, Your Grace," she said, offering him a demure smile. "I would never suspect a man such as yourself of being capable of such a thing."

He held her gaze, and she willed herself not to blink. She was not going to let this man intimidate her anymore—because, like it or not, he was now her father-in-law, and she supposed she'd better get used to him.

His eyes narrowed slightly. "I've had interest in the property, you know," he said, his eyes flicking back to West. "Somehow word got out that I was thinking of selling and I've had someone in touch with an offer. A very good offer, I might add."

"How nice," West said blandly. "Please let me know if the prospective owner needs any information from me, beyond the account books I've already sent you. I hope you received them?" he added politely.

"The carriage stuffed full of them was rather hard to miss," the duke said, his gaze locked on his son's. "If you think that you are playing a game of poker with me, West, then I would remind you that I don't play games I don't know I can win."

West inclined his head. "On the contrary, Father—I look forward to doing anything that I can to assist with the sale of Rosemere to its new owner." He smiled at his father; when, Sophie wondered, was the last time he'd had cause to do that? "I don't think this is the time or place for such a discussion, but I'd be happy to continue it later. But"—and here, his smile vanished, and he took two steps closer to his father—"I wish to make it perfectly clear to you that if Rosemere is the price I must pay for my marriage, then I would pay it a thousand times over. Indeed, I am *happy* to pay it, if it means that you no longer have any leverage over me." He stepped back again, reaching behind him, and Sophie slipped her hand into his once more.

West turned slightly, so that he and Sophie were no longer facing his father directly, but rather were including the group at large. "I'm sorry that we have doubly deceived all of you, but I hope you will wish us both happy—and perhaps we can now turn our attention to where it belongs." He nodded at Alexandra and Blackford, then turned to Sophie's mother. "Lady Wexham, would you do me the honor of saving a waltz for me?"

This simple question somehow broke the dam, and in short order Lady Wexham had swooped down upon them both, raining kisses on cheeks and shedding a few discreet tears into the handkerchief that West handed her. Their siblings and friends followed suit, and for some time there was little sense to be had from anyone amid the melee of well-wishes and joyful exclamations.

At one point, Sophie found herself back at West's side, and she turned to him. "My cheeks hurt," she said, raising a hand to her face, where a helpless smile seemed to have been permanently stuck.

West leaned down and—mindless of the impropriety involved—pressed a soft kiss to her forehead. "I would see that smile on your face every day for the rest of my life."

Sophie, in that moment, did not think this would be a difficult wish to fulfill.

It was later, when Sophie was enjoying a brief respite from dancing and had left West chatting amiably with Blackford and Belfry and their brother-in-law, the Earl of Risedale, that Alexandra found her.

Sophie had just accepted a flute of champagne from a passing footman and had ducked behind a potted palm to enjoy it—not entirely out of sight, but just hidden enough that one would have to be properly looking for her to spot her—when her sister appeared beside her.

Alexandra looked very pretty this evening, her dark hair gleaming in the candlelight, wearing a gown of bright yellow that somehow made her skin glow radiantly, though a similar shade would no doubt have made Sophie look sallow.

"I just escaped a five-minute lecture from Maria about how I was very wrong to taunt you with threats of a double wedding and leaving the church on horseback," Alexandra said, not sounding remotely apologetic.

"I'm surprised she was so defensive of my tender sensibilities," Sophie said, taking a sip of champagne.

"Oh, she's not," Alexandra said cheerfully. "I've no doubt your own lecture will be forthcoming."

"I'll look forward to that," Sophie said wryly, though Maria *had* pressed her hand and wished her happy with obvious sincerity, and the satisfied air of someone who felt that a great wrong had been corrected.

Alexandra craned her head around. "Do you think it would draw attention to our hiding place if I were to summon a footman to a bit of greenery? I'm parched." Not waiting for an answer, she hissed, "Pssst!" The footman she was attempting to summon, standing about ten feet away, paused, then glanced around as if suspecting someone had let a snake into the ballroom. "Psssst!" Alexandra hissed, a bit louder this time, and when he at last turned she waved him frantically over, relieving him of two glasses from his tray before sending him on his way.

"I do not think the War Office will be recruiting you for intelligence work," Sophie said.

Alexandra ignored her, taking a hearty gulp of champagne. A silence descended between them as they both leaned against the wall, one that Sophie was slightly hesitant to break. But this was Alexandra—her sister, yes, but also, these past few years, her very dearest friend. She could not bear this slightly strained note that now existed between them.

"I'm sorry, you know," Sophie said, turning her head toward her sister without lifting it away from the wall. Alexandra mirrored the movement.

"So am I."

Sophie hesitated. "West says . . . he says that I worry too much over you."

Alexandra lifted her champagne flute in salute. "For that reason alone, I should toast your marriage. If he can finally make you see sense, then I am even fonder of him than I already was."

Sophie gave a wavering smile. "It is just—for so long, I worried so much about you—about *all* of you. As the eldest, it was my job to marry well, to ease the way for the rest of you."

"Our father is a viscount, Soph, and thanks to Mama, we are positively rolling in money." Sophie was shocked into a laugh, which had no doubt been her sister's intent in speaking so bluntly. "I do not think we would have found our paths unduly difficult—so long as we had the good sense not to fall in love with the heirs to dukedoms who had fathers with giant sticks up their—"

"Thank you, point taken," Sophie interrupted hastily, laughing again. "I suppose my experience with the duke did make me overly concerned for the rest of you. But I hadn't really *taken*, you know, in my first two Seasons, before I met West. All of the gentlemen who were highest in the instep didn't want to marry the daughter of some upstart viscount with a fortune from trade."

"But would you want to marry any of *them*?" Alexandra pressed.

"I—I suppose not," Sophie said, rather startled.

"Then why were you so concerned about what they'd think of the rest of us? Do you think Mama and Papa so obsessed with rank that they'd set their sights on some appalling snob, just so that they could say their daughter married an earl? Even Maria settled for a second son, after that disaster with Sandworth, and if anyone among us would care about such things, it would be her."

"Well . . . no." Sophie sighed. "Being the eldest, though, I think I've always considered it my responsibility to worry over the rest of you."

"That's why we have *parents*," Alexandra pointed out. "They worried over us plenty, if you'll recall. It's not as though we grew up in an orphanage trying to elbow our way to the front of the line for a bowl of porridge. And even if there was cause for concern, we're all well-settled now—you're allowed to care for yourself, you know."

"But *you* were the one who wasn't going to marry if I was unwed!" Sophie pointed out, half-laughing, half-exasperated. It was a bit galling to be criticized for the same behavior that Alexandra had employed herself.

"As a matter of fact," Alexandra said carelessly, "that's not actually true, which you'd know if you'd bothered to ask me, instead of taking matters into your own hands. I tried to tell you as much this afternoon."

"I—you—"

"I was hesitating, yes, for all the reasons Blackford told you," Alexandra said, "but I was hoping to discuss it with you at some point, without Harriet and Betsy present. I *was* worried that you and West would never work things out, that you'd never be happy, but you've always gone so stubbornly silent whenever anyone mentions his name that I wasn't certain how to raise the subject. So you can imagine my surprise," she added, "when you suddenly informed me that you were engaged."

Sophie rubbed a hand over her face, and drained the rest of her champagne. "Did you smell a rat immediately?"

"More or less," Alexandra said. "And once Blackford told me about the conversation he'd had with you, I was fairly certain I knew what you were about."

"You might have spared me the torment of the double wedding planning," Sophie said severely.

"I wanted to see how far you'd be willing to take this ruse." Alexandra sounded quite pleased with herself. "And then I grew annoyed with you, and kept making things more and more ludicrous, to see if you'd just admit that you were lying. But the more I watched you and West together, the more convinced I became that you were still in love—and the more irritated I was that you continued agreeing to all my plans, which I knew you wouldn't do if you'd really intended to marry him." She shook her head. "It all grew a bit mixed up in my head, I'll admit. But whilst Blackford and I *were* planning our own, much smaller wedding all the while, I promise you that I would have walked down the aisle in something utterly horrifying and departed on a white horse, if that was what it took to see you and West married."

"Fortunately, a special license was actually all it took." Sophie attempted a stern look at her sister, but couldn't quite manage it; how could she be annoyed, when Alexandra was essentially doing precisely what she'd done to *her* for years? "Did Harriet and Betsy know?"

"Oh no, I knew I couldn't possibly trust them with this," Alexandra said. "Though that has been troubling in its own way, as it means they've been sincere in their enthusiasm for every one of my unhinged ideas." She frowned. "Should we be concerned about their mental states?"

"We shall simply blame Betsy's on the baby, and Harriet's on the all-consuming fervor of her rivalry with Hyacinth Montmorency." Sophie smiled, and Alexandra smiled back at her.

"We're allowed to worry for you, Soph," Alexandra said a bit tentatively, and Sophie swallowed. "Just because you're the eldest doesn't mean that you're the only one who cares for us. We love you—we want you to be happy. And I would have welcomed anyone who made you happy, but . . . well, I'm just so glad that it's West."

Sophie's smile wavered at this point, and her lower lip was a bit unsure of itself, but she blinked away the tears that threatened to blur her vision and took the extra glass of champagne from her sister's hand. She lifted it to Alexandra's glass in a toast.

"So am I."

Chapter Twenty-Five

Combining two households—and two household staffs—was proving to be more complicated than West had anticipated.

"Briar, for the love of God, I *do not care*," West said, after the fifteenth interruption in the past two hours, all to do with the question of whether the footmen who were joining their household from Sophie's were properly matched in height. "If you think one of them needs to wear stilts, then feel free to see that it is taken care of, so long as the footman in question is amenable."

Briar, aquiver with wounded dignity, drew himself up to his full height, puffed out his chest, and offered a stiff, "Indeed, my lord," before bowing himself out, narrowly avoiding bumping into Sophie as he did so. He was full of apologies and inquiries as to *her* needs; it seemed that Briar approved of marriage in general, and Sophie specifically. There had been a few hairy moments before he'd realized that Sophie's elderly butler was happy to take this opportunity to be pensioned off, but once that was sorted he'd been full of nothing but solicitous concern for the new lady of the house.

"Why does he like you more than he likes me?" West asked darkly, rising from his desk as Briar bowed himself out with one last adoring look at Sophie before the door clicked shut behind him.

"Perhaps because I told him that I thought the infusion of new staff into your household was an excellent opportunity to rethink the bedrooms for the servants, and in all the upheaval and redecorating, I saw to it that he and Hawthorne were moved into adjoining rooms." She sauntered toward him clad in a fetching dress of white muslin, her hair simply arranged, a few loose curls escaping; waving him back into his seat, she perched on the edge of his desk in a way that was likely not intended to look seductively inviting, but which had that effect on his body all the same.

He rubbed his jaw thoughtfully. "Why are you so much more clever than I am?"

She leaned forward to press a quick kiss to his mouth. "Because I am a woman, and I've had to be. How else would we ever get anything done?"

She made to pull back, but he reached out and slid his hand into the loose knot at the nape of her neck, pinning her in place. He leaned forward again, tipping his head up to give her a more thorough kiss. Her lips parted on a sigh and her breath mingled with his own. His free hand made slow, steady progress from her waist up her side, tracing the curve of a breast, cupping its weight in his hand. She made a needy noise in her throat, her hands tugging on his hair just hard enough to send a bolt of pleasurable pain straight to his cock, and he was about to rise from his seat when there was yet another knock at the study door.

He tore his mouth from hers. "Briar, I do not wish to answer any more questions about the height of our footmen!" Sophie stifled a laugh in his shoulder.

There was a brief pause, and then a rather ostentatious clearing of the throat from the other side of the door. "It is His Grace, the Duke of Dovington, here to see you, my lord." West did not think he was imagining the faintly smug note to Briar's voice. *Accuse me of frivolous, footman-related interruptions ever again, and see where it leads you!*

Sophie was out of his arms and off his desk like a shot, smoothing her hair back into place as she turned to face the door. She glanced back at him, and he took three seconds to think very innocent, *cold* thoughts before he nodded at her.

"You may send him in, Briar," she called, and the door opened and West's father walked in.

He paused briefly and allowed his gaze to flick back and forth between West and Sophie, fast as a blink, and West had the sense that he knew precisely what they'd been up to approximately thirty seconds earlier. Unfortunately for the duke, West did not give a damn.

"Father," he said, rising.

"Your Grace," Sophie added, dipping a polite—but not terribly deep—curtsey.

"West." The duke nodded at him, and then at Sophie. "Lady Weston. I apologize for the interruption, but I have something I wish to discuss with you—some new information that has come to light."

West gestured at one of the chairs opposite his desk, and his father took a seat as soon as Sophie had. "Is something amiss?" West asked.

"Hmm." Despite being seated on the wrong side of the desk, the duke still looked like a man holding court: he reclined in his chair, bracing his elbows upon the armrests, and brought his fingers together before his mouth in thoughtful contemplation. "An interesting question. I do not know if 'amiss' is the correct word, however."

"Oh, are we to have a lesson on vocabulary?" Sophie inquired innocently. "How delightful. There are a number of invectives I'm positively desperate to learn polite synonyms for." She paused briefly. "Not that I would need to use them in present company, of course."

"Of course," the duke agreed dryly; West did not think he imagined the brief, faintest hint of a twitch at the edge of his father's mouth, almost as if he were amused. He had not known the Duke of Dovington to be capable of such an emotion.

"I was intrigued, last week, to receive interest in purchasing Rosemere, as you will recall," the duke continued. "I have corresponded further with the potential buyer, and their offer is certainly a tempting one." He paused. "But not *too* tempting, you see. It is a fair offer, but not overly generous—the buyer clearly has some knowledge of the estate and its potential yields."

"I would hope that anyone looking to purchase an estate would do some research before making an offer," West said blandly.

"Hmm," the duke said again. "Well, I grew frankly curious about this man making the offer, who was being quite mysterious. The correspondence I had was all from his solicitor, you see; this solicitor proved to be distressingly unforthcoming when I asked for specifics regarding the identity of his client." Next to the duke, Sophie had gone very still, though the duke gave no indication of having taken note of this. "So, to assuage my curiosity, I had my own solicitor do a bit of digging, and was intrigued to learn that this very solicitor is employed not just by your parents, Lady Weston, but by your mother's entire extended family, and their various shipping companies."

"What a coincidence," Sophie said calmly, lacing her hands together on her lap. "My mother's family does often employ the services of a reputable solicitor, given all the legal matters that tend to crop up in their line of work—they run quite a profitable set of businesses, you know." She paused delicately. "I believe it is this very fact that made me so objectionable to you as a potential daughter-in-law, in fact. Unless my memory fails me—it is all so *very* long ago now." She smiled at the duke.

West was tempted to applaud.

"Indeed," the duke said, and his gaze was steady on Sophie; she met his eyes unblinkingly. She should not, in her simple afternoon gown, have looked anything like a future duchess—she was not draped in fine fabrics, elegantly coiffed, dripping in jewels. But there was a certain set to her chin, and a look in her eye, that made it quite obvious that she was not remotely intimidated by the man seated next to her, whose wife had once held the title that would someday be hers.

At last, the duke gave a nearly imperceptible nod. He rose to his feet. "I'll notify this solicitor that the sale can go through," he said curtly, and West and Sophie exchanged a single, startled glance.

"But—" Sophie said.

"Lady Weston," the duke interrupted her, "I am not a man who takes kindly to having my own will subverted, so I would prefer not to linger on this any longer than necessary. But I can recognize a worthy opponent." He extended a hand to Sophie then, and she seemed to realize, after a brief, surprised pause, that he wished to shake hands with her. West doubted his father had ever shaken hands with a woman in his entire life—women were to be flattered; they were to be waltzed with, made love to, given idle, meaningless compliments. But West thought now, watching his wife and father shake hands warily, that there was something like respect in the way his father looked at Sophie.

Respect was not admiration, or affection, or even acceptance—but it was something. And in this instance, it was a concession.

His father dropped Sophie's hand, picked up his hat, and cast West a wry glance. "I'll have that paperwork regarding the estate returned to you, shall I? And in the future, perhaps you'll refrain from wasting my time with such absurd stunts?"

West gave the duke a thin smile. "Only if you'll refrain from meddling in my marriage, Father."

The duke pressed his lips together into a grim line, but did not offer a rejoinder. Instead, he merely tossed imperiously over his shoulder on his way out the door, "You might see to providing me with an heir, at least."

The door shut behind him.

"You know," Sophie said thoughtfully, as she and West stared at the door through which the duke had departed, "I simply cannot *wait* to disappoint him on that score."

West was inclined to agree; he felt the familiar irritation creeping through him that so often came on the heels of discussions with his father, even as he knew that the conversation that had just occurred was likely the best they could ever hope to exchange with the duke on the matter of their marriage. He rose to his feet and, ignoring his cane, walked slowly toward Sophie. He reached down a hand, pulling her to her feet, and she tilted her head back slightly to look him directly in the eye.

"I love you," he said simply. He would never tire of saying it—not after so many years of feeling it and yet keeping it so carefully tucked away.

She dimpled. "I know." She reached up to rest her hands on his shoulders. She gently pushed against him, until he took a step backward. "Now, you are going to sit in that chair, and I'm going to get down on my knees and do something that you're going to enjoy very much indeed, and then, if you'd like to thank me, you can bend me over your desk and have your way with me." A commanding note entered her voice as she described this program of events, one that was like an invisible finger stroking down his cock.

"Unless," she added graciously, "you have any complaints about this proposed plan?"

West most emphatically did not, and he leaned down to kiss her by way of reply.

"So you did it, then," Violet said admiringly the following evening, leaning back in her seat and taking a sip of sherry with a happy sigh. "You outsmarted the duke. I'm tempted to applaud, really."

It was the first time Sophie had played hostess as a marchioness; they'd invited their friends to dinner, and then, instead of the ladies withdrawing to leave the gentlemen to their port and conversation, they'd all moved to the library. It was a warm evening, and they'd opened the French doors leading to the terrace, allowing a breeze and the scent of roses to waft in from the back garden. They were scattered around the room in odd configurations: Harriet and Betsy had their heads together, laughing over something in a book they'd pulled from the shelves, while their husbands were deep in conversation with Blackford and Risedale. The Countess of Risedale and Alexandra were debating something good-naturedly with Maria and Grovecourt. Diana, Jane, and Penvale were cheerfully arguing about—unless Sophie had entirely misheard—the size of seagulls in Cornwall; Emily was attempting to reclaim her overgrown kitten, Cecil, from Belfry and Jeremy, who had it chasing a feather in increasingly tight circles. (Sophie remained unclear as to why, exactly, the kitten was in attendance at all this evening; Belfry had informed her in apologetic tones upon their arrival that he'd learned not to question the emotional needs of a woman in a delicate condition, which Sophie could not argue with.)

That left Sophie, West, Violet, and James sitting rather cozily together on a settee and a couple of armchairs set against one wall, near the open doors. West and Sophie had just finished regaling the other two with the tale of the duke's visit.

"I just wish I could have seen the look on his face," James said, taking a sip of brandy. He was reclining on the settee, his arm resting along its back, his fingers playing lazily with a loose curl of dark hair on Violet's shoulder.

"I will cherish the memory for the rest of my life," Sophie assured him. She was seated in an armchair at one end of the settee, facing West, who sat in the matching chair opposite her. He lifted his glass of brandy to her in a silent salute, one side of his mouth curving up in a private smile that was just for her. There was something looser, more relaxed to him as he reclined in his own chair, she thought; not as pertained to his appearance, which was as immaculate as ever—cravat neatly tied; dark hair combed back from his face; shoes shined to a dark gloss. But there was an ease to his limbs, to the lines of his face, that she had not been accustomed to seeing in him in recent years. Despite the faint lines in his forehead—a product, no doubt, of repeated skeptical lifting of a brow—and the occasional strand of gray hair she'd taken to gleefully informing him of when she spotted them at his temples, he reminded her, very forcefully, of the man she'd met seven years earlier.

"And he just gave you Rosemere?" James asked, his voice laced with faint incredulity; he was, after all, quite familiar with the perils that came from accepting any gifts of real estate from their father.

West rolled his eyes heavenward. "He did not; he sold it to us—to Sophie, really; it's her dowry that went to the purchase—and had the gall to haggle with her solicitor."

"Mr. Edwards drove a hard bargain, though," Sophie said cheerfully, taking a sip of her own brandy. It was liberating, she thought, to drink it from a tumbler, as the gentlemen did, rather than surreptitiously from a teacup, as had been her previous habit. "But it is safely ours now, and the duke can't touch it, nor threaten to steal it out from under our noses." She rolled her own eyes in turn. "No doubt he was mollified by the thought that we'll be raising future generations of little dukes there."

Something about her tone must have tipped her hand, for Violet looked at her curiously. "Won't you be, then?"

Sophie's gaze flicked to West, who was regarding her steadily, warmth in his green eyes. "I'm not certain," she said lightly. "I wasn't fortunate in that regard in my first marriage, you know, and . . ." She trailed off, the idea of voicing this thought to anyone other than West suddenly very frightening. But this was Violet and James—they were family. And why should she be frightened, or ashamed, when nothing about her own inclinations and wishes felt shameful to her? "And I've never felt terribly maternal," she said, her voice still light. "So if we are not so lucky, I don't know that I'll be all that cut up about it."

Violet's and James's eyes remained on her, thoughtful, not straying to West, and for this Sophie was grateful; she didn't know what she'd been expecting, precisely—for them to turn to West and exclaim at his courage in daring to wed a woman who might be barren? Who, even if she *were* to have children, was not at all certain she'd enjoy it terribly much? Instead, Violet merely nodded consideringly. "Having witnessed Emily's experiences with being enceinte so far, I think you might have the wiser philosophy, Sophie," she said. Emily had apparently been quite ill that winter, in the early days of her pregnancy; there was something slightly wistful in Violet's voice, however, that told Sophie that her sister-in-law would be willing to risk that condition, should she be so fortunate in the future. James dropped his hand from Violet's shoulder and reached down to squeeze her hand instead, dropping a kiss onto her head.

"Not," Violet added more brightly now, though her hand was still gripping James's tightly, "that now would be a terribly convenient time for us to have a baby anyway—we've pyramids to see!"

"There aren't pyramids in Italy," James said patiently. He and Violet had travel plans for the end of summer and autumn, once the Season was over; Violet had always been curious to see more of the world, and wildly indignant that ladies were not offered the opportunity for a Grand Tour the way gentlemen of means were, and so James had resolved to take her on an extended journey across the Continent. Violet had spent much of the past fortnight since the plan was announced trying to convince him to take her to increasingly remote locations; in addition to the Egyptian pyramids, Sophie had personally heard her advocating for both Constantinople and, to James's mild horror, Boston.

"Violet," he'd said in pained tones, "I get *seasick*."

"Which means you'll keep yourself quite occupied below deck for the duration of the journey, leaving me free to explore the ship without you underfoot," she'd said cheerfully. The actual journey—rather than the increasingly elaborate one that Violet was fabricating in her imagination—would take them to France, Switzerland, and Italy, as Sophie understood it. She personally thought the entire undertaking sounded equal parts thrilling and exhausting, and was herself looking forward to a quiet autumn at Rosemere instead.

At this juncture, Violet was summoned by Diana, while James wandered over to have a word with Risedale about the racing stables they were planning to open on his estate in Oxfordshire, leaving West and Sophie momentarily alone. West met her eyes, and tilted his head at the open French doors onto the terrace.

"Fancy a stroll in the garden?" he asked in a low voice.

Sophie rose to her feet as West followed suit. "Are you trying to seduce me in the open air?" she asked, reaching out to flick an invisible speck of dust from his shoulder. He reached up and caught her hand tight in his. The lamplight loved the angles of his face, casting his cheekbones into sharp relief, and turned his green eyes warm as they locked with hers.

"Perhaps." The word was lazy, low. "Are you amenable?"

She lifted her face to press a quick kiss to his mouth, not caring who saw—not here, in the safety of the home they shared, surrounded by their friends. "Perhaps."

And then she kissed him again, and allowed him to lead her onto the terrace, into a shadowy corner hidden from view, where he did several shocking things with his hand without so much as dislodging her bodice, and where she in turn demonstrated—to their mutual satisfaction—the delightful effect that a bit of friction in precisely the right location could have.

Some time later, as they stood, a bit breathless, leaning against the wall, gazing up at the night sky, his arm keeping her tucked close to his side, she said, "I wondered, you know—whether it would have been worth it. Worth seven years and all the pain. Whether I'd built you—*us*—up into something in my mind that reality could never match." She shook her head, letting out a half-incredulous laugh at the joy coursing through her. "And yet, it's even better." She turned her face up to his. "Can you believe it?"

He turned to look down at her in the shadowy darkness, just outside the edge of a pool of torchlight. "Yes," he said quite simply. "I've always believed it." He didn't say anything else; he didn't need to.

And Sophie reached up and kissed him again, alight with joy at the simple knowledge that she could.

Epilogue

One year later

September was Sophie's favorite month at Rosemere. The heat of summer had passed and the days were growing shorter, but the afternoons were still warm and sunny, the hills that surrounded the house still green. It was the perfect month for long walks along the river that the house overlooked, for quiet evenings before the fire in the drawing room, for long nights spent—sleeping or otherwise—in a warm bed, with a window open to admit the increasingly chilly night air.

It was also the perfect month to host a house party—something Sophie had suggested with great anticipation, but which she was now having cause to regret, when faced with the prospect of explaining Pass the Bread to her friends.

"Does this not seem like it might be dangerous for the baby?" Belfry demanded, once Sophie had finished explaining; much to everyone's surprise, fatherhood had turned him downright paranoid about anything that might vaguely be construed as a threat to the health and safety of baby Theodore, including—but not limited to—Emily's cat Cecil Lucifer Beelzebub, overly warm days, overly cold days, dangerously quick pushing of the pram, and, now, flying baked goods.

"It's bread, Belfry, not a cannonball, don't be hysterical," Diana said impatiently. "I do not think fatherhood is good for the brain," she added severely, though she smiled a gentle smile down at her own daughter—born just a couple of months earlier—currently cooing in the arms of her entirely besotted father.

"We shall be certain the twins give all the babies a wide birth," West assured Belfry, who looked only somewhat mollified, though he was distracted at this juncture by the sight of Emily slipping a scrap of food under the table for Cecil, who most assuredly was *not* supposed to be in the dining room, and did not protest further.

It was the first evening of the house party, and none of Sophie's sisters had arrived yet—they, and the rest of the guests, were expected the following day. Tonight, however, it was merely James and Violet, Diana and Jeremy, Emily and Belfry, and Penvale and Jane. They had finished dinner and the plates had been cleared, but they were lingering over glasses of wine as the candles burned low. The various small, chubby offspring had been brought in by their nannies for a few minutes with their parents before being tucked away in the nursery; Sophie, at the moment, was holding Penvale and Jane's daughter, who was frowning up at her wearing an expression eerily reminiscent of her mother.

"Isn't Harriet expecting again?" Jane asked with a frown, making the mother-daughter resemblance even more pronounced. "I cannot imagine wishing to do anything more active than necessary in that state."

"I could not agree more," Diana said, and she and Jane exchanged glances of dark empathy; both had been horribly ill during their own pregnancies, to the point that Diana had flatly informed Jeremy that, if they did not have a boy on a second attempt, "the title can go to a sentient turnip, for all I care." Having observed Jeremy in the company of baby Isabella, who already had him wrapped around her (exceedingly tiny) finger, Sophie did not think he cared much about having an heir.

"And yet," Penvale said to his wife, "you *did* manage to muster sufficient energy to arrange a one-night encore performance of the haunting of Trethwick Abbey, a mere month before Nora was born."

"I could not allow our wedding anniversary to pass without marking the occasion," Jane said serenely.

"Yes," Penvale said darkly. "What a special treat."

"You have no appreciation for romance," Jane said, crossing her arms, though her frown slipped a bit when Penvale winked across the table at her.

Sophie glanced down the table at West and caught his eye; he offered her a small, private smile. On the first anniversary of their own wedding, earlier that summer, she had awoken to a single rose in a vase beside her bed, next to a handwritten itinerary for the day, including items such as *Eat as many breakfast pastries as you can* and *Compromise your husband's virtue out of doors.* (This had been a particularly enjoyable one to check off.)

Nora, as if sensing that her parents had mentioned her, gave a brief squawk in Sophie's arms; she glanced down, startled, to see the baby blinking up at her, her face growing more red by the second.

"Why does she look like this?" Sophie asked, alarmed, with a glance at Penvale and Jane. Despite the abundance of—entirely beloved—babies in her life, she was not remotely sorry that there had been no sign of one forthcoming for herself and West.

"She always looks like that," Penvale said, even as he rose to come collect his daughter. "She inherited it from her mother." He skirted Jane's chair, successfully dodging her attempt to elbow him in the stomach, and scooped Nora from Sophie's arms. He sniffed, then grimaced. "Or there might be another reason."

"Aren't you looking forward to the miracle of parenthood?" James asked Violet, as Nora began to squall in earnest. For a moment, the others—so distracted by Nora's cries, which seemed to be spreading to the two other babies, like some sort of alarming plague—took no notice. After a couple of seconds, however, West blinked, then slowly turned to his brother and sister-in-law, who were seated next to each other at one end of the table.

"Do you mean . . . ?"

"I hope so," Violet said, smiling. "Otherwise I've been feeling decidedly awful for no reason at all." She did, now that Sophie looked at her more closely, seem a bit pale, something that, if Sophie had noticed it earlier, she'd thought nothing of; it had been two years since Violet and James had reconciled, with no sign of a baby. Sophie hadn't liked to pry, but she knew—thanks to one tearful confession, some months earlier—that Violet was growing concerned.

"Oh!" Emily squealed, and flung herself out of her seat ("Don't jostle the baby!" Belfry howled, as she passed Theodore to him hastily on her way) and into Violet's arms, nearly knocking her from her chair. "I'm so pleased for you."

"Emily, for heaven's sake, don't knock her over or she'll be sick all over you," Diana said, with a faint shudder and an expression of grim recollection. She, too, however, rose to squeeze Violet's shoulder. West, meanwhile, had clapped a hand on his brother's back, and was now murmuring something in James's ear, even as the rest of the room joined in the chorus of congratulations. West leaned back in his seat after a moment, making space for Jeremy to reach over and ruffle James's hair affectionately; James, for his part, had a bit of color in his cheeks, and looked absurdly pleased. Sophie felt an overwhelming rush of fondness for her brother-in-law; unbidden, the memory arose of a ride in Hyde Park two years earlier, Jeremy by her side. They'd been in the process of ending their short-lived affair when they'd crossed paths with Violet and James, clearly in the midst of some serious discussion. James had proceeded to behave like an utter lunatic; bizarrely, that encounter had led to everything that had come after, up to and including this moment.

There was movement next to her, and she started; she'd been so wrapped up in her thoughts that she hadn't noticed that West had risen from his seat and made his way to her side, sinking down in the empty chair next to hers. He reached an arm out, resting it on the back of her chair, his hand toying with the spot where the short sleeve on her evening gown met the bare skin of her arm. Gooseflesh rose in the wake of his touch, and she glanced sideways at him, smiling.

"Are you regretting hosting yet?" she asked, tilting her head toward him so that she could be heard amid the cacophony of well-wishes and crying babies.

The lines around his eyes deepened, and one side of his mouth curved up. "No." He leaned over, unheeding of whoever might be looking, and pressed a quick, soft kiss to her lips. "I don't regret a single moment that has passed since the day you agreed to marry me."

Sophie regarded him skeptically. "Not even accepting Penvale's invitation to go swimming in the Serpentine on Christmas Day?"

West grimaced at the memory. "It was invigorating."

"I recall some more colorful language being employed at the time."

"It certainly taught me a lesson about the merits of cold-water swimming."

"Oh?" Sophie tilted her head. "Which are?"

"The lesson," West said, straight-faced, "is that there are none."

Sophie let out a peal of laughter at that, and West smiled—a real smile, one that lit his face and made him look years younger.

And then she said—because it was true, and the first thing that sprang to mind, even if it did sound slightly mad—"I'm so glad that Violet decided to feign a case of consumption."

West's smile softened slightly as he gazed at her. "I am, too."

Soon, the babies would be retrieved by their nannies; later, the group would retreat to the library for a game of charades and ill-advised quantities of brandy and sherry; even later than that, West would take her by the hand after bidding the last of their guests good night, leading her up the stairs and along the winding corridors to their bedroom, where he would remove her clothes slowly, and take her to bed while moonlight spilled into the room through an open window. The next morning, she would awaken to sunshine and the knowledge that her sisters would soon be here, and she would wander downstairs to breakfast with a smile on her face that she could not suppress, possessed by the joy that filled every corner of her life.

But for now, she sat with West's arm curled around her shoulders, in a noisy room surrounded by their friends—and this, in and of itself, was enough.

Acknowledgments

Despite the fact that I write romance novels, I am extremely allergic to sentiment when it comes to my own life, which is why I find myself very daunted by the task of writing acknowledgments for the fifth and final book in the Regency Vows series. These books changed my life—I write this from my cozy apartment in Maine, a state in which I would not live were it not for the freedom these books have given me. And, too, as I write this, it is the end of August 2023, and I am in the midst of preparing for a move to the UK, where I have dreamed of living for most of my life; this move is solely possible because of my writing career. So, it is extremely difficult for me to begin to properly thank everyone who has made my life as it currently exists possible, but I am going to do my best.

Taylor Haggerty and Kaitlin Olson are the greatest agent and editor I could hope for. They were the first people to fall in love with this group of fictional characters I love so much; I still remember my first phone calls with each of them, and the surreal feeling of hearing them discuss Violet and James, Diana and Jeremy and the rest, with

ACKNOWLEDGMENTS

the same warmth that I felt. With each book, I feel more and more fortunate to get to work with them; it is impossible for me to put into words how smart and talented they both are, so I won't even try. I'll just say: thank you both, for everything.

Megan Rudloff, Zakiya Jamal, Ifeoma Anyoku, Karlyn Hixson, Morgan Hoit, and all of the other incredible and hardworking people at Atria Books are a dream to work with, and I'm so appreciative for all that they do to bring my books into the world (and ensure that anyone reads them).

Other behind-the-scenes folks who need to be acknowledged include the all-star team at Root Literary—an agency I still feel incredulously lucky to be represented by—and the various foreign publishers who have published my books overseas. (And especially Kate Byrne, who brought my books to the UK, and therefore made my next adventure possible.)

I've had such incredible support from so many independent bookstores, and feel so grateful for every single one who has ever hosted me for an event, or invited me to a book club, or put my books on a display, or hand sold one of them. I'm particularly indebted to Flyleaf Books in Chapel Hill, NC, and Print: A Bookstore in Portland, ME, which have been my bookstore homes for these past few years, and which have been a pure delight to work with.

There are so many authors who have treated me with such kindness in the beginning years of my career. From offering blurbs to doing events with me to hosting giveaways to just generally being sympathetic ears and relentless cheerleaders, I'm so grateful to know so many great, talented people. I won't attempt to name them all, because I know I'd forget people, but I'd be remiss not to specifically mention

ACKNOWLEDGMENTS

Sarah Hogle, who rescued me when I was floundering while trying to write this book, and helped me see the way to the finish line.

My friends and family are an incredible source of support no matter how far apart we live. They're a far-flung bunch—in Florida, in North Carolina, in Maine, and lots of other places, too—but I know they know who they are, and I hope they know how much I love them, even if I am terrible at actually saying it. This time, I'd particularly like to thank: Allie, Hettie, and Elsie, who let me (sort of) steal their names; everyone who made Maine feel like home so quickly (especially Leah, Lila, Meg, and Megan); and my mom, who was the original West and Sophie fan.

Finally, to every reader, reviewer, blogger, librarian, and bookseller who has ever sent me a kind message, or helped spread the word about my books—and especially to those of you who have, from the very start, been asking for this particular story: Thank you, thank you, thank you. This one is for you.

About the Author

Martha Waters is the author of the Regency Vows series, which includes *To Have and to Hoax*, *To Love and to Loathe*, *To Marry and to Meddle*, *To Swoon and to Spar*, and *To Woo and to Wed*. She was born and raised in sunny South Florida and is a graduate of the University of North Carolina at Chapel Hill. She recently moved from snowy Maine to rainy England, and loves sundresses, gin cocktails, and traveling.

Discover Martha Waters's
"SWEET, SEXY, AND UTTERLY FUN"
(Emily Henry)
Regency Vows series